Wolff,

Shadows over
 paradise.

060993

$15.00

DATE			

BY ISABEL WOLFF

Shadows Over Paradise
The Very Picture of You
A Vintage Affair

Shadows Over
Paradise

BANTAM BOOKS

NEW YORK

Shadows Over Paradise

A Novel

ISABEL WOLFF

A Bantam Books Trade Paperback Original

Published in the United States by Bantam Books, an imprint of Random House, a division of Random House LLC, a Penguin Random House Company, New York.

BANTAM BOOKS and the HOUSE colophon are registered trademarks of Random House LLC.
RANDOM HOUSE READER'S CIRCLE & Design is a registered trademark of Random House LLC.

LIBRARY OF CONGRESS CATALOGING-IN-PUBLICATION DATA
Wolff, Isabel.
Shadows over paradise : a novel / Isabel Wolff.
pages ; cm
ISBN 978-0-345-53318-0
eBook ISBN 978-0-345-53317-3
1. Authors—Fiction. 2. Families—Fiction.
3. World War, 1939–1945—Fiction. I. Title.
PR6073.O355S53 2015
823'.914—dc23   2014029819

Printed in the United States of America on acid-free paper

www.bantamdell.com

2 4 6 8 9 7 5 3 1

Book design by Dana Leigh Blanchette

IN MEMORY OF MY MOTHER

The past is never dead. It's not even past.

—WILLIAM FAULKNER,
Requiem for a Nun

Prologue

31 August 1987

Holiday makers speckle the beach, reclining behind brightly striped windbreaks, hands held to eyes against the late-afternoon sun as they gaze at the glittering sea. On the horizon squats a huge gray tanker; in the middle distance a scattering of white-sailed yachts, their spinnakers billowed and taut. At the shore-line a young couple in surfing gear are launching a yellow canoe. He holds it while she climbs in, then he jumps on and they paddle away, the boat rocking and bumping through the swell. Two little girls in pink swimsuits stop paddling for a moment to watch them, then dash in and out of the water, shrieking with laughter. Behind them, a family is playing French cricket. The ball soars toward the rocks, pursued by a dog barking wildly, its claws driving up a spray of wet sand.

On the cliff path behind the beach, people are queuing at the wooden hut for tea and biscuits, or an ice cream, or a bucket and spade or a ready-inflated mattress, which is what a couple of teenage boys are buying now. "Don't take it in the sea," warns the woman behind the counter. The taller boy shakes his head, then he and his friend carry the airbed down the worn granite steps to the beach.

Here the sand is pale and dry, glinting with mica. As they head for the water, the boys throw a covetous glance at a blond woman in a black bikini, who's lying on a white towel, perfectly still. She's enjoying the warmth of the sun and the sound of the sea pulling in and out, as steady as breathing. A sand fly lands on her cheek, and she brushes it away, then pushes herself up, resting on her elbows. She gazes at the headland, where the grass has dried to a pale gold, then she looks at the dark-haired man sitting beside her and gives him an indolent smile. Now she turns onto her front, reaches behind to unclip her bikini top, then hands him a tube of Ambre Solaire. The man hesitates, glancing at the woman's two children building a sandcastle a few feet away, then he removes the cap and starts rubbing the cream onto the woman's shoulders. As his palm strokes her skin, she sighs with pleasure.

Her daughter, kneeling in the sand, looks up. Seeing the man's hand moving over her mother's waist, the girl reddens, then stumbles to her feet. "Let's go rock pooling," she says to her little brother.

He shakes his blond head and continues digging. "No."

"But I want you to."

"I'd rather stay with Mum."

The girl picks up her plastic sandals and bangs them together. "You have to come with me."

"Why?"

She puts on the right shoe. "To help me."

"Don't want to help you."

"Well, you've *got* to." She shoves her left foot into the other sandal, bends to do it up, then grabs the bucket that the boy was filling and empties it. "I'll carry this; you take the net."

The boy shrugs his narrow shoulders, then stands. He hitches up his red swimming trunks, which are hand-me-downs and much too big; he picks up the net lying nearby.

Their mother lifts her head. "You don't have long," she says. "We'll be leaving at six, so you're to come back when you hear the bell from the tea hut. Did you hear me?" she adds to her daughter. "Hold his hand now. You must hold his hand." The girl gives a sullen nod, then starts to walk toward the rocks that spill down from the low cliff to the sea. Her brother follows her, dragging the net, its stick leaving a sinuous trail, like the tail of the yellow kite that he now notices, swaying high up, against the blue. He cranes his neck to watch it, one eye closed against the sun.

The girl glances behind and sees that he's not following her. "Ted!" she calls. "Come *on*!" She wants to get as far as possible from their mother and her so-called friend.

"Teddy!" The little boy tears his gaze from the kite and follows his sister, jumping onto her footprints, leaving no tracks of his own. A toddler wobbles across his path, naked except for a sun hat, then tumbles over, wails, and is hastily scooped up.

Now they're passing a boy and girl who are digging. The

trench they've made is six feet long, and so deep that they're visible only from the waist up.

Ted stops, entranced. "Look, Evie!" She turns. "It's 'normous."

"It is," she agrees seriously. "Must have taken ages," she says to the girl, who is about her own age, although tall and long-limbed. She's wearing a white T-shirt with a large black *J* on it. Evie wonders what it stands for. Julie? Jane?

"It did take ages," the girl replies. Her face is a pale oval framed by long dark hair. She tucks a hank behind her ear and nods at the rampart of displaced sand. "We've been digging all afternoon, haven't we, Tom?"

Tom, a thickset boy of about eight, straightens up.

"We're making a tunnel." He leans on his spade. "Like that Channel Tunnel they're going to build."

"It was my idea," the girl adds. "We've done it all by ourselves." She turns to Tom. "Mum'll be surprised when she sees it."

Tom laughs. "She'll be amazed."

"You making a real tunnel?" Ted asks him.

"Yes." Tom points to a deep recess at the back of the hole.

Ted peers at it. "Can I go in?"

"Maybe." Tom shrugs. "When it's finished. But we'll have to be quick because the tide's coming up."

"The time's coming up?" Ted looks at the sea.

"The *tide*, silly," says Evie. "Come on, Ted, we'd better go."

On the other side of the beach, the children's mother closes her eyes as her companion's hands caress the swell of her hips. "That's lovely," she says. "Can you hear me purring?" she adds with a laugh. Someone nearby is listening to Radio One. She can hear the Pet Shop Boys. "Always on My Mind."

Her boyfriend lies down beside her. "You're always on *my* mind, Babs," he murmurs.

She puts her hand to his chest, spreading her fingers against his skin. "This is the best holiday I've had for years."

By now her children have reached the rocks—jagged gray boulders thinly striped with white quartz. They clamber up, and Ted peers into the first pool. He stares at the seaweed, some brown and knobbly, some as green and smooth as lettuce. He pokes his net at a sea anemone, and to his delight, it retracts its maroon tendrils. Then he spies a shrimp and thrusts the net at it. "Caught something!" he shouts, but as he inspects the mesh, his face falls—all that's in it is a brown winkle. "Evie!" he calls, dismayed to see that she is fifty or sixty feet away. "Wait for me!" But Evie keeps on jumping across the rocks, the bucket swinging from her arm.

As Ted follows her, he looks out to sea and spots a yellow canoe with two people in it, lifting and twisting their paddles. He hears a distant roar and sees a motorboat rip across the water, the wake fanning out in widening chevrons that make the canoe rock and sway. Then he returns his gaze to Evie. She's peering into a pool. "Evie!" he yells, but she doesn't respond.

Ted steps onto the next boulder, but it's crusted with tiny black mussels that cut into his feet. The rock beside it looks smooth, but when he stands on it, it wobbles violently, and his thin arms flail as he tries not to fall. Sudden tears sting his eyes. The rocks are sharp, and his trunks won't stay up and his sister won't wait for him, let alone hold his hand like she's supposed to. "Evie . . ." His throat aches as he tries not to cry. "Eee-vieeee!"

At last she turns. Seeing his distress, she makes her way back to him. "What's the matter, Ted?" She stares at his feet. "Why didn't you wear your beach shoes?"

He sniffs. "I forgot."

Evie heaves an exasperated sigh, then turns toward the sea. "Then we'd better go this way—the rocks are easier. Mind the barnacles," she adds over her shoulder. "Ooh, *there's* a good pool." It's long and narrow, like a little loch, with bands of leathery-looking weeds that sway to and fro. As Evie's shadow falls onto the surface, a small brown fish darts across the bottom. "Give me the net!" Ted passes it to her and takes the bucket as Evie crouches down, thrusts the net under a rock, and swiftly withdraws it. There's a glint of silver. "Got it!" she yells. "Fill the bucket, Ted! Quick!"

Ted dips the bucket into the pool, then hands it to her. Evie tips the fish in, and it swims to the bottom, then scoots under a shred of bladder wrack. "It's *huge,*" Evie breathes. "And there's a shrimp!" She feels a sudden euphoria—her loathing of her mother's "friend" forgotten. "Let's get some more." As she dips the net into the water again, she hears, faintly, the bell that the woman in the tea hut rings when she's closing.

A few yards away the waves are breaking over the rocks; the two children can feel the spray on the backs of their legs.

Ted shivers. "Is it high time yet, Evie?"

Evie remembers Clive's hands on their mother's flanks. She thinks of his hairy chest and his thick arms, with their tattoos, and of the grunts that she hears through the bedroom wall.

"It isn't high tide," she answers. "Not yet."

Ted picks up the net again. "The bell's ringing."

Evie shrugs. "I can't hear it."

"I can, and 'member what Mum said, she said—"

"Let's find a crab!" Evie yells. "Come on!"

Thrilled by the idea, Ted follows his sister, relieved that she's going more slowly now, even if it's only to avoid spilling their precious catch. Here the rocks are not sharp with mussels but treacherous with seaweed, which slips like satin beneath Ted's feet. He longs for Evie to hold his hand but doesn't ask, not wanting to seem babyish.

"We should have brought some ham," he hears her say. "Crabs like ham. We'll bring some tomorrow, okay?"

Ted nods happily.

On the beach, the man flying the kite is reeling it in. The mother of the girls in the pink swimsuits is calling them out of the sea. They run toward her, teeth chattering, and she wraps a towel around each one while the encroaching waves lick at their footprints. The family that was playing French cricket is packing up; the father hurls the ball and the dog tears after it.

People are folding their chairs, or packing up baskets and bags as the sea advances, then retreats, then pushes forward again.

"Five more minutes, Clive," Barbara says.

He winds a lock of her hair around his finger. "So what's happening tonight?"

"Well, I thought we'd walk to Trennick and get some fish and chips; we could buy a nice bottle of wine, and *then* . . . I'll get the kids into bed early."

"You do that," Clive whispers. He kisses her. "You do that, Babs." Barbara smiles to think that she's only known Clive for eight weeks. She remembers the rush of desire when she saw him—the first time she'd felt anything for a man in years. She thinks of how she'd loathed the job—sitting at her desk all day with nothing to see through the window but lorries and trucks with JJ HAULAGE on them, the only thing on her wall a road map of the United Kingdom. Just as she was wondering how much more of it she could stand, Clive had walked in. Tall and dark, with the shoulders of an ox, he'd reminded Barbara of a drawing of the Minotaur in one of Evie's books. He'd come about his pay slip—five overnights to Harwich that were missing. Flustered, Barbara had promised to correct it; then he'd suggested, cheekily, that she could "make it up to him." She'd laughed and said maybe she would . . .

She'd told him that she had two kids—though no ex, God rest Finn's soul; but Clive said that she could have had ten kids in tow and it wouldn't have mattered. The fact that—at thirty-eight—he's ten years older than she is makes Barbara feel light-headed.

The tricky thing had been introducing him to Evie and Ted. Ted took little notice of him, turning back to his Legos, but Evie was hostile, and when Barbara told them that Clive would be coming on the holiday, she'd run to her room, slamming the door. But, as Barbara had said to her, Evie had friends—why shouldn't Mummy have a friend? Why shouldn't Mummy have a bit of happiness? Didn't Mummy deserve it after all she'd been through? But Evie had simply stared at her, as though trying to drill a hole in her soul. *Well, she'll just have to get used to him,* Barbara decides as Clive kisses her fingertips.

Suddenly Barbara realizes that the bell has stopped ringing. She sits up.

On the rocks, Ted is getting tired. But now Evie has found another pool, a few feet from the water's edge.

"There'll be crabs in here," she says authoritatively. "Okay, Ted, you hold the bucket. Be careful," she warns as she passes it to him. She takes the net. "What's the matter?"

"I want to hold the net."

"You're too young." Confident that this has settled the matter, she returns her gaze to the pool.

Ted thumps the bucket down on a ledge. "I'm five!"

"Well, I'm nine, so it's better if I do it. It's not easy catching crabs."

"It's my turn. You caught the fish—*and* the shrimp. So it's my turn with the net now, and—"

"Shhhh!" Evie is holding up her left hand, her eyes fixed on the water. "I saw one," she hisses. "A big one."

"Let me get it."

Evie leans forward, very slowly, then jabs the net at a clump of weed. As she lifts it out, a khaki-colored crab, the size of her hand, is dangling from the mesh with one claw.

Ted lunges for the net. To his amazement he manages to wrest it from her; as he does so, the crab falls back into the water then scuttles under a rock.

Evie's mouth chasms with outrage. "You idiot!"

Ted's chin dimples. "I'm not."

"You *are*." She glares at him. "You're an idiot—and a baby— a stupid little *baby*! No wonder Mum calls you Teddy Bear."

His face crumples. "Sorry, Evie." He offers her the net. "Catch it again. Please."

Evie's tempted, but then she notices how close the waves are now. "No. We've got to get back." She tips the bucket into the pool, and the fish and shrimp dart away. Then she sets off for the beach, which looks improbably distant, as if viewed through the wrong end of a telescope. She can just see Tom and his sister, flinging sand out of that hole as though their lives depended on it. She turns back to Ted. He's still standing by the pool, his bangs blown by the breeze. "What are you doing?"

"I want to get the crab!" Ted's eyes glisten with tears. "I want to show it to Mum."

"You can't."

"I *can!*" A sob convulses his thin rib cage. "I can get it, Evie!" He squats down and thrusts the net into the pool frantically.

"It's too late! You ruined it—now come on!" Ted doesn't move. "I'm wait-ing." Her hands drop to her hips. "Right! Ten, nine, eight . . ."

Ted glances at her.

"Seven, six, five . . ."

He looks longingly at the pool. "But—"

"Three, two . . . *one!* I'm going!"

Still sobbing, Ted starts to descend, but Evie is already springing across the rocks, the soles of her shoes slapping the stone. "This way," she calls as she moves higher up, toward the cliff. "Put your hand on that rock there." She points to it, then leaps across a gully. She jumps onto the next rock, then the next, stepping from boulder to boulder until, at last, she's yards from the beach. Evie jumps onto the sand, surprised at how relieved she feels. There's the girl with the *J* T-shirt, sitting by the trench, observing Tom with a blend of curiosity and admiration. Evie stands beside her as he wriggles into the tunnel, then she walks on, looking for shells. She stops to pick up a piece of sea glass but decides that it's too new-looking to keep. As she straightens up she can hear gulls crying, and the barking of a dog. Then she sees her mother coming toward her, in her dress now, scanning the rocks, one hand to her eyes, lips pursed. Evie lifts her left arm and waves. Her mother waves back, smiling with relief. Then her expression changes to one of consternation, then alarm. She starts running toward Evie.

Evie turns and looks behind her. Her heart stops.

Shadows Over
Paradise

One

I knew that Nina's wedding was going to change things between Rick and me, though I could never have guessed by how much. Up until then, it had all been so easy—he and I had fitted into each other's lives as though we'd always known one another. And now we were going to a wedding—our first one together—and suddenly being with Rick was hard.

"They've got great weather for it," he remarked as I locked the door of our small North London flat. The early haze had given way to a pristine blue sky.

"A good omen," I said as we walked to the car.

Rick beeped open his old Golf. "I didn't know you were superstitious, Jenni. But then I don't know everything about you." There was a slight edge to his voice.

"Well, I *am* superstitious." I put our gift, in its silvery bag, on the backseat. "But then I was born on Friday the thirteenth."

Rick smiled. "That should make you immune."

We drove west, talking pleasantly but with an unfamiliar re-
serve, born of the anguished conversations that we'd been having over the past two or three days.

We sped down the A40 and were soon driving along rural
roads past fields still stubbled and pale from the harvest. It
was very warm for mid-October, and clear—an Indian summer's day, piercingly beautiful with its golden light and long
shadows.

Nina's parents lived at the southern end of the Cotswolds.
Over the years I'd visited the house for weekends or the occa-
sional party—Nina's twenty-first, and her thirtieth, which was
already five years ago, I reflected soberly. For fifteen years, she
and Honor had been my closest friends. And today it was Nina's
wedding, and before long, no doubt, there'd be a christening.

Rick glanced at me. "You okay, Jen?"

"Yes. Why?"

He downshifted a gear. "You sighed."

"Oh . . . no reason. I'm just a bit tired." A bad sleeper at the
best of times, I'd lain awake most of the night. As I'd stared into
the darkness, I'd longed for Rick to hold me and whisper that
everything would be all right, but he'd turned away.

"So where do we go from here?" For a moment I thought
that Rick was talking about us. "Which way?"

I spotted the sign for Bisley. "Go right."

Minutes later we turned on to Nailsford Lane, where a clutch
of white balloons bobbed from a farm gate.

"Looks like we're the first," Rick remarked as we drove into
the parking field, which was empty except for an abandoned

tractor. He parked in the shade of a huge copper beech; as he opened his door, I could hear its leaves rustle and rattle. "Is it going to be a big do?"

"Pretty big—about eighty, Nina told me."

"So, who will I know, apart from her and Jon?"

I pulled down the visor and checked my reflection in the mirror.

"I'm not sure—she's invited quite a few of the people we knew at Bristol; not that I've stayed in touch with that many . . ." I winced at my red-veined eyes and pale cheeks. "I've only really kept up with Nina and Honor." I wound my long, dark hair into a bun, then pinned onto that the pale-pink silk flower that matched my dress.

Rick pulled a blue tie out of his jacket pocket. "So I guess Honor will be here?"

"Of course." Rick grimaced; I glanced at him. "Don't be like that, Rick—Honor's lovely."

"She's exhausting."

"Exuberant," I countered, wishing that my boyfriend was a bit keener on my best friend.

He groaned. "She never stops talking. So she's in the right job, not that I listen."

"You should—her show's the best thing on Radio Five." As Rick looped and twisted the blue silk, I suppressed a dark smile. He's tying the knot, I thought.

Reaching into the back for the gift, I saw more cars arriving, bumping slowly over the field. We made our way across the grass, which was studded with dandelion heads, their downy seeds drifting like plankton. We strolled up Church Walk, then

pushed on the lych-gate, which was garlanded with moon dai-
sies, and went up the graveled path.

Jon was waiting anxiously by the porch with his brothers, all
three men in morning dress with yellow silk waistcoats. They
greeted us warmly and we chatted for a minute or two; then the
photographer, who had been sorting out his camera on top of a
tomb, offered to take a picture of Rick and me.

"Let's have a smile," he said as he clicked away. "A bit
more—it's a wedding, not a funeral," he added genially. "*That's*
better." There was another volley of clicks, then he squinted at
the screen. "Lovely."

Tim handed Rick and me our Order of Service sheets, and
we walked into the cool of the church.

I'd been to Saint Jude's before but had forgotten how small it
was, and how simple the interior, with its plain walls, wooden
roof, and box pews. There was the smell of beeswax and dust
and age, mingled with the scent of the oriental lilies that festooned the columns and pulpit. It was also very light, with clear
glass, except for the east window, which depicted Christ blessing the children. The sun streamed through its colored panes,
scattering jeweled beams across the whitewashed walls.

"Lovely church," Rick murmured as we sat down.

"It is," I agreed, though today its beauty was a shard in my
heart. Rick and I glanced through our service sheets as the
church filled up, heels tapping over the flagstones, wood creaking as people sat down, then chatted quietly or just listened to
the Bach partita the organist was playing.

Jon's parents went to their seats. Behind them I recognized a
colleague of Nina's, and now here was Honor, in a green bomb-
shell dress that hugged her curves and complemented her

creamy skin and blond hair. She blew me and Rick an extravagant kiss, then sat near the front.

Now Jon and his older brother, James, took their places together, while their younger brother, Tim, ushered in a few latecomers. Nina's mother, in a turquoise opera coat and matching hat, smiled benignly as she made her way to her pew.

I turned and caught a glimpse of Nina. She stood on the porch, in the white silk dupion sheath that Honor and I had helped her choose, her veil drifting behind her.

As the Bach drew to an end, the vicar stepped in front of the altar and welcomed everyone. Then there was a burst of Handel, and we all stood as Nina walked down the aisle on her father's arm.

After the opening prayers we sang "Morning Has Broken," then Honor stepped up to the lectern to read the sonnet that Nina had chosen.

"My true love hath my heart, and I have his," she began, her dulcet voice echoing slightly. *"By just exchange one for the other given. I hold his dear, and mine he cannot miss. There never was a better bargain driven . . ."*

As Honor read, I felt a sting of envy. The lovers understood each other so well. I'd thought I had that with Rick . . .

"My true love hath my heart—and I have his," Honor concluded.

The vicar raised his hands. "Dearly beloved, we are gathered together here in the sight of God, and in the face of this congregation, to join together this Man and this Woman in holy Matrimony . . ." I looked at Nina and Jon, side by side in a pool of light, and wondered whether these words would ever be said for Rick and me. "Nor taken in hand wantonly," the vicar was saying, "but reverently, discreetly, advisedly, and soberly, and in the fear of God, duly considering the causes for which Matrimony was ordained." At that I felt Rick shift slightly. "First, it was ordained for the procreation of children . . ." I stole a glance at him, but his face gave nothing away. "Therefore, if any man can show any just cause, why they may not lawfully be joined together, let him now speak, or else, hereafter, forever hold his peace."

I tried to follow the service but found it suddenly impossible to focus on the music, or the sermon, or on the beauty and solemnity of the vows. As Nina and Jon committed themselves to each other with unfaltering voices, I felt another stab of pain. The register was signed, the last hymn sung, and the blessing given; then, as Widor's Toccata mingled with the pealing bells, we followed Nina and Jon outside.

We showered the couple with petals and took snaps with our phones; then the photographer began the formal photos of them while we all milled around by the porch.

"Great to see you! Fantastic weather!"

"Lovely service—much prefer the King James."

"Me too. Well read, Honor!"

"Should we make our way to the house?"

"Not yet. I think they want a group pic."

Rick and I, keen to get away from the crowd, strolled through the churchyard; we looked at the gravestones, most of which were very old and eroded, blotched with yellow lichen.

Rick stopped in front of a slate headstone. "That's odd. It's got a pineapple on it."

I looked at the carved image. "A pineapple means prosperity, as do figs, and I guess this was a prosperous area, probably because of the wool trade."

We walked on in silence, past stones that had angels on them, and doves and candles, the symbolism of which was clear.

We could hear the chatter of the guests, a sudden burst of Honor's unmistakable laughter, then the photographer's voice. *"Could you look at me, Nina?"*

Rick approached another grave, by a yew. He peered at it. "This one's got a bunch of grapes carved on it."

"Grapes represent the wine at the Last Supper."

Rick glanced at me. "How do you know all this, Jen? I didn't think you were religious."

"I had to research it for one of my books. It was years ago, but I've remembered a lot of it."

"Now look at each other again."

"Here's a rose," Rick said, pointing to another headstone. "I assume that means love?"

"Oh, very romantic."

"No. Roses show how old the person was when they died." I studied the worn emblem. "This is a full rose, which was used for adults." I read the inscription. "Mary Ann Betts . . . was . . ." I peered at her dates. "Twenty-five. The stem's severed, to show that her life was cut short."

"I see." Our conversation felt stiff and formal, as though we were strangers, not lovers.

"Can we have a kiss?"

"A partially opened rose means a teenager."

"And another one. Lovely."

"And a rosebud is for a child."

"Hold his hand now."

Rick nodded thoughtfully. "A sad subject."

"Yes . . ."

"Okay, all stand together, please—nice and close!"

Rick and I joined everyone for the group photo, for which the photographer climbed onto a stepladder, wobbling theatrically to make us all laugh. We smiled up at him while he clicked away, then, hand in hand, Nina and Jon led us down the path, across the field, to the house.

The Old Forge was just as I remembered it—long and low, its pale stone walls ablaze with pyracantha and Virginia creeper. A large marquee filled the lawn. In the distance were the hills of Slad, the plunging pastures dotted with sheep, their bleats carrying across the valley on the still air.

We joined the receiving line, greeting both sets of parents, then the bride and groom.

Nina's face lit up, and as we hugged I had to fight back sudden tears. I didn't know whether they were tears of happiness for her or of self-pity. "You look so beautiful, Nina."

"Thank you." She put her lips to my ear. "You next," she whispered.

Jon kissed me on the cheek, then clasped Rick's hand.

"Good to *see* you both! Thanks for coming!"

"Congratulations, Jon," Rick said warmly. "It was a lovely service. Congratulations, Nina."

Now we moved on into the large sunny sitting room where drinks were being served. I put our gift on a table among a cluster of other presents and cards. A waiter offered us a glass of champagne. Rick took one and raised it. "Here's to the happy couple."

I sipped my fizz. "They are happy. It's wonderful."

"How long have they been together?"

"About the same as us. They got engaged on their first anniversary," I added neutrally, then laughed at myself for ever having thought that Rick and I might do the same.

I looked at Rick, so handsome, with his open expression, dark hair, and blue gaze. I tried, and failed, to imagine life without him. We'd agreed to talk things over again the next day. Before I could think about that, though, a gong summoned us into the marquee, which was bedecked with white agapanthus and pink nerines, the tables gleaming with silver and china. We found our names and stood behind our chairs while the vicar said grace.

Rick and I had been placed with Honor, and with Amy and Sean, whom I'd known at college but hadn't seen for years, and an old schoolfriend of Jon's, Al. I was glad that Nina had put him next to Honor; she'd been single for a while now, and he was very attractive. Also at our table was Nina's godfather, Vincent Tregear. I vaguely remembered him from her twenty-first birthday. A near neighbor named Carolyn Browne introduced herself. I steeled myself for the effort of making small talk with people I don't know; unlike Honor, I'm not good at it, and in my frame of mind I knew it would be harder than usual.

I heard Carolyn explain to Rick that she was a solicitor, recently retired. "I'm so busy though," she confessed, laughing. "I'm a governor of a local school; I play golf and bridge; I travel. I was dreading retirement, but it's really fine." She smiled at Rick. "Not that you're anywhere *near* that stage. So, what do you do?"

He unfurled his napkin. "I'm a teacher—at a primary school in Islington."

"He's the deputy head," I volunteered proudly. Carolyn smiled at me. "And what about you, erm . . . ?"

"Jenni." I turned my place card toward her.

"Jenni," she echoed. "And you're . . ." She nodded at Rick.

"Yes, I'm Rick's . . ." The word *girlfriend* made us seem like teenagers; *partner* made us sound as though we were in business, not in love. "Other half," I concluded, though I disliked this too; it seemed to suggest, ominously, that we'd been sliced apart.

"And what do you do?" Carolyn asked me.

My heart sank—I hate talking about myself. "I'm a writer."

"A writer?" Her face lit up. "Do you write novels?"

"No," I replied. "It's all nonfiction. But you won't have heard of me."

"I read a lot, so maybe I will. What's your name? Jenni"— Carolyn peered at my place card—"Clark." She narrowed her eyes. "Jenni Clark."

"I don't write under that name."

"So is it Jennifer Clark?"

"No—what I mean is, I don't write under *any* name."

I was about to explain why when Honor said, "Jenni's a ghost."

"A ghost?" Carolyn looked puzzled.

"She ghosts things." Honor opened her napkin. "Strange to think that it can be a verb, isn't it? I ghost, you ghost, he ghosts," she added gaily.

I rolled my eyes at Honor, then turned to Carolyn. "I'm a ghostwriter."

"Oh, I see. So you write books for people who can't write."

"Or they can," I said, "but don't have the time, or lack the confidence, or they don't know how to shape the material."

"So it's actors and pop stars, I suppose? Footballers? TV presenters?"

I shook my head. "I don't do the celebrity stuff. I used to, but not anymore."

"Which is a shame," Honor interjected, "as you'd make far more money."

"True." I rested my fork. "But I didn't enjoy it."

"Why not?" asked Al, who was on my left.

"It was too frustrating," I answered, "having to battle with my subjects' egos, or finding that they didn't turn up for the interviews; or that they'd give me some brilliant material, then the next day tell me that I wasn't to use it. So these days I only do the projects that interest me."

Honor, who has a butterfly mind, was now discussing ghosts of the other kind. "I'm *sure* they exist," she said to Vincent Tregear. "Twenty years ago I was staying with my cousins in France; it was a warm, still day, just like today, and we were exploring this abandoned house. It was a ruin, so we could see right up to the roof. And we *both* heard footsteps, right above us, on the nonexistent floorboards." She gave an extravagant shudder. "I've never forgotten it."

"*I* believe in ghosts," Carolyn remarked. "I live on my own, in an old house, and at times I've been aware of this . . . presence."

Amy nodded enthusiastically. "I've sometimes felt a sudden chill." She turned to Sean. "Do you remember, darling, last summer? When we were in Wales?"

"I do," he answered. "Though I believe it was because you were pregnant."

"No—pregnancy made me feel hot, not cold."

"A few years ago," said Al, "I was asleep in my flat, alone, when I suddenly woke up, convinced that someone was sitting on my bed."

I shivered at the idea. "And you weren't dreaming?"

He shook his head. "I was wide awake. I can still remember the weight of it, pressing down on the mattress. Yet there was no one there."

"How terrifying," I murmured.

"It was." He poured me some water, then filled his own glass. "Has anything like that ever happened to you?"

"It hasn't, I'm glad to say. But I don't dismiss other people's experiences."

"I've always been skeptical about these things," Sean observed. "I believe that if people are sufficiently on edge, they can see things that aren't really there. Like Macbeth seeing the ghost of Banquo."

"Shake not thy gory locks at me!" intoned Honor, then giggled. "And Macbeth certainly is on edge by then, isn't he, having murdered—what—four people?" Then she went off on some conversational tangent about why it was considered unlucky for actors to say "Macbeth" inside a theater. "People think it's because of the evil in the story," she prattled away as a waiter took her plate. "But it's actually because if a play wasn't selling well, the actors would have to quickly rehearse *Macbeth,* as that's always popular, so doing *Macbeth* became associated with ill luck. Now, what are we having next?" She picked up a gold-tasseled menu. "Sea bass—yum. Did you know that sea bass are hermaphrodites? The males become females at six months."

Al, clearly uninterested in the gender-switching tendencies

of our main course, turned to me. "So what sort of books do you write?"

"A real mix," I answered. "Psychology, health, and popular culture; I've done a diet book, and a couple of gardening books . . ."

I thought of my titles, more than twenty of them, lined up on the shelf in my study.

"So you must learn a huge amount about all these things," Al said.

"I do. It's one of the perks."

Carolyn sipped her wine. "But do you get any kind of credit?"

"No."

"I thought that with ghostwritten books it usually said 'with so-and-so' or 'as told to.' "

"It depends," I said. "Some ghostwriters ask for that. I don't."

"So your name appears nowhere?"

"That's right."

She frowned. "Don't you mind?"

I shrugged. "Anonymity's part of the deal. And of course the clients like it that way. They'd prefer everyone to think they'd written the book all by themselves."

Carolyn laughed. "I couldn't *bear* not to have any of the glory. If I'd worked that hard on something, I'd want people to know!"

"Me too," chimed in Honor. "I don't know why you want to hide your light under a bushel *quite* so much, Jen."

"Because it's enough that I've enjoyed the work and been paid for it. I'm happy to be . . . invisible."

"You were always like that," Honor went on. "You were never one to seek the limelight—unlike me." She giggled. "I enjoy it."

"So, are you still acting?" Sean asked her.

"Not for five years now," she answered. "I couldn't take the insecurity anymore, so I went into radio, which I love."

"I've heard your show," Amy interjected. "It's really good."

"Thanks." Honor basked in the compliment for a moment. "And you two have had a baby, haven't you?"

"We have," Amy answered. "So I'm on maternity leave."

"And what are you working on now, Jenni?" Carolyn asked.

I fiddled with my wineglass. "A baby-care guide."

"How lovely," she responded. "And are you a mum?"

My heart contracted. "No." I sipped my wine.

"Doesn't that make it difficult? Writing a book about something you haven't been through yourself?"

"Not at all. The client's talked extensively to me about her experience—she's a midwife—and I've written it up in a clear and, I hope, engaging way."

"I must buy it," Amy said to me. "What's it called?"

"*Bringing Up Baby*. It'll be out in the spring. But I always get a few complimentary copies, so if you give me your address, I'll send you one."

"Oh, that's kind. I'll write it down." Amy began looking in her bag for a pen.

"You can contact me through my website," I suggested. "Jenni Clark Ghostwriting. So . . . how old's your baby?"

At that Sean took out his phone and swiped the screen.

"She's called Rosie."

I smiled at the photo. "She's gorgeous. Isn't she lovely, Honor?"

Honor peered at the image. "She's a little beauty."

"She's what, six months?" I asked.

Amy's face glowed with pride. "Yes—she'll be seven months a week from Wednesday."

"So is she crawling?" I went on. "Or starting to roll over?" Beside me I could feel Rick stiffen.

"She's crawling beautifully," Amy replied. "But she's not rolling over yet."

Sean laughed. "It'll be nerve-racking when she does."

"You won't be able to leave her on the bed or the changing table," I said. "That's when lots of parents put the changing mat on the floor—not that I'm a parent myself, but of course we cover this in the book . . ." Rick had tuned out of the conversation and was talking to Carolyn again. Al turned to me. "So can you write about any subject?"

"Well, not something I could never relate to," I answered, "like particle physics—not that I'd ever get chosen for a book like that. But I'll do almost any professional writing job: not just books, but corporate reports, press releases, business pitches, memoirs—"

"Memoirs?" echoed Vincent. "You mean, writing someone's life story?"

"Yes—usually an older person, just for private publication."

"Do you enjoy that?" Vincent asked.

"Very much. In fact it's what I like doing best, my favorite kind of project. I love immersing myself in other people's memories."

Vincent looked as though he was about to say something, but then Carolyn began asking him about golf, Amy was telling Rick about yoga, and Honor was chatting to Al about his work as an orthodontist. She was drawn to him, I could tell. Good old Nina for putting them together. Suddenly Honor looked at me, grinned, then tapped her teeth. "Al says I have a *perfect* bite."

I raised my glass. "Congratulations!"

"Not just good," Honor said. "Perfect!"

"Don't let it go to your head," Al said.

She laughed. "Where else is my bite supposed to go?"

Soon it was time for the speeches and toasts; the cake was cut, then after coffee there was a break before the evening party was to start.

Amy and Sean had to leave, to get back to their baby. Vincent also said his goodbyes. As the caterers moved the tables back, Rick and I went out into the garden.

We sat on a bench, watching the sky turn crimson, then mauve, then an inky blue in which the first stars were starting to shine.

"Well, it's been a great day," Rick pronounced. The awkwardness had returned, squatting between us like an uninvited guest.

"It's been a lovely day," I agreed. "*We* should . . ."

"What?" he murmured after a moment.

My nerve failed. "We should go inside. It's getting cold."

Rick stood up. "And the band's started." He held out his hand.

So we returned to the marquee, where Jon and Nina were dancing their first waltz. Soon everyone took to the floor. But as Rick's arms went round me and he pulled me close, I felt that he was hugging me goodbye.

Two

"So . . . what are we going to do?" Rick asked me gently the following day.

We'd had lunch—not that I'd been able to eat—and now faced each other across our kitchen table. I shook my head helplessly. I didn't trust myself to speak.

"We've got three options," Rick went on. "One, I change my mind; two, you change your mind; or three . . ."

I felt my stomach clench. "I don't want to break up."

"Nor do I." He exhaled, hard, as though breathing on glass, then he looked at me, his blue eyes searching my face. "I do love you, Jen."

"Then you should be happy to let me have what I want."

He flinched. "You know it's not that simple."

A silence fell between us, and we could hear the rumble of traffic from the City Road.

"I keep thinking about this quote I once read," Rick said after a moment. "I can't remember who it's by, but it's about how love doesn't consist in gazing at the other person, but in looking together in the same direction." He shrugged. "But we're not doing that."

I cradled my coffee mug, with its pattern of red hearts, in my hands. "We've been together for a year and a half," I said quietly. "We've lived together for nine months, and we've been happy. Haven't we?" I glanced at the framed photo collage that I'd made of our first year together. There were snaps of us on top of Mount Snowdon, walking on the South Downs, sitting on the swing seat in his parents' garden, cooking together, kissing. Then my eyes strayed to Nina's wedding invitation on the kitchen dresser. I bitterly regretted having teasingly asked Rick when we might take our relationship forward.

"We have been happy," Rick said at last. "That's what makes it so hard."

Another silence enveloped us. I could hear the hum of the fridge. "There is a fourth option," I said, "which is to go on as we were. So let's just . . . forget marriage."

Rick stared at me as though I were speaking in tongues. "This isn't *about* marriage, Jen."

I glanced at my manuscript, the typed pages stacked up on the table. *Bringing Up Baby: From Newborn to 12 Months—the Definitive Infant-Care Guide.* A page had fallen to the floor.

"So what are we going to do?" Rick asked me again.

"I don't know." A wave of resentment coursed through me. "I only know that I was always *honest* with you." As I picked up the sheet, random sentences leapt out at me. *Great adventure of parenthood . . . bliss of holding your baby for the first time . . . what to expect, month by month.*

"You were honest," Rick agreed. "You told me right from the start that you didn't want to have children and that this was something I had to know if we were to get involved."

"Yes," I said hotly, "and *you* said you didn't mind, because you work with children every day. You said that your brother has four kids, so there was no pressure on you to have them. You told me that you'd never been bothered about it and that people can have a good life without children—which is true."

"I *did* feel like that, Jenni. But I've changed."

"Well, I wish you hadn't, because now we've got a problem."

Rick pushed back his chair; he went and stood by the French windows. Through the panes the plants in our small walled garden looked dusty and withered. I'd been too distracted and upset to water them. "People do change," he said quietly. "They're allowed to change. And it's crept up on me over the past few months. I've wanted to talk to you about it but was afraid to, precisely for this reason. But now you've brought the issue into the open."

"Why have you changed?"

He shrugged. "I don't know—probably because I'm nearly forty now."

"You were nearly forty when we met."

"Or maybe it's seeing the kids at school develop and grow, and wishing that I could watch my own kids do that."

"That didn't seem to worry you before."

"True. But now it does."

I glanced at the manuscript. "I think it's because I've been working on this baby-care book." I felt my throat constrict. "I wish I'd never agreed to do it."

"The book has nothing to do with it, Jen. I wanted to be with you so much that I convinced myself I didn't want children. Then I began to believe that because we were in love we'd naturally *want* to have them. So I thought you'd change your mind."

"Which is what you're hoping for now?"

Rick sighed. "I guess I am. Because then we'd still have each other, but with the chance of family life too. I'll be applying for head teacher posts before long. I'd like to try for jobs outside London, if you were happy to move."

"I'd be happy to be wherever you were," I said truthfully.

"Jen . . ." Rick's face was full of sudden yearning. "We could have a *great* life. We'd be able to afford a bigger place." He looked around him. "This flat's so small."

"I don't care. I'd live in a bedsit with you if I had to. But yes, it would be wonderful to have more space—with a bigger garden."

He nodded. "I've been thinking about that garden a lot. I see a lawn, with children running around on it, laughing. But then they fade, like ghosts, because I know you don't want any." Rick sat down again, then reached for my hands. "I want nothing more than to share my life with you, Jen, but we have to want the same things. And the question of whether or not we have children isn't one that we can compromise on, and if we can't agree about it—"

I withdrew my hands. "Let's imagine that I do change my mind. What if we then find that I can't *have* kids?"

"At least I'd know that we'd tried. Or maybe, I don't know . . . we could try IVF."

"A bank-breaking emotional roller coaster with no guarantees. The other day Honor interviewed a woman who's spent forty thousand pounds on it and still isn't pregnant."

"Well, we might be luckier. If not, we could adopt."

"Could we?" I echoed. "Would we really want that? In any case, this is all academic, because I won't *be* changing my mind, and if you really do love me, you'll accept that. Can't we just go on as we were?" I added desperately.

Rick blinked. "I don't see how we can."

My throat ached with a suppressed sob. "Why not? Because now you've decided that you *would* like kids, you want to go right out there, as soon as possible, and find some woman to have them with? Is that it? Should I start knitting a matinee jacket for the baby right now?"

Rick flinched. "Don't be silly, Jen. It's because we'd only be putting off the inevitable. I'd come to resent you, then you'd be upset with me, and we'd break up anyway." He shook his head. "What I don't understand is why you won't at least explore *why* it is that you feel—"

"No," I interrupted. "I won't."

"Why not?"

"Because I'm not prepared to bare my soul to some stranger! In any case there's nothing *to* explore. Yes, lots of women want children, but there are lots who don't, and I'm one of them. So seeing a counselor won't make any difference. I mean, you're the one who's changed, Rick, not me, yet you're making the condescending assumption that I don't know my own mind!"

"No, Jen, I'm just trying to work out why you feel as you do. Because you *like* children. You go out of your way to be with them."

"That's not true."

"It is—you come into school every week and read to them."

"I . . . do it for you."

"Jen . . ." Rick looked bewildered. "That's how we *met*." Another silence fell. I could hear a magpie chattering in a nearby garden. "Well, it's hardly a big deal, especially as my flat was practically next door. And liking children doesn't mean I want to have them myself. I don't."

"Yet you've said that if I'd been divorced, with children, you'd happily have had those kids in your life."

"Yes."

"But you won't have a child of your own."

"No."

"I wish I knew why *not*. If you told me that it was because you felt that having children would wreck your career, or your lifestyle, or your body, I could at least understand that. I could try to accept it. But to say that you won't have children because you'd be too scared . . ."

I put my hand on the table, tracing the grain with my fingertips. "I would be," I insisted quietly.

"Why?"

I looked up. "I've told you. I'd be scared that something would go wrong. Or that I'd make a terrible mistake—that I'd drop the baby, or forget to feed it or give it enough to drink."

"Babies don't let you forget, Jen; that's why they cry. And you've just written a *book* about babies. Hasn't that made you feel you could cope?"

"It's given me knowledge of how to care for them," I conceded. "But it hasn't taken away my fear that something bad would happen." Panic swept through me. "Like . . . crib death, God forbid, or that I'd turn my back for a few seconds—that's all it would take—and the child would fall down the stairs, or run into the road, or that there'd be some terrible accident that I could never, ever, get over." Tears stung my eyes. "Parenthood's a white-knuckle ride, and I don't want to get on."

Rick gave a mystified shrug. "Most people probably feel the same way, but they control their fears. You let them govern your life. You're normally so levelheaded, but with this I think you're being—"

"Don't tell me—irrational?"

"Yes."

"It's *not* irrational to avoid anxiety and stress."

"It *is* irrational to presume that things will go terribly wrong—especially as you've no reason to think you wouldn't be a good, careful parent. What's your real fear, Jenni? That you wouldn't love the child?"

"On the contrary; I know that I would—which is precisely why I don't want to have one."

He groaned. "But you know, Jen, this isn't just about whether or not we have a family."

"What do you mean?"

Rick gave a frustrated sigh. "We get on so well, Jen." I nodded. "We respect each other. We love being together, we talk easily—and we're attracted to each other."

"We are," I agreed with a pang.

"But you're just not . . . open with me. Every time I ask you about your childhood you avoid my questions, or change the subject. And you never mention your mother, or explain why it is that you're virtually estranged."

"I *have* explained."

"You haven't—at least not in any way that I can understand. And as time's gone on, it's bothered me more and more. This feeling I have, that although I love being with you, and desire you, I don't really *know* you." He sighed. "You said that your mother neglected you."

"No. She looked after me. But she was distant and cold."

"That *is* neglect." Rick chewed his lip. "So . . . was she always like that?"

"No." I saw my mother playing with me, reading to me. Holding my hand. "But as I grew older, it got worse; and it wasn't as though I had a father to make up for it."

"Maybe that's why she was so remote—though you'd think what happened might have brought her closer to you."

"Well . . . it didn't."

"Is this the real reason why you don't want kids?" Rick asked. "Out of a fear that you'd be like that with your own child? Because you wouldn't be, Jen."

"How do you know?" I said bleakly. "I might be *worse*."

"Jenni, I wish that you'd at least talk to someone who might be able to help you overcome your fears."

I laughed. "With a wave of their magic, psychotherapeutic wand? No. In any case, there's nothing *to* resolve. I don't want to have children. I like talking to them, and reading to them, and playing with them, and yes, I can see that having a child must in many ways be wonderful. But against that I set the never-ending, heart-wrenching anxiety of parenthood. I intend to protect myself from that."

Rick stood up, then walked over to the patio doors and unbolted them. He went out and sat on the wooden bench at the end of our small garden. After a moment he took a pack of cigarettes out of his breast pocket, lit one, released a nebula of smoke, then sat with his hands on his knees, head bowed.

I pushed back my chair, gathered up the manuscript, then went down the hall into my study. I dropped the pages beside the computer and sat staring at the darkened screen.

Three options . . . allowed to change . . . not open with me . . .

I heard an email come in but ignored it. Was there any way Rick and I might resolve our problem? I refused to see a counselor. I didn't *need* counseling, and it would be more likely to destroy us than help us. Without thinking, I clicked the mouse and the screen flared into life.

I looked at the list of messages, desperate for distraction. The first three offered me laser lipo, cut-price hair extensions, and 50 percent off a pocket-sprung mattress. The fourth was headed *Ghostwriting Enquiry* and had been automatically forwarded from my website. I was surprised to see that it was from Nina's godfather, Vincent Tregear. It was a two-line message, asking me to call him. I was too upset to speak to him now. Instead, I opened the baby-guide document and stared listlessly at the screen, seeing the words but not taking them in. Then I closed the document and, with an effort of will, forced my mind away from Rick. I wiped my eyes, reached for the handset, and dialed the number that Vincent had given.

After three rings the phone picked up, and I recognized Vincent's voice.

He thanked me for getting back to him. "I know we hardly spoke at the wedding," he went on. "But I was very interested in what you were saying about writing memoirs. So I made a mental note of your website, and last night I took a look at it and was impressed. The reason I've got in touch is because I'm wondering whether you might be able to help my mother write her memoirs."

"I see."

"She's seventy-nine," he explained. "She's in good health, and her memory's fine. For years my brother and I have suggested that she write something about her life. She's always been against the idea, but recently, to our surprise, she said that she would like to. But it won't be easy, as there are some parts of her life that she's never talked about." Broken love affairs, I speculated, or marital difficulties. "She's never talked about what happened to her during the war."

My thoughts were racing, my mind already trying to shape a possible story for Vincent's mother. She would have been a child at the time. Perhaps she'd lived in London, was evacuated, and treated badly. Perhaps she'd stayed, and seen terrible things.

"She doesn't have a computer," I heard Vincent say. "So I offered to help her get her reminiscences onto paper; but she said that she'd find it too awkward, sharing such difficult memories with her own child."

"That's completely understandable. I know I'd find it hard myself."

"So for a while we left it there; then last week, out of the blue, my mother suggested that we find someone for her to talk to. I thought about commissioning a journalist, but then at the wedding I heard you talking about what you do. So . . . how exactly would it work?"

I explained that I spend time with the person, and record

hours of interviews with them. "With their permission I also read their diaries and correspondence," I went on. "I look at their photos and mementoes—anything that will help me to prompt their memories."

"Then you transcribe it all," he said.

"Yes—except that it's much more than a transcription. I'm trying to evoke that person, in their own voice. So I don't simply ask them what happened to them, I ask them how they *felt* about it at the time; how they think their experiences changed them, what they're proud of, or what they regret. It's quite an intense exploration of who the person is and how they've lived—there's a lot of soul searching. Some people find it difficult."

"I can understand. And how long would it take?"

"Three to four months. So, have a think," I added.

"I don't need to think about it," Vincent responded. "I'm keen to go ahead. In fact I wanted to ask if you could start next week?"

"That's . . . soon."

"It is, but we'd like to have it done in time for my mother's eightieth in late January. It's to be our present to her."

"I see. Well, I'd have to check my work diary." I didn't want to let on that there was precious little in it. "But before I do, could you tell me a bit more?" I reached for a pad and pen, glad to have this distraction and wondering what his mother's story might be.

"My mother's farmed for most of her life." I scribbled *farmer*. "It's not a big farm," he explained, "just a hundred and twenty acres, but it's been in my father's family since the 1860s. He died ten years ago."

Widowed, I wrote. *Farm. 150 yrs.*

"Mum has always worked very hard, and still works hard," Vincent went on. "She runs the farm shop, and she grows most of what's sold in it."

"And what sort of education did she have? Did she go to university?"

"No. She married my father when she was nineteen." *Married @ 19 . . . Mrs. Tregear.*

"And what's her first name?" Vincent told me and I wrote it down. "That's pretty."

"It's Klara with a *K*."

"So . . . is your mother German?"

"No. Dutch."

As I turned the *C* into a *K,* I imagined Klara growing up in Holland, under German occupation. Perhaps she'd known Anne Frank, or Audrey Hepburn—they'd have been about the same age. I saw Klara standing in a frozen field trying to dig up tulip bulbs to eat.

"My mother grew up in the tropics," I heard Vincent say. "On Java. Her father was the manager of a rubber plantation."

Plantation . . . Java . . .

"When the Pacific war started, after Pearl Harbor, she was interned with her mother and younger brother." *Interned . . .* I imagined bamboo fencing and barbed wire. "We know that internees suffered terrible privation, as well as cruelty, but she's rarely talked about it, except to mention the odd incident in this camp or that."

I'd have to do some research. I scribbled *Dutch East Indies,* then *Japanese occupation.*

"Vincent, I *would* like to take on this commission."

"Really? That's great!"

"And in fact I could start next week." My pen had run out. I yanked open the drawer and rummaged in it for another one. "If you give me your address, I'll send you my standard letter of engagement. Where do you live?"

"In Gerrards Cross, near Beaconsfield."

"I know it. It'll be easy to get there. It can't take more than, what, half an hour by train, or I could borrow my boyfriend's car—that's Rick, he was there yesterday; he doesn't use it much, and so—"

"Jenni, I must stop you," Vincent interjected. "My mother doesn't live with me."

"Oh." Why had I assumed that she did?

"She lives with my brother, Henry; he runs the farm."

"I see. And where is it?"

"In Cornwall." My heart sank as I wrote it down. "At a place called Polvarth." My pen stopped. "It's just a coastal hamlet," I heard him say. "It's beautiful, with small fields going down to the sea, and there's a wonderful beach . . . Jenni? Are you still there?"

I closed my eyes. "Vincent, have you contacted anyone else about this?"

"No. As I say, I was going to try and find a journalist, perhaps someone from the *Cornish Guardian*, but then yesterday I heard you talking about your work and was very taken with what you said, especially that you love immersing yourself in other people's memories."

"I do," I said quietly. It distracts me from my *own*.

"And on your website you say that being a ghost isn't just about being a writer; it's like being a midwife—you're helping to deliver the story of someone's life."

"But I also say that it's a very intense, emotional process, and that it's therefore important to choose the right person."

"I can't help feeling that you are. I also think that my mother would like you. I must say, I'm rather confused," Vincent added. "Didn't you just say that you wanted to do it?"

"I did say that . . . but I always advise prospective clients to, well, shop around. So that they have a choice," I went on, trying to keep the tension out of my voice. "I can recommend some other ghostwriters."

There was a pause. "Are you unsure about it because of the distance?"

"Yes," I said gratefully. "That's the reason. It's such a long way."

"We'd pay your travel expenses. And my mother would put you up—"

"That's kind," I interrupted, "but I never stay with the client—it's one of my rules."

"Fair enough, but she has a holiday cottage just down the lane. It's not that big, but it's comfortable."

"I'm sure it's lovely, but—"

"You'd be completely independent. You could come up to the farm during the day. My mother's a very pleasant person."

"I'm sure she is, Vincent, but that's not why . . ."

"You just want to think about it," he said after a moment.

"I do. And I'd need to talk to Rick."

"Of course. I'm sorry, Jenni. I didn't mean to push you. But if you could let me know, either way."

"I will."

I hung up, then sat staring at the computer screen again, seeing nothing. I raised my eyes to the shelf above my desk. *Battling the Enemy Within: Regain the Confidence to Be Yourself*. I'd bought that book a year before but still hadn't summoned the courage to read more than a few pages. Nor had I even opened the one beside it, *Transcending Fear: How to Face Your Demons*.

I'd never faced my demons. I'd buried them, in the sand.

I heard Rick's footsteps; then there he was in the doorway. "Are you okay, Jen?" He smiled, as if to reassure me that things were fine, when we both knew they weren't. "I heard you talking," he went on. "You sounded agitated." I told him about Vincent's call. "But that sounds interesting. And it's work." He lifted a pile of magazines off the armchair, put them on the floor, then sat down. I could smell the lingering scent of his cigarette. "Do you have much to do at the moment?"

"No. I have to get the baby guide to the publisher by Thursday, then there's nothing."

Rick stretched out his long, lean legs. "So why aren't you sure about this job?"

I couldn't tell him the truth. I'd wanted to, many times, but the dread of seeing shock and disappointment in his eyes had stopped me. "It's so . . . far."

He looked puzzled. "But you went up to Scotland to do that memoir last year. We emailed and Skyped, didn't we? It was fine." I nodded. "If you did this one, how long would you have to go for?"

"The usual." I put the top on my pen. "A week to ten days."

"Well . . ." He shrugged. "Perhaps it's come up now for a reason. It might be good for us to have some time apart."

"So that we can get used to it. Is that what you mean?" I dreaded hearing his answer, but I had to ask.

"No, so that we have some breathing space, to think about everything. It could . . . help." He didn't look as though he believed that it would. "So where exactly is Polvarth?"

"It's in south Cornwall, close to a fishing village called Trennick. It's very small—just one long lane that leads down to a beach. At the other end of it there's a farm." The Tregears' farm, I now realized.

"You've been there before?"

I nodded. "There are a few holiday homes, built in the sixties." I pictured the one that we'd stayed in, Penlee. "There's also a hotel." It had a big garden with a play area at the end of it with swings and a seesaw. "Just below the hotel is the beach. And on the cliff path behind the beach is a tea hut—or there was. Perhaps it's gone now."

"When were you last there? You've never mentioned the place to me."

"I . . . forgot about it. I was nine."

"So you went there with your mother?" I nodded. "And was it a happy holiday?" I didn't answer. Rick exhaled loudly, clearly frustrated by the conversation. "Obviously not. Then perhaps you shouldn't go—if it's going to upset you, it won't be worth it. But you're thirty-four, Jen. You're not a child." He stood up abruptly. "I think I'll walk up to school. I've got to plan tomorrow's lessons, and I might as well do it there." His smile was tight. "Whether you go to Cornwall or not is your decision. See you later, darling."

I wanted to throw my arms round him and implore him to

stay. Instead, I sat perfectly still. "Yes," I said coolly. "See you later."

After Rick left, I sat at my desk, frozen with misery, as the daylight began to fade. The nights were drawing in. I dreaded the thought of another winter in the city.

I took the phone out of the cradle. "It's my decision," I murmured. "I don't have to do it." I tapped in Vincent's number. "I don't want to do it." My finger hovered over the button. "And I'm not going to do it." I pressed Call.

The phone was picked up after three rings. "Hello?"

"Vincent? It's Jenni Clark again."

"Hello, Jenni. Thanks for phoning me back."

"Vincent . . ." I steeled myself. "I've thought about it."

"Yes?"

"I've also discussed it with Rick. And the thing is . . ." My eyes strayed to the shelf. *Transcending Fear.* "The thing is . . . that . . ."

"So . . . what have you decided?"

How to Face Your Demons.

"I'll come."

Three

The following Saturday I went to Paddington station and boarded the train for Cornwall. The week had rushed by, with the final edits on the baby-care guide due. I was glad to finish the project and to stop thinking about babies. I'd then thrown myself into researching the Dutch East Indies and the Japanese occupation.

Rick and I hadn't really discussed our problems again. In any case we'd hardly seen each other. He'd been busy at school with parents' evenings, and he'd spent time at the gym. He was clearly avoiding being with me. But when we did finally talk, we decided that it would be better if we didn't phone, text, or Skype while I was away.

"We need to find out how much we miss each other," Rick had said as he drove me to the station. "Perhaps that'll give us the answer."

"Perhaps it will," I responded bleakly. I hated the uncertainty between us but didn't know what else to say.

On the train, I stowed my case in the luggage rack, then found my seat. Soon there was the slamming of doors, a shrill whistle, and the creaking and groaning of the train cars as we pulled away from the platform. As we trundled through West London, my mind was in turmoil; my future with Rick hung in the balance, and I was heading for Cornwall, a place I'd shunned for twenty-five years. I'd been unable even to look at the county on a map without a stab of pain. Now, for reasons I didn't even understand, I was going back.

Desperate to distract myself, I got out my laptop.

The Dutch East Indies was a colony that became Indonesia following World War II . . .

Through the window the urban sprawl had already given way to fields and coppiced hills that were tinged with gold.

Java lies between Sumatra to the west and Bali to the east. . . . A chain of volcanic mountains forms a spine along the island . . . four main provinces . . .

Soon we were passing through the Somerset levels, where weeping willows lined the riverbanks. A heron shook out its wings, then lifted into the air.

On 28 February 1942 the Japanese 16th Army landed at three locations on the coast of West Java; their main targets were the cities of Batavia (now Jakarta) and Bandung . . .

The train was running beside an estuary. The tide was out and flocks of wading birds had gathered on the silty shore. My mind filled with thoughts of Rick again, but I forced them away. I returned to my research and read on about the fall of Java.

At the next station, a woman got on with a small girl and boy, and they sat at the table across the aisle.

The girl had short brown hair, held off her pretty face with a yellow clip. She read a book while her little brother, seated opposite her, played on a Nintendo.

The Japanese began interning nonmilitary European men— mostly planters, teachers, civil servants, and engineers—from March 1942. Their wives and children were interned from November of that year. For many, this was the start of an ordeal that was to last three and a half years.

"Fear!" I looked up. The boy had put down his Nintendo and was looking at his sister. "Fear!" he repeated. Absorbed in her story, she ignored him.

"Feear . . ." He grabbed her arm. "FEAR!"

Their mother, who'd been texting, lowered her phone. "Sophia, answer your brother, will you!"

Sophia glared at him. "What?"

He held up his Nintendo. "Could you do my Super Mario for me, Phia? I'm stuck."

She peered at it. "Okay."

The boy passed the console to her, and she began tapping the screen with the stylus while he watched, rapt, resting his face in his hands.

Some 108,000 civilians were herded into camps, where they were held in atrocious conditions; 13,000 died from starvation and disease. I tried to imagine the dreadful reality behind those figures. Klara must have been through so much, and at such a young age.

As we left Plymouth, the woman put her phone down again. "I want you to stop playing and look out the window," she told her children. "What huge ships," she said as we passed the dockyard. "We'll be crossing the river in a minute. *Here* we go," she sang as the train rolled onto Brunel's great railway bridge.

The girl stood up to get a better view through the massive iron girders. "It's like flying!"

A hundred feet below, the Tamar glittered in the sunshine.

"Look at all those boats," said her mother. "Now we're in Cornwall," she added as we reached the other side.

"Yay!" the children exclaimed.

After Saltash the train proceeded slowly through steep pastureland, then through a conifer plantation. We passed Liskeard and Par, then St. Austell with its terraces of pale stone houses.

The loudspeaker crackled into life. "This is your train manager speaking. Next stop, Truro."

My hands shook as I gathered up my things. I smiled goodbye to the children's mum; then, as the train halted, I stepped off with my case.

At the Hertz office at the front of the station I collected the keys for the small car I'd reserved. Then, my heart pounding, I drove off, past Truro's cathedral with its three spires, out of the city. Following the signs for St. Mawes, I went down a winding road canopied by oak and beech, their branches pierced here and there by shafts of sunlight that dappled the tarmac.

I drove through Glendurn and Trelawn, then, seeing the sign for Trennick, I turned onto a still narrower road, ringed with blackthorn and alder, the banks thick with brambles that scratched the sides of the car.

I rounded the next bend. Then I stopped.

Before me was the sea, shimmering in the sun. This was Polvarth, a place I'd vowed never to return to, yet which I saw, in my mind, every day.

It was my idea.

I closed my eyes as the memories rushed back.

We did it all by ourselves.

Beneath the sign that said HIGHER POLVARTH FARM was an old kitchen table on which had been left a crate of cauliflowers (50p each), a box of cabbages (50p), and a yellow bucket holding bunches of dahlias (75p). A jam jar contained a few coins. A smaller sign had a black arrow on it, pointing right. FARM SHOP, 200 YDS. CRABS, LOBSTERS & FISH, CAUGHT DAILY. OPEN 9 A.M.–11 A.M. & 5 P.M.–7 P.M., MON TO SAT.

I turned in, bumped carefully down the track, then braked.

In front of me rose the farmhouse, a square, white-painted building with a low-pitched slate roof and tall windows. Beside it were parked an old Land Rover and a white pickup, the back of which was piled with lobster pots. Behind me was a big, open-sided shed housing a wooden boat on a trailer; a stone barn served as the farm shop. A ginger cat lay curled in the sun-light.

The door of the farmhouse opened, and a well-built man in blue overalls came out.

"Jenni?" He held out his hand as he came closer. "Henry Tregear."

I shook it, feeling shy suddenly. "Good to meet you. I can see the resemblance to your brother."

Henry patted his head, grinning. "Vince has got rather more hair. You'll meet my mother later—she's just nipped over to Trelawn to see a friend. But in the meantime I'll show you where you're staying—if I could just hop in your car with you."

Henry got into the passenger seat, and I drove a few hundred yards down the lane to the modern cottage that I'd passed on the way up. I parked on the forecourt, then Henry got out, opened the boot, and carried my suitcase to the semi-glassed front door.

There was a slate sign on the wall: LANHAY. The interior was quite plain, with wooden floors and neutral furnishings. On the walls hung framed prints of flowers and fish—typical of a holiday house. But in one of the bedrooms was an original oil painting—a striking seascape. I stared at the churning blue and green water, low cliffs, and jagged rocks.

Henry noticed me looking at it. "That's by my son, Adam. He sells quite a few; in fact he's having an exhibition the week after next, at Trennick."

I shivered in recognition. "It's the beach here, isn't it?"

"It is. How did you know? Have you just driven down there?"

"No . . ." I tried to quell the thudding in my rib cage. "I've been to Polvarth before."

"I see. Anyway, the house is simple," Henry remarked as we went downstairs again, "but comfy." He fiddled with the boiler, then touched the nearest radiator. "You've got everything you need; the washing machine's there. Give the door a little thump if it won't start. Dishwasher, microwave, fridge . . ." He opened the latter, revealing milk, cheese, bacon, a dozen eggs, and a bottle of wine.

"There's some salad stuff as well, some veg, and a loaf of bread in the bread bin."

"That's so kind. Thank you."

"Tea and coffee's here." He opened a cupboard. "But there's a general store at Trennick for anything else you might want.

It's a couple of miles by road, or you can easily walk to it. You just go down to the beach, up the steps onto the cliff, then carry on round the coastal path for five minutes."

"Yes, I remember that path."

"Course you do—you've been here before. So, when was that?"

"Oh . . . years ago."

"Well, we're very glad that you've come again. Having my mother's memoirs will mean a lot to her family; having said that, we're not sure how forthcoming she'll be." He smiled ruefully.

"Well, I'll try to draw out her story, but what she says is up to her."

"Of course," Henry agreed. "She has to feel happy with it."

I set my laptop on the table. "This will be a good place to work. Is there a broadband connection?"

"There is, but I'm afraid the phone only takes incoming calls."

"That's okay—I've got my mobile."

"Just to warn you, the signal's patchy; you get better reception if you stand in the lane."

I walked to the window. There was a small garden, enclosed by a fence. In the center of the lawn was a windswept cherry tree, crusted with tufts of green lichen, and in the far corner, a battered-looking palm. On the other side of the fence a herd of tawny-colored cattle grazed peacefully, occasionally lifting their heads, as if enjoying the view. Beyond that was the sea. I could see a scattering of white sails, and to my right, the headland jutting out, like a prow.

"It's beautiful!" I exclaimed. I had forgotten how beautiful it was.

"It is," Henry agreed. "I still have to pinch myself after fifty-four years spent staring at it. Anyway, here are your keys. So come up to the farm at around seven and have supper with us."

I thanked Henry and promised that I would.

After Henry left I texted Rick to say that I'd arrived. I wished that he could be with me. If he were, I'd take him down to the beach and I'd finally tell him what had happened there all those years ago. I tried to imagine his reaction—shock, swiftly changing to bewilderment that I could have kept my secret from him for so long.

I sat at the garden table as the shadows stretched across the lawn. The sea was pewter now, patched with silver where the sun's rays streamed through a bank of low clouds. A week ago I'd been at Nina's wedding; now her wedding had brought me back to Polvarth. I repressed a shudder.

I went inside and unpacked. As I opened my wash bag I looked at the pink blister pack of pills that Rick had come to hate but which made me feel safe. I took one, then, having showered and changed, I walked the few hundred yards up to the farm. I was looking forward to meeting Klara. What would she be like? I wondered. Would she be easy to work with?

The knocker on the farmhouse door was in the shape of a hand. I hesitated for a moment, then rapped.

Henry, now in green cords and a blue checked shirt, ushered me into the large square kitchen with its red-and-black floor tiles, cream-colored Aga, and pine furniture. He took my jacket, then introduced me to his wife, Beth.

"Welcome, Jenni," she said. She was a fair-haired, cheerful woman in her midfifties. "Is everything okay at Lanhay?"

"Oh yes, it's great, thank you. It's a gorgeous cottage." Henry smiled at the elderly woman who was setting the table. "Mum, meet Jenni." The woman set down the last plate, then turned and held out her hand.

I took it. "Hello, Mrs. Tregear. I've been looking forward to meeting you."

"Please, call me Klara."

Klara Tregear was slim and upright, with high cheekbones and blue-gray eyes; her hair was a pure white, cut to the chin and held with a clip, like the little girl on the train. Her face was seamed with age, and tanned from the sun and wind.

"So . . ." The smile she gave me was anxious. "You're going to take me down memory lane." Her voice was soft, and she spoke with a slight Dutch inflection. "I find the thought a little daunting."

"I completely understand. But I'll try to make the process as pleasant as possible. Just think of it as a long conversation with someone who's really interested in you."

"So you will be hanging on my every word," she remarked wryly.

"I certainly will." I glanced around the kitchen. "Will we be doing the interviews here?"

"No—at my flat." Klara pointed through the window to the barn. "I live above the shop. But please, you must be hungry." She gestured to the table.

As I sat down I looked through the French windows. Clumps of agapanthus and scarlet sedums framed the long lawn. Beyond the garden, the land sloped down to the sea, indigo in the deepening dusk. A distant light glimmered from a boat or buoy.

Klara poured me a glass of wine, then sat down beside me. "How long will we talk for each time?"

"It's quite an intense process, as you can imagine." She nodded. "I usually aim to record three hours of material a day. Could we do two hours in the mornings? Would that be okay?"

"Yes, after eleven would be best, when the shop shuts."

"Then another hour in the afternoon?" I suggested.

"That would be fine. Tomorrow, being Sunday, we're closed, so that's a good day for us to start. I go to church first thing, but I'm usually back by ten. Could you come then?"

"Ten will be fine." I sipped the wine and felt my tension slip away. If I could just keep a grip on my emotions, I told myself, I'd be able to do this job.

Beth carried a big earthenware dish to the table. "I hope you like fish pie, Jenni." She put it on a trivet.

"I do, very much."

"Then help yourself."

"Thanks." But Klara had already picked up my plate and was spooning a huge portion onto it. "Oh, I couldn't eat that much," I protested.

"Try," Klara said firmly as she handed it to me.

"It looks delicious. Is it made with your own fish?"

"It is," Beth answered. "Our son, Adam, goes to the cove every morning and puts down lobster pots. He also uses short nets that he stakes to the sea floor, just a few yards out. He gets plaice, monkfish, scallops, and sole, and we buy them from him to sell in the shop. It's an important part of the business, especially in the season."

I took some salad. "Is it still the season now?"

Henry joined us at the table. "Just about—it finishes at the end of the month. But we have local customers, and we supply the hotel, so we stay open nearly all the year round."

"And the cattle, I presume they're yours."

"They are." He unfurled his napkin. "We rear them for beef, which provides the greater part of our income. They're South Devons. We used to have Friesians when this was a dairy farm."

"I remember them," I said without thinking. "I remember them being herded down the lane; I remember the big silver churn at the end of your track. We used to scoop the milk out with a ladle and put the money in a jar."

Klara glanced at me in surprise. "You've been here before?"

"She has," said Henry.

Klara put some fish pie on her own plate. "When was that?"

"Oh, a long time ago; I was . . . a child."

Klara picked up her fork. "And where did you stay?"

"At one of the holiday houses near the beach. I can't remember which one." I resorted to my usual strategy of deflecting unwelcome questions with questions of my own. "But could you tell me about the farm?"

"Well . . ." Beth shrugged, smiling. "It's a busy life. There's always something to be done, whether it's mending the fences, hedge cutting, bucket feeding a calf, or pulling up ragwort and nightshade. We work very long days, especially in the summer."

"Not that we complain," Henry added. "We love this place." He smiled at Klara. "And we're very lucky in that my mum still does so much."

Klara laughed. "I'm sure I'd drop dead if I stopped! After sixty-three years, my body wouldn't be able to cope with not working."

I studied her. She had a wiry vigor, her movements quick and efficient. Her hands were rough and callused, her fingertips bent with arthritis. Her shoulders were round, as though shaped by the wind.

I had another sip of wine. "So Adam does the fishing . . ."

"He does," answered Beth. "He also paints."

"Your husband was telling me. I love the seascape in the cottage; he's very talented."

"He lives in Porthloe," Beth went on, pleased to hear her son praised, "with his girlfriend, Molly, and their baby. Klara runs the shop and grows most of our fresh produce. I prepare the shellfish, and I make the bread and preserves that we sell. Henry looks after the cattle and does the accounts."

"An unending task." He rolled his eyes.

Beth poured herself some water. "He's also a Coastwatch volunteer."

"Really?"

Henry nodded. "There are a few of us who do it from the old coast guard hut on Polvarth Point. We keep a lookout for any incidents at sea, or on the beach or the cliff paths."

"People do such silly things," Klara said.

"Like what?" I asked faintly.

Henry sighed. "They walk too near the cliff edge and slip, or they go out in a kayak, with no knowledge of the currents, and get carried out to open sea. We have kids floating away in rubber dinghies, or getting stuck on the rocks at high tide."

"Sometimes people dig tunnels in the sand," said Beth. "If I see that, I always warn them not to." She looked at Klara. "Do you remember what happened to those boys?"

"Oh, I do," Klara responded quietly, then turned to me. "In fact I might talk about that to you."

Heat spilled into my face. "Why?" I asked, too abruptly.

"Well . . ." Klara was clearly taken aback by my reaction. "For the book. I've been thinking about some of the more memorable things that have happened here over the years."

"Of course." I sipped my wine to cover my growing distress. Why on earth had I *come* here? I should have followed my instincts and stayed away.

Now Henry was talking about a calf that, the year before, got lost in the fog. "It ended up in the sea," he told me.

"In the sea?" I echoed.

"Something must have spooked it," Beth explained. "A dog or a fox, because it had swum two hundred yards out from the beach. Luckily, a friend of ours was out fishing, saw it, and managed to get a rope round it and hauled it into his boat. When we got it back, its mum kept pushing it away because it smelt of brine."

"We had to tie them together," Henry added. "In the end she let it feed and all was well. But it was a miracle it didn't drown."

"Jenni . . ." Klara was looking at me reproachfully; she nodded at my plate. "You've hardly eaten."

"Oh. I'm sorry. It was delicious, but a bit too much . . ."

Henry laughed. "You have to eat up round here, otherwise my mum gets upset—don't you, Mum?"

"Don't worry," Klara told me. "He's just teasing you. But you'll have some ice cream."

"I've eaten so well, Klara, I couldn't manage another thing, but thank you."

"Coffee, then?"

"Oh, yes please. I never say no to that; I drink so much, it probably flows in my veins."

Over coffee and the petit fours that Klara pressed on me, I learned a bit more about Vincent. He was three years older than Henry, a civil engineer, divorced with one grown-up daughter.

"I met Vincent years ago," I told them, "at my friend Nina's twenty-first—he's her godfather."

"That's right. He and her dad were at Imperial College together."

"We were at the same table at Nina's wedding."

"That was lucky," Henry remarked. "Otherwise I don't suppose you'd be here now."

"No." I fiddled with my napkin. "I don't suppose I would."

"Vince never wanted to be a farmer," Henry went on. "Fortunately for our parents, I did. Adam will take over in years to come." He asked me about my book projects and how I got the memoir-writing work.

"I advertise in magazines and on genealogy websites," I replied. "I also put up notices in local libraries."

"You live in Islington, don't you?" Beth topped up my coffee.

"Yes—at the Angel."

"Are you from London?"

I shook my head. "I grew up in a village near Reading, but we moved to Southampton when I was ten."

"Do you have any brothers or sisters?" Klara asked.

"None." I gave her a quick smile in case she thought me

abrupt. "Well . . ." I put my napkin on the table. "I think I should be getting back."

"Of course," Beth agreed warmly. "You must be tired after the journey. Are you okay to walk on your own? Or would you like Henry to go down the lane with you?"

"Oh, I'll be fine," I assured her. "I'm not scared of the dark."

"Well, let me give you a flashlight. It's pitch-black out there." As I put on my coat, Beth opened a cupboard under the sink, took a torch out, and handed it to me.

"Good night, Jenni. It was lovely meeting you."

"Good night, Beth. Thanks for supper—it was delicious. Good night, Henry." I turned to Klara and smiled. "I'll see you in the morning."

"Yes. See you then, dear. Sleep well."

"Thanks. You too." I knew that I'd be lucky to sleep at all.

I switched on the flashlight, then walked up the track, raking the ground with the beam. The evening had been fine—I liked Klara, and Henry and Beth had been warm and welcoming. But I'd given too much away. As I turned toward the cottage, I resolved to be more careful.

The blackthorn trees, sculpted by the wind, hunched over the lane. The stars glittered in a blue-black sky. I turned off the torch and looked up. I could see Orion's Belt, and Venus, and there were the seven points of the Big Dipper. And now, as my eyes adjusted to the dark, I could see the pale band of the Milky Way. I craned my neck, drinking in its nebulous beauty. "Wonderful," I whispered as I gazed at its star clouds and clusters. "It's wonder—" A sudden jolt ran the length of my spine. I froze, my pulse racing, and listened. The sound that had startled me must have been the wind. I was about to walk on when I heard it again. Adrenaline flooded my veins. It wasn't the wind. There was someone there. I couldn't see anyone, but I could feel a presence; someone was very close, so close that I could hear breathing. I tried to cry out but could make no sound; I wanted to run, but my feet seemed clamped to the ground—and there it was again! So loud that it filled my ears; and now my own breath was ragged, my heart pounding. Then I felt it suddenly slow. I exhaled with relief as I realized that what I'd heard was just the slow gasp of the sea.

Four

I slept fitfully and, as usual, woke before dawn. In my half-asleep state I reached out for Rick, longing for his warm body, then, with a pang, remembered where I was. I lay staring into the darkness for a while, then I showered and dressed and drank a cup of coffee. Steeling myself, I set off for the beach.

I strolled past villas screened by dry-stone walls and fuchsia hedges still speckled with red flowers, then a converted barn that offered B and B. I came to Lower Polvarth, where, set back from the lane, a row of houses stood with pretty front gardens and evocative names—Bohella, Sea Mist, and Rosevine.

I stopped in front of Penlee. I remembered the bank of hydrangeas and that lilac tree—I'd snapped a branch trying to climb it, and Mum had been cross. The bedrooms were on the first floor. We'd had the one on the left, with bunk beds; she was in the room next to it.

Suddenly the curtains in "her" room parted and I saw a woman framed in the window. She was in her midfifties—my mother's age now. She gazed out to sea but then saw me standing there. I looked away and walked quickly on, past the old red phone box; and here were the stone gateposts of the Polvarth Hotel.

I turned in, my feet crunching over the gravel. The large Georgian house had been old-fashioned and shabby; now it looked smart and sleek, with two Range Rovers and a Porsche parked outside and a pair of potted bay trees flanking the door.

The garden was just as I remembered it, framed by a cedar of Lebanon and a Monterey pine with a wind-blasted crown. The trees might look the same, but I had changed beyond all recognition.

I crossed the lawn, then went down the steps to the play area. There were still swings, a slide, and a wooden playhouse.

I lifted my eyes to the view. Before me was the bay, a perfect horseshoe, and just beyond it the village of Trennick, its Victorian villas and snug cob cottages jostling for position along the harbor walls.

I stepped back onto the lane through a gap in the hedge and continued downhill. Gulls wheeled above me, crying their sharp cries. The lane curved to the left, and there was the beach.

Ignoring the thudding in my chest, I kept walking, past the wooden signs pointing to the coastal path and the life buoy in its scarlet case.

I stopped halfway down the slipway. The waves were flecked with white, and there were the cliffs, the tea hut, still there, the cobalt rocks and the crescent of sand. I felt a sudden, sharp constriction in my ribs, as though my heart was hooped with a tightening wire.

We're making a tunnel . . .

I forced myself forward, the wind whipping my cheeks. A boy was walking a Labrador; the dog ambled beside him, sniffing at the seaweed. A young couple in wet suits ran into the waves, scattering the spray in glittering arcs.

Mum'll be surprised . . . She'll be amazed.

Can I go in?

As I crossed the sand, I felt the wire in my chest tighten. I saw the ambulance pull into the field behind the hut; I saw the medics with their stretcher and bags. I remembered the other holiday makers standing there, in their eyes a strange blend of distress and avid curiosity. Now I recalled an arm going round me, drawing me away; then I saw the doors of the ambulance slam shut.

It was nine when I got back to Lanhay. As I unlocked the cottage door, my hands were trembling. I sat at the table, head bowed, perfectly still, struggling to absorb the blow to my soul. My mother had been twenty-eight then—six years younger than I was now. I remembered the drive home, in the police car, her fingers clasped so tightly that her knuckles were white. I'd put my hand on hers, but she didn't take it.

I stood up, went into the sitting room, turned on the radio, and tuned it to Honor's show. Just the sound of her voice consoled me, bringing me back to myself. Honor had always had that effect on me, making me feel better when I was low. Her cheerfulness and exuberance were the perfect counterpoint to my shyness.

There was the usual miscellany—a funny interview with Emma Watson about her new film, then some Coldplay, followed by the news, and then a heated discussion about whether the world was going to end on 21 December, as predicted by the ancient Mayans using their Long Count calendar.

"So what you're saying," said Honor to her interviewee, "is that just two months from now, what we can expect is not so much Christmas as the Apocalypse."

"Yes," the woman replied grimly. "Because on that day the sun will be in *exact* alignment with the center of the Milky Way, which will affect the earth's magnetic shield, throwing the planet completely out of kilter, resulting in catastrophic earthquakes and flooding that could wipe us all out."

"But astronomers have trashed this theory," Honor pointed out. "As has NASA."

"They can trash it all they like, but it's going to happen."

"Well, on the twenty-second of December I guess we'll know who was right," Honor concluded. "But thanks for joining us today—and speaking of mass extinctions . . ." There was a deafening roar, then she introduced the producer of a new documentary about the last days of the dinosaurs.

"Weren't they wiped out by an asteroid?" Honor asked her guest. "Sixty-five million years ago?"

"That's the accepted theory," the man replied; "which is known as the Late Cretaceous Tertiary Extinction, but the truth is, no one really knows. So in the program we explore alternative explanations, such as climate change caused by a massive volcanic eruption, or the evolution of mammals that ate dinosaur eggs. We also look at the possibility of a major change in vegetation, resulting in the plant-eating dinosaurs becoming unable to digest their food."

"And getting fatal constipation?"

"Well . . . yes."

Honor laughed. "I think I'd have preferred the meteor strike. But what's your favorite dinosaur? I've always liked Ankylosaurus, with that terrific club on the tail."

"Yes, a feature shared by Euoplocephalus, though that had spikes, not armored plates. But my personal favorite *has* to be Spinosaurus, with that marvelous dorsal sail . . ."

By now Honor's lively chatter had lifted my mood so much that I felt able to face the day. I had a job to do, and I was going to do it.

It was twenty to ten. I switched off the radio and read through the notes I'd made, then opened my laptop and created a new document: "Klara." I labeled five microcassettes, put one in the machine, tested it, then walked up to the farm.

On the way there I stopped to look at a chaffinch swinging about on a cluster of elderberries; I realized that this was where I'd been so frightened the night before. Closing my eyes, I could hear the sea pulling in and out, but now it seemed distant, not near at all. Perhaps the darkness had amplified it, or perhaps it was just the effect of the wine. Even so, I shuddered as I remembered the sound.

As I approached the farm, I saw Klara, in a blue striped dress and white apron, setting out vegetables on the table. She put a jam jar down next to them and then turned at my footsteps. "Jenni! Good morning."

"Morning, Klara." I nodded at the cabbages and cauliflowers. "It's nice that you do this."

She shrugged. "We've always done it."

"Do people put the money in the jar?"

"Usually, although I couldn't care less if they don't. I care only that good food shouldn't be wasted." She folded the carrier bag that she'd been using and tucked it into her apron pocket. "Before we start talking, I've a few chores I need to do. Will you come with me?"

"Of course—I'd love to see the farm."

We crossed the yard and went into the shed. "This is our second boat," Klara explained. "It's a Cornish cove boat like our first one—my grandson's been repairing it." We stepped around the tins of black paint, then picked our way through various bits of farm machinery and several sacks of animal feed. Klara half filled a plastic bowl with corn. I followed her into a small field. There were two large wooden coops there with long runs, in each of which were a dozen or so hens. At our approach there was a burst of frenzied clucking.

"Ladies, please!" Klara called as the hens rushed forward. "No pushing or pecking!" She tossed the grain through the mesh. "These are Rhode Island Reds; they have dreadful manners, but they lay well." She threw in another handful. "I give them these corn pellets in the morning, then vegetable scraps at night." I stared about me in fascination as she topped up the water bowls from a rain barrel. The hens in the second coop were black with tufty faces, like Victorian whiskers. "These are Araucana," Klara explained. "They're very sweet-natured, and their eggs are a beautiful blue." She gave them the rest of the corn, then wiped the bowl with the corner of her apron. "All done. Now we go up here."

I dutifully followed Klara through another gate into the adjacent field. A large greenhouse on a brick plinth stood there. Its panes flashed and glinted in the sun.

As we went inside, we were hit by a wall of warm air mingled with the scent of damp earth and the tang of tomatoes.

Klara took a pair of secateurs out of her apron and snipped some off a vine and laid them in the bowl. Then she snapped two cucumbers off their stems.

"We grow peppers too," she told me as a bee flew past. "We have aubergines, okra, galia melons . . ."

"And grapes." I glanced at the thick vine that trailed along the roof.

"Yes, though they're rather small and prone to mildew. I give them to the hens, as a treat." We walked on past grow bags planted with Lollo Rosso and Little Gem lettuce, coriander, and thyme, then Klara stopped again. "These are my pride and joy."

Before us were six lemon trees in big clay pots.

"I love growing lemons." Klara twisted off three ripe ones, put them in the bowl, then indicated the two smaller trees to our left. "Those are kumquats. They're too bitter to eat but make good marmalade."

"And you sell all this in the shop?"

"We do. Everything that we sell we have produced ourselves. Come."

I followed her out of the greenhouse and toward the field to our left, where I could now see a huge stone structure, like a little fortress.

"What's that?"

"You'll see," Klara answered as we approached it, then entered through a wooden gate.

Inside, the air was still, the deep silence broken only by the silvery trills of a blackbird perched high on the wall. The air was fragrant with a late-flowering rose.

We strolled along the gravel path, in the sunshine, past gooseberry and red currant bushes and teepee frames for peas and runner beans. There were rows of cabbages, cauliflowers, and leeks, a strawberry patch, a bed of dahlias, and a small orchard of dwarf apple trees.

"It's amazing!" I exclaimed, utterly charmed. "But it must be so much work."

"It is," Klara said as she twisted a few last apples off the nearest tree. "But I have a gardener who does the weeding and the heavy pruning. The watering is automated, and the rest I can manage."

"How long is it?" I asked as we walked on. "A hundred feet?"

"A hundred and twenty, and thirty feet wide. The walls are eighteen feet high and two feet deep."

"It's magnificent."

"It was my husband's wedding present to me. He asked me what I wanted, and I said that what I wanted, more than anything, was a walled garden. So he and his farmhand, Seb, built this, using stones that they carried up from the cove. It took them a year."

"And when was that?"

"They started it in 1952. I'd just arrived here, never having been to England, let alone Cornwall."

"You must have been very much in love with your husband."

"I was." I felt a sting of envy, that Klara's love had clearly been so deeply reciprocated. "When I saw the farm for the first time, I made it my ambition to grow any crop, from A to Z."

"Really?" I laughed. "And did you achieve that?"

"Oh, I did," she replied as we passed a row of pumpkins. "We have everything from asparagus to . . . zucchini."

"What's Q?" I wondered aloud.

"Quince." Klara pointed to a glossy shrub growing against the wall.

"And Y?"

"Yams. Though I don't grow many, as they tend to go mad and take over the place."

We'd stopped by a peach tree that had been trained against the south-facing wall. Its leaves had yellowed and its fruit was all gone, except for one or two shriveled ones that were being probed by wasps.

Klara pressed her hand against the thick, twisted trunk. "This was the first thing I planted. We've grown old together— old and rather gnarled." She smiled; wrinkles fanned her eyes. "I planted that too." She nodded at a huge fig tree. "I planted everything—it was an obsession, because when I was a child someone told me that the word *paradise* means 'walled garden.' And from that moment, that was my dream, to have my own little paradise, that no one could ever take away."

Klara's flat occupied the upper floor of the barn. It had a high, raftered ceiling with skylights and a galley kitchen.

Klara put the bowl on the counter, then began to rinse the fruit and vegetables. I was enjoying being with her but wondered whether she was ever going to sit down and start the interview.

"I used to live in the farmhouse," she was saying. "I moved out after my husband died so that Henry and Beth could have it. But this flat suits me quite well. My bedroom and bathroom are downstairs, and this is my living and dining area."

"It's wonderfully light." A floor-to-ceiling unit was crammed with books; I peered at the shelves. There were orange-and-green Penguin Classics, a complete set of Dickens in maroon leather bindings, and novels by Daphne du Maurier, Jane Austen, Georgette Heyer and the Brontës. There were some Dutch titles—*Max Havelaar* was one I vaguely recognized—and several biographies. "You read a lot, Klara."

"I do. And I'm lucky in that my eyesight's still good—*afkloppen*. Touch wood." She rapped on a cupboard and then untied her apron. "I'd much rather read than watch TV, though I do have a small television in my bedroom."

On the bottom shelf were a couple of dozen Virago Modern Classics. "You like Elizabeth Taylor," I said. "She's my favorite writer in the world."

"Mine too," Klara responded warmly. "My dearest friend, Jane, was a terrific reader, and she introduced me to her books. I used to adore *Sleeping Beauty*, but now that I'm old, it's *Mrs. Palfrey at the Claremont*."

"I love that one too," I said, feeling sad for Klara that her best friend had died.

"Please excuse the clutter," she said, changing the subject.

"I hadn't noticed. But it's a lovely flat. And you can see the sea." Now I glanced at the wooden dresser; on it were rows of blue-and-white china plates decorated with flowers, peacocks, and boats. "Is that Delft?"

Klara lifted up the kettle. "It is. It's from my grandparents' home."

"Which was where?"

"In Rotterdam, which is where I was born—I'm a Rotterdammer." She filled the kettle. "Coffee?"

"I'd love some. In fact I need some—I'm incredibly tired."

Klara studied my face. "Didn't you sleep well, my dear?"

"Not really, no. I . . . was just excited from the trip," I lied.

"I hope it's not the bed."

"Oh, the bed's very comfortable, Klara; but I never sleep well, wherever I am. My internal alarm goes off at an unspeakable hour."

A look of sympathy crossed Klara's face. "What a nuisance. So what do you do when that happens? Read?"

"Yes, sometimes, or listen to the radio. Usually I get up and work."

"Well, I'm sorry you have that problem. I shall pick some valerian for you and dry it; it helps."

"Thank you. That's kind." I felt a little flustered by Klara's concern.

She opened the fridge, took out a Victoria sponge, and put it on the kitchen counter. "You'll have some cake." I realized that this wasn't so much an invitation as a command.

"Yes, please—just a small piece."

"It needs a little caster sugar on the top." She sprinkled some on, then got a knife out of the drawer.

"It looks delicious. May I look at your pictures, Klara?"

She glanced up from her cake cutting. "Of course."

Arrayed on the sideboard were photos of Klara with her husband, and of Henry and Vincent. I stared at them avidly. I always love being with clients in their homes—it gives me a strong sense of who they are before we even begin the interviews. Then, once they start to talk, I feel as though I'm right inside their head; plunged into their thoughts and memories. It's as close as I can get to being someone else.

Amongst the snaps were some formal portraits in silver

frames. It wasn't hard to guess who the people in these ones were—Klara's parents on their wedding day; Klara herself at eight or nine, sitting on a pony. There was also a studio portrait of Klara, aged about six or seven, with her arm round a little boy. They both had short blond hair and stared solemnly at the camera with the same large round eyes.

"This is you with your brother?"

She looked at me, then glanced away. "Yes."

"What's his name?"

"Peter." Klara's face filled with grief. "His name was Peter." I immediately wondered when, and how, he'd died.

"All those older photos belonged to my grandparents," Klara went on as she spooned coffee into a heavy brown jug. "Fortunately my mother always enclosed a few snaps in her letters to them, otherwise we'd have had no record of our ten years on Java. Everything we'd ever owned there was lost or destroyed."

The kettle was boiling. Klara tipped the water into the jug, and the aroma of coffee filled the air.

"Let's use the Delft, as we shall be talking about Holland." She took down some plates and cups and put them on a tray. So Klara was ready to start. I began asking her more direct questions.

"How old were you when you went to Java?"

"I was almost four. My father decided to try his luck in the NEI—the Netherlands East Indies, as it then was. He got a job on a rubber plantation, not far from Bandung."

She picked up the tray and I stepped forward. "Let me help you."

"If you could take the jug, I can manage the rest." Klara carried the tray to the low wooden table and set it down; then she sat on the right side of the sofa while I took the armchair opposite. She poured me a cup of coffee, then handed me an enormous wedge of Victoria sponge that almost covered the plate.

"Oh, could I have half that?"

Klara passed me a fork. "I'm sure you can manage it."

"Well . . ." I didn't want to argue with her. "It does look good." I tasted it. "It's delicious."

"We really ought to be eating madeleines," she quipped. "Not that I need help in summoning the remembrance of things past. My memory is quite undimmed. Which I sometimes feel is a disadvantage."

"What do you mean?"

Klara poured herself some coffee. "A few months ago, my dearest friend, Jane, was diagnosed with dementia."

"Oh, I see. When you said she 'was' a great reader, I assumed that she'd died. I'm glad that's not the case."

"Oh, she's in good health—physically at least. But in a way, the Jane I've known for fifty-five years *has* died. When I talk to her about some of the happy times we've had, the people we've known or the books we've both loved, she looks at me blankly, or becomes confused."

"That must be heartbreaking."

"It is. It makes me feel . . . lonely." Klara sighed. "But I assume that Jane's *un*happy memories are also disappearing, and I must say there are times when I envy her this. How wonderful it must be, to be unable to remember things that once caused us distress. Yet we should embrace all our memories, whether joyful or painful. They're all we ever really own in this life."

As I murmured my agreement I wondered what painful memories Klara was thinking of and whether she would want to talk about them for the book.

Klara sipped her coffee, then looked at me. "One might say that you're in the memory 'business.'"

I nodded. "You could put it that way. It's my job to draw memories out of my clients." *While fiercely protecting my own memories,* I reflected wryly. I glanced at the old leather albums piled up on the table in front of us. Rick had sometimes remarked on my own lack of family photographs. "You've got quite a few photos, Klara."

"I have."

"They'll help hugely in the interview process—and we can reproduce some of them in the book, if you'd like to."

"I would. Having committed myself to this memoir, I want it to be as vivid as possible."

"I think it will be, Klara—not because of any photos that we put in it, but because of what you say. The key to it is not just to remember what happened to you at this time or that, but to think about how those events affected you then, to make you the person that you are now."

"Put that way it sounds a bit like . . . therapy."

"Well, it's a journey of self-discovery, so the process *can* be therapeutic, yes—cathartic, even."

"I've been thinking hard about the past." Klara laid her hand on one of the albums. "I've been looking at the much-loved faces in these pages, and remembering what they meant to me—still mean to me."

"When you talk about them, try to recall not just what they

looked like, but how they talked or walked, or laughed, or dressed. Any little details that will bring them alive."

Klara nodded and sipped her coffee again. She flashed me an anxious smile. "How strange to think that I barely know you, Jenni, yet I'm about to tell you so much about myself—more than I have ever told anyone in my own family—my own husband, even."

"It must feel very strange," I agreed. "But try to think of it as a conversation with an old friend."

"We aren't friends though, are we?"

I was taken aback by her directness. "No . . . But we'll get to know each other over these next few days."

"Well, you'll get to know me." She put her cup on the table. "But will I get to know *you*?"

"Of . . . course."

"Because this has all come up so quickly; and now that we're sitting here, I realize that I simply *can't* talk to you about myself, unless I know at least a little about you."

"You already . . . do." I wondered whether we were ever going to start the interview. Klara was expertly deflecting my questions, beating me at my own game.

"I don't," she countered. "All I know is that you live in London and grew up near Reading, an only child, then moved to Southampton. I know that you're a friend of Vincent's goddaughter, and that you came here on holiday, many years ago. So please, Jenni, tell me a bit more about yourself."

This was the last thing I wanted to do. I forced a smile. "What would you like to know?"

"Well, are you married? I don't get the impression that you are."

"I'm not. But I live with someone—Rick. He's a primary school teacher." Klara was looking at me expectantly.

"He's . . . easygoing," I went on, feeling myself flounder under her gaze. "He's decent and attractive—at least I think so. He's the same height as me, which I like, because we can look straight into each other's eyes. His are the color of the sea." Was that really all I could find to say about the man I loved?

Klara nodded approvingly. "He sounds lovely."

"He is. We've been together for a year and a half."

"So, you must feel that you know each other pretty well by now."

"I do feel that I know Rick, yes." Whether he really knew me was a different matter.

"And do you hope to get married?" Klara was certainly very direct.

"I do," I answered. "We both do. If it's right," I added, then wished that I hadn't.

Klara nodded thoughtfully. "And why did you become a ghostwriter, rather than, say . . ."

"A 'proper' writer?" I suggested, smiling.

Klara flinched. "Oh, I didn't mean to be rude."

I laughed. "I do get asked that question."

"How annoying."

"Not really. People don't mean to be insulting; they genuinely want to know why I don't write my own—"

"Story?"

"Yes."

Klara stared at me. "So why don't you?"

"I guess I . . . prefer other people's."

"I see. But how did you *get* to be a ghostwriter? Is that what you always wanted to do?"

"Not at all. I was a researcher for a breakfast television show. It was my job to invite the studio guests and brief the presenters about them. One day I had to book a well-known actor; he was in his seventies—"

"Can you say who he was?"

"I can't—I signed a confidentiality agreement—but he's a household name. We got on well, and while I was chatting to him before he went on, he told me that he'd been approached by a publisher to write his memoirs. He said his agent was keen for him to do it, but that he didn't want to, because he hated writing. He added that he wished he could find someone to write it *for* him. Without even thinking, I said that *I* could."

"And you did."

"Yes—and the book was a success and got good reviews. More important, I'd loved doing it—taking someone into his past, like a personal historian, helping him see the fabric and shape of his life—helping him tell his story; it fascinated me. I'd never done anything I loved as much. So I quit my job and set myself up as a ghostwriter. That was twelve years ago."

"Who else have you worked with?"

"A few athletes, several actresses, a famous milliner, a couple of TV personalities, a well-known explorer . . . a fashion designer."

"Celebrities, then."

"Yes, but after a while that sort of work palled. I found myself more intrigued by the lives of 'ordinary' people—not that they ever are ordinary. Far from it." I put my cup down. "But that's how I got into ghostwriting—quite by chance."

"I don't think it *was* just chance," Klara remarked. Her eyes were thoughtful.

"What do you mean?"

"I mean that you must already have wanted to do it. Otherwise you'd simply have said to that actor, 'How interesting; I hope you find someone,' and carried on with your job. I suspect that he simply showed you a path that you were already looking for."

"Perhaps. Anyway . . ." I opened my bag. "I hope you feel a bit better acquainted with me now, Klara."

"I do, Jenni. Thank you." She cocked her head. "The odd thing is, I feel I've met you before."

I looked at her, surprised. "I don't think so."

"Perhaps when you came here on holiday that time? Maybe I chatted to you when you collected the milk. You'd have been a little girl, and I'd have been in my fifties." Klara cocked her head. "Something about you is familiar."

I had no recollection of her. "I'm sure we've never met."

"I think we have," she insisted. "It'll suddenly come back to me."

I knew that Klara was wrong, but there was no point in disagreeing with her. I took out the tape recorder and placed it on the table in front of her.

She glanced at it anxiously. "So what do I do? Just . . . start talking?"

"No; I'll guide the conversation with my questions. I already know quite a bit about you from Vincent." I glanced at my notes. "I'd like to divide up the interviews more or less chronologically, starting with your early life in Holland." Klara nodded. "Then we'll talk about the move to Java, and your memories of the plantation, of your family, and your childhood friends. After that I thought we'd talk about the war. You would have been, what, nine, when Java was occupied?" She nodded again. "Vincent told me that you were interned." She didn't respond. "So . . . I imagine we'll be talking about that," I pressed on. "Then we'll come to the liberation of Java and the turmoil that accompanied the struggle for Indonesian independence. Following that I'd like to talk about Holland, and what it was like going back there." At that Klara smiled a grim little smile. "Then we'll come on to your meeting your husband. He was in the Royal Navy, wasn't he?"

"He was. We met in September 1949. His ship, HMS *Vanguard*, had berthed in Rotterdam for a few days; he had some shore leave, and I met him at a dance. I was sixteen, he was nineteen, and he began chatting to me."

"Could he speak Dutch?"

"Not a word." Klara smiled. "Fortunately I spoke good English, otherwise I don't suppose we'd have clicked in the way that we did. Harry told me within a week that he'd fallen in love with me and hoped to marry me. But he had two more years to do in the navy and I had to finish school; so we got engaged in 1951 and were married the following year."

"What a romantic story," I said wistfully. "I shall love writing about it. We'll also talk about your life in Cornwall. Does that all sound okay?"

"It sounds fine," Klara replied. "Except for one thing."

"Yes?"

"I'll find it extremely difficult to talk about some of the things that happened during the occupation. I'll talk about the historical facts, of course, and about the kinds of things that people suffered."

"During internment, you mean? In the camps?"

"Yes. But there are some things . . . particularly toward the end, in the last camp that we were in, Tjideng. I don't think I'd be able to find the words to describe what we . . . what I . . ." She inhaled, her breath juddering.

"Klara," I said gently, "you don't have to talk about anything you don't want to. Memoirs can take people into quite dark emotional territory. But it's up to you how far, or how deep, you want to go. You have to feel comfortable with what you say."

"Yes." She swallowed. "I do."

"So you'll see the manuscript before it's printed, and you can add any further stories or reflections; and I can delete anything that you're unhappy about, or regret having said."

"Really?"

"Yes. So don't worry. This is *your* story. You'll be in control."

Klara gave a little sigh of relief. "I'd been feeling quite apprehensive, but that does make me feel . . . better."

"I'm glad. I want you to be comfortable. So . . ." I put my pad on my lap, then turned off my phone. "Are you ready to start?"

Klara folded her hands in her lap. Her eyes were steady on me. "I'm ready."

As I pressed Record, I felt the frisson that I always feel when I begin a new memoir.

"Klara, could you tell me what your earliest memory is?"

Five

Klara

I remember the little *tjik-tjaks,* dainty beige lizards that used to run across our sitting room walls. I used to stare at them as they zipped about, mesmerized by their miraculous ability to cling to vertical surfaces, and even ceilings, without falling off. They were called *tjik-tjaks* because that was the noise that they made, and we loved them, because every night, when the lamps were lit, they would eat the mosquitoes that might otherwise have given us malaria. Less welcome were the snakes that would sometimes slither across our verandah, especially during the rains. I recall once seeing my mother throw boiling water over a deadly black-and-yellow krait. I stood in the doorway while she did this and, with appalled delight, watched it writhe.

My mother told me, before we left Holland, that we were

going to live in a faraway land that was warm and colorful—an "earthly paradise," I remember she said. To me this description seemed to be true. From our windows we could see mountains swathed in jungle that was every shade of green, yet was also filled with the hot pinks and reds of hibiscus, bougainvillea, and oleander. These flowers not only looked gorgeous, they attracted butterflies—scarlet and yellow, emerald and black, burnt orange and shimmering blue.

When we first got there, I'd lie in bed, unable to sleep because of all the weird noises of the tropics—the trilling of crickets, which was always especially loud at night, or the sudden shriek of a bird or a macaque, one of the monkeys in the rubber forest that surrounded our house. Sometimes there'd be the howling of pye-dogs, and the strange, guttural cries of the *tokeh*, large stripy salamanders that sounded like frogs. If you heard the *tokeh* seven times in a row, you could make a wish; so I'd listen to their croaks, and would get upset if I lost count and had to start all over again.

Our house was large, single-story, like most houses in the East Indies, and built of brown brick with a roof made of curved red tiles. It had a circular drive and low, wide steps on which my mother placed pink and white orchids in big pots. All the rooms had high ceilings and ceramic floors, which were polished with slices of coconut tightly wrapped in muslin. I still think of this house as my childhood home.

Around the sides of the house were covered walkways called *émpérs*, and behind it was a smaller house called a pavilion, in which were the kitchen, the *gudang* or storeroom, plus the washing facilities, bathroom and loo. We had an enormous garden, with a banana palm, a mango tree, a cherimoya, and, at the end, a big waringin—an Indian fig, with a thick, rippled trunk and long aerial roots. Bats roosted in that tree. At dusk we'd see them spread their cloaklike wings and swoop out.

My mother loved gardening and created wonderful flower beds in which she grew roses, gerbera, and lilies, and I'd make the petals into dresses for my dolls. The garden was full of exotic birds—hoopoes, golden orioles, and hummingbirds, which hovered over the jasmine like iridescent bees. But my favorite bird was the Java sparrow because it looked like a puffin.

As Dutch colonials we had a privileged life. We employed a gardener, Ismail, who I thought of as extremely old, because his hair was gray, but he was probably only in his forties. We had a maid named Jasmine, who was married to the plantation's head foreman, Suliman. They were in their midthirties but had no children, which caused them great sadness. Because of this, I think, Jasmine was very affectionate to my little brother, Peter, and me.

Jasmine and my mother were always cleaning, because in the tropics mold and mildew take hold very quickly. They'd hang the rugs up in the sun and bang the weevils out of them. They'd take books off the shelves and wipe the covers and give all the clothes a vigorous shake. I remember once my mother being very upset about a favorite dress of hers that Peter, ill with typhoid, had thrown up on. She had taken it off and left it in the pavilion; when she went to wash it the following morning, the part he'd been sick on had been eaten away.

Every week the floors had to be disinfected or the insects would move in. If termites showed up, we'd have to place the furniture legs in saucers of carbolic acid. Once, we forgot to do this with our piano, and they destroyed it from inside, leaving hillocks of sawdust beneath. And I remember, once, seeing a huge bird spider scuttle across my bedroom floor. It was so large that I could hear its feet clicking on the tiles, a memory that still makes me shudder seventy years later! So I remember this constant battle we all waged against bugs—cockroaches and moths, stick insects and giant centipedes the length of a forearm, creatures that I could never even have imagined back in Holland. But I always thought of the East Indies—never the Netherlands—as *home.*

Although I'm Dutch, I have almost no childhood memories of Holland. I know about my early years there only from my parents, Anneke and Hans, and from my grandparents, Oma and Opa, who lived near to us in Rotterdam. My grandfather worked on the canals, leading the horses along the towpath as they pulled the barges. I'm sad to say that I can barely remember him, because by the time we returned home he had died, in the terrible "hunger winter," before Holland was liberated from the Nazis. I know that Opa was a simple man, with little learning, while Oma was well educated, well read, and determined that her daughter be the same. So my mother went to high school, then on to college, where she studied to be a teacher. She met my father ice-skating, and they were married within a few months.

My father worked for an electrical engineering company, but in 1936 he was laid off because of the slump. According to my mother, he was in despair, especially as by that time they had two children; but then he got a job as the manager of a rubber plantation in West Java. He went out there first. Three months later my mother, Peter, and I followed.

We left for Java on New Year's Eve. I know this because my

mother used to say that it had seemed such an auspicious day for us to be setting off for our new life. But she could never have imagined that the "earthly paradise" to which we were sailing would, within a few years, become a living hell. But to Java we went, taking with us a single crate that contained my parents' wedding china, their books, and our clothes.

We sailed from Amsterdam on the SS *Indrapoera,* which was a wonderful white steamship, like a floating castle. I remember the icy cold as we stood on the deck waiting to leave. My mother held Peter, who wasn't yet two, in her arms, and she and I waved hankies at my grandparents—two dark-coated specks on the quay far below. Some passengers had brought white towels to wave, and I wished that we had done so too, as I was certain that it must have been hard for Oma and Opa to spot us in the crowd. My mother was smiling and crying, and as the foghorn sounded our departure, she called out to her parents, "Goodbye . . . we'll miss you . . . we love you," even though they couldn't possibly have heard. As a goodbye gift they had given her an expensive new Agfa camera, and she'd promised to send them photos whenever she could.

The journey to Java took four weeks. It must have been hard for my mother, because she had to cope with a toddler while also looking after me. I remember how rough it was as we went through the Atlantic, becoming warm and calm as we turned in to the Mediterranean. It was strange going through the Suez Canal and seeing the palm-tree-dotted desert stretching away on either side, as though we were sailing across the land.

There were games and entertainments on board. I remember the children's fancy-dress parade. My mother said that I was to be Assepoester, or Cinderella. I thought I'd be wearing a wonderful gown, but my mother explained that as she didn't have any fine material with which to make me one, I was to be Cinderella in her everyday rags. So she cut down an old green petticoat of hers, shredded the hem, then tied string round my waist for a belt. She messed up my hair, dabbed smuts on my face with her mascara, and found a brush for me to hold. Then she took a photo of me to send to Oma and Opa. Years later, when we really *were* in rags, filthy and barefoot, my mother told me that she had come to see that costume as an omen; and I remember, after the war, when we returned to Holland, and my mother saw that photo of me again, she cried.

At the end of January we sailed into Batavia, the old name for Jakarta, and as we walked down the gangway we saw my father waving at us. I was so excited! I remember him kissing my mother, passionately, and in that instant I realized how much he loved and needed her. He kissed and hugged Peter and me, then carrying Peter in one arm, he picked up our case and shepherded Mum and me through the crowd.

We traveled to Bandung in order to buy the things that we'd need. The buildings there were different from any I'd ever seen: mosques with oriental domes, elegant teahouses, and gorgeous emporiums. There were beautiful women, dressed in batik sarongs and *kebayas*, elegant, fitted blouses, with frangipani flowers pinned in their hair. There were expensive cars, but we went everywhere by *delman*, a pony trap, a mode of transport I adored. After a few days in Bandung we drove up into the mountains, to the plantation, which was called Sisi Gunung, which means "mountainside."

I often think how brave my parents were to go halfway across the world to start a new life, in a place they had never even seen—especially as neither had ever traveled outside Holland. On Java they had to get used to so many new things, not least the local language, Malay, which they both had to learn. There was the constant threat of malaria, typhoid, cholera, and dysentery; adjusting to the equatorial climate must have been hard. There were two seasons—wet, when we were often deluged, and dry, when it could be blisteringly hot. But against these hazards and discomforts my parents weighed the freedom of not having to wear winter clothes, and the bliss of seeing blue skies for much of the year. Added to which they loved the Javanese landscape with its mountains, waterfalls, and shining rice fields.

I find it strange, to think that I've lived for so much longer than either of my parents. They're so often in my thoughts, and I see them as they were when I was a child. My father was big and strong with fair hair and deep brown eyes; my mother was short and plump, with moss-green eyes and long auburn hair that she'd twist into a bun. She was always wonderfully calm. I remember once she was reading to me when Jasmine came running, screaming, with Peter, then two, in her arms. She'd found a python curled around the toilet. When my mother went to look at it she didn't even cry out; she simply called Ismail, who killed it, then stretched it out on the lawn. It was, he said, a "baby"—five feet long.

Another time I lifted a rock in our garden and a scorpion ran toward me, its stinger raised. But my mother just stamped on it, then warned me not to lift up rocks again. She had terrific sangfroid. She was also very good at first aid. She'd never scold me for my cuts and grazes, usually sustained doing things that I'd been told *not* to do; she'd just get out the iodine and dressings, bandage me up, then firmly tell me not to do it another time.

During the war she was going to need those healing skills, and every bit of that inner calm, as, like thousands of women, she would be tested to destruction.

My father was full of energy and drive. I used to love going out into the forest with him to watch him supervise the rubber harvest. Sometimes he'd let *me* cut the diagonal line into the tree and tie the coconut shell beneath it to catch the milky-white drips. Then we'd go back a few hours later and collect the latex and take it to the shed, where it was mixed with acid to make it congeal. It was then pressed into dark yellow sheets, which were hung up on wooden ceiling racks to dry. Peter and I used to scour the floor for bits of "scrap" and try to make balls by binding them with raffia, but they never bounced very well.

My father also managed the forest, planting saplings, disinfecting the diseased trees, and clearing the dead or dying ones. He walked miles every day and worked from dawn until dusk. He was a gentle, good-humored man. But if he thought that a worker wasn't pulling his weight, he would take him to task. He could also be tough with me. I remember once—I must have been about six—I found a pair of scissors and impulsively cut off my long, fair hair. When my father saw me, he marched me to the barber and asked him to give me a short back and sides, like a boy, to punish me for trying to make myself look like one. But I adored my new, cropped style, and I have worn my hair short ever since.

I used to love going with my mother to the market in the local village or kampong. The stalls would be piled high with mangoes, papayas, and spiky red lychees, the air filled with the scent

of cinnamon, vanilla, and coffee beans, and the delicious smell
of nasi goreng. Often there'd be gamelan music playing, and
the shopkeepers would stand outside their stores, enticing us in.
Sometimes vendors would cycle up to our house with bales of
batik, silks, and shantung, and we'd sit with them on the verandah and look through their wares.

I remember how excited Peter and I were when our father
bought his first car. It was a dark green Ford, and on weekends
we'd all get in it and drive into the forest. Dad would turn off
the engine, and we'd sit very still, hardly daring to breathe as
the wildlife came out—troops of gray monkeys with rust-
colored babies clinging to their chests and tiny deer as well as
peacocks and toucans. Just once, when I was eight, we saw a
panther. I can still see its dark beauty as it slinked past us in the
shadow of the trees.

My favorite place was the swimming pool. It was high up,
and commanded a wonderful view of the mountains all around
us and, below us, of the forest, the plantation buildings, the
houses and kampong. On Sundays we'd spend the whole day at
the pool, usually with the Jochens, who were the only other Europeans at Sisi Gunung. Wil Jochen was the boss. He did the
general administration and the rubber exporting, while my father supervised the day-to-day agricultural work.

Wil was short and fat, with thick calves, a barrel chest, and a
voice that could be heard all over the plantation. But his wife,
Irene, who was English, was very gentle and softly spoken, as
were their daughters, Susan and Flora. Susan was six years older
than Flora and was slender and pale, like Irene, with waist-
length blond hair that she would let Flora and me brush. Susan

was always sketching and painting and told us that she longed to be an artist when she grew up.

Flora, who was my age, looked more like her father, sturdy and short. She had dark brown eyes and blunt-cut chestnut hair that had a wonderful shine, which I envied. Almost from the day we met, Flora and I were inseparable; always at each other's side as we played around the plantation and at school.

The nearest Dutch schools were in Bandung, three hours away. So Flora's parents and mine rented a house there and our mothers took it in turns to look after us all, a month at a time. On the holidays we'd return to Sisi Gunung.

I could sense that my father didn't much care for Wil—I think he disliked his overbearing manner. But my mother and Irene were great friends. I became very fond of Irene too, and because of the time I spent with her, I picked up a good deal of English. I used to like looking at the copies of the *Home Notes* magazine that her parents sent her each month from their home in Kent. In particular, I enjoyed reading the recipes. I'd copy them out so that my mother could make cottage pie or brandy snaps or scones, although the imperial measurements mystified me. Why should the word *ounces* be abbreviated as *ozs* when there was no *z* in it? And why was there no *l* or *b* in the word *pound*?

I think I was an inquisitive child, nosy even, always fascinated by what the grown-ups were saying. I remember one summer, walking up the Jochens' drive and hearing Irene and Susan talking in English on the verandah. Susan was very upset, and Irene was trying to placate her, reassuring her that her father would "soon calm down" and to "ignore him." But when they saw me, they immediately started chatting to me in Dutch as though everything was fine.

Later, when I asked Flora about it, she told me that her father had discovered that Susan was in love with one of the rubber tappers, Arif. Arif was sixteen to Susan's fourteen, tall and very attractive, with a warm smile and an athletic grace. Even I, at eight, could sense his appeal. That morning Wil, idly looking through Susan's sketchbook, had found a portrait of Arif.

"Dad went *berserk*," Flora told me, her eyes wide.

"Why?"

"Because you can tell, from Arif's big moony eyes, that he's in love with her too. But Dad shouted at Sue that he wouldn't have her 'throwing herself away' on an *Inlander*. Mum said that it was just a teenage crush and that he was being ridiculous. But Dad tore the portrait up, then told Arif that he'd sack him if he even *looked* at Sue again."

I remember trying to imagine what my own parents would say if I'd been Susan's age and it had been me. I decided that they wouldn't mind. They'd never tried to stop Peter and me being friends with the local children. Peter's best friend was a boy named Jaya who lived in the kampong. He and Peter fished together in the pond, digging up ant eggs for bait. Jaya would bring his wooden chess set up to our house, and they'd set it out on the verandah and play. Because Peter was too young to start school, Mum taught him his letters and numbers. If Jaya was around, he'd join in, and my mother used to say how good he was at maths.

A few of the Dutch people we knew had criticized my parents for their "naïve" attitude toward the local people. Wil Jochen sometimes muttered about it. Ralph and Marleen Dekker, tea planters at Tasikmalaya, a few miles away, openly disapproved. Their son, Herman, was two years older than Peter, and our families occasionally visited each other, though my mother disliked Mrs. Dekker's air of superiority; her mother had been a lady-in-waiting to Queen Wilhelmina, and Mrs. Dekker made sure that everyone knew it. But my dad wanted to be on good terms with the other planters in the area; and so one April Sunday—it was Peter's birthday—the Dekkers came over for lunch.

I remember Mrs. Dekker's expression as she watched Jaya splashing about in the pool with Peter and Herman. Then she turned to my mother. Was it "quite wise," she asked her, to "cross the social boundaries"?

"Jaya's a dear little boy, Marleen," my mother responded. "He and Peter are great friends."

"But Anneke—to let him *swim*!"

"Herman and Peter don't seem to mind, Marleen. Why should you?"

"Because this sort of familiarity isn't . . . right."

"It's right in our home," my mother retorted calmly.

"No good can come of it," Mrs. Dekker insisted. "It's my belief that you'll regret it."

My mother's face flushed. "What is there to regret about a happy friendship? As for no good coming of it, I believe that you're wrong. It surely *is* good for children of different cultures to have fun together, because that builds understanding, which, heaven knows, the world needs more than ever at the moment."

"But the fact is—"

"Don't *tell* me," my mother interrupted, "that 'east is east and west is west.' How often have I heard *that* in this country?"

"That's because it's true," Mrs. Dekker insisted. "We're not the same as the *Inlanders*, Anneke. You shouldn't pretend that we are."

My mother flinched. "I'm not pretending anything, Marleen. I'm simply surprised that you would object to a nice little boy having fun—especially as it's *my* home that he's having fun in, not yours. And to be frank, I find your high-and-mighty attitude rather ridiculous, given that we planters are really no more than glorified farmers!"

Mrs. Dekker didn't answer, but I remember being aware of a sudden chill in the air, and shortly afterward, the Dekkers left.

This incident seemed, on the surface, a trivial matter, but afterward my mother said she felt bad about it and wished that she'd restrained herself. My father assured her that it would soon be forgotten. It wasn't, and it would come back to haunt my mother in a devastating way.

As for the views that she had expressed, they were consistent with what she and my father had always taught Peter and me—that we were no better or worse than anyone else on Java. We were simply lucky to be living in such a beautiful and bountiful country—over which a shadow was falling.

As children we were vaguely aware that war was coming to Europe—a place that, to us, seemed so remote, it might as well have been another planet. But the grown-ups talked of little else. At that time everyone listened to the Dutch East Indies radio station. From this we knew that Britain and France had declared war on Nazi Germany, and that Canada had then done so too. As Germany seized one country after another, the adults became more and more somber. They kept talking about the "neutrality of the Netherlands."

"What's that mean?" Peter asked as we all ate supper one night.

"That Holland has chosen to stay out of the war," my mother explained. "Which means that Hitler wouldn't dare to invade it."

"He would," my father countered bleakly. "And he will." Then in May 1940, during half term, my mother switched on the radio and we heard the newscaster announce that the Kingdom of the Netherlands had fallen. My mother closed her eyes. I looked at my father.

His head had sunk into his hands.

Six

I was surprised at how easily Klara confided in me that first day. The diffidence that she'd shown at first quickly evaporated, and she'd revisited her past with a passionate immediacy, as though describing very recent events. I felt myself warm to her, though she seemed almost oblivious to me as she spoke, in a low voice, her hands clasped, looking slightly away.

Many of Klara's anecdotes were about her brother, Peter: Peter learning to swim, Peter catching a carp, Peter getting malaria and spending a month in hospital, Klara's joy when he came home. Then, at the end of the afternoon, I'd reached forward and turned off the tape.

"That's probably enough for today, Klara."

"Is the hour up?" She looked surprised. "It's gone by so quickly."

"For me too. I've absolutely loved listening to you. I feel I'm there, on Java, with you and Flora, and Peter." I glanced at my pad. I'd scribbled *tested to destruction*, which must surely be a reference to what her mother had faced during internment. I'd also written *Mrs. D—come back to haunt*. "Klara, you mentioned that you've lived a lot longer than your parents."

"I have. My father was only forty-eight when he died."

"That's young." I tried to work out the dates. "Did he die during the war?"

"No. Miraculously, he survived it, but his health had been ruined. So many men didn't make it into their fifties because of what they'd been through. A vast number were held in prison camps, where they were starved, or got beriberi, or were tortured by the Kempeitai—the Japanese military police, who were utterly brutal. As we know, huge numbers of POWs were transported to build the Burma-Thailand Railway, where a third of them died. What isn't widely known was that thousands more were taken to Japan to be slave labor in factories and coal mines. And that"—Klara blinked, as though still struggling to comprehend it—"was what happened to my father."

"Did your mother survive the war?"

"She did. She lived to sixty-three, which, though better than forty-eight, is still not what you could call a long life."

"And . . . Peter?"

Her eyes clouded. "Peter was ten."

"How terrible," I murmured. "Did he die in the camp?"

"Yes. In early August 1945."

"So close to the end."

"So close," she echoed bleakly. "Five days."

"I'm *so* sorry. You've talked about Peter a great deal."

"Have I?" she said absently.

"Yes. You obviously adored him."

Klara's face grew pale. For a moment I thought she was going to cry. "I did adore him," she said quietly, "and I still miss him. I think about him every day, every hour; he's nearly always in my thoughts, and I just *wish*, with all my heart, that I . . ." She bit her lip. "Siblings share the same childhood memories," she went on. "They even share the same genes. So to lose a brother or sister is to lose a part of oneself. People say that it's like losing a limb, but it's much more than that. It's as though a piece has been gouged out of your heart."

"I know . . ." I'd said it impulsively. "I mean, I . . . understand."

Klara's face hardened. "I'm sorry," she said quietly, "but I don't see how you *could*, unless the same thing had happened to you." I was silent. "Not long after Harold died, a friend from church told me that she knew how I felt. But she was only fifty, and her husband was very much alive. She was simply showing sympathy, but sympathy is very different from genuine fellow feeling based on shared experience. I'm sorry, Jenni," Klara went on quickly. "I didn't mean to sound judgmental. I'm just glad, for your sake, that you *don't* know how I feel." I nodded my assent, then pretended to look for something in my bag while I composed myself. Klara stood up stiffly. "I'm a little tired," she said softly.

"It's not surprising." I put the top on my pen. "The memoir process is exhausting, physically and emotionally." She nodded. "So I'll leave you in peace for now. Thanks for all the coffee and cake you've plied me with; it was delicious."

I gathered up the cups and plates and took them to the kitchen; then I came back and picked up my bag.

"So I'll be here in the morning, Klara." I smiled my good-bye, then walked to the door.

"I see him," I heard her say.

I turned, my heart thudding. "What do you mean?"

"Peter," Klara murmured. "I see Peter. Or rather, I feel his presence."

"His presence?"

"Yes. There are times when I'm certain that he's with me, right beside me. Sometimes I even imagine that I can hear him breathing, but then I realize it's just the sound of the sea. He'd be seventy-seven now," she went on, "with white hair and wrinkled skin, like me. But he'd still be my little brother and we'd still be great friends, and we'd be able to talk to each other about our parents, and Jasmine, and Susan and Flora, and about all the happy times we had on Java before . . ." Tears glittered in her eyes.

"I'm sorry you're upset, Klara. I wish there was something I could say to make it easier, but I know there isn't." I opened my bag and passed her a tissue.

"How can one look back on one's whole life, and remember beloved family members and friends *without* being upset? I expected to be, which is why it's taken me so long to agree to this memoir. Anyway . . ." She gave me a watery smile. "Until tomorrow, Jenni."

"Until tomorrow."

As I walked back I wondered what Klara had been about to say. *I just wish with all my heart that I* . . . What did she wish? It had been a cry of regret. And why, after so many years, was her grief so raw? It was clear that she was still profoundly affected by whatever had happened to Peter.

As I went into the cottage, I switched on my phone and, to my surprise, saw a missed call from Rick. It jolted me out of Klara's world, back into the dismal reality of my own failing relationship. I pressed the green button but couldn't get a signal. Then, remembering what Henry had advised, I went back outside and walked down the lane. As the number rang, I could hear the soft roar of the waves.

When Rick answered, the longing I felt for him overwhelmed me.

"Jen—how are you?"

"I'm all right. It's *so* nice to hear your voice, Rick. How are things?"

"Not bad, though I'm missing you." I allowed myself to hope. "And how's your Dutch lady?"

I watched a thrush foraging in the hedgerow. "She's fine. I've been with her most of the day."

"Is she a good talker?"

"She was reserved at first, and nervous, but now she talks quite fluently, almost as if I'm not there. It's as though she's on her own, explaining her life to herself." I shivered in the wind and walked on. "How's everything with you?"

"Pretty good. I went to see the folks today." Rick's parents, Tony and Joy, still lived in the house near Oxted that Rick had grown up in. "Mark and Becky were there with the kids; everyone sends you their love."

I imagined the noisy family lunch, the adults chatting over coffee while the four children squabbled over toys or ran around in the garden. "I'm sorry not to have seen them." This was only half true. There were times when I found it a strain being with such a happy and close-knit family group.

"Rick, I hope you didn't talk to them about us." His parents had always welcomed me, but I'd sensed their disappointment that their son was with a woman who didn't want to have children.

"Of course I didn't. I just told them that you were in Cornwall, for work, and that I was missing you, which is true."

"And I've missed *you*, Rick, so much. But I thought we'd agreed not to contact each other for the first week."

"I wouldn't have done," he responded, "but your mother's just phoned. As that happens so rarely, I felt I should tell you."

I'd come to a gap in the hedge; beyond it lay fields, then the lapis sea, filmed with gold in the sinking sun.

"So . . . what did she say?"

"Not much—only that she hadn't spoken to you in a long time; she sounded regretful about it." We hadn't been in touch since February, I realized guiltily, when she'd rung to wish me a happy birthday. "She asked where you were, so I explained that you were in Cornwall, working."

"You didn't say where, did you?"

"I did." I imagined the blow that this would have given her. "I mean, why not?" Rick went on, clearly irritated by the conversation. He always hated the way I refused to talk about my mother. "You didn't say that I shouldn't tell her."

"True—but then I didn't think that she'd phone. So . . . how did she react?"

"She'd been chatting to me—she was friendly, but when I told her where you were, she went very quiet. Before she could hang up I said that you'd phone her."

"I will. When I'm back in London."

"Why not call her from there?" Rick heaved a frustrated

sigh. "It's really sad, Jenni, this thing you have about your mother. And it's weird that I've never met her."

"I've told you why—"

"No," he interrupted vehemently. "You haven't, at least, not in any way that I've been able to understand."

"She and I just don't . . . get on." I thought of Rick's parents, still together after forty years, still in the same house in which they'd brought up their children. Rick had had only stability and continuity. All I'd known was tragedy and change.

"It's a shame, Jen. Especially as your mum's so young: She's going to be in your life for a long time, so why shut her out? I feel sorry for her." He wouldn't if he knew the truth, I reflected. I turned and headed back up the lane. "What I really wanted to say, though, is that if things do, somehow, work out, then I'd like us to visit her." I stopped, my heart pounding. "Is that okay, Jen?"

No, it isn't, I wanted to say, *because if we went to her house, then you'd know the truth.*

Instead, I closed my eyes and said, "Yes."

The next morning I woke at dawn, as usual; I lay there thinking about my mother. I'd texted her to say that I'd phone her when I was back in London. She hadn't responded. But then it must have been a shock for her to learn where I was. She must think me callous, I reflected, going back to Polvarth—and for work, as though it was just another job. She wouldn't understand it. As the light filtered in, my thoughts turned to Peter. How had he died? Klara clearly wasn't ready to tell me, and every instinct told me not to ask.

I got up and worked, transcribing the last part of our first interview. When I'd finished, I walked up to the farm. As I strolled down the track, the ginger cat came up to me and I bent to stroke it. I saw Henry lifting lobster pots off the pickup truck.

"Morning," I called out.

He smiled. "Morning, Jenni." A young man stepped down from behind the wheel. "This is my son, Adam. Adam, this is Jenni; she's helping Granny with her memoirs."

Adam was in his late twenties, with his mother's fair coloring and his father's lean face. His blond hair was long, dreadlocked, and tied in a ponytail. As he lifted his right hand in greeting, I saw that it was flecked with green and blue paint. I imagined him behind an easel, gazing at the sea.

"Hi, Adam. Caught much?" I gestured toward the pots.

"Not bad," he answered. "Two monkfish, five sole, eight bass, and six lobsters." He lifted two of the pots off the truck, and I saw the speckled blue creatures, their antennae quivering through the ropework. The cat jumped up and batted its paws at them. "Cut it out, Ruby." Adam lifted the pots out of the cat's reach, then handed them to his father, who took them into the farmhouse, leaving a trail of water on the dusty ground. Adam turned back to me, squinting into the sunlight.

"So how's it going with my gran?"

"We've made a good start. She's a remarkable person."

He nodded. "Gran's the bees' knees. We're really glad she's doing it. I'd given up believing that she ever would."

"Why do you think she's changed her mind?"

"Turning eighty?" he suggested. "Becoming a great-grandmother probably had something to do with it too; my girl-friend, Molly, and I have a six-month-old. What do you think,

Dad?" he asked his father, who'd just emerged from the farm-house.

"What do I think about what?"

"Jenni was wondering why Gran's decided to write her memoirs. I said it was probably the big eight-oh."

"Partly," Henry answered. "But I suspect that it's mainly because of Jane." He swung two more pots off the truck. "She's my mother's best friend," he explained to me.

"She talked to me about her," I said.

"I think seeing Jane losing her memories has shocked my mother into wanting to preserve her own—she hasn't said as much, but that's what I believe. Anyway, my boy, we'd better get moving."

"Sure, Dad." Adam gave me a broad smile. "See you then, Jenni."

"Yes. See you."

I went into the shop. It was large and cool, the walls painted white, with a refrigerated counter containing dressed lobsters and crabs, gleaming plaice and Dover sole and fat white scallops still in their shells. There were sacks of potatoes and, on the tables, neat piles of vegetables and fruit. The shelves were stacked with jars of Polvarth marmalade, Polvarth quince jelly, assorted Polvarth jams, and lemon curd. There were homemade loaves and cakes, and trays of eggs. By the door, in steel buckets, were bunches of red and yellow dahlias. Four of what I now recognized to be Adam's paintings hung on the wall, next to a poster for the exhibition of his work at the Driftwood Gallery in Trennick.

Klara was serving someone. She put the woman's purchases

into a paper carrier, then tore off the receipt and handed it to her.

The customer left, then a moment later returned. "Sorry, I meant to ask if you'll have any pumpkins. My grandchildren are coming down for half term next week. They'll want one for Halloween."

"I'm growing a dozen," Klara answered. "Shall I set one aside for you?"

"Please," the woman said. "The biggest, if you don't mind." She gave Klara her name and then left.

As Klara wrote the woman's name down, I glanced round the shop. "You do all this on your own?"

She looked up. "I do, but it's only open for two hours in the morning and two in the afternoon, so it's not too bad, and Adam helps me when he's got time. I saw him unloading—did he catch much?" I told her. "That's good. All the lobsters will sell. So . . . let's go." She untied her apron and hung it on a hook. Then she turned over the Open sign and closed the shop door.

Up in her flat, everything looked familiar, except for one change. On the table, next to the photo albums, was a large, intricately carved wooden box.

As she made the coffee, Klara started chatting. "Before we begin, Jenni, do tell me about your friends. I've met Nina—many years ago. She came here with her parents. She was about twelve, and seemed a lovely girl." It was odd to think of Nina being here, walking down the lane and playing on the beach that held such difficult memories for me. "What does she do?" Klara asked as she filled the coffee jug. "Vincent did tell me, but I've forgotten."

"She's an account manager for one of the big advertising agencies. She's run some very successful campaigns—for cars, and hair-care products and mobile phones. She's done really well."

"Are you a close friend of hers?"

"I am."

"So how did you meet?"

"At Bristol; we were both reading history but didn't become friends until the first summer term, when we took part in a student production of *A Midsummer Night's Dream*. Nina was Titania, and the girl who was to become my other great friend, Honor, was Hermia. That's how we all met."

"Who did *you* play? I can see you as Helena, with your height."

"The director did ask me to audition for the part, but I didn't want to—I was happy just to do makeup."

"So you preferred a backstage role."

I nodded. "Always have done."

"And your friend Honor—tell me about her."

"Well . . . she's very effusive, and expressive. She used to be an actress—she read English and drama—but she gave it up to become a radio reporter. Now she presents a chat show on Radio Five. It suits her, because she's always talking and laughing, engaging with other people, looking for common ground. She's friendly and upbeat and—"

"Extrovert?"

"Yes. I've always found that very attractive in a person, perhaps because I could never be like that myself."

"You're . . . not shy, Jenni; I don't think you could do this job if you were shy. But you are reticent."

"I guess I am, but Honor charges straight in, which makes her easy to know." Talking about Honor made me want to call her; we hadn't spoken since the wedding.

"So Honor and Nina are your closest friends."

"They are. After fifteen years, I don't know what I'd do without them."

"I expect they feel the same way about you."

I smiled. "I hope so. Anyway, Klara, it's nice to talk—I enjoy our conversations—but—"

"We need to get on," Klara concluded.

"We should really. So . . . where had we got to?" I glanced at my notes. "The fall of Holland."

Klara heaved a painful sigh. "That was so dreadful, because there was a ceasefire in place, but the Germans bombed the country anyway, destroying the center of Rotterdam. Hundreds were killed." She glanced at the tape recorder. "Is it running?"

I pressed the button. "It is now. So shall we start?"

"Yes," Klara agreed. "Let's start." She clasped her hands in her lap.

I leaned forward and turned on the tape.

Seven

Klara

Holland was now *bezet*—occupied. My mother was distraught, believing that her parents must have been killed. But as the weeks went by we learned, to our relief, that their part of Rotterdam had escaped the devastation. I used to terrify myself, imagining them looking out of their windows and seeing German soldiers in the streets below.

Peter had a wooden popgun that my father had made. He'd wave it about and say it was a machine gun, and that he'd use it if the Germans tried to occupy *us*.

"That's not going to happen." My mother put her arm round him. "Java is very far from the war."

"How far?" he demanded.

"Eleven thousand kilometers," my father answered. "So you mustn't worry, Pietje. There won't be any fighting here."

Reassured, we found our lives went on more or less as before. The trees were still being tapped, and the rubber continued to be processed. Peter and Jaya played their games, and Flora, Susan, and I went back to school, running up the steps each morning in our blue tartan skirts and white shirts. The sun continued to shine down on our corner of paradise. The war seemed far, far away—so much so that I remember this period as a particularly happy time. We went on a trip to East Java and spent a few days in Surabaya, where we visited the zoo, full of different kinds of monkeys, a Java rhino, and a sad-looking white tiger. There were birds, including an eagle with which Peter was very taken. We visited a beautiful bay called Pasir Putih, where we stayed in a small guesthouse, right on the beach, and were lulled to sleep by the waves. Every day Dad caught fish, which he cooked on an open fire, and we ate it with semanggi, a wild clover that has four heart-shaped leaves. Dad laid one on his palm. "This is how I think of our family," he told us.

Perhaps to distract us from our worries about the war, my parents indulged Peter and me. When we returned to the plantation, Peter announced that he wanted a rabbit; so my parents got him a pale brown-and-white one with long lop ears and a coat like swansdown. Peter called it Ferdi, and my father built a big hutch, and made a wire run on the lawn for it, with a coconut shell for water, and a section of split bamboo "roof" to give it shade.

More happiness was in store when, one morning, my mother

asked me to go onto the verandah to fetch her book. As I opened the front door, I stopped. Standing in the middle of our lawn was Jasmine, holding the reins of a small white pony.

I stared at it, my heart racing, scarcely daring to hope.

"Whose is it?"

Jasmine laughed. "Yours!"

"Mine?" With a cry of joy I ran up to it.

I'd wanted a pony for so long. I'd count the croaks of the *tokeh,* and each time I heard seven I'd squeeze my eyes shut and wish for one. Now my wish had come true.

"Is he *really* mine?" I asked my mother, unable to believe it.

"He really is." She crossed the lawn toward us. "He's called Sweetie."

I stroked Sweetie's velvety muzzle and felt his warm breath on my hands. "But where did you get him?"

"We bought him from the Bosmans, tea planters near Solo. He belonged to their daughter, Lara."

"Doesn't she *want* him?"

"She does," my mother replied, "but they're going back to South Africa and can't take him with them. We heard that they were looking for a good home for him, so Daddy went to see him last week. He promised Lara that you'd take great care of him."

I flung my arms round Sweetie's neck. "I *will.*" I ran to my mother and kissed her. "*Thank* you!"

At first, Jasmine would lead Sweetie round the garden, while Flora or I sat on his back making clicking noises; then Susan, who'd done some riding in England, showed us how to make him walk on, turn to the left or right, and trot. She used to come with us on rides into the rubber forest, though somehow we'd always end up wherever Arif was working. He and Susan would sit next to each other on the ground, chatting quietly in Malay, their heads and hands almost touching, while Flora and I kept a lookout for Wil.

And so, despite all the trouble that was in the world, I remember the summer of 1940 as a very happy time.

My parents tried to stop Peter and me from listening to the radio, but it was on so much that we couldn't help but hear what was happening in Europe. The main news was that the Germans were using Holland as a base from which to attack Britain. The British were fighting back, though no one seemed to think they could win. But they had a new plane, the Spitfire, which everyone was excited about. We all listened to a broadcast by the Dutch prince Bernhard, in which he said that the RAF needed hundreds more of these wonderful planes. He talked about the Spitfire Fund and asked the Dutch in the Indies to contribute whatever they could to this important cause. He appealed for money and, just as important, aluminum.

I remember my mother and Jasmine taking saucepans and cake tins from the shelves in the *gudang*, and I used to collect our used toothpaste tubes. My father raided his tool shed for nuts and bolts and old paint tins. The Jochens even donated their aluminum kitchen table—I remember it being carried onto their lawn, where it got hot in the sun. All these things were packed up and sent to the docks at Batavia to be shipped to England.

There were Spitfire Fund parties at the Rotary Club in Garut, our nearest town. For one of these gatherings, my father made a huge plywood caricature of Hitler's face, which Susan painted and Flora, Peter, and I varnished. People queued up to throw coins into its horrible, shouting mouth, and I was thrilled to think of all that money going to the fund.

Even with this activity, we felt removed from the conflict. So I was shocked one day to hear a classmate, Corrie van der Velden, tell our teacher, Miss Vries, that there was going to be a war with Japan.

"What makes you think that?" Miss Vries responded calmly. As she began to wipe the blackboard, her engagement ring sparkled. She'd told us that she was getting married.

"My father says it's going to happen," Corrie answered, "and he's a major. He says that the Japs will come here and fight *us* and that it's going to be terrible. I overheard him telling my mother, and she got very upset."

Miss Vries put the blackboard wiper down. "I really can't imagine that that's going to happen, Corrie, so let's have no more talk of it. Now, would you all get out your maths books?" After school I tearfully asked my mother if the Japanese really were going to invade Java.

"Of course they're not," she answered. "I suspect Corrie's only saying that because she thinks it makes her seem important. What do you think, Flora?"

Flora looked up from her book. "I agree. Just because her dad's in the army. I'm not taking *any* notice of it."

"Nor should you, Klara," my mother told me. "The only thing you're to worry about is your schoolwork." But the idea of the Japanese fighting us wouldn't go away. During the summer of '41 I heard my father and Wil arguing about it one evening as they sat on our verandah.

"It's a ludicrous notion," Wil declared.

My father lowered his beer. "Why—given that the Japanese

have already invaded Manchuria, Korea, Formosa, and most of eastern China?"

"All right, but they'd never dare attack *us* in those planes of theirs—they're just tin cans! I tell you, Hans, it's *not* going to happen."

Even when the Dutch government asked plantation managers to start a Landwacht, unit or home guard, to train units of local men for guerrilla warfare, Wil scoffed. But my father took it seriously. He formed a platoon.

He chose twenty of our best plantation workers, including Suliman and Arif, and drilled them on our drive, using rifles that the Dutch government had provided. Peter, Flora, and I used to like watching the "cadets" being put through their paces. Susan would join us and pretend to be chatting to my mother, though she'd shoot glances at Arif as he marched up and down. I can still remember the commands that used to ring across our garden:

"Schouder geweer*! Pre-sent* arms! *Links, rechts! Links, rechts!"*

But the months went by, and to everyone's relief, our small army didn't seem to be needed.

Early in December, Flora, Susan, and I were at school. It was almost the end of term, and we were looking forward to our Christmas concert. But at assembly one morning the headmistress, Miss Broek, announced with a grim expression that the holiday would begin that very day.

"The reason," she told us, "is that yesterday Japanese planes attacked the U.S. Pacific Fleet in Pearl Harbor, sinking eight of their ships. America is now at war with Japan."

As a gasp rippled through the hall, Miss Broek added that the

Netherlands, as a close ally of the United States, had declared war against Japan too.

"So we must all pray that the brave Dutch soldiers will protect us," Miss Broek went on. "Please bow your heads."

Prayers were said—I heard stifled sobs—then we all filed out and collected our bags.

As Flora, Susan, and I walked down the school's front steps, I saw Corrie being met by her mother, a blond Australian woman who was always smiling. Normally petite, she was hugely pregnant, with twins, Corrie had told us.

I went up to Corrie. "So you were right."

"Well, not me—my *papa*." Corrie flashed me a rueful smile. "It's scary, isn't it?"

I nodded. "Very."

"Oh, it'll be *fine*, girls," Mrs. Van der Velden said. "It just means you'll have a bit longer for Christmas. Enjoy it, though, because I'm sure you'll be back in class soon enough!"

The next day, as we decorated the house for Christmas, I put on the radio and heard that the Japanese had attacked the Philippines. A few days later the announcer told us that Japanese pilots had made strikes on Singapore and Borneo. Then, as we sat down to lunch on Christmas Day, we heard that the Japanese had captured Hong Kong.

"*Surely* they'll stop there!" my mother cried. Her face had grown pale, and I was suddenly frightened. The war seemed horribly close.

"No," my father said grimly. "They'll come here, because they want oil, and this is where the oil is."

Now every adult conversation was about the war. On the radio and in the newspapers, citizens were advised how to prepare for it, where to hide in case of air attacks, what to pack if your home had to be evacuated.

"Where should *we* hide if the Japs attack?" I asked Flora anxiously. "Under the verandah?"

Flora thought for a moment. "No," she replied. "Because of the snakes."

"That's true. Maybe our dads will build an air-raid shelter," I suggested. "Let's ask them to do that."

The next day Flora came to me, her eyes red with weeping. Her father wouldn't be making an air-raid shelter, she told me.

I was horrified. "Why not?"

Flora's eyes shone with sudden tears. "Because we're leaving Java."

It was as though I'd been pushed off a cliff. Then I heard approaching voices and saw Wil, with my father. I ran to them.

"Mr. Jochen . . ." I was so upset that I could hardly get out the words. "Is it true, Mr. Jochen? That you're leaving Java?"

He nodded. "We are. I've just been discussing it with your dad. As my wife and the girls have British passports, I've decided that we'll get a boat to Singapore and stay there until the hostilities are over."

"But . . ." I felt a wave of dismay. I was losing my best friend.

"What if the Japs take Singapore?" my father asked Wil.

Wil laughed, then slapped Dad on the back. "My dear Hans, Singapore is *invincible*!"

The day before the Jochens left, I went to their house. I could see that Susan had been crying, largely because of having to leave Arif, I suspected, and I had to swallow my own tears as I watched Flora pack. I helped her choose the clothes that she was to take, and her mother said that she could bring one or two toys, so she packed her favorite dolls: Lottie, a china doll with brown ringlets, and Lucie, a rag doll with big button eyes. Flora also had a brass lizard that she treasured. It had delicate hands, a wonderfully sinuous tail, and green agates for its eyes. I'd always coveted it and hoped, with the selfishness of a child, that Flora might leave it behind for me to look after. But to my disappointment, she put that in her case too.

The next day the Jochens drove away. My father was angry that Wil had decided to leave; it would hugely increase his own workload; he would now have to be the plantation administrator as well as the manager. I heard him tell my mother that he thought Wil Jochen a fool to put his family at such risk, given that the sea was full of Jap submarines. But my mother, Peter, and I saw them all off with hugs and smiles, and promises to write. I watched Flora waving to me through the rear window until the very last moment. Then, as their car disappeared from view, I burst into tears.

My mother put her arm round me. "Don't be upset," she said, though she was almost crying herself. "Two such good friends can't be parted for long. I'm sure you and Flora will see each other again."

My mother could not have known then that we *would*, but in circumstances that none of us could have imagined.

Everyone was talking about Singapore. Most people insisted, as Wil had done, that it was an "impregnable fortress" that would "never be taken." But in mid-February, Singapore fell. Knowing that many people had been killed, I was terrified for Flora's safety. Then, as the Japanese swept farther south, taking Borneo and Sumatra, I began for the first time to fear for our own.

"Will they *definitely* come here?" I asked my father.

He hesitated. "I'm not going to lie to you, Klara—I believe that they will." He touched my cheek. "But you mustn't worry because there are rules about what they can and can't do—international rules." Despite this, I had a dreadful sense of foreboding.

My mother began sewing rucksacks for us all. Into them she carefully packed tins of beef and beans, milk powder, packets of biscuits, and medical supplies, especially quinine tablets against malaria. Her great fear was that Peter would get malaria again. She also made some outfits for him and me to grow into.

"We need some clothes for the future," she told us, "because we don't know what will happen, or where we'll be."

My parents kept the radio on constantly during this time. The news was terrifying. We heard of naval battles in the Java Sea and of two Dutch warships that had been sunk.

"What about the sailors?" I asked, imagining them flailing in the water.

"Some may have survived," my mother said after a moment. "But I'm afraid that many won't have done, and we must pray for them."

One day it was announced that the retreating Dutch had managed to destroy half the oil wells on Borneo and Sumatra.

"What heroes," my father murmured.

Then the announcer said there were rumors that the Japanese had beheaded these men, or hacked off their limbs, and that their wives and daughters had been raped.

My mother gasped.

"What does raped mean?" I wanted to know.

"It means that they were . . . tortured," she answered after a moment.

"Tortured?"

"Yes. Hurt very badly, on purpose."

I turned to my father, bewildered. "What about the rules, Dad? You said there were rules." But he just shook his head.

It was reported that there was now fighting on Java itself, around Surabaya, near the beach where we'd had such a wonderful holiday. I imagined the white sand being strafed by Japanese planes, and couldn't sleep.

A week later, Peter and I were in the garden when we saw a red glow in the sky and heard low rumblings. It was as though one of the island's volcanoes was awakening.

Frightened, we ran to Mum, who told us that it was just thunder, but I knew it must be gunfire, because by then we'd heard that the Japanese had made landings in West Java. Peter and I sat together on the verandah. How, I marveled, could something as dreadful as war make the sky look so lovely? Within days, Batavia had been taken, soon followed by Bandung. Java was now in Japanese hands.

The day after the invasion I went with my mother to the market to get extra supplies of rice, sugar, and flour. There was an eerie silence as we walked through the streets. The shopkeepers, who usually stood outside their stores chatting, were all inside. Many of the shops were closed. When we got to the square I saw that the Dutch flag that always flew there was gone. In its place was a white flag with a blood-red ball in the center of it.

My mother looked stricken. "They're already up here—in

the mountains; we must go home." So we hurried back, got everyone inside, then locked all our windows and doors.

The knowledge that we were now occupied was terrifying. Everyone knew of the atrocities that the Japanese had carried out on other islands. We'd also heard that in some parts of Java, gangs of youths were taking advantage of the situation and were *rampokking*—looting—the houses of Europeans and killing anyone who tried to fight back. It was reported that the soldiers of the Royal Netherlands East Indies Army, having surrendered, were being sent to prisoner-of-war camps. I imagined Corrie's father among them, his hands shackled.

"Should we leave Java too?" I asked my father. "Like the Jochens did?"

"No, Klara," he replied. "There's nowhere for us to go; we must just pray that the occupation doesn't last long." Stories of cruelty began to circulate. We heard that in the towns and cities, European civilian men were being herded into schools and government buildings, but that their families were not being allowed to visit them. We were told that in Bandung a *kawat,* or barbed-wire fence, had been put around the perimeter of these buildings, turning them into a prison camp.

One night, we learned, three men who'd been interned in one of these camps were caught climbing out. The next day the Japanese lined them up outside the gates. They left the men standing there, in the sun, for two days, without shade, food, or water. Then they were severely beaten and brought back inside. A few days later three other men had been caught doing the same thing. But they weren't made to stand in the sun. They were tied to posts and bayoneted in front of all the prisoners.

There were also rumors that the European civilian men would now be transported to an old military barracks, called Tjimahi, and that their wives and children would be moved into "protected areas."

"To be protected from what?" I asked my parents. My father's mouth became a thin line. "From the local people, with whom we've lived, peacefully, for more than three centuries."

"I don't need to be protected from Jaya," Peter volunteered. "He's my friend."

"These 'protected areas' are really camps," my father explained. "They're for holding lots of people, so that they can't go round causing trouble for the Japs."

"Will *we* have to go into a camp?" I asked.

"Fortunately, we won't," my mother answered. "The Japs have said that they'll leave the planters alone, as they need us to go on growing our crops."

"Which they'll then send to Japan," my father added sourly.

"Yes, but at least we'll be together, Hans," my mother reminded him gently, "and still in our home. We must just be thankful for that."

My father gave a defeated sigh. "I am."

All the Europeans had to go and register with their local police station, as though we were now aliens on Japanese territory. So we drove to Garut, where my parents were given ID cards by an official. He told my parents that within the week all privately owned cars would be confiscated. "They're not taking *my* car," my father said furiously as we drove back home. "I won't let them!"

Two days later we were in the living room. My mother was doing some darning while Peter and I played cards with Dad. Suddenly Mum looked up; we heard the crunch of wheels on the gravel.

She froze, then lowered her sewing.

My father went to the window. "They're here," he said quietly. "Klara and Peter, go and sit with your mother."

As we did so, she looked at my father, alarmed. "Do *whatever* they ask, Hans," she whispered. "If you don't, God knows *what* they might—"

We heard heavy steps on the verandah, then loud banging. Dad opened the front door, and two Japanese soldiers marched in. The first man was an officer, with a brown uniform and gleaming black boots. At his waist was a gun, and a long curved sword in a leather scabbard. Was he going to shoot us, I wondered? Or behead us? The second man was an ordinary soldier. His uniform was green; he wore a cap with a strip of white cloth at the neck, and carried a rifle with a steel bayonet. I stared at the blade with horrified fascination, imagining it being plunged into human flesh.

The officer's eyes swept the room. Seeing the rack that held the weapons for our platoon, he barked an order at the soldier, who took the rifles and carried them outside, piled in his arms. The officer opened Dad's gun cabinet and took out his pistol, his hunting rifle, and the ammunition; these he handed to his subordinate too. Next, he went into the dining room and, to my dismay, emerged with the radio, my mother's beloved Agfa, and the Bolex Cine camera that Dad had given her for her birthday. Then the two soldiers went outside.

Mum, Peter, and I ran to the window. We watched them walk

toward the garage. The officer looked at the Ford, then turned to my father and held out his hand. My father hesitated. Beside me, I felt my mother stiffen.

"Just *do* it, Hans!" she hissed.

As if he'd heard her, Dad handed over the key. The officer opened the car door, removed his sword, then slid behind the wheel. He drove the Ford away, followed by his minion in the other car, the back of which was filled with our things.

Now, without any means of self-protection or escape, we felt very vulnerable. All we could do was to carry on, as best we could, thankful that we were at least still together as a family, which was rare, as by then nearly all the European men had been interned.

One big problem was that without a car it was much harder to bring back food from the market. Dad walked Sweetie down there, and loaded him up with sacks of rice and flour; but getting there and back took a long time. And all the while I knew that there'd be shortages.

"We'll grow our own food," my father said to Peter and me. "We'll grow enough to feed all the families on the plantation. We'll dig up the lawn for corn and we'll use the flower beds for spinach, carrots, and sweet potatoes. Sorry, Annie," he added to my mother, who looked stricken at the thought of her roses being destroyed, "but we're going to need every bit of spare land. We'll plant the Jochens' garden too—Wil can hardly complain, given that the wretch has abandoned us."

I wondered again if Flora had managed to get to Singapore and, if so, whether that was better or worse than being on Java. I'd watch Arif as he went about the plantation and wonder whether he was still thinking about Susan or trying to forget her.

We all set to work. Dad showed Peter and me how to germinate seeds and taught us to space the seedlings out, with the tallest crops at the back and the shorter ones at the front so that every plant would get the sun. He stressed the importance of watering only at night, so that the earth would stay damp for longer. We'd run out of sugar but received an unexpected gift one afternoon when we heard a high-pitched sound that was getting louder and louder. I looked up and saw a black cloud flying toward us.

"Bees!" my mother screamed. We all ran inside and banged the shutters closed. The swarm went past the house, but we could still hear the buzzing. When we ventured out, we saw a black ball on a low branch of the cherimoya.

My father stared at the seething mass. "If only we could put them in a hive . . ."

"Suliman knows how to do that," Jasmine said. So she fetched him and he looked at the swarm; then he and my father found an old keg, took it to the workshop, made some frames to go inside it, and cut a hole in the lid. Then, while we all retreated onto the verandah, Suliman went right up to the bees.

"He should wear a veil," my mother said anxiously. "Jasmine, let me get him a muslin."

Jasmine shook her head. "He'll be fine, Mrs. Anneke." To our amazement, Suliman plunged his hands into the buzzing mass.

My father's jaw slackened. "What are you *doing*, Suliman?"

"I'm looking for the queen," he replied, then carried on

pushing the bees aside, as if parting hair. "Ah, *here* she is." Gently, he pulled her out; we saw the long, golden body wriggling between his thumb and forefinger. Suliman lifted her to his mouth.

Peter gasped. "Is he *eating* her?"

"No," Jasmine answered. "He's just biting the tips of her wings so she can't fly away, which means the bees will stay."

Suliman took the queen over to the keg and dropped her inside; then he carefully sawed off the branch and shook the swarm inside. Once he'd closed the lid, he and my father carried the hive to a clearing in the forest, by the stream.

I never forgot Suliman's courage. And the bees must have liked their new home, because a few weeks later we tasted our first honey.

"This will help us to survive," Dad said as he scraped the honeycomb.

By now three months had gone by. The school was closed indefinitely, and I kept thinking about my classmates. What had happened to Corrie and Greta, I wondered, and to Edda and Lena? Were they still in their homes, or were they in camps too? What about Miss Broek and Miss Vries and all the other teachers?

Without a radio we had no idea what was happening in the world, and so, oddly enough, this was for us an almost innocent time. The rubber production continued; we tended our crops, swam in the pool, and went for rides on Sweetie, though never very far from home, for fear of meeting Japanese soldiers. Peter still had Jaya to play with, but I missed Flora so badly and prayed that, wherever she was, she was safe. Every night I thanked God that my family was at least still together, and still at Sisi Gunung, just as my mother had said. Then, in March 1943, our lives changed.

I was with my mother and Peter in the garden one morning when Dad came to find us. Looking shaken, he told us that he'd just had a telephone call from the local police. They'd told him that the official policy of not interning planters had now ended.

My mother looked alarmed. "Which means what?"

My father frowned. "That I have to leave the plantation."

"So they've gone back on their word?"

"They have. The Japs believe that the planters are hiding weapons on their land, and they don't like it. So a truck will come for me at the end of the week."

My mother closed her eyes, as though trying to shut out the image. "This will be hard," she said quietly.

"It will be," my father agreed, "but we must just keep our heads up, and hope it won't be for long. But Annie, I'll need you to run things while I'm away. Suliman will help you."

Dad spent the remaining days with my mother, going over the rubber production and showing her the accounts. Then, the day before he left, he took Peter and me aside.

"You both have to make me a solemn promise," he said, "that you'll help your mother and do everything she tells you, with *no* argument." His concerned eyes shone into us. "Do you understand?"

We said that we did and solemnly promised to do as he asked. Then we went inside and tried not to cry as we watched Mum pack our dad's suitcase.

Early the next morning, a big open-topped truck rumbled up to the house. When the back was dropped down I saw five men, three of whom I knew from our neighboring plantations, including Ralph Dekker. As there were no seats, all five were sitting on the floor, by their suitcases. They were guarded by four soldiers with rifles and bayonets. One opened Dad's suitcase and inspected its contents. He took out Dad's razor, compass, and penknife, then thrust the bag back at him.

"*Lekas!*" he shouted, jerking his head at the truck. "*Lekas!* Hurry!"

Dad kissed Peter and me, hugged us hard, and told us that everything would be fine. "Keep your heads up, children," he whispered. Then he held Mum, kissed her, and climbed on. The tailgate was slammed shut and the vehicle moved off.

Peter and I ran after it. "Bye, Daddy!" we shouted. "Take care! We'll see you soon! We love you!"

As the truck disappeared down the drive, Peter burst into tears. Mum put her arms round him. "There's no need to cry, darling."

"There *is*," he said, sobbing, "because Daddy's gone and I'll never see him again! Never!"

It breaks my heart to think that Peter was right.

Eight

"Are you all right, Jenni?" Klara asked when I went up to the flat the next morning. "You look pale."

"I'm rather tired. I didn't have a good night."

"If you're cold in bed, you'll find more blankets in the wardrobe."

"Thanks, Klara, it's perfectly warm; it's just that, as I say, I don't sleep well."

Klara handed me a cup of coffee. "I'm sorry. I've been drying some valerian for you to infuse—I'll give it to you this afternoon." It would take more than herbal tea to calm my tormented mind, I reflected. "It must be hard for you, though, being in Polvarth."

"What do you mean?" I asked sharply.

Klara looked puzzled at my tone. "Well . . . having to work away from home. It must be difficult."

I exhaled with relief. "It's hard. Yes . . . Some ghostwriters do the interviews over the phone, or by email; but for me that would be like trying to paint someone's portrait from photos. I can only draw a person's story out of them face-to-face."

"I can understand that," Klara responded. "But you must be missing your boyfriend."

"I am," I answered. "Very much."

"He's a teacher, you said."

"Yes—a good one. The children adore him."

She sipped her coffee. "And how did you meet—if you don't mind my asking?" Klara clearly wanted to chat. She seemed to need to talk about me for a few minutes before every session.

"I don't mind at all," I responded. "I like talking to you, Klara. Rick and I met at his school. I read to the little ones every Wednesday. I've been doing it for three years."

"So the children are what, four and five?"

"Yes. They're lovely. I really enjoy it. One day the class teacher was away and Rick was standing in for her. He talked to me for a minute or two afterward, and . . ."

"That was that?"

I smiled. "I just thought how nice he looked, and how sweet he was with the children. Then, a few days later, I was leaving my flat and he walked past. He stopped to chat, and he asked me if I'd have lunch with him sometime. So I did."

"Did you still do the reading?"

"Yes—there was no need to stop; in any case, no one knew that Rick and I were involved. Then, as my lease was due to end, he suggested that we get a place together. So we found a flat a bit farther away, and we've been there for nine months. It's small, but . . . what was that Dutch word? *Gezellig.*"

She smiled. "Is he the same age as you?"

"Four years older—he's thirty-eight."

"And he's never been married?"

"No. He's had a few relationships that didn't work out; he was with his last girlfriend, Kitty, for three years." I thought of the photos of Kitty that I'd once found at the back of a cupboard. Kitty, blond and pretty, lying on a sun lounger somewhere in the Mediterranean; Kitty in hiking gear by a lake; Rick with his arm round Kitty in his parents' kitchen; Kitty dolled up for some black-tie event. "He was very keen on her," I went on, "but she was eight years younger than Rick and didn't want to settle down. So she left him, went traveling for a few months, then came back. But he said it wasn't the same after that and they soon split up. I think she regrets it now."

"What makes you say that?"

"Because she emails him from time to time."

"Surely she knows he's with you?"

"She does, but I think she's keeping the door open." I shrugged. "Just in case."

"Well . . . you and Rick live together," Klara said. "And you seem very happy."

"Yes . . . we are . . ."

Her face lit up. "Isn't it half term, next week?"

"That's right."

"Then why don't you ask your Rick to come and stay with you here? It would be fine by me."

"Oh, that's kind, Klara, thank you—it would have been great, but to be honest I don't think I will, because actually, Rick and I . . ." Impulsively, I told her what had been happening.

"I see," she said, when I'd finished. "I did feel that you were troubled about something." I didn't tell Klara that this wasn't the only thing that was troubling me.

"Often the man will go along with whatever the woman wants; but I suppose some men are keen to have a family."

"Yes, and I now know that Rick's one of them." I got out my pad. "So we're in limbo at the moment, not phoning each other for a few days to try and see whether or not we can get over this problem." I realized that Klara was the first person I'd confided in about this.

"Do you think you might change your mind?"

"I don't think so, no."

"Have you always felt this way about having children?"

"When I was little, I wanted to have four—two girls and two boys. I even named them: Harriet, Marcus, Katie, and James." I saw them lined up in clean clothes and gleaming shoes.

"So what happened to that dream?" Klara asked. "Is it that you're too busy with your career?"

"No. My career's got nothing to do with it. I just decided, a long time ago, that I didn't want to be responsible for another human being."

Klara frowned. "Well … it does seem daunting—particularly at the beginning when they're so tiny. But I can only say that Nature helps us to meet that responsibility. Do tell me to mind my own business, Jenni …"

"It's okay."

"But it seems a shame to let that perfectly natural anxiety stop you." She sipped her coffee. "At least these days, women aren't *expected* to have children."

"That's true. It's a personal choice." I tucked my hair behind my ear. "Did you always want to be a mother?"

"I longed to be one," she answered without hesitation. "Not least because I'd been told that I never would be."

"Because of what happened to you during the war?"

"That's right. After I'd been married for three years and still wasn't pregnant, I saw a specialist. He said that having been starved as a young girl had affected my fertility." I flinched at the word *starved*. "Then, a year later, by which time we were waiting to adopt, I conceived. It seemed a miracle, and I thanked God." Klara put her coffee cup down. "And tell me about your parents, Jenni. Are you close to them?"

"No. My father died when I was five."

"How sad," she murmured. "And how hard for your mother."

"It was, although they'd split up the year before. They were very young; she was nineteen when she had me. It was a shotgun wedding, I think. Anyway, my father left us when I was four; he'd got involved with a woman at work. A few months later he was in Scotland with this girlfriend when a van slammed into their car. She survived, but he died at the scene."

"How awful for everyone. And dreadful for your mother."

"She was devastated. She'd adored him and had always hoped he'd come back."

"Bringing up a child on her own can't have been easy."

I shifted on my chair. "To make things worse, she discovered that my father hadn't had life insurance, so things were tough for her financially as well. So she did a bookkeeping course and got a job."

"Did she ever marry again?"

"No. But then it would have been a lot for a man to take on."

Klara looked puzzled. "One little girl?"

"But, to answer your question, I'm not close to her. In fact, we have very little to do with each other."

Klara blinked. "That's a great shame; one draws a lot of strength from one's family."

"Not always, Klara. It depends on the relationship that you have with them, and my relationship with my mother is . . . not good."

"But *why*?"

By now I was used to Klara's directness.

"Because there are old resentments, things she said to me that I can never forget." I sipped my coffee before going on. "It's odd, isn't it—that old saying about sticks and stones breaking bones but words never hurting. I'd much rather have had the sticks and stones, because to this day, my mother's words still cause me great pain." Now I tried to turn the attention back to Klara. "But it's probably hard for you to understand, as you seem to have been close to your own mother."

"Not always," she answered to my surprise. "In fact there was a time—quite a long time—when my mother would barely speak to me."

"You mean there was a rift?"

"Yes. A terrible one." She looked away. "Perhaps I'll tell you about it, when I feel ready."

"If you want to, Klara. If you don't want to, that's fine." She nodded. "But you have a good relationship with your sons."

"I do. I see less of Vincent, obviously, although he phones me every week. But both he and Henry have been very good to me. Children are a huge comfort, Jenni. And you know, parenthood is a great adventure."

I bristled. Klara was pushing the idea of children at me. "I'm sure it is, Klara. But it's not the only adventure that life has to offer. Anyway . . ." I'd opened up to her enough. I got out my tape machine. "Let's get back to work."

Nine

Klara

I missed my father so much—his physical presence, his voice, his steps on the verandah as he came and went. I missed having him tease me, and read to me and Peter at bedtime. Day after day I'd try to imagine where he was. Did he sleep in a dormitory or in a cell? Was he warm enough at night? Had he been able to hang up his *kelambu,* his mosquito net? Did he have enough to eat?

"You mustn't worry about your father," my mother told me. "He's a big, strong man, he's very robust. He'll just think about how much we love him, and he'll be fine—we'll *all* be fine. But please, darling, my life isn't easy without him, so I need you to be *good.*"

I'm ashamed to say that Peter and I weren't good. Without

two parents to keep us in check, my brother and I ran wild, or squabbled incessantly. I took to bossing him about, and Jasmine and my mother were too busy to intervene. Jasmine was looking after things at home while my mother kept the rubber production going. It was strange seeing her, rather than my father, checking that the trees had been tapped and the latex collected, or inspecting the pressed sheets in the shed. It was even stranger seeing Mum opening the safe every Friday to pay the workers, or listening to their complaints.

Being a child, I thought only of my own sadness. I didn't think about how hard life must have been for my mother or how much she must have missed my father. I gave no thought to how afraid she must have felt, especially at night, in case any *rampokkers* decided to try their luck, or any Japanese soldiers came up to the house. Worse, though, than any of these fears, was still not knowing where my father *was*.

We'd heard that most of the civilian men were being held in Tjimahi, so twice a week we wrote to him there. Peter and I would tell him how our crops were growing, and we'd enclose drawings of ourselves, standing in the sunshine by the cherimoya, all smiles. One day Peter drew tears onto his face, but I made him rub them off.

"It's bad enough for Dad," I said crossly. "Don't make him feel sad!"

For weeks we heard nothing. Then, one morning, Mum received an envelope stamped *Tjimahi*. Inside was a card from our father. We were thrilled to hear from him at last, but the card was very strange. It was typed with a list of prescribed phrases that he had circled to say that he was "eating healthy food" and doing "useful work." He was also allowed twenty-five free words, in Malay, as Dutch had been banned. He wrote that he was "fine," but that he missed us and that we must all keep our "heads up." In one corner he had drawn a four-leaf clover.

A couple of months after this, my mother called Peter and me to her. In her hand was an official-looking letter.

"Now *we* have to leave the plantation," she told us.

"Where will we go?" Peter asked.

"Are we leaving Java?" I wanted to know.

"No." My mother sighed. "We can't, because of the Japanese. Java seems to have become a prison, from which we can't escape. In any case, we wouldn't want to leave without Daddy, would we?"

"Of course not!" Peter exclaimed. "I'd *never* leave Java without him."

"So where *are* we going to go?" I demanded.

My mother frowned. "We have to go into a camp."

Peter clapped his hands. "Perhaps it'll be the same one that Daddy's in!"

She shook her head. "It will be a camp just for women and children. This letter doesn't say where it is, only that a truck will come to pick us up tomorrow, at dawn. So let's go inside and pack, quickly, as we don't have much time."

"Are you sad?" I asked her in Malay as she and Jasmine got down our leather cases.

"I am," my mother replied. "I'll be very sad without Jasmine." Jasmine was weeping. "We'll miss everyone here. We'll miss our home."

Tears sprang to my eyes as the reality of what was happening sank in. "What about Sweetie? And Ferdi?"

"What about *Jaya*?" Peter wailed. "Can't he come with us?"

Mum stroked his hair. "Of course he can't, darling. What would his mother say? As for the pets, Jasmine will look after them until we're back."

"I will," Jasmine promised. "Don't worry, children. You will be home very soon."

"The Allies will come, and they'll drive the Japanese out of Java," my mother reassured us. "But until that happens we just have to be cheerful, and look on this time as an adventure."

The letter stipulated that we were to take a roll-up mattress each, plus whatever other *barang*, or luggage, we could carry. Mum got out the rucksacks that she'd made us, with the clothes and rations inside; then she and Jasmine filled our suitcases with mosquito nets, sheets and towels, cups and plates and books. Onto her own case Mum tied a wok, and a small Anglo stove. Into Peter's she tucked his teddy bear, his Meccano erector set, and a small wooden Spitfire that Dad had made him. Then Peter went to his cupboard and pulled out his best navy blazer.

"You won't need that smart jacket, darling," my mother said to him.

"I will," he replied as he packed it. "Because I'm going to wear it on the day we see Daddy again."

At that I got out my yellow silk party dress and gave it to Mum. Without saying anything, she laid it in my case.

I asked her what would happen to everyone on the plantation. She answered that for now the rubber production would stop. Then she went into Dad's office, opened the safe, and asked Suliman to call the workers. She gave them each two months' pay; then, when she'd done that, she paid Suliman and Jasmine six months' wages, to look after the house and our pets, and to distribute the crops to the plantation families. The rest of the money, Mum put in her bag.

Peter was desperate to tell Jaya what was happening, but Mum said that it was too late to go and see him.

"We'll write to Jaya when we get to the camp," she said soothingly.

The next day marked the start of our internment. It's a day that's remained etched on my mind.

We rose before dawn and had our last breakfast at Sisi Gunung. As a pink light filled the sky, I went into Sweetie's stall, put my arms round his neck, and promised that I'd come back to him soon. While Peter and I were saying goodbye to Ferdi, we heard the crunch of heavy tires on the gravel and saw an open truck, like the one that had come for my father, bumping up the drive. Three soldiers with rifles jumped down and opened the back. It was crammed with women and children, all standing, their hair matted, their faces filmed with dust.

"*Lekas!*" the soldiers shouted at us. "*Lekas! Goh!*" Jasmine kissed Peter and me, hugged us, then put her arms round my mother. Suddenly I heard rapid steps and the sound of the gravel being scattered, then Jaya hurtled up to us, out of breath. He was clutching a batik bag. He gave it to Peter. Inside was Jaya's beloved chess set. In Malay, Jaya told Peter that he was "lending" it to him and that he had to "bring it back soon." Peter smiled and promised that he would, then he and Jaya hugged until a soldier forced them apart, pushing himself between them. Suliman put our bags and mattresses on the truck, then he lifted Peter and me up and clasped our hands in both of his. Then he helped my mother to climb on. We waved to him, and to Jasmine and Jaya, then, as the tailgate was shut, I took one last look at my beloved home.

The drive down from the hills was hell. The truck was so full that there was no floor space for anyone to sit, and we had to hold on to one another as we swung round the bends. The sides of the vehicle were very high, and we couldn't see anything except the sun blazing down on us, and the crowns of the palm trees waving above us. Where *was* the camp, we all wondered—in the jungle? Or was it in a former prison or a disused barracks? These, we knew, were the kinds of places that had been turned into the "civilian internment centers" that had sprung up all over Java.

The truck was painfully slow and kept on breaking down. At one point we all had to get out while it was fixed. This was a blessing, as we were desperate for water, which some local women, seeing our sorry state, brought us.

"Drink," they whispered as they handed round coconut shells. "*Minum.* Drink."

At last the truck was fixed and we got back on.

As we recognized the tops of the buildings, we realized that we were entering Bandung. We drove past our school—I recognized the green-tiled roof and the moon-and-stars weather vane. I thought of the smart uniform that I had worn there each day, my face washed, my hair brushed and braided. Now we were disheveled and dirty. I panicked at the thought of Miss Vries seeing me like this, then remembered that the school had been closed for a year and a half, and that I had no idea where Miss Vries was. I wondered whether she was still called Miss Vries, given that she had been due to get married.

We came to the north part of the city, which, we now understood, was our destination, and the truck stopped. As the back was dropped down we saw that the whole area was enclosed by a plaited bamboo fence, called a *gedék*, topped with barbed wire. There was one gate, with a watchtower that was manned by four soldiers armed with rifles and bayonets. Someone said that the camp was called Bloemencamp, as the streets here were all named after flowers.

The truck made several stops, as women and children climbed out with their belongings. When we got to a street called Orchideelaan, it stopped again. This time Mum, Peter, and I were told to get down; we picked up our luggage and were escorted to a bungalow. As we looked at it we thought that it would be bearable, though smaller than what we were used to. But when we went inside we saw, to our amazement, that it was already full of people—about thirty women, girls, and boys, one family group to a room. We were assigned a small storeroom at the back of the house.

My mother and I put the mattresses inside, then laid them down beneath the shutterless window. Our rucksacks, stuffed with towels, became pillows; our suitcases, small tables. It was *gezellig*, my mother said, as she pinned a picture to the wall. Cozy. Then she put her arms round us and told us that there was nothing to fear. We had shelter, gas to cook with, electricity, and water. We must just keep our heads up, as Daddy had urged us to do. We were with other women and children, and we'd all help one another get through this stressful time.

"Let's play chess," Peter said. He put Jaya's set out on top of his suitcase, and he and I had a game. Peter no longer had Jaya,

I reflected, and I no longer had Flora. We would keep each other company.

Just before nightfall, my mother hung up our *kelambus*, but there wasn't room for all three, so she had one, while Peter and I shared another. I had never shared a bedroom with him, so it was strange to be cocooned together, inside the net. In a short while we heard "Lights out!" and the room was plunged into darkness.

"It's noisy, isn't it?" Peter murmured after a while.

"Very," I murmured back.

I could hear people talking, coughing, yawning, and praying. Several children were crying; someone was singing a lullaby—*Sleep, baby, sleep.* I realized that Peter had drifted off. But I stayed awake, listening to his soft, steady breathing. It reminded me of the sound of the sea.

We were woken early. Everyone rushed out of bed. I soon understood why: There was only one loo in the house and one basin, and a mad dash for both.

"I wonder what happens now," my mother said to us as we waited in the line to wash. "Could you tell us, please?" she asked the woman standing in front of us. She was about twenty-five, blond, with a broad face and hazel eyes that were flecked with gold.

"What happens now?" The woman laughed. "What happens now is what happens every morning—and evening— blooming *tenko*."

"Blooming *tenko*?" Peter echoed. "What's that?"

"Roll call," the woman replied wearily. "*Tenko* means 'counting.' You'll soon know your Japanese numbers, young man."

We had some of the food that we'd brought with us for breakfast, then we followed everyone out of the house, down the street, onto a field where soldiers were harrying the women and children into rows and columns, five across and about a hundred deep.

"Now what?" I asked my mother as we lined up on the pale, dry grass.

She bit her lip. "I don't know." It was the first time I'd ever seen my mother look vulnerable and unsure. It scared me.

As I looked around, still exhausted and confused from yesterday's journey, I spotted a classmate in the row behind me. Greta and I had never been especially close, but I was elated to see her and we grinned at each other. She had coppery hair and very pale, freckled skin, except that her skin wasn't pale, I now saw; it was brown, as though all her freckles had joined up. Standing next to her was her grandmother, Mrs. Moonen, who was also her guardian, Greta's parents having died of typhoid when Greta was three.

My mother turned to Mrs. Moonen. "What are we all waiting for?" she asked.

"We're waiting for the commandant to come," Mrs. Moonen whispered. "But don't talk, or they'll punish you." *Punish*. It was a word that we were to hear again and again.

We faced forward, and now saw that at the front of the field was a platform on which a woman was standing. She was *Belanda Indo*—a person of Dutch and Indonesian parentage. Holding up a megaphone, this woman informed us, in Malay, that she was the camp's translator. She told us that during *tenko* we must all face east toward Japan. She explained that the commandant would soon arrive, and that when he did, she would shout *Kiotsuke!*—"Attention!"—and then *Keré!* which meant "Bow!" It was important to bow in the correct way, she went on, because we were really bowing to the Japanese emperor. To bow in a sloppy way would be to insult His Imperial Majesty, and we would be punished. She then explained that we had to bend from the waist at an angle of thirty degrees, and that we must stay like that until we heard *Naore!*—"Stand up!"—after which would come the command *Yasume!*—"Dismiss." The translator added that we must also bow to any and every Japanese soldier, but must never look them in the eye, since we were "not worthy." Should we dare to do so, we would be severely punished.

Peter looked stricken. "We'll be punished?"

"Yes. If we look the soldiers in the eye," my mother whispered, "or don't bow correctly."

"Why do we have to bow?" he demanded. "It's silly. I won't!"

"You *must*," my mother hissed.

I remembered the promise that we'd made our dad.

"I'll bow," I whispered. "And you have to do it too, Pietje. No arguments, remember?"

Our mother sighed with relief. "Thank you, children." Her face shone with perspiration. "Let's just hope the commandant comes soon."

But he didn't come, and the temperature was rising by the minute. We'd been standing there for three hours. Sweat trickled down our foreheads, stinging our eyes; it plastered our clothes to our backs. We had to brush ants off our feet and an-

kles and swat away flies. As the sun rose ever higher, I thought
of Ferdi, and of how concerned my father had been to provide
shade for that little animal; but here we were, women and children, exposed for hours to the sun's rays with no hats or sun-
glasses permitted, and not even the elderly or infants allowed to
sit down. Now I understood why Greta, normally so pale, was
dark brown.

All around us babies wept and screamed; people sobbed and
begged for water; a woman in front of us collapsed but was
jerked onto her feet by two guards. Peter, exhausted, kept trying
to lie on the ground, so Mum and I held him upright between us.

At last the commandant arrived. He carried a whip, and his
tall black boots shone in the sun. His sword hung from his waist.
I couldn't help staring at it, imagining it slicing and slashing . . .

"*Keré!*" screamed the interpreter. We all bowed.

"Lower," my mother whispered to Peter and me. "Get right
down!"

"Why?" Peter asked.

"Just *do* it!" I said.

"*Naore!*"

We all straightened up.

The interpreter jumped off the platform, and the commandant sprang onto it, like a fox. He planted his legs wide, folded
his arms, then shouted that we were extremely fortunate to be
guests of the Japanese emperor, and to be under the benevolent
protection of the Imperial Japanese Army. In return for this benevolent protection, he went on, we had to behave well, never
try to escape, keep ourselves clean, and dress modestly. We
weren't to gamble, drink alcohol, or brawl, and we had to speak

only Japanese or Malay, not Dutch, which was forbidden. Most of all, we must do "useful work."

"*Keré!*" shouted the interpreter again. Everyone bowed as the commandant strode off.

"*Yasume!*" We were dismissed. I felt giddy with relief. As Greta and I walked off the field, she told me that she and her grandmother had been in this camp for a year. We talked about our classmates, but she didn't know what had happened to any of them; she said that there were many other camps where they might be. "We're all prisoners now," she added quietly.

When my mother, Peter, and I reached our new home, the woman that we'd spoken to in the morning told us that her name was Kirsten, and that she'd been here in Bloemencamp for a year.

"Could you tell me where the school is?" my mother asked her.

"School?" Kirsten roared with laughter. "There's no school! The Japs have forbidden education."

"I see." Mum looked at Peter and me. "Then I'll just teach you myself."

"Oh, you won't be up to it," Kirsten said. "You'll be too tired."

Mum bristled. "I shall be fine, thank you."

"You won't," Kirsten insisted. "You'll be exhausted." My mother bit her lip but didn't reply. I could see that she didn't much like Kirsten.

The next day Mum was assigned work, as a "furniture lady." Her job was to haul furniture out of abandoned houses and load it onto a two-wheeled wooden cart that would normally be pulled by a horse or a buffalo. Once the cupboards, tables, and chairs were piled high, my mother, along with Kirsten and a woman called Loes, had to pull the cart to another, already emptied house, and carry in the furniture to be stored there ready for any Japanese people to use in the future.

Within a week of starting this, my mother was noticeably thinner, her face and shins bruised from the heavy work. At the end of each day she would cook for us on the Anglo, but after that, just as Kirsten had predicted, she was too weary to do anything but sleep.

As I was ten, I was made to do chores. Some girls my age had to look after the babies and younger children while their mothers worked, or they had to sweep the streets or sort through the huge pile of rubbish by the gate. I was told that I would be pulling up weeds. This wasn't easy, as the ground was baked hard and we had to watch out for scorpions. We weren't allowed to kneel but had to squat on our haunches, which was very uncomfortable. Greta was doing this work too, a few yards from where I was working. One day I saw her succumb to the desire to kneel down. Within seconds a soldier had run over to her, grabbed her by the arm, and yanked her upright. I thought that he'd make her squat down again; instead, he raised his hand and struck her on the cheek. Instinctively, she turned her head and received a second blow on that side of her face. She fell to her knees, then was jerked upright and slapped again. I scrambled to my feet and ran to help her, but another soldier pushed me down, his face twisted with fury.

That night I told my mother what I'd seen.

She closed her eyes for a moment. "Poor Greta," she murmured. "Poor little girl."

"But why did that soldier hit her? He didn't have to *hit* her, did he?"

My mother explained that Japanese soldiers despised prisoners because they themselves would rather commit suicide than suffer the dishonor of surrender. So, to them, European *women* prisoners were beneath contempt, and they hated having to guard us. To make themselves feel better, they vented their rage and frustration on us.

"So, in order not to be hurt by them, we must do whatever they say," Mum concluded. "We must always bow to them, at once, and *never* look them in the eye. Do you both understand?" We nodded solemnly.

As the days passed, Mum worried about Peter, who was eight, being left alone while she and I worked. She didn't want him running around the camp, like some of the other boys did, for fear he'd get into trouble with the soldiers. So Mum asked a woman called Ina, who was in her sixties and therefore exempt from work, to look after him. Ina was tall and thin, with hooded eyes, high cheekbones, and a curved nose; she reminded me of the eagle that we'd seen at the zoo. She'd never had children, but she looked after Peter very well. She cooked his food rations, played chess with him, and got him to write his numbers and letters using a stick in the dirt. Whenever she did this she would have to pretend that they were just chatting, because if it had looked as though a lesson was going on, she would have been beaten. In return for her care of Peter, Ina got items of my mother's clothing.

"Why does Ina *want* your clothes?" I asked Mum. "She's much taller than you are; they'll never fit her." Mum replied that Ina didn't want to wear the clothes, only to barter them with the locals. At that time the Japanese still tolerated *gedekking;* crawling under the fence to trade money or jewelry for food or medicine with the people outside.

"Why doesn't Ina barter her own things?" I demanded. My mother answered that Ina had very few possessions, as she'd already been in two other camps, and so most of what she'd had to start with was gone. "But why do the locals *want* our old clothes?" Mum explained that throughout Java the supply of cotton had dried up, and so the camp inmates traded their garments with the local people for food—a hanky would fetch one egg, a blouse six eggs or a "hand" of bananas. A dress would fetch ten eggs.

"Don't ever give Ina my silk dress," I told my mother. "Or Peter's jacket."

"I won't," she promised, "because I know you're going to need them."

As time went on, we got to know the people in "our" house, all except for a woman called Marjolein, who spoke to no one.

"Why doesn't she speak to anyone?" my mother asked Kirsten.

"Because it's her house," Kirsten replied. "She loathes having to share it with thirty strangers; can't say I blame her."

Many of the families had been in more than one camp; some had been in Solo and De Wijk in the east, others had been in Muntilan and Ambarawa, in Central Java.

"The Japs are moving everyone westward," Kirsten remarked.

"Why?" my mother asked.

"They're herding us into one big ghetto," Kirsten answered, "to make it easier to control us. That's why it's so crowded."

Every day more trucks arrived, loaded with women and children. We recognized some from the other plantations, and there were more pupils from my school.

One day, to my joy, I saw Corrie van der Velden getting off a truck with her mother and her twin sisters, who by then were two and a half. They were allocated a room in our house, in the pavilion, and we were so glad to see them, though the twins cried a lot, which made sleeping—never easy—harder than usual. Corrie told me that they had been held in another camp, Karees, for the past year, in southeastern Bandung. They'd been in a house with twenty others, and had lived in the garage. "But now the camp's being cleared," Corrie explained, "so they've brought us here." Her father, she added, was in Tjimahi. She had last glimpsed him sitting blindfolded, in the back of a truck, with the rest of his regiment. It had been a shock, she said, to see him like that. Had my own father been blindfolded? I tried to push the awful thought out of my mind.

What I remember most about the house on Orchideelaan was the noise. Day and night we heard the constant mumble of people talking, arguing, shouting, and weeping. One woman sneezed a lot—it sounded like a pistol being fired. Ina was always reading aloud from her Bible—to comfort us, she said, though I found it annoying and upsetting. But the worst thing was hearing babies cry. Their mothers were often too exhausted to comfort them, and too undernourished to be able to breast-feed them.

At that time everyone did their own cooking, using the rations that were provided, as well as food that could be bought from a shop called a *toko* that each family could go to on one day per month. When it was our turn, Peter and I would go there with our mother, but the *toko* had very little on sale and what there was was very expensive. Dutch money had been banned and replaced with Japanese "guilders," which were worth far less; worse, the quantities that we could buy were tiny: a teaspoon of salt, a few grams of sugar or bread; a single papaya.

A few weeks after we'd arrived, soldiers burst into the house and took away our stoves. Then the gas supply was shut off, and kitchens were turned into bedrooms to accommodate yet more prisoners. The *toko* was closed. Now we all had to collect our food from the *dapur,* a central kitchen that was just a bamboo shed with old oil drums serving as massive saucepans. These were suspended over open fires and were lifted off them by two of the teenage boys using wooden poles. You had to stand in line with your pans to receive some watery soup, one spoon of horribly starchy rice with a tiny bit of meat and a sliver of onion or carrot stirred into it. There'd be half a slice of rubbery bread, and occasionally an egg or a banana, though these treats would have to be shared between three or four mouths. But even these meager rations were dwindling, and people were getting thinner, though the soldiers always looked well fed.

At *tenko* one morning the commandant informed us that in order to supplement the rations, we now had to grow our own food. We were given spinach and tomato seeds and our back garden was divided into ten sections, one for each family. It was the dry season, and the ground was bone hard. I remember watching Corrie's mother struggling to break the baked soil with a pickaxe that was nearly as big as she was, while the twins and Corrie napped inside, watched over by Ina, who had taken on the role of benign aunt.

"Are you all right, Mrs. Van der Velden?" I asked. "Can I help you?"

"That's kind, Klara." Mrs. Van der Velden leaned on the pickaxe, out of breath. "But you're far too young to do this sort of work." She smiled. "And you don't have to call me Mrs. Van der Velden. Kate will do just fine."

My mother and Kirsten both helped Kate, and soon the rock-hard earth was dug over and watered and we were able to plant the seeds. They grew well, but we had to watch the plants at night because if we didn't, people would steal them.

One guard stole in broad daylight. Everyone called him Johnny Tomato, and he'd ride around the camp on his bike, which was too small for him, his neckcloth flapping. If he spotted a ripe tomato, he'd get off his bike, pick it, then eat it right there on the spot. Once I saw him doing this at the house opposite ours; then, just as he was about to get back onto his bike, he stopped. As he stared down the street I followed his gaze and saw Marjolein, her head drooping with exhaustion as she returned from her shift in the *dapur*. Suddenly she looked up, stopped, and bowed. Perhaps she bowed a few seconds too late, or perhaps Johnny was just in a bad mood, but he threw his bike down, ran up to her, and started screaming at her in an enraged staccato that bounced off the walls. Then, to my horror, he took off his rifle and struck her with the butt; then he hit her again, and now he was pounding her shoulders and back, until she lay in the dust, her arms curled round her head. Then, as Kirsten and I rushed to help her, Johnny climbed back onto his bicycle and pedaled away.

We saw so many women and girls being hit that it became the norm. Slapping was the preferred way; the soldiers would strike first with the flat of the hand, then the back of the hand, then the flat again, snorting with the effort. *Slap, slap, slap!* Some liked to kick, or chop or punch. Others were more cunning, jabbing their fingers into soft parts with agonizing precision. A few, like Johnny Tomato, used their rifles, breaking collarbones and ribs or knocking out teeth.

My mother feared that being exposed to such violence would affect Peter and me. She worried that it would make us hate the Japanese.

"Why shouldn't we hate them?" Peter demanded. "They're horrible to *us*."

"I don't want you to hate *anyone*," my mother replied. "Hatred is destroying the whole world."

Not long after this, one of the twins, Sofie, became ill with dysentery. There was no hospital, and Kate was frantic. One morning I saw her run outside holding Sofie. She stopped two soldiers who'd been passing the house. Still cradling Sofie, she bowed, then implored them to get medicine for her "very sick child."

"Imatin," she said. "I need Imatin for my baby."

The first soldier stared at her, then shook his head. Kate fell to her knees, still clutching the little girl, and begged him to help. But the pair just shrugged, then walked on. Kate sobbed as she carried Sofie inside.

That night my mother and I were woken by footsteps on the *émpér* that ran along the side of the house. We pulled back our *kelambus* and saw, standing by the open window, the second soldier. Without speaking, he handed my mother a small brown bottle; she looked at the label, then ran with it to Kate, who let out a cry of joy.

"You *see*," my mother said triumphantly to Peter and me once Sofie had recovered. "That just proves that there's good and bad in everyone; we must *never* forget that."

My mother had said that running the plantation on her own had been too hard; but life in Bloemencamp was far worse. Peter and I hated having to see her doing such backbreaking work; we hated being hungry all the time. We loathed being crammed into such a confined space, with so many others that you could hear every cough, snore, and burp. I couldn't bear the filth, the dreadful food, or the utter boredom. But what I hated, more than anything else, was *tenko*. *Tenko* was hell.

Morning and night we'd have to stand there as the soldiers counted us in our rows, shouting out the numbers:

Ichi! Ni! San! Shi! Go! Roku! Shichi! Hachi! Kyuu! Ju!

If they made a mistake, which they nearly always did, they'd go back and start all over again. There'd be people groaning and crying and leaning on one another, then they'd jerk straight up to bow as the commandant would stride past. We'd have to listen to him ranting at us, that we had been defeated and must therefore be obedient, polite, and grateful for the "hospitality" and "protection" that we were being given. As if this wasn't enough, it was made far worse by the soldiers' always finding someone to pick on. It could be for anything. Once they picked on Greta's grandmother, Mrs. Moonen. Her mouth lifted up a little on one side; perhaps she'd had a stroke, I don't know, but she was standing at the front when the commandant suddenly seemed to notice her. He must have thought that she was laughing at him, because he barked an order at a guard and the next second she was being dragged off the field. The following morning I saw Greta winding a bloodied bandage around Mrs. Moonen's shorn head.

Of the many punishments that the Japanese used, head shaving was the most common. It was done in public, very badly, and was humiliating. Most would just tie a scarf around their head and carry on. Often, other women would cut off bits of their own hair and glue it to the front of the shaved woman's scarf. My mother had done this so often that her once luxuriantly long hair now barely reached her collar.

"Why don't we just escape?" Peter suggested one morning.

"Why don't we?" I agreed. "After all, there are thousands of us, and just a few of them."

"But they have guns and bayonets," my mother responded. "And they'd use them."

"In any case," added Kate, "it would be hard to hide. We'd soon be spotted, brought back, and probably executed. Don't worry, darling," she said to Corrie. "That's not going to happen."

"I shan't try and escape," my mother stated. "My priority is just to stay alive, for my children."

"Exactly," agreed Kate, "and I shall stay alive for my girls— even if it kills me!" she added with a grim laugh.

I remember how painfully slowly time went by. We lost all track of it, though my mother tried to keep count of the passing weeks and months by making a daily mark on the wall. Our main aim was not to be noticed by the guards, so that we wouldn't be punished. So during *tenko* I'd stand there, my face a mask, thinking about my father, and about the plantation, and about Ferdi and Sweetie and about how much I'd like to eat a mango, barely listening to the commandant ranting away. Then, during one *tenko,* after we'd been in Bloemencamp for about a year, I heard the interpreter announce that we were to be moved. A murmur of surprise rippled through the lines. My mother whispered to Peter and me that we were going to another camp, called Tjihapit. Then the interpreter raised her megaphone again, and told us that we were to go and pack immediately. We were to bring whatever we could carry, but were not to try to smuggle in any "forbidden items." Our bags would be searched at the gate.

Back in the house, we all discussed what was forbidden.

"Anything Dutch," said Kirsten. "That means no Dutch money—notes or coins—or anything with an image of Queen Wilhelmina on it."

"Nothing orange," Ina added, *"although . . ."* She lifted up her dress to reveal an orange ribbon sewn along the hem of her pants. She grinned. "Like my royal knickers?"

"They're lovely," said Loes. "At *tenko* I tie a piece of orange wool to one of my toes so that I feel I'm bowing to Holland, not to the rotten Japs."

"No Dutch flags," Kirsten went on as she packed her suitcase. "No radio parts," she added in a singsong voice. "No scissors or knives or—even more dangerous—*books!*"

This grieved my mother, as reading was, as she often put it, a way of "restoring" herself at the end of each day. But we had to leave our books piled up in the front gardens to be collected and burned; not even Bibles were allowed. Ina beckoned to me and opened her jacket; hidden inside the lining were a few pages that she said she'd torn out of her Old Testament. "A few of my favorite psalms," she whispered, then put her finger to her lips.

"No paper or pens," Kirsten intoned as she packed her bag. "No playing cards, and no board games."

My mother turned to Peter. "You'll have to leave Jaya's chess set behind."

"But I said I'd bring it back to him! I can't leave it!" His eyes had filled. "I *can't*, Mummy."

"You'll have to, Pietje," she said. "We can't risk them finding it."

"Because if they *did*," I said crossly, "it's Mummy that they'd punish, not you. Do you want that?"

My mother wiped away his tears. "After the war I'll buy Jaya a beautiful new chess set for you to give him."

Peter swallowed. "Do you promise?"

"I do. I'll get him one that's *even* nicer."

This seemed to cheer Peter. "He's always wanted one made of onyx and marble."

Mum smiled. "Then that's what he'll have. I'll get him the most beautiful onyx and marble chess set that I can find. This is my solemn promise to you, darling."

Peter sniffed, then he took Jaya's chess set out of his suitcase. With a regretful sigh, he put it in a corner of the room.

Family photos had also been banned, but my mother refused to leave behind the photo of our father, so she stitched it into Peter's teddy bear along with the one postcard that we'd received from him.

We all tried to figure out why we were being moved. No one seemed to know. There were all sorts of rumors flying around: that the Japanese were losing the war; that they were winning it; that the Allies were on their way, advancing across the Pacific, island by island. Someone said that Tjihapit was a punishment camp, run by the Kempeitai, which no one came out of alive. Someone else said no, it was better than Bloemencamp, with more food and fewer people.

But I didn't care what it was like. It was at least a change—something to break us out of our harsh routine.

Ten

Klara and I had been recording for about an hour on Tuesday afternoon when I suddenly realized, guiltily, that she was exhausted.

"You're tired, Klara," I said. "Let's stop for today. I was so engrossed in what you were saying, I didn't notice."

"Yes." She heaved a weary sigh. "I don't think I can do any more reminiscing today." She glanced at her watch. "In any case, I have to open the shop soon."

I turned off the tape recorder. "I'll leave you to have a little rest before that." I put the recorder into my bag, then stood up.

"Don't go yet, Jenni," Klara said. "There's something I want to show you."

I sat down again, pleased that Klara wanted to share something with me, unprompted. She lifted the lid of the wooden box, which had been intriguing me. "As I told you, we left Java with nothing," she said quietly. "But I do have a few mementoes, which I treasure, as a reminder of what we survived. This is one." She took out a white handkerchief, neatly folded, opened it out, and laid it on the table. Edged in lace, it was made of fine cotton lawn and embroidered in a red-and-blue script. In the center of it was a circle, inside which, in small square capitals, was sewn BLOEMENCAMP, BANDUNG, JUN 43–44. Around this, in tiny letters, were thirty or so names.

"My mother made this," Klara explained. "She stitched onto it the names of every woman and child who'd been in the house with us."

"Loes van Rozelaar," I read. "Lisbeth de Jong, Kate van der Velden, Hanke Sillem, Martha Tromp." I stared at the hanky, fascinated. KIRSTEN SWAAN. "Here's Kirsten—there's no other Kirsten, so it must be her." MARJOLEIN DE BRUIN. "That's Marjolein, whose house it was. And there's Ina." INA BOGAARDT.

"And here's my mother," added Klara. ANNEKE BENNINK. "She worked on this hanky at night. I remember thinking how hard it must be, doing such minuscule stitches by lamplight, but she said that it was important to her, because in years to come she wanted to be able to remember everyone's name."

"Some have just the first names." I peered at them. CORRIE, ANGELIKA, YAN.

"Those are the children," Klara explained. "My mother did it like that in order to differentiate them from the adults." SASKIA, SOFIE, KLARA, PETER . . .

"I'd like to photograph it, for the memoir. I'll bring my camera either tomorrow or the day after. Would that be okay?"

Klara folded the handkerchief. "Of course." As she put it back into the box, I caught a glimpse of something else.

"What's that?"

She lifted it out. It was a bound notebook. The green leather cover was sun-stained and scratched. Klara looked at it, then passed it to me. I gazed at the embossed initials. AKB. "This was your mother's?"

"Yes. Anneke Katrien Bennink."

"Is it her diary?"

"No. She didn't keep a diary."

"May I open it?" Klara nodded. Gently I turned the first few pages. The edges were yellowed and brittle.

Irish Stew, I read in a small neat hand. *Een pond rundvlees . . . twee uien . . . vijf wortels.* I turned the page. *Apple Charlotte . . . Vier Kookappels . . . 200 gram bloem . . . 200 gram poedersuiker . . . een theelepel vanille . . .* I went to the next page. *Rice Pudding . . .*

"She compiled it when we were in Tjihapit," I heard Klara say.

I looked at her, bewildered. "Why would anyone compile a recipe book in a concentration camp?"

"I *will* tell you why, Jenni." She nodded at the clock. "But not until next time, because I have to go down now." She stood up stiffly. "I hate to keep people waiting—it's bad manners and bad business."

I carried the coffee things to the kitchen and put them on the counter. "It must be hard for you," I said, "recalling these very painful events, then having to go and chat to your customers as though it's just a normal day."

"I'm fine," she replied. "It's very intense, as you said it would be; but it's less difficult than I imagined—perhaps because I find you so easy to talk to, Jenni. I find that I *want* to talk to you—I feel you pulling my story out of me, like a length of wool."

"As though I'm unraveling you?" I teased.

"Yes, which, in a way, you are." Klara studied my face for a moment. "But I've been racking my brains as to where we met."

"We didn't," I asserted gently.

She shook her head. "I feel sure that we did. Perhaps we chatted in the lane, or on the beach." She sighed. "Or perhaps my memory is failing, like Jane's."

"But why *should* you remember, given that it was twenty-five years ago?" I felt my face flush.

"So you came here in . . . 1987?"

My pulse was racing. "That's right."

Klara blinked. "Something will jog my memory and I'll suddenly remember." We walked toward the door. "And are you happy with what we've recorded so far?"

"Very happy," I answered, glad to change the subject. "But there's another element I'd like to include, which is to get your family to share something about you; one or two anecdotes, or just a paragraph about how they see you as a person and what you mean to them. This will add some other perspectives as well as involving your nearest and dearest in the creation of the memoir."

"That's a nice idea. So you'd ask Henry and Beth? And Vincent?"

"Yes, and your grandchildren. I could chat to Adam when I see him around the farm; and I could interview Vincent's daughter over the phone, or she could email me something."

"I'm sure Gill would do that. She lives in Rome. I'll give you her contact details tomorrow."

"I thought I'd also ask one or two of your friends."

"Well, Jane of course," Klara suggested. "Some things she *can* still recall, though I can never predict what. Her memories seem to wash in and out, like waves."

"Does she live nearby?"

Klara nodded. "She's in sheltered accommodation in Trelawn. I see her every week, so I could take you with me, or I could bring her here, or we could meet in St. Mawes." We walked down the stairs into the yard; Klara unlocked the shop door, then turned to me. "Can I give you some bread, or a cake? Would you like some fruit? We've got lots of eggs, so do take a box."

"I'm fine, thanks, Klara, I've still got plenty of food in the fridge, and I can buy anything I need in Trennick."

"That's true—the shop there's open until nine, and the Boathouse does good fish and chips if you don't want to cook. Or you could always have supper with us—just knock on the door."

I hesitated. I didn't want to appear ungrateful, but I didn't think I could face another big family meal. "That's very kind, Klara, but I think I'll stay in."

"I understand. So"—she smiled—"I'll see you tomorrow."

It was still light as I walked back to Lanhay. Klara's story filled my thoughts: her mother hauling the furniture cart; Kate trying to pickaxe the dusty ground; Greta and Marjolein being slapped and hit; hatless babies, crying in the sun. My own life, and my own problems, receded.

There was an email from Honor waiting for me when I got back to the cottage. I'd been trying to speak to her since the wedding but had kept on missing her. I emailed her back to say where I was and why. As the mobile signal was so poor, I gave her the number for the phone in the cottage. A minute later it rang.

"Jenni!"

"Honor!" I laughed. "That was quick."

"I really wanted to talk to you. I'm sorry I haven't called—I've been busy—but hey, what's been happening with you? I turn my back for a second, and you disappear to the other end of the country!"

"Well, it all happened very quickly. And where are you?"

"In the studio, waiting to do an interview for Sunday's show. So you're in Cornwall—let me get this right—ghosting the memoirs of the mother of Nina's godfather?"

"Correct." I told her how the job had come about.

"I did notice that he was listening to you rather intently," she said. "I know you can't say much, because of confidentiality, but has she got a good story?"

I explained, in general terms, what it was.

"So these were concentration camps?"

"Yes, in which people were neglected, starved, and often brutalized."

"My God—you'd carry that with you all through your life!"

"Klara has. This is the first time she's talked about it."

"So you sit with her and just listen?"

"I ask a few questions, but yes."

"You must find it pretty harrowing."

"I do, but it's worse for Klara, having to talk about it when she still feels the pain of it so strongly. It's as though it was yesterday for her."

"Does she get upset?"

"Yes. Sometimes she cries."

"So do you stop recording?"

"No. I just pass her a tissue and carry on. It may sound harsh, but her tears are an important part of the story."

"I can understand that—it happens to me too, at times, when I'm interviewing people about something sad. And where in Cornwall does she live?"

"In the south, on the Roseland Peninsula."

"Oh, I don't know it; I've only ever been to the north. Anyway, I have some news."

"Yes?"

"Nina's back from her honeymoon."

"Great. Did they have a good time in Provence?"

"Lovely, apparently; she said they wished they could've stayed longer. She *also* said that she's—" There was a theatrical pause.

"What? Gone back to work?"

"No—or rather she has, but she's . . . oh, can't you guess, Jen?"

"Pregnant?" I murmured.

"*Yes!* Isn't it fabulous?" To my surprise, I felt my eyes fill. "She's *just* told me," I heard Honor say. "She hadn't dared breathe a word, even to us, until she was sure."

"That's understandable."

"But she had her first scan this morning and everything's fine. She tried to call you but couldn't get through, so she gave me permission to tell you."

"It's wonderful." I blinked back a tear, then began to work out the dates. "The first scan's done at twelve weeks."

"Is it?"

"Yes; which means that the baby will arrive in . . . early May."

"That's what Nina said. She's hoping to have the christening on their first wedding anniversary—so we're to save the date. What do you hope she'll have—a girl or a boy?"

"A boy."

"I'd like it to be a girl so that I can buy her some gorgeous dresses, but we'll love it whatever."

"Oh, we will." I saw myself with Nina's baby in my arms, its dimpled hand clutching my finger. "We'll adore it . . ."

"And how's Rick?" Honor prattled on happily.

"He's fine . . ."

"Will he be coming down to Cornwall while you're there?"

I hesitated. "I don't think so."

"But it would be a chance to have a few days together outside London—and isn't half term coming up?"

"Yes, but—"

"You don't have time? Too busy?"

"It's not that. In fact Klara did suggest it, very kindly. But . . . things are a bit tricky between Rick and me at the moment."

"Oh . . . I did think you seemed a bit subdued at the wedding." Honor gave a frustrated sigh. "I wish you'd told me before, Jen—I blab away to you about everything in my life, but you always bottle things up. So . . . what's happened?"

"Nothing dramatic. We've simply realized that we want . . . different things. But I'd rather not talk about it now, if that's okay. I need to concentrate on getting the job done. One thing at a time."

"Sure." Honor knew better than to push me. "But call me at home if you want. I'll be there later."

"Thanks, Hons. I might. But, just quickly, have you heard from Al?"

She exhaled painfully. "No. I'm a bit upset about it, as we swapped cards. Al's short for Alastair, by the way—not Alexander or Alan, in case you were wondering."

"Ah. That question *was* keeping me awake at night, yes."

"I did think that he'd phone," Honor wailed. "We talked a *lot* at the wedding."

"Why don't you ring him?"

"*No*. Too pushy."

"Not in this day and age. You could always pretend that you want to interview him about modern orthodontics."

"Actually, that's not such a bad idea. Did you know that kids with perfectly straight teeth are having braces put on because they think it gives them a geeky kind of chic—isn't that weird? But I still can't get over what Al said about my bite. No one, apart from my mother, has ever told me that *any* part of me was perfect. Though my gynecologist did once say that I have a *very* nice—ooh, my producer wants me; I'd better go. But call me anytime, Jen! I mean it. Bye."

As I put the phone down, smiling, I wished that I could have told Honor what was happening with Rick. But it wasn't a conversation I wanted to have over the phone. And I'd meant what

I said—I did need to concentrate on Klara's story. I wanted to do it justice.

I sat at the kitchen table and began to transcribe the day's material. As I typed out the part about the handkerchief, I wondered how many of those women had survived. I thought of Klara's mother, stitching her son's name onto it, unaware of the sorrow to come. Peter was so alive in Klara's narrative. It was awful waiting for the tragedy—whatever it was—to unfold.

By seven thirty I'd finished the transcription and read through it twice. Feeling wrung out, I opened the wine and had a large glass. I made myself some pasta and drank two more glasses, after which all I wanted was an espresso, but there was no ground coffee left—I'd already finished it. But so strong was my craving that I decided to go and get some.

The car key was next to the phone. I picked it up; then I glanced at the half-empty bottle and set it down. What had I been thinking? I couldn't possibly drive. Instead, emboldened by the wine, I slipped on my coat, grabbed the torch, and set off on foot.

The moon was low and large, bathing everything in a milky light. As I went down the lane I could hear an owl, then the faint roar of the sea, growing louder as I approached the beach. As I stepped onto the slipway the wind rushed up, slapping my cheeks and tugging at my hair. The sand was half exposed, the jagged rocks black against the moonlit sea.

The tide's coming up.

The time's coming up?

The tide, *silly* . . .

We'll have to be quick.

I crossed the beach, inhaling the scent of the sea, then went up the granite steps onto the path, followed it round the cliff through a screen of wind-sculpted trees, then found myself on the edge of the village. The scent of wood smoke hung in the air. I remembered Trennick's narrow streets and white-painted cottages, the Three Feathers pub, and the Boathouse café. I walked up to the square, where the light from the shop window cast a yellow rectangle onto the road. I bought the coffee, dropped it into my bag, then walked back the way I'd come.

I stood on the cliff for a few moments and looked out; the moonlight had pooled on the sea, like a slick of molten silver. I went down the steps, then instead of crossing the beach, I walked to the water's edge. I stood there, watching the waves curl over the sand, listening to the gentle scrape and rattle of the pebbles. I turned to go, started walking, then suddenly stopped, my pulse racing. I'd heard a cry.

Evie . . . Evie . . . Wait . . .

Eleven

Klara

On the day of our move we piled our mattresses in front of the house ready for a truck to pick up, then we walked to the gate with our *barang*. Our packing had been quick. After a year in Bloemencamp we possessed only a fraction of what we'd arrived with. Ina had just one small bag, and so she carried one of the twins, Sofie, while Corrie carried Saskia. Kate strapped on her rucksack and picked up their bags, and we all walked together to the gate.

There were already hundreds of women in the queue, many of them wearing several layers of clothing, surrounded by their suitcases, trunks, baskets, bags, and impromptu sacks made of knotted sheets. Most had saucepans strapped to their rucksacks, as well as kettles, potties, feather dusters, enamel buckets, and even folding chairs.

"How can they possibly carry all that stuff?" I asked Kirsten.

"Because they know they don't have far to take it," she answered. "I just heard someone say that Tjihapit is only across the street."

"Really?" said my mother.

Kirsten nodded. "Seems it's just another part of northern Bandung."

We moved forward with painful slowness; this was because, far ahead of us, we could see that the soldiers were inspecting every piece of luggage, unfolding clothes, checking pockets, shaking things out, their fingers probing for any forbidden items.

By now the sun was high. A woman standing near us fainted and had to be revived. All around us children were crying. Sofie began screaming; I remember wanting to scream too. Suddenly she was sick on Ina's shoulder.

"Never mind, darling," Ina crooned. "Let's clean you up." She took the water flask that Kate passed her and wiped Sofie's little mouth with a rag, then dabbed at her front, and at her own dress. "We'll soon be there, poppet, and then Mummy will make you feel better. That's what mummies—"

We heard shouting, then gasps. A rumor rippled back to us that a woman had been caught trying to smuggle in forbidden items—an atlas, it was said, and a ten-guilder note. As we got closer, we saw her standing to one side, her arms stretched above her head. She was no more than fifteen. There was a red welt on her cheek; one eye was swollen shut. Her clothes were streaked with dust where she'd been hit to the ground.

"Now you understand why I wouldn't let you bring the chess set," my mother whispered to Peter. He nodded miserably.

"Poor girl," Kate whispered. "They'll make her stand there all day—that's what the bastards do." Two hours later, as we reached the head of the queue, the girl *was* still there, her hands still raised, her head drooping onto her chest, whether from exhaustion or a desire not to be stared at, I didn't know.

The soldiers looked through Ina's bag, then searched her jacket pockets. I was terrified that they'd find the Bible pages, but they didn't, and we all got through the inspection unscathed.

Tjihapit seemed much bigger than Bloemencamp and was far busier. The streets thronged with newcomers carrying or dragging their possessions as they looked for their accommodation. There were also women and teenagers walking to and from work, or fetching cans of food from the *dapur*. There were furniture ladies pushing carts loaded with chests of drawers, tables and chairs—even pianos. Children played in the street with improvised toys; some clattered along on stilts made of tin cans with string threaded through them; others had a bicycle wheel and a stick. Many were so thin and listless that they simply sat on the curb, pretend-playing with their hands.

"Nice houses," said Kirsten with a sour smile.

Front gardens, festooned with lines of washing, grew wild; broken windows resembled missing teeth; shutters were askew, like drooping eyelids; paint peeled and lifted, like diseased skin.

Kate, her girls, and Ina were to be in the same house, on Riowstraat, while Kirsten and my family were very close by on Houtmanstraat.

I felt a wave of relief as we looked at the house—it was twice as big as the one on Orchideelaan. But as we went inside, my heart sank. There were already at least fifty women and children living in it. The utility room that we'd been assigned over-looked a scrubby backyard, beyond which rose the *gedék*, crowned with barbed wire.

We settled in as best we could. Kirsten put her mattress down in a corner of the sitting room, a few feet away from us.

"Home sweet home," she said as she hung up her *kelambu*.

Because Houtmanstraat was on the very edge of the camp, sounds from the world outside would drift in—the clucking of chickens being taken to market, the rumble of a bus, or the tin-kling of a bicycle bell. Sometimes we'd hear passing vendors hawking their wares, their voices becoming louder, then fading away.

We had a stroke of luck in that my mother's job at Tjihapit was not shifting furniture but preparing vegetables in the *dapur*. Peter and I urged her to take advantage of her position, so once or twice she hid a carrot in her clothes. But when one *dapur* worker, who'd taken a piece of pork, was chased down the street by a mob of furious women hurling stones, Mum vowed that she'd never steal any vegetables again.

Snails, though, were there for the taking. One day, in the damp alley behind our house, my mother found a giant snail, or *kéong*, and brought it back to the house.

"We're going to find some more," she said, showing it to us, "and we're going to cook them. Well, the *French* like snails," she protested when she saw our disgusted expressions. "They consider them a delicacy and eat them in the finest restaurants."

So the three of us went on a snail hunt, and on our first foray we came back with ten. My mother heated a can of water on the back of her clothes iron and boiled them—they made an awful, hissing sound, I remember. As they were still tough, she boiled them again, then she covered them with a cloth and thumped them between two bricks, to tenderize them. Finally, she cut them up and put them in our rice, giving Kirsten some, as she had shared some of her food with us.

Kirsten kissed her fingertips. "Hmmm! *Best* snails I've ever eaten."

"Have you had them before?" Peter asked her.

"No. So those were the best."

To our amazement the snails did taste good; but word soon got round about them and within a short time Tjihapit's *kéongs* had gone. Nor, soon, were there any slugs, frogs, snakes, or rats to be found and, to my distress, the lucky croaks of the *tokeh* could no longer be heard.

Gradually we got to know some of the people in this new house. There was a woman named Ilse who came from a tea plantation in Central Java. The Japanese had shot her husband because he'd refused to hand over his car keys. I thought of my mother, desperately willing my father to hand over his. Then there was Shirin, who was beautiful, with long dark hair and expressive brown eyes, though they often held a sad, defeated look. I assumed that Shirin was *Belanda Indo,* but one day, as we chatted on the front steps, she told me that her father was Persian. She'd been living in Balikpapan, on Borneo, where her husband had worked for Dutch Oil. As the Japanese approached, Shirin explained, she had been evacuated, with other women and children. Her husband and his colleagues stayed behind, and had managed to blow up the oil refinery, partially destroying it. In a low, calm voice, Shirin added that they had all been beheaded. So the rumors that we'd heard were true.

There was another woman, named Vena, who was very pretty. She had blond hair and wore a tightly fitting black skirt with a lacy white top, through which you could see her bare skin. She used to put on red lipstick in the mornings, then go and stand by the main gate. I asked Kirsten why Vena dressed like this, and why the women in our house often called her rude names.

"They can't stand Vena," Kirsten replied, "because she's being nice to the Japs in the hope that she'll get more food and better treatment."

I thought about this for a moment. "Couldn't *we* be nice to them too?" It seemed sensible, given how thin we were getting.

Kirsten laughed darkly. "*No*, sweetheart. Better to starve."

It *wasn't* better, I reasoned. Then I wondered what Vena had to do to be "nice" to the Japs. Did she have to chat with them? Tell them jokes? Sing songs? Whatever it was, it must have worked, because sometime later I saw Vena leaving with her suitcase, presumably for a life outside, and we didn't see her in the camp after that.

One problem that we had in Tjihapit was that the soldiers were always searching our rooms, ordering us out while they ransacked the place for forbidden items. In addition, they were always putting a stop to this activity or that. There had been lectures and knitting circles, but these were now banned; there was also to be strictly no *gedekking*, although it still went on in secret. One woman in our house managed to get out of the camp by going through the sewer ditch, and came back with some bananas. Had she been caught, she would have been beaten. A few days later, we heard, someone had swapped a cocktail dress for ten eggs. After she'd been given the eggs, the woman had thrown the dress over the fence, but it caught on the barbed wire. The Indonesian had tried to lift it off with a stick, but a guard saw him and the man was dragged away.

The following day was an ordeal that still haunts me. At dawn the whole camp was ordered onto the field. The commandant arrived and shouted for the woman who'd traded the dress to step forward. No one stirred.

"You will stay here until she does!" he screamed.

We stood in the sun all morning and were still standing there in the afternoon. Children cried. Adults groaned. Women fainted with sunstroke and, inevitably, wet themselves, or worse. We knew that the commandant would, if necessary, make us stand there for days. He had to, in order to "save face"; because for inmates to be *gedekking* implied that the rations weren't enough, which would reflect badly on his running of the camp.

By the time we'd been on the field for eight hours, I just wanted the ordeal to *end*, no matter what the outcome. An elderly woman had died. Several children were ill with sunstroke. Babies screamed with hunger and pain.

There were furious whisperings.

"Why doesn't the wretched woman step forward?"

"How can she *bear* to let everyone else suffer like this?"

"Who *is* she? Does anyone know?"

Toward sunset, by which time we'd been standing in the sun for ten hours, someone gave an officer the *gedekker*'s name.

The commandant was duly fetched. He walked through the rows, then stopped. My heart lurched.

"My *God*," I heard Kirsten whisper. "It's Kate . . ."

I braced myself for the commandant's rage, but he simply looked at Kate for a few moments, sadly almost, then took her by the elbow.

"Wait," Kate said to him. "Please . . ." She turned to Corrie and hugged her tightly, kissed her, then whispered something to her. Next, she kissed each of the twins; they'd been asleep at her feet but were now awake, screaming, their arms stretched toward their mother. As she was led away, Corrie tried to console them, though she was crying herself.

From that day on it was Corrie who looked after her little sisters, with Ina's help. But Kate was never seen again.

For weeks afterward I dreamed about Kate. I understood why she hadn't confessed—she knew she might be killed. Then I wondered who had informed on her, and whether that person felt bad about it or believed that it had been the right thing to do. I prayed that I myself would never face such a dilemma. But the time was going to come when I would.

By now the rice allowance had dropped to one cup a day. Most women gave half their food to their children, but my mother didn't. She told Peter and me that the women who did this were falling ill.

"You *mustn't* be ill, Mum," I said, suddenly terrified. "We *need* you."

"I know," she responded, "which is why I'm determined to stay strong." Even so she was, by now, pitifully thin, her pillowy plumpness long since gone. At night she would get the photo of my father out of Peter's bear and hold it to her sunken cheek.

Once more we were ordered to grow food. We planted tomatoes and carrots, which grew very well, but to our despair they would always be stolen, either by our neighbors or by soldiers. One day, when I was tending the plants with Shirin, I burst into tears at the frustration of having to work so hard to grow food that we would never get to *eat*. Between sobs, I said I wished we could build a wall round our plot to keep the plants safe. Shirin agreed. She told me that in old Persian, the word *paradise* translates as "walled garden." From that moment I dreamed of having such a paradise myself one day.

"How ironic," Kirsten said bleakly, "that we live on Java, where everything grows like mad—yet we're starving." She sighed wearily. "Do you ever think about that, Klara?"

"I try not to," I answered bitterly.

As the time went on we became obsessed with food. A little water, heated on a clothes iron with a few grains of salt, became "lovely soup"; rice with a sliver of onion became "delicious rice." Being given a tiny lump of sugar in our rations was a sensation that would be talked about in the camp for days afterward.

Then a strange mania started, for collecting recipes. We'd all sit round and read our favorite ones aloud to one another, mentally assembling the ingredients, discussing the preparation method, then mentally "eating" the finished dish, savoring it over and over again. We found that doing this did, somehow, alleviate our hunger. I was able to remember the recipes that I'd copied out from Irene's *Home Notes* magazines. Because they were English recipes, the other women didn't know them, which seemed to make them especially appealing. So they would rush into our room and ask me to recite them, then they'd sit on the floor, get out their pads, and feverishly scribble down the ingredients for Irish stew or Lancashire hot pot or Victoria sponge, though they'd often argue about the quantities because I wasn't good at converting pounds and ounces into grams. My mother kept a recipe book and said that after the war she was going to cook every single thing in it.

Yet the truth was, we shouldn't have starved. We knew that the Red Cross was sending food parcels, but we never saw them because the Japanese didn't distribute them. We got just one, on 8 June 1944; I remember the date because it was my mother's birthday, and she said it was the best present that she'd ever had. In the boxes were tins of butter, ham, sardines, sugar, and coffee—ordinary items, yet to us, manna from heaven, and we eked it out for as long as possible, relishing every morsel. But even more sustaining than the food inside were the labels on the outside, stating that these things had been sent by the American Red Cross in Washington, D.C. Up until that moment we felt that the world had forgotten us. Now we knew, for the first time, that people far away were trying to keep us alive. This knowledge gave us a huge psychological lift.

The food situation continued to get worse. The allowance had dropped again, this time to less than half a cup of cooked rice a day. By now, women and children were falling ill. They had tropical ulcers that wouldn't heal, and dysentery. Worse, some people were starting to show the swollen legs of beriberi. The gravity of our situation was unmistakable.

"I feel almost nostalgic about Bloemencamp," Kirsten told us miserably. "There we could just about cope. But in *this* dump . . ." She pinched her fleshless hip. "For the first time I know I might die."

"You're *not* going to die," my mother said to her. "You're going to be fine. We're *all* going to be fine, and we're all going to—"

Kirsten grimaced. "Live happily ever after?"

My mother pursed her lips. "Who knows what the future holds? But we're going to help each other to *survive*."

Kirsten shrugged. "Not all women are helping each other, are they?"

This was true. There was a lot of bickering and arguing, even fights. The day before, there'd been a vicious argument over a bar of soap—there'd been slaps and hair pulling before the two women were separated. There was a furious squabble going on right now, with voices being raised because someone's *kelambu* was taking up too much room.

Under such pressure it was impossible to maintain a civilized veneer. A woman in our house went to the *gedék* and traded her wedding ring for a piece of bacon, which she then cooked for her three children on her iron. She stuffed a sheet under the door of their room, but the delicious aroma still drove us insane. Some women wept, but others called her names and swore that they'd betray her to the Japs.

"They can't cope," Kirsten said as we listened to this. "They can't cope with the fact that she's been able to feed her children, where they haven't been able to feed theirs."

"Exactly," Ina agreed. "And the courage she showed only makes them feel worse."

Seeing other mothers crack under the strain, Peter and I worried that our mother would crack too. But she had enormous self-control. She kept out of trouble at work, and avoided getting into arguments with other women. Sometimes she got angry with Peter and me, especially if we squabbled, which we often did. But we were living on top of each other, we were always hungry, and bored, too, because we had no toys or books.

Although our bickering grieved our mother, she never smacked us. But some mothers did hit their kids, not caring who saw.

By this time there were several thousand of us in Tjihapit, yet every day hundreds more arrived. The Dutch and other Europeans had long since been rounded up, but now it was the turn of the *Belanda Indos*. They'd previously been exempt, on the basis that they were really Asian and therefore on Japan's side, even though most felt themselves to be Dutch. They were being interned because, we now knew, Japan was losing the war and its leadership wanted to eradicate *any* Western influence. So we watched the *Belanda Indos* stream through the gate.

They had a lot of possessions, which we eyed covetously: more important, they had food—baskets of chickens and ducks and sacks of flour and rice, which we stared at like ravenous dogs. I have never forgotten their horrified expressions as they first laid eyes on us. We were all desperately thin, our hair matted and louse-ridden, our bodies filthy, our clothes heavily patched or in rags.

"Welcome, ladies," Kirsten called out to them as they walked by. Some of them held hankies to their faces because we stank. "Welcome to our delightful camp, and we very much hope that you enjoy your stay—not that we've the slightest idea where you'll all fit."

More houses were cleared, and everyone had to squeeze up. But with so many extra people, the water supply became a trickle. The sanitation was revolting, and we were catching illnesses from one another. Worst of all, there was even less food.

One morning Shirin announced that the Japs had figured out how to solve the overcrowding problem.

"How?" Kirsten demanded indolently. "Are they going to kill us?"

"No," Shirin answered seriously. "They're going to send more boys to the men's camps."

Mum looked up, alarmed. "From what age?"

"Thirteen."

My mother closed her eyes with relief.

At the start of internment, boys up to the age of fifteen had been allowed to stay with their mothers, but some women had complained that the boys were staring at them, or flirting with their daughters. So these fifteen-year-olds, having been deemed a "danger to women," were transferred to the men's camps. Then fourteen-year-olds were sent away too; and now it was to be the thirteen-year-olds. Some of the mothers in Greta's house mounted a protest against it. They all wore white—the Buddhist color of mourning. They told the commandant that these boys were still children and begged him to reconsider. Instead, he had them beaten and locked up. The women were let out three days later, to be told that their sons were to be transported at first light.

"They don't even know where they're being sent," my mother murmured as the boys walked past our house to the waiting trucks. Some of the mothers were brave and refused to cry; but as the engines started, many of them wailed and surged forward, clawing the air as they tried to reach their sons. The soldiers crossed rifles and pushed them back. Then the trucks drove away through the gate.

Now, with no teenage boys left in Tjihapit, we girls had to do the heavy work. I remember having to lift the huge food drums in the *dapur,* or wheeling the garbage cart out through the gate. Yet, still more people were arriving, and now, in August 1944, we heard that boys of twelve were to be transported. A few weeks later, it was announced that boys of eleven would have to go into the men's camps. Then it was rumored that soon even boys of ten would be picked up. At this my mother became distressed, because Peter was coming up to nine and a half.

Once, when she and I were alone together, she told me how worried she was.

"I *must* keep Peter with me," she said. "We don't know what these men's camps are like; the conditions might be worse than they are here, with even less food. And I don't think he'd survive another bout of malaria if he were on his own."

I don't think he'd survive . . .

The words sliced into my heart. But at the same time I was aware that my mother was now treating me as though I were another adult, not a child, and I wanted to help her. "So what can we do, Mummy?"

She lifted her finger to her lips. "No one, apart from us, knows how old he is," she whispered. "So we'll simply lie about his age."

"Yes," I whispered back. "And because he's so small, I'm sure we'll be believed." I felt proud to be my mother's ally, taking important decisions with her.

"You will help me protect Peter, won't you, Klara?" my mother asked.

"Of course I will," I promised.

But soon we were distracted from our anxiety by two startling events. We learned that a month before, Paris had been liberated. Without a radio, we hadn't known. We were so euphoric that we had to be careful not to smile or sing in front of the guards. A few days after that, we were informed, at *tenko*, that the camp was to be "liquidated." At this there were wails of despair, because many women thought it meant that we were all going to die. It had been whispered for months that once the Japanese realized that they were losing the war, we would all be machine-gunned, or locked inside churches and schools, which would be set on fire. We'd heard rumors of a plan to send us all to Borneo and release us into the jungle without food or water. So at the word *liquidation*, there were screams and cries. Then the translator raised her megaphone again and ordered us to be calm.

"Liquidation," she explained, meant only that Camp Tji-hapit was to be closed. We were to be transported again.

Twelve

On Wednesday morning Klara and I covered a lot of ground, though I'd found it hard to focus. We would soon come to the part about Peter's death, and I dreaded it. I needed to think of him being alive, surviving, growing up.

"Are you still not sleeping well?" Klara asked as I turned off the recorder. "You look pale."

"I'm sleeping better, in that I *go* to sleep—I think the valerian helps—but the problem is, I have these . . . dreams."

"What do you dream about?"

I hesitated. "Peter," I answered quietly.

Klara looked puzzled. "You dream about my little brother?"

"I do. It's as though your memories of him have brought him to life. I feel that I know him myself, and I'm worried about what's going to happen to him. In fact I can't bear to think of it . . . because . . ." Klara's face had blurred. "I'm sorry," I whispered.

Klara looked bewildered. "You don't have to apologize, Jenni—I'm very touched; it's as though you feel my sadness, and just as deeply."

"I do feel it—and I know how hard it's going to be for you to talk about what happened to him."

"It will be. But then it's hard for me every day—even without this memoir it's still so much on my mind."

I wondered again why Klara's grief seemed not to have been softened by time. Then I remembered something I'd once read about trauma: that if a traumatic event isn't integrated into a person's life, so that the person can at least accept it, then they're destined to relive it, again and again.

Evie . . . Evie . . .

"I dream about someone else too," I went on softly. "Someone I knew a long time ago."

"Your father?" Klara asked after a moment.

"No." My voice fractured. "It's . . ."

Klara looked shocked. "Jenni, my dear, please don't cry." I groped in my bag for a tissue. "I don't know who this person is, but couldn't you perhaps get in touch again, if not seeing them upsets you so much?"

"I can't. It's too late."

"Well, I . . . wish I could help you, Jenni."

I fought the urge to tell Klara everything, fearful that if I did, it might destroy our rapport. In any case, I was here to do a job, I reasoned, not to talk about myself. I blinked back my tears, then looked at my notes.

But the time was going to come when I would.

"Klara, you talked about having faced a dilemma; I wondered what you'd meant by that."

She grew pale. "I had to make a very difficult choice—one that's haunted me ever since. I do want to tell you about it, Jenni, but I'm not ready to do so yet. So please bear with me until I am."

As I unlocked the cottage door, I could hear the landline ringing. I picked up the phone.

"Jenni?" It was Honor. "Listen, I'm going to take a few days off. I've done all the pre-records for Sunday's show, and as the rest of the program's going to be live, I've got a little gap in my schedule."

"Well, make the most of it."

"I intend to. That's why I'm calling—because I thought I'd come and see you."

"What? Down here?"

"Yes—if it's okay."

"You mean you want to stay with me?"

"Well, I don't have to stay—I could go to a B and B. But it would be great if I could spend some time with you and see a bit of south Cornwall. I thought I might even get tonight's sleeper train so that I can be there by the morning. They've got berths available—I've just checked."

"Honor, it would be *great* if you came. I'd love you to stay, but let me ask Klara and call you back."

I rang Klara. "Of course Honor can stay," she said at once.

"It'll be good for you to have company, Jenni. I worry that you're working too hard."

So early the next morning I drove to the Truro station. As I arrived, the sleeper train was just pulling out. Honor walked toward me, dragging her pink-and-black suitcase behind her like a huge Liquorice Allsort, its wheels thundering across the platform.

"Jen-ni!" She grinned. "This is so nice of you!" She wrapped me in one of her hugs. "And thanks for picking me up at ungodly o'clock."

"Of course I'd pick you up! It's so nice that you've come. How was the journey?"

"Gorgeous—I was rocked to sleep. I love night trains, and it gives me a bit more time with you. But I won't interrupt your work," she promised as I beeped open the car. "I'll go for walks, and I've got a couple of books, and my iPad; then we can chat in the evenings." I put her suitcase in the boot. "So is it going well with your Dutch lady?"

"I think so; we're making progress, at any rate."

We drove off, Honor admiring Truro's Georgian architecture; then, as we sped toward Roseland, she talked about Al, who'd finally phoned, and asked her to have dinner with him the following week. She chatted about Nina, who was having acupuncture for her morning sickness. I was enjoying listening to Honor and felt comforted by her presence. As we wound our way through Trelawn, I remembered that this was where Klara's friend Jane lived. I stopped and bought some groceries at the village store, then we drove on to Polvarth.

Honor exclaimed over the cottage, the cows, and the sea.

"It's all so lovely," she said as I showed her first her room, then mine. She studied the seascape on my bedroom wall. "That's good."

"It's by Klara's grandson, Adam."

"Do you know where it is?"

"It's the local bay, just at the end of the lane here."

"Oh, I'll walk down there later."

The thought of Honor being on the beach gave me a strange, hollow feeling.

We went downstairs, and now, over breakfast, Honor asked me about Rick.

"Oh God," she murmured when I'd explained. "You've always said that you don't want kids. I assumed that Rick knew and didn't mind."

"He did know, and *said* he didn't mind; but now he does, which gives us a huge problem."

"That issue *is* a deal breaker. So what will you do if . . . ?" Honor's meaning hung in the air.

"I suppose we'll split up." The thought of not being with Rick made me feel ill. I imagined leaving him, my clothes and books packed into suitcases and crates. But where would I live? Not nearby, as Rick would still be at the school. I'd have to stop doing the reading; I suddenly realized how much I'd miss the children. I saw them crowded round *Stick Man* or *The Tiger Who Came to Tea* or running to the Book Corner. Would Rick and I say goodbye, never to meet again? Or would we stay friends? If so, how would I be able to bear it when he met someone else? I imagined another woman in our flat, cradling their baby—Rick's baby. Then I realized that the woman I was imagining was Kitty, only too happy to commit to Rick at last.

At eleven I walked up to the farm.

"Has Honor arrived?" Klara asked me.

"Yes, she got the night train. She'll be here until lunchtime on Saturday."

"Will she be okay on her own?"

"Oh, she'll be fine. She's good at keeping herself busy. She's going to go for walks and read."

Klara looked anxious. "I do hope you've got enough to eat."

"We've got plenty; and thanks again for letting her stay. I promise it won't interfere with the memoir."

"Well, you must take *some* time off while she's here. In fact, Jenni, it would suit me if we didn't do our four o'clock session today."

"In that case I'll do something with Honor this afternoon. But before we start recording I'd like to take photos of the hand-kerchief." I took out my camera and the piece of black card that I'd brought as a background.

Klara opened the carved box. "I've been wondering when you could meet Jane." She took the hanky out and laid it carefully on the card. "I think it would be best if I brought her here. We could chat over a cup of tea and some cake." I zoomed in on the handkerchief, focusing the names. "That would be great," I said as I snapped away. I peered at the screen. "These are good."

Klara folded the hanky and put it back in the box. "Do you want to photograph the recipe book too, Jenni?"

"Yes, please."

She took out the green notebook. As she did so, I caught a glimpse of some of the other things in the box: a large brown envelope, a thick blue airmail letter, and something wrapped in white cloth.

Klara handed me the notebook. I put it on the card, then photographed its front cover and several of the inside pages. I tried to imagine the desperate hunger that had inspired its creation. I checked the photos, then returned the camera to my bag and got out the recorder. "So how did you and Jane meet?"

"Through our children." Klara put the notebook back in the box and closed the lid. "Jane's son, Frank, was at school with Vincent. That was fifty years ago, goodness me."

"And did Jane work?"

Klara nodded. "She did dressmaking and alterations—she was very skilled. That's what she'd do in the winter. In the summer months she ran the tea hut."

A warmth rose in my chest. "For how long?"

"Oh, all day. She used to ring a bell when she was about to close."

"I meant . . . how many years did she run it for? I just wondered," I added as I registered Klara's puzzlement at the question.

"Let me think." Klara narrowed her eyes. "Jane and her husband bought it in the early eighties, and she only sold it in 2006, after he died, so . . . twenty-five years. But it used to be open every day from Good Friday until Halloween, rain or shine. It was lovely then; now it's a bit posh. When Jane ran it, it was teas and coffees, ice creams and sweets, buckets and nets; it was so nice."

"It was."

"Oh, of course you'd remember it yourself—you were here in '87, didn't you say?"

"I think that's when it was; I'm not quite sure." I tried not to stutter. "But you know, Klara, if Jane's memory's not going to be reliable enough, perhaps I could interview someone else—another friend of yours?"

Klara looked at me in surprise. "Well, as I say, Jane's memory *is* erratic, but she means a lot to me, and I'd love you to try. So let's stick to the plan for you to meet her—perhaps early next week?"

"Sure," I said, my heart sinking. "Anyway, where had we got to? Oh yes." With a shaky hand, I pressed Record.

I returned to Lanhay just after one.

"I've been exploring," Honor reported as I hung up my coat. "I went down to the beach, but it was high tide and completely covered, so instead I walked round the headland. I got to a place called Carne, had a scrumptious hot chocolate from an ice cream van, gazed soulfully at the sea, then came back."

I took the finished tape out of the recorder and labeled it. "Sounds lovely."

"It was glorious; there are still masses of wildflowers. I saw lots of pink valerian. It's terrific for sleeping problems."

"I know. Klara gave me some."

"Do you still sleep badly, Jen?" Honor looked concerned.

"Not too well, no."

She gave me a compassionate glance. "Well . . . it must be very hard at the moment, wondering what's going to happen with Rick." I didn't tell Honor that that wasn't the only thing preoccupying me. "It's a shame you don't want to have kids," she went on. "I mean, it would make everything so easy if you could just—"

"Having children *doesn't* make things *easy*."

"Right . . . I just meant that it would make the *decision* easy. Of course having children is a huge challenge and exhausting—everyone knows that. But it must be wonderful, if you've always wanted them, to get that chance—I hope *I* do. Maybe I won't." Honor shrugged. "But Jen, you've found a man who you really like, and who feels the same about you, so I hope you don't throw your chance at happiness away. Anyway . . . lecture over. Shall I make lunch?" She opened the fridge and peered inside. "Ham and cheese omelette?"

"That would be nice."

Honor took out the box of eggs, then lifted the lid.

"Ooh—blue ones."

"They're from the farm. Araucanas," I added as Honor rummaged in the cupboards and pulled out a frying pan. "Klara told me that she's busy this afternoon, so I'm going to take the rest of the day off. Would you like to go to St. Mawes? I've never been."

"I'd love to."

An hour later we made our way there along the narrow, winding road, turning off at St. Just in Roseland to look at the church set in a subtropical garden beside a tidal creek. We drove on, and as we rounded a bend, there was St. Mawes, rising steeply up from the harbor, the houses interspersed with Monterey pines, giving the village a Mediterranean air. At the far end was the small castle. The gardens sloped down to the wide waters of the Carrick Roads.

"It's beautiful," Honor murmured. "All those boats, and that lovely promontory."

"I guess that's St. Anthony Head—and that'll be Falmouth Docks across the water."

We drove slowly up to St. Mawes Castle, parked, then crossed the drawbridge and went in.

After we'd explored its battlements, we walked into the village, strolling along the waterfront past steep, narrow streets where romantically named houses—Smugglers' Corner, Trevarth, and Sea-Spray—jostled for space.

On Marine Parade we passed an art gallery, and a gift shop in the window of which were some knitted baby hats and booties in the shape of penguins and lions. We gazed at them.

"How adorable," Honor breathed. "I want to buy them right now, for Nina's baby."

"No," I said firmly. "Too early."

"True. We don't want to jinx it." We walked on. "So what are you going to wear to the christening?"

"Can't say I've decided yet."

"Do you think one should avoid white, so as not to upstage the baby?"

"I think it would be tactful, yes . . ."

We passed the St. Mawes Hotel and the tiny post office with its racks of postcards and buckets and nets. We came to the harbor, where a small ferry was moored by the quay. A few people were waiting to board it.

"Let's see where that ferry goes," Honor remarked. As she went up to the ticket kiosk to ask, I noticed a café on the other side of the road. Sitting at a table in the window was Klara. She was with another silver-haired woman. As Klara leaned forward and dabbed at her companion's jacket with a napkin, I realized, with a sinking feeling, that this was probably Jane. Suddenly Klara looked up. Her face broke into a smile, and she waved to me while the other woman followed her gaze with an impassive air.

Honor came back. "Who's that you're waving at?"

"It's Klara. So . . . where does the ferry go?"

"Oh, to Falmouth and up the Helford Passage, but look, I'd love to meet Klara. Can we say a quick hello?"

There was no getting out of it. "Sure." We crossed the road and went into the café. Klara was on her feet, pulling out chairs for us.

"This is Honor," I said.

"It's great to meet you, Klara. Thanks so much for letting me stay."

"It's a pleasure," Klara responded. "And this is my friend Jane."

Honor beamed. "Hello, Jane. I'm Honor."

Jane gave her a sweet but vacant smile. "Honor? Honor . . . ," she repeated, then narrowed her eyes as though mulling over a difficult question.

"I'm staying at Lanhay," Honor explained.

A frown pleated Jane's brow. "Lanhay?"

"My cottage," Klara interposed. "Don't you remember, Jane? Harry and I built it ten years ago. In fact you made those lovely curtains for it."

"Did I?" Jane asked. "Well, I do *like* curtains. I always have." She turned to me, and as she held me in her clear, childlike gaze, I felt a rush of recognition that made me feel weak. I saw again Jane's features animated by compassion; I remembered her voice, as she'd chatted away, doing her best to reassure me. I remembered her beautifully manicured hands, shuffling cards. I prayed that she wouldn't remember me. To my relief, her expression remained blank. She hadn't a clue who I was. Suddenly her eyes widened and she grinned at me. "Snap!"

"Snap?" said Klara.

"Snap!" Jane repeated.

"You're being silly, sweetie," Klara said to her patiently. "Jane, this is Jenni," she persevered. "Jenni's staying at Lanhay while she helps me write a book. I told you that she'd be coming down for a few days—do you remember?"

"Yes." Jane nodded. "I *do* remember, and curtains *are* nice, yes, yes, very nice, *but* . . ." She sighed. "This isn't Jenni."

"Of course it is," Klara said gently. "Now let's have some more tea." She waved at the waitress, then turned to Honor and me. "What would you girls like? My treat, of course."

"It *isn't* Jenni," Jane insisted, a little petulantly.

"It is," Klara responded evenly. She picked up the menu, then glanced at me. "They do a delicious lemon cake here; let me get you some."

Jane was shaking her head, her lips pursed. "It's *Genevieve*."

Klara looked at her. "No, Jane. Her name's Jenni—as in Jennifer."

Honor laughed. "Actually, Klara, Jane's right: It *is* Genevieve." She looked at Jane. "But how funny that you should know that, because no one ever calls Jenni Genevieve, do they?" she added to me.

My mouth had gone dry. "Only my mother."

Klara stared at me, bewildered. "I thought you were called Jennifer."

"No. People always assume that's my name, but it's not. Jane's right." I felt as though I were hurtling toward an abyss. And now I was falling . . .

"Of *course* you're Genevieve," Jane said. "And we played snap!" She gave me an indulgent smile. "Didn't we?"

"Genevieve?" Klara echoed. She looked at me searchingly. Then her expression changed from one of confusion to clarity. "Of *course*," she murmured. Her eyes filled with concern. "I remember you now." And in that moment I remembered her too.

"How did Jane know who you were?" Honor asked as we drove back to the cottage.

"We met," I answered tersely. "Many years ago."

"Down here?" I nodded. "So you've been to Polvarth before?"

I changed down a gear. "Yes."

"You haven't told me that. So, you came here on holiday?"

"Yes. When I was a child."

"And you met Jane then?"

"That's right. She used to run the tea hut down on the beach."

"How amazing that she remembered you after so long, especially as she's a bit confused. You must have made a great impression on her." I didn't respond. "And Klara said that she's met you as well."

I turned off the main road. "She has. I'd . . . forgotten."

"It was great to see St. Mawes," Honor said as I parked the car at Lanhay a few minutes later. "But, Jenni, the tide's low now. Can we go and look at the beach before it gets dark?"

"Of course."

We set off down the lane.

"Are you okay, Jen?" Honor asked after a minute or two. "You seem a bit distracted. Is it because of Rick?"

"No. It's got nothing to do with him." We came to the row of holiday houses, and I stopped at Penlee. "This is where I stayed when we came here before. It was twenty-five years ago."

Honor looked at the house, then we walked on, past the old red telephone kiosk and the stone gateposts of the hotel. "So you'd have been nine," she said. "You came with your mother?"

"Yes." It was true. Suddenly the beach came into view.

Honor clapped her hands. "It's beautiful! And the tide's *right* out!" The rippled sand glimmered in the low sunlight.

As we walked down the slipway I heard his voice again, thin and high, drifting toward me.

Evie! Wait! Please. Evie! Evie . . .

"There's the tea hut," I heard Honor say. "It's closed—for the winter, I suppose." We walked across the beach, stepping round the clumps of brown seaweed that strewed the high-tide line. Honor bent down and picked up a piece of driftwood. "Look at this, Jen, it must have been in the sea for years; it's so white, and as smooth as satin." She held it out to me, but I barely glanced at it. "Are you sure you're okay, Jen?"

"I'm fine."

She looked about her. "It must be fantastic here in the summer."

You don't have long. . . . Hold his hand now.

"And the rocks are great," Honor remarked as she walked toward them. "I couldn't see them yesterday because they were covered up by the sea. Can we look in the rock pools?"

Don't want to help you.

Well, you've got to.

"If you like," I said absently. I followed Honor across the pale sand, and we climbed up.

"Ooh, tiny mussels!" Honor exclaimed as she stood on the first rock. She tiptoed between them. "Don't want to crush them." She jumped onto the next rock, then peered down, her hands on her knees. "This is a good pool—lots of nice seaweed. That's bladder wrack, isn't it?" she asked as I came and stood beside her. "I think that wide one's called sea belt . . . Oh, look! A shrimp! Just there, by those limpets." She straightened up and stepped onto the next boulder, then bent down to the water again, her blond hair lifting in the breeze. She stared into this pool for a few moments, then frantically beckoned to me. "*Fish!*" she whispered, her eyes wide. She stooped a little lower as she tried to spot it again.

I want to hold the net. . . . It's my turn.

"It's gone under that rock. But it was huge—at least two inches, a speckled brown color with frilly fins." Honor laughed. "I could do this for hours!"

The bell's ringing, Evie.

I can't hear it.

. . . 'Member what Mum said.

Honor leapt across a gap. "Be careful," she warned. "There's a gully here—it's quite deep." I didn't follow her. "I'd love to see a crab," she called over her shoulder.

You're . . . a stupid little baby*!*

I can get *it, Evie!*

It's too late! You ruined it . . .

"I adore rock pooling." Honor stepped onto the next boulder. "In fact I wouldn't mind doing it again tomorrow. We could buy a net and bucket. What do you think, Jen? Jenni?" She turned. "*Jenni?* What's wrong?" She hurried toward me, jumping back over the gully again. "What's the matter, honey?" She put her hand on my arm, her blue eyes filled with concern. "You're crying—please tell me what's wrong. If it's because of Rick, crying won't help," she rushed on. "You've just got to decide what you mind most—losing Rick, or having a child when you don't really want to, though God knows a lot of women our age would be thrilled to have a man who was keen to start a family with them."

"It's not *about* Rick," I murmured. "I told you it's not."

"Then what *is* it about? What's happened, Jen?" Honor's expression cleared. "It's to do with Jane, isn't it? She *was* a bit strange with you, but she's obviously a bit confused, so I wouldn't get upset about it." She shoveled her hand into her pocket, pulled out a pack of tissues, and handed me a couple. "Please don't cry, Jenni. I mean, why should what poor old Jane said upset you like this?"

I felt a tear seep into my mouth with a salty tang. "She remembers," I said brokenly. "They probably *all* remember round here."

"Remember what?" Honor frowned, baffled. "What do they remember, Jen?" She sat on a rock, then stretched out her hand for me to sit beside her. As I did so, she tucked her arm through mine. "Jen, honey, I hate seeing you like this. And I worry that I talk so much, I don't give you the chance to confide in me. I wish you'd tell me what's wrong," she coaxed. I didn't answer. "Maybe I can help."

"You can't." My throat ached with a suppressed sob. "No one can help me." I looked at the sea, dotted with white sails. "I should never have come back! I'd persuaded myself that it might be a *good* thing to come back; that I might be able to find some peace at last—but I never will. It'll always scratch at my soul."

Honor was staring at me. "Jenni, what are you talking about?" she asked quietly. I didn't answer. "Please, Jen, in the name of our friendship, tell me what's upsetting you so much."

"All right." I closed my eyes. "I will."

Thirteen

Klara

In October 1944 we left Tjihapit to go to our next camp. Because there were so many of us, we were transported in groups. Our group was one of the first to go.

As I walked to the gate I saw that, as usual on these occasions, everyone was weighed down with suitcases, sacks made of knotted sheets, and bulging canvas backpacks to which clanking pots and pans had been tied. Just in front of us were Greta and Mrs. Moonen, Shirin and Ilse. Mum, Peter, and I stood with Kirsten, and with Corrie, Ina, and the twins. In Corrie's eyes was the usual blend of grief, outrage, and determination. Weighed down by her rucksack, she held Saskia, while Ina carried Sofie. Kirsten and I picked up the rest of Corrie's *barang*. As we shuffled forward, I felt that we were no longer just a group of women and children but a family, doing our best to help and protect one another.

As I passed through the gate, I saw two large trucks. Onto the back of these, some European prisoners, stripped to the waist in the searing heat, were loading our mattresses and luggage. It had been two years since I'd seen any European men. I was shocked at how thin they were, with corrugated chests and sunken eyes. They worked slowly despite the repeated *Lekas!* from their guards.

We had to line up to be counted; then we were told to stay in our rows and wait for the bus, which would transport us to our destination.

"It's so good to be outside the camp," Ina said wonderingly. She stroked Sofie's hair. "Isn't it, darling?"

"It really is," I murmured. "Even this little bit of freedom is wonderful."

We stared at the people as they just walked around, chatted, or rode bikes. A street seller with a basket of bananas approached us, and I longed to buy one—not that I had any money—but a guard chased him away.

Finally the buses arrived.

"The windows are painted black," my mother remarked as the vehicles pulled up in a cloud of exhaust.

"The Japs obviously don't want us to see where we're going," Ina said.

"Or to be seen," Kirsten pointed out. I repressed a shudder.

The doors were opened and we piled on.

"Lekas!" the soldiers yelled at us. *"Lekas!"*

The engines started. We had braced ourselves for a long

journey, but after just a few minutes the bus juddered to a stop and we were ordered off.

As I descended, I saw that we had been brought to a railway station. We sat on the platform in the rising heat, slumped against our bags. I wondered where the shining train tracks led.

Finally, a small locomotive pulled in, and a cloud of gray-white steam blanketed the platform, making us cough. The soldiers pushed us aboard. The carriages were fourth-class coaches with no seats, just a backless wooden bench that ran along the sides. Miraculously, my mother managed to find places for us on this, while Kirsten, Ina, and Corrie sat opposite us, with the twins on their laps. Our view of one another was soon blocked by the crowd of people getting on.

The windows, which would normally have been open to the air, were screened with split bamboo that darkened the interior. Once again, I reflected, we were being made to feel like vermin, not fit to be seen.

"Did you see the toilet?" Peter whispered. "It's just a hole in the floor, with no door." He grimaced. "I shan't use it!"

"I don't know how anyone will be able to get to it," my mother pointed out. "Let's hope we're not on the train for long."

An elderly woman near to us was clearly in distress; a teenage girl stood up and gave her her seat. The woman sank gratefully onto it, breathing heavily. The heat was intensified by the crush of so many bodies, and by the metal roof on which the sun beat down.

"It'll be better when the train moves," my mother said. "Not long now, my darlings." But, to my dismay, the train just waited on the track. An hour later we were still there, drenched in sweat, gasping for air. Then, just as the ovenlike heat seemed impossible to bear a moment longer, the train squealed, clanged, and lurched forward. A collective sigh ran through the coach, like a zephyr.

"Thank you, God!" Ina shouted from the other side of the coach. "Nice to know you were listening!"

As the train picked up pace, some women parted strands of the bamboo, letting a few shafts of light into the dim interior.

"We're going through northern Bandung," my mother said. Luxuriating in the breeze, I began to feel I could cope. But after a few minutes the train stopped again.

"Oh *no*," Peter murmured.

"They're doing it on purpose!" someone shouted. "To make us suffer as much as possible, God damn those rotten Japs!"

We remained stationary for another two hours. In the suffocating atmosphere, women and children wept. Someone asked for a rag, as her child had had an accident. The elderly woman was wheezing badly, her shoulders hunched with the effort of drawing air into her lungs. She managed to tell us that she had lost her flask, so my mother gave her some of our water in a tin cup.

Eventually the train jerked forward again. A few miles later, we pulled in at a station. The name Tjimahi rushed through the carriage. Tjimahi was where so many husbands and fathers had been interned. I parted the bamboo and peered out, desperate for a glimpse of my own father, or at least of the place where we still believed him to be. On the platform I saw soldiers, their bayonets at the ready should any of us try to escape.

The train waited at Tjimahi for two hours. The temperature in the coach was over one hundred degrees, and the air was acrid with sweat. There were other foul smells too, as people had to relieve themselves where they stood. There were shrieks and sobs. I could hear Corrie trying to comfort the twins.

"Don't cry, girls," she crooned. "Don't cry, my darlings. We'll be there very soon."

I heard Ina's voice. She was reciting a psalm—something about lifting our eyes to the hills. Someone else began to sing "Ave Maria." Now we heard an argument start; it quickly escalated, with shouting and crying, then there was the sound of a slap.

"Stop it!" Kirsten yelled. "For God's sake, stop it, and stay *calm*!"

At long last, the train jerked forward.

At dusk the heat died down, and so did the anguished voices and the weeping. Late at night we stopped at a station and someone made out the name: Purwakarta. At daybreak we reached another town, Tjikampek. There again we waited, hunger clawing our insides.

To my joy, we now moved off again, and as the sun rose I caught glimpses of the landscape through which we passed; a paradise of palm trees, woodland groves, and flowering jacarandas. Everywhere were rice paddies, the shining water reflecting the blue sky and puffs of white cloud.

"This land is so lovely," my mother murmured. Suddenly Peter began to cry. Then he pressed his face against my mother's arm, his thin shoulders heaving with distress.

"Don't be upset, Pietje," she whispered. "It doesn't matter. I'll clean you when we get there."

"I've done the same, Peter," I said. "Everyone has—we can't help it. Don't cry."

"They transport cattle with more dignity," Kirsten remarked bitterly.

"Where are we *going*?" someone else wailed.

As the air now became ever more humid, we realized that we were heading for the coast. After a while we stopped yet again, this time in a siding. Two hours later we lurched forward with a squeal of metal. I saw that we were traveling past suburban villas surrounded by lawns and trees. Finally, we drew to a halt. Looking out, I saw that we were at another small station. But this time we could hear guards running up and down, yelling and banging sticks on the sides of the train and shouting, *"Turun! Turun!"* Get out!

"Where are we?" I asked.

My mother shook her head. "I don't know."

Peter sniffled. "What will happen now?" His face was streaked with dust, sweat, and tears.

"We have to get off."

Mothers were shaking their children awake. People were picking up their bags. The soldiers unlocked the doors and we slithered across the soiled floor, then stumbled, blinking, onto a platform. It was drizzling. A dilapidated sign read TANAH ABANG.

"We're in Batavia," my mother said.

The journey from Bandung normally took four hours. We had been on the train for twenty-eight. We huddled together, exhausted, frightened, hungry, and filthy, and gratefully turned up our faces to the rain.

As I looked back at the train, I saw that some passengers had been so shattered by the journey that they couldn't walk and were being lifted out. I saw soldiers carrying several women, holding them by the shoulders and feet, one of them the elderly woman who'd been sitting near to us. A soldier held a little girl in his arms; she was limp, like a doll, a thin arm dangling. Another soldier carried a baby. They laid them all on the platform, side by side.

We stared at them, shocked.

"Dead?" Peter whispered to my mother.

She nodded, then looked away.

Suddenly an officer barked an order, and now we were being herded out of the station toward big trucks that were covered in tarpaulins. The soldiers yelled at us to climb in. The motionless bodies and a knapsack were left behind on the platform.

The truck started off, and once again we were riding along in a darkened interior, not knowing where we were going, completely hidden from human eyes. Here and there the tarpaulin was torn, and I caught glimpses of fine houses on residential streets. Then the truck drew to a halt, the cover was raised, and we were ordered out. We were on a long, wide avenue. My mother handed Sofie to Ina, while Corrie carried Saskia.

"This is Laan Trivelli," Corrie said. "I've been here before."

On our right was a canal with a bridge, and the soldiers prodded us toward it.

As we inched forward, I was able to see where it was that we were going. Ahead of us, beyond the bridge, was a gate. It was like the one in Tjihapit, but taller and wider, the watchtowers on either side of it much higher. As we passed through it, I saw a guardhouse. It had a verandah on which stood a long rack, full of guns.

As we shuffled forward, three emaciated women in heavily patched clothes came toward us. In a loud voice, one of them told us that we had arrived at Camp Tjideng.

Suddenly we became aware of a commotion.

"What's going on?" Kirsten asked.

A few feet ahead of us another *barang* inspection was being carried out, but this time the officer in charge of it was behaving like a madman. If people didn't open their bags immediately, he would slap them. If a suitcase had a lock that didn't work, he'd kick it, and its contents would spill onto the road. He wore the uniform of an officer, but on his feet were bedroom slippers.

Our turn came. My mother gathered our bags and put them on the table. She then bowed, a few seconds too late it seemed, for as she straightened up, the officer leaned forward and gave her a blow on the head that knocked her to her knees.

Peter gasped and rushed forward. "Leave her *alone*!" he screamed. "Leave my mummy alone!"

I lunged for him and dragged him to one side. "Be *quiet*," I whispered as Mum got to her feet, "or he'll hit her again!"

We waited there while Mum went silently, white-faced, through the inspection; then she rejoined us, still shaken, and we walked on.

"So this is Tjideng," I said. It was as though we had passed through the very portals of hell.

Peter was tugging at my arm. "Look!"

Following his gaze, I saw, beside the gate, a large cage on stilts. From inside it peered out two pairs of quizzical, dark brown eyes.

"Look, girls, monkeys," I heard Corrie say cheerfully.

Suddenly the creatures began to screech. They hurled themselves at the bars, making the cage rock. The twins shrieked in terror, then began crying. Corrie tried to comfort them.

"Why do they have monkeys?" Peter asked me.

I shuddered. "Don't know."

Now we saw that the avenue, Laan Trivelli, stretched all the way ahead of us, flanked by a row of broad-canopied trees. A group of women had gathered nearby and were staring at us. As we trudged by, they called out, "Dirty Tjihapiters!" and "Fatsos!"

We were too shocked at their appearance to take offense. The expression "just skin and bones" sprang to mind. Most were barefoot, but some wore rough wooden sandals, tied on with string or strips of old tires. Others wore what looked like tea towels round their breasts, and many had wound bandanas around their shaved heads.

A tall, gaunt-looking woman in a heavily patched yellow dress approached us. She wore an armband and clearly had some sort of official role.

"Good afternoon," she began as we gathered round. "My name is Mrs. Cornelisse, and I'm your *hancho*, or group leader. It's my job to help you settle in. Those six houses there have just been cleared for you." She pointed to a row of villas nearby.

My mother's jaw slackened. "Six houses?" she echoed. "For *five hundred* people?"

Ignoring her, Mrs. Cornelisse explained that the man who'd inspected our luggage was the commandant, Lieutenant Sonei, and that we should keep away from him, as he could be nasty. My mother nodded knowingly. Mrs. Cornelisse then told us that the building on the left of the gate was the camp office. The big villa on the right of the gate, she added, was Sonei's. My heart sank to know that our accommodation was so close to the living quarters of this monster.

Mrs. Cornelisse led us to our house. It was a large bungalow with the usual verandah, covered walkways, and red-tiled roof. Once it would have been considered attractive, but now the door and window frames were shattered and the front garden was a patch of bare earth. We went inside. Kirsten, Ina, Corrie, and the twins came with us, as well as Greta, her *oma*, Shirin, and Ilse.

The living room was already crammed with women and children, the bedrooms taken, but my mother found three floor spaces in the dining room, beneath the open window.

"Please take no more than fifty centimeters!" Mrs. Cornelisse shouted. "No more than fifty centimeters per person!" Once we had put down our things, she summoned us all into the front yard. There she explained that we needed to choose two people to go to the *dapur* with a basin big enough to hold fifty liters of food. There was a frenzied search for one, and a metal washtub was found. Mrs. Moonen and Shirin agreed to go, and returned an hour later with the heavy tub, which they had struggled to carry. The sago porridge that it contained was enough to provide each person with just one cup of food. It tasted like wallpaper paste, but we were so famished that not a speck was left. There were also some tiny lumps of translucent gray bread.

That evening Mrs. Cornelisse stood in the front garden again, raised her megaphone, and summoned us to *tenko*—our first in Tjideng.

We came out of the house and began to line up a little farther down the road, opposite a large building, on the front of which the words JULIANA SCHOOL could be seen. The young woman standing on my right told me that it was no longer a school—it was the camp hospital.

"But it's where you go to die, not to get better," she added cheerily. Judging by her emaciated body, and the tea towel tied round her chest, she'd clearly been in Tjideng a long time.

Mrs. Cornelisse carefully ticked off all our names on her list, but I noticed that she kept casting anxious glances at Sonei's villa.

As we stood looking down the wide, deserted street, a high-pitched noise could suddenly be heard. It reminded me of the sound that the bees had made as they swarmed toward us that day. It was growing louder and louder; and now I was amazed to see a seemingly endless stream of women and children pour onto Laan Trivelli. They came by the hundreds from the streets to the left and right. In Tjihapit, *tenko* had taken place in groups throughout the day. Here it seemed to be done in one vast gathering, along what we now knew to be Tjideng's main road.

As I gaped at the sea of people surging toward us, a sudden jolt ran down the length of my spine. I gripped Mum's arm so hard that she yelped.

"What's the matter?" she demanded crossly.

I pointed to three distant figures. My mother followed my gaze, shielding her eyes against the sinking sun. I heard her gasp.

"*Is* it?" she murmured. "It *is* . . ." A euphoric smile lit up her weary face. "It's *Irene*! But oh, she's so *thin*, Klara; I wouldn't have known her." I wondered, with our own altered appearance, how easily Irene would have recognized us. "There's Susan," my mother added happily. "But her hair's short. And there's darling Flora." My mother's eyes shone with tears. "My God, Klara—they're safe and they're *here*!" She turned to Peter. "We've spotted the Jochens," she told him excitedly. "Let me lift you up, darling, so that you can see them."

"Sssshhhh!" said Mrs. Cornelisse into her megaphone. "Quiet now, everyone!"

Behind us the huge gate had swung open. A phalanx of soldiers strode toward us, led by Sonei.

Mrs. Cornelisse raised her megaphone again.

"*Kiotsuke!*" she shouted. "*Kere!*" We all bowed. After we had spent what felt like an age at thirty degrees, the order "*Naore!*" rang out and we straightened up. Then the endless counting began, out loud.

"*Ichi! Ni! San! Shi! Go!*"

Sometimes a column had to be counted twice or even three times before Sonei was satisfied.

"*Roku! Shichi! Hachi! Kyuu! Ju!*"

Sonei was running up and down the rows, clutching his whip, his sword bouncing against his leg. He was immaculately dressed, but on his feet were those strange slippers, which made a *sluff-sluff* sound as he raced around. He was followed by Mrs. Cornelisse, who now had to go forward and call the next group to order. So a wave of megaphoned *Kiotsukes* and *Keres* echoed all the way down Laan Trivelli, gradually drowned out by the resumed chatter of the women and children around us.

I could still see Flora and longed to run to her. But we had to stay in our lines until every one of the prisoners—several thousand—had been counted, and this took more than two hours. During this time I speculated with my mother as to how long the Jochens had been in Tjideng, and where Mr. Jochen might be.

"Perhaps he's in a camp with Daddy," Peter suggested.

"Perhaps he is," Mum agreed, though I saw her face cloud. We still had no idea where our father was.

The young woman who'd spoken to me earlier introduced herself as May. She said that she was living in the house next door to ours, and that she'd been in Tjideng from the start of the occupation. Her fair hair had been bleached by the sun; her skin was the color of tea from having spent so much time outside.

I asked May how many people there were in the camp. She explained that there were more than ten thousand of us, adding that until a year before there had been only twenty-five hundred, in a much bigger area. But Sonei had repeatedly reduced the camp in size.

"Why?" I asked.

"The smaller the camp, the easier for him to keep an eye on us," May answered. "One tip: When you bow, you must put your little fingers on the side seams of your skirt, like this." She demonstrated. "If you don't, Sonei will thrash the daylights out of you or get his clippers out. Isn't that right, Louisa?" she said to the red-haired woman standing next to her.

"Dead right," Louisa confirmed. "The man's a fiend. In his last camp he tore people's hair out by the roots." She pointed to the gate. "You saw the monkey cage?" I nodded. "One of the women in this camp gave those apes to Sonei, hoping to get favors from him. He placed the cage inside the camp as 'entertainment.' Sometimes he starves them for a week, then lets them out—for 'fun,'" Louisa added contemptuously. "But the creatures terrify everyone. They've bitten several of the children."

My mother put her arms around Peter and me. "How horrible," she murmured.

"Oh, they're nasty things," Louisa continued. "Mrs. Ament—she was the camp head then—complained to Sonei about them. He listened to her very carefully." She paused. "Then he opened the cage, grabbed one of the monkeys, and smashed its head against the wall; there was blood everywhere. He said he'd done it to punish Mrs. Ament for her 'ingratitude' for the 'entertainment' that the monkeys provided." She shuddered. "She was lucky that Sonei didn't kill her too. Once, he beheaded a woman at *tenko*."

My mother, horrified that Peter and I were hearing of such brutality, murmured that Sonei must be mad.

"He *is* mad," May agreed. "He's a lunatic—a real one. Just wait until the next full moon! That's when he puts on his steel-capped boots and things get really scary."

We watched Sonei lead his soldiers back to the gate, which seemed to signal the end of *tenko*. Everyone sighed with relief, and our group broke ranks. I wanted to run to Flora, but it was dark, and my mother said that we had to get back to the house. She promised that we would find Flora and her family the next day.

Inside the house, the floor was a sea of mattresses covered by ghostly mosquito netting. Mum had managed to hang a *kelambu* from the ceiling; it just covered Peter, herself, and me. As "Lights out!" was heard, we lay under it, cocooned together. They both fell asleep, but I lay awake, comforted by their breathing and by the wonderful knowledge that I had found Flora again.

Fourteen

On the beach, Honor's face was slack with shock. "You had a little brother?" she said weakly.

I nodded. "Ted. His name was Ted. He was five."

She blinked, bewildered. "How can I have known you for fifteen years, and not known that?"

"Because no one knows," I answered. "Not you. Not Nina. I've never told anyone."

"Surely you've told Rick?" I shook my head. "My God . . ." In Honor's eyes was a blend of compassion and astonishment. "But . . . what happened?"

"It was August," I began quietly. "We were here with my mother and her new boyfriend, this man Clive. I hated him being on our family holiday, and wanted to get away from him. So I went rock pooling with Ted. He hadn't wanted to come with me, but I made him, which makes me feel even worse about

what happened . . ." I exhaled painfully. "As we walked across
the sand we met a boy and girl, about the same age as us, who
were making this huge hole." I looked across to the patch of
sand where they'd been digging. I half expected to see them
there. "The girl had a *J* on her shirt," I went on. "I don't know
why, but that detail really stuck in my mind. She was tall and
thin like me, with dark hair, except that hers was very long;
mine was short in those days. Her brother was sandy-haired and
stocky, and Ted and I chatted to them about this big tunnel that
they were digging; then we left them and went on the rocks. But
the tide was coming up."

"Oh, Jenni," Honor murmured.

"We went a long way—too far, almost to Trennick." I nodded into the distance. "But we were enjoying ourselves, catching fish and shrimps, and it was very sunny, and then . . ." I
paused. "We heard the bell."

"The bell?"

"The woman who ran the tea hut always rang a bell at six to
let everyone know she was closing. Our mother had told us to
come back when we heard it. Ted said that he could hear it, but
I pretended I couldn't, because I didn't *want* to go back.
But"—my fingers clenched around the tissue—"when I saw
how close the waves were, I said we *should* go back, and so I
started for the beach . . . I thought Ted was following me."

"Oh God."

"Eventually I reached the sand, and I had another look at the
tunnel; it was huge by then. After that I walked on, looking for
shells, and as I glanced up I saw my mother in the distance,
looking for us. So I waved, and she waved back with a relieved
smile. Then I remember her smile fading. She started running

toward me; she was shouting frantically at someone behind me. As I turned, I could hear a dog barking. Then I saw Ted. He was some way away, but he was very visible because of his red swimming trunks. He was standing on a rock, and there was this dog snapping at him, and Ted was screaming."

Honor's eyes were full of anguish. "Did the dog bite him?"

"No. I don't think it was going to—it was just excited; it had been on the beach all day, chasing balls. I think its ball must have gone onto the rocks near Ted and it just wanted Ted to throw it. But he was terrified of dogs. My mother had seen what was happening, and she was running toward him, trying to call the dog off. She was shouting at it to get away from him, but that only seemed to make it bark more. Just as she got near to it, it jumped up." I swallowed. "And Ted disappeared."

"Disappeared?"

"In that instant I knew where he'd been standing. Just there . . . He'd been standing by that gully, then the dog had startled him and he'd lost his footing. My mother was scrambling over the rocks in her bare feet. She was still screaming at the dog to get away, not realizing that by then it had already gone, because its owners were calling it."

"Didn't they realize what had happened?"

"I don't think they had any idea, because I saw them walking toward the slipway with all their stuff. My mother dropped down into the gully and lifted Ted up, then she carried him over the rocks—her feet were bleeding—while I tried to help. As she laid Ted on the sand I could see a swelling on the side of his face. His eyes were closed. There was spit on his lips, like seafoam, and my mother kept saying his name, over and over, and stroking his face, but he wasn't responding. Then her boyfriend ran

down to us, and when he saw how Ted was, he yelled that he'd
call an ambulance from the hotel; he raced up the beach again.
In the meantime people had gathered round. They all had this
strange expression on their faces, as though they were very
upset, but also fascinated."

"Oh, *Jen*," Honor whispered.

"A woman came up to us and said she was a nurse. As she
examined Ted, Mum explained, through her sobs, what had happened and said that she thought he was concussed. The woman
said that he was breathing okay, but that we had to get him to
hospital as soon as possible. So my mother picked Ted up and
carried him up the beach. The girl and boy who'd been digging
were just staring at us, in shock. Within a few minutes I heard a
siren, and the ambulance drove onto the field behind the hut—
that was the closest it could get to the beach. Two ambulance
men jumped out and ran down to us and gave Ted first aid; then
they laid him on a stretcher and my mother followed them to the
ambulance and waited while they lifted him in. I started to get in
too, but Mum told me that I wasn't to come—I think she didn't
want me to see Ted in such a bad way. But as her boyfriend got
in, my mother said that she needed someone to look after me.
The woman who ran the tea hut said that she would. She told
Mum that she'd take me to the hotel, and that she wouldn't leave
my side until Mum came back, however long that might be. Mum
thanked her and told me to go with her." I inhaled. "The woman
asked me my name, then told me that hers was Jane; which I'd
forgotten—until today," I added quietly. "I remember now—it's
all coming back to me in perfect detail. As the ambulance doors
shut, Jane put her arm round my shoulder and drew me away."

"Oh, Jenni," Honor breathed again.

"She helped me pick up our towels and our beach things. She said that we were going to need them the next day because it was going to be hot again. Then we walked up the lane to the hotel.

"We were shown into a corner of the lounge, where there was a TV and a box of games for the children. Jane chatted away to me, telling me that my mum would soon be back. The manager brought me something to eat, but I didn't want it. Jane and I watched television, though it might as well have been a blank screen. Then she got out some board games and we played Snakes and Ladders; after that we played snap. We played it over and over again. Then, sometime in the early hours, my mother returned.

"I'd fallen asleep on a sofa, and Jane had put a blanket over me. I remember hearing my mother's voice, then opening my eyes and seeing her, and feeling so relieved. Mum was back, and everything was going to be okay, and Ted would be fine, and we could carry on with the holiday and I didn't even mind Clive being there, because he'd been nice, running to call the ambulance like that. It was even going to be sunny again the next day. Then, in a low, flat voice that I barely recognized, Mum thanked Jane for looking after me, and we walked up to Penlee. On the way there I asked my mum how Ted was, but she didn't answer. I asked her if he was still in the hospital, and she said yes. As we went into the house I asked her how long he was going to be there because I really wanted to see him. It was then that my mother sat me on her lap and told me that Ted had died."

"I wish I'd . . . *known*," Honor said again, later that evening. We sat in the kitchen, hardly talking. The window was open, and we could hear the sigh of the sea. "I hate to think of you carrying something so huge, for so long, all by yourself. It must have made you feel . . . lonely."

"I did feel lonely," I responded quietly. "But whenever I think about that day, which I do nearly all the time, I think about the boy and girl who were making the tunnel. Perhaps it's because that was the last 'normal' conversation I had with anyone before Ted died. Or perhaps it's simply because they were there—but I associate them with it profoundly."

"It must have been so hard for you just to walk on the beach today, let alone to go out on the rocks. It must have been difficult, just coming here, to Polvarth."

"It was. When I realized where the job was, I could have said no, and I was going to say no; then, somehow, I found myself saying yes. A part of me *has* wanted to come here again, because it's haunted me all these years."

Honor looked at me, still stunned by what she'd learned. "And you've never told *anyone?*"

"Not a soul. You must be wondering what else you don't know about me," I added bleakly. "But there isn't anything."

She pushed away her plate. "I'm just so sad about it, Jen. But I still don't understand why you couldn't tell your close friends; and I can't fathom why you've never told Rick. How could you want to share the rest of your *life* with him, yet not tell him something so important about yourself?"

"I did *want* to tell Rick. Of course I did."

"Then why didn't you?"

"I . . ." I couldn't bring myself to tell Honor the truth. "I was just . . . waiting for the right time, but it never seemed to come.

And the longer I left it, the harder it got. But this is why he's never met my mother, because if we went there, he'd see all the photos of the brother he didn't know I'd had."

"I've only met your mother once," Honor said. "At our graduation. I remember thinking that she looked sad, but I assumed it was because you and she aren't close—I'd always known that. I also thought it might be because of what had happened to your dad. But it was something even worse—poor woman." She exhaled. "So . . . was it a head injury?"

I nodded. "What they call a catastrophic head injury. They carried out emergency surgery, but he died in the night."

"So is that why you left Goring?"

"Yes. My mother couldn't bear the house anymore without Ted; she couldn't bear going up to the school to collect me but having to go home without him. It upset her to see the children in his class, and she couldn't cope with the sympathy of their parents, or of the local shopkeepers. Goring was such a small place that everyone knew what had happened—they already knew what had happened to my dad."

"Did *you* want to go? Leave your schoolfriends?"

"Probably not; but I guess I was too traumatized to protest, so I went along with what my mother wanted, which was to escape. She only ever went back there to visit the cemetery." I thought of Ted's small headstone in the children's corner of the churchyard. It was carved with his name and dates, a rosebud, and the inscription SLEEP, MY DARLING.

"Why did she move to Southampton? Did she know people there?"

"She didn't know a soul—which was the whole point. It was

a large city in which she felt she could be anonymous. She found a job, in the accounts department of a big printing firm, and enrolled me in a local school."

"Didn't you tell any of your new friends what had happened?"

"Absolutely not. I kept myself to myself. And if anyone asked me whether I had any siblings, I'd just say no, which wasn't a lie."

"But wasn't exactly the truth."

"I didn't see why I had to *tell* the truth. These people were strangers. What did it have to do with them?"

"But, Jenni, *I'm* not a stranger; neither is Nina—or Rick. So why you felt you couldn't tell even us, I don't know."

I looked at my hands, unable to tell her. "It was just too sad to talk about. I was struggling with it, as I still do to this day. And by the time I'd met you and Nina, I'd buried it so deep inside that it had almost . . . fossilized." I lifted my eyes to the sea. "But now I'm here, and it's cracked open, and I'm tormented by it all over again."

"Tormented?" Honor echoed softly. "But what happened was a tragedy, Jen. It was just one of those terribly sad things— a small boy, an overexcited dog. It was an accident. It was no one's fault."

I stood up, went to the window, and pulled down the blind against the night.

The following morning Honor set off on a coastal walk, while I went up to the farm. As I walked down the track, I saw Henry and Beth in the yard. We chatted briefly, but their friendly smiles were tinged with sympathy and I saw at once that they knew my story. It would have been natural for Klara to have told them about our encounter with Jane. The thought made me feel naked, exposed.

I went up the stairs to the flat. As Klara opened the door, I sensed that she was looking at me in a different way, as though now unsure how to treat me.

"Jenni." She smiled at me solicitously. "Come in. You'll have some coffee and cake?"

"Coffee, please, but no cake, thanks. I'm not hungry." This time Klara didn't press it on me.

"It was lovely to meet Honor," she said as she brought the tray over. "What's she doing today?"

"She's walking to the lighthouse at St. Anthony Head. I'm going to pick her up at half one, and then we'll have a pub lunch somewhere. *So . . .* " I got out the recorder. "I've transcribed what we did yesterday morning—the hellish journey to Tjideng . . ." I quickly changed the batteries. "I found it hard, listening to it again."

Klara smiled grimly. "The experience has remained seared on my mind all these years; and you can be sure that having been through *that*, I never complained about any train journey that I ever went on."

I nodded. "I wondered if we could talk about what happened when you got there. I know from my research that Tjideng was one of the worst camps."

"Yes, because of Sonei. He was . . . a devil."

"So, Klara, it's now October 1944, and you've just settled in to your third camp. The war is almost over, though you didn't know that at the time. Can you tell me what you remember about your first few days and weeks there?"

Klara didn't respond. She sat staring at her lap. For a moment I thought that she was too upset at the prospect of having to talk about Tjideng. She'd told me that there were some experiences that would be too difficult for her to describe, let alone discuss. Perhaps we'd come to those now. She'd spoken of so many harrowing incidents that I didn't dare imagine what these ones might be. I was just thinking that we'd have to find some way to skirt round them when Klara looked up. "So I was right," she said softly.

Realizing that we were not going to be talking about Java, I reached forward and turned off the tape recorder.

"Yes," I said. "You were."

"I *knew* I recognized you. From the moment I saw you. Of course you've changed—you were just a child—but I was certain that we'd met."

"I really didn't remember you, until yesterday—I must have blocked it out." How odd, I thought, that my mind had obscured some memories, while preserving others with crystal clarity. "Then seeing you with Jane brought it all back. You were at the hotel."

Klara nodded. "I spent most of last night thinking about what happened that day. I remember it quite clearly. I was in the farmhouse and had heard the siren. Then Henry came back and told me what had happened; he'd been walking back from Trennick and had seen the ambulance. Later, Jane phoned me. In a low voice, she told me that she was at the hotel, looking after a young girl while her mother was at the hospital with the little boy who'd fallen on the rocks."

"Then you came and sat with us."

"Yes. I thought I'd keep Jane company in a sensitive situation. It was late by then, and I imagined you'd be asleep; but you were playing snap. I remember thinking how brave you were being."

"I wasn't brave at all, Klara—far from it! But I remember you coming into the room and chatting with Jane and me as though everything was perfectly normal. We all played cards, and after a while you left and I fell asleep. Then, at last, my mother returned." My throat ached. "And then . . ." The albums, the carved box, and the coffee cups had blurred. I fumbled in my bag for a tissue, then pressed it to my eyes.

I heard Klara sigh. "It was just so sad, Jenni." I was silent. "I've never forgotten it," she said. "I think everyone in this small community felt the tragedy of it for a very long time. There've been a few close calls on the beach; five years ago two boys made a tunnel that collapsed on them; they were dug out just in time. But there's only been one death, and from time to time people here do mention it." A silence enveloped us. I could hear the hum of the fridge. "Now I understand why you were so vague about when it was that you came here."

"I didn't want you to know."

"I've been thinking too about you saying that you don't have any siblings."

"I don't—not for a long time now."

"The thing is that I *had* been thinking about it, for the book. So I would have mentioned it to you when we got to that part of my life."

"I knew that, and I was dreading it. I don't know how I would have reacted; I think I'd just have kept quiet and pretended that it had nothing to do with me."

"But if it's still *so* painful that you couldn't bring yourself to say who you are, or what your connection with Polvarth is, then why come back at all?"

"I've been trying to work that out." I clutched the tissue. "When Vincent phoned me about doing your memoirs, I was immediately excited by your story and felt very drawn to it. But just as I accepted the commission, he told me where you lived."

"That must have given you a shock."

"It was like a physical blow; the thought of not only coming here again but of having to stay here was agony. So I tried to get out of it. And I was making these increasingly desperate excuses when I suddenly heard myself telling Vincent that I *would* do it. I don't even know why."

"Perhaps you wanted to—what's the expression? Lay a ghost?"

I laughed grimly. "I did. And I thought I could, just by being here, but I can't. I feel Ted's presence. I feel haunted by him."

"Haunted?"

"I hear him saying my name; he always called me Evie because when he was little he couldn't say Genevieve. Now his voice is always in my head."

Klara lowered her cup. "That's how I feel about Peter. So you *do* understand that."

"Oh, I do! Except that I probably feel worse than you do, Klara." I closed my eyes. "Because what happened to Ted was my fault."

"But"—Klara's voice was sharp suddenly—"it was an accident, Jenni. He fell."

"Yes—he was startled by a dog and lost his footing."

"So, how could that have been your fault? If anything, it

would have been the fault of the people who owned the dog. It shouldn't have been off its lead if it wasn't safe with children."

"I think it was just trying to play. But Ted was terrified of dogs. He was screaming, and perhaps that made the dog more excited; I'll never know. I only know that I didn't look after him."

"Was it your job to look after him?"

"Yes. I was four years older."

"You were only a child yourself. You were what? Eight?"

"I was nine—nine and a half," I added. The extra six months seemed to matter. "But my mother had told me to hold Ted's hand, and I didn't, not because I was 'only' a child myself, but because I was angry with him."

"Angry?"

"We'd argued over the net. Then he'd grabbed it and we'd lost a crab that I'd just caught and I was furious. Then I saw that the tide was coming up and said we had to go back. But I was still angry—not just about the crab, of course; I was angry with my mother for bringing her horrible new boyfriend on the holiday. I hated him being there with us, on the beach, and in the house, and in my mother's bedroom; it was embarrassing, ruining everything, and I'd been looking forward to the holiday so much. So I took my anger out on Ted, and I walked away."

"Did you know where he was?"

"I knew that he was following me."

"How did you know?"

I felt a wave of shame. "Because I could hear him crying. He was calling my name, begging me to wait. But I pretended not to hear, and then his voice became fainter and fainter as I got farther and farther away."

"What did you think would happen to him?"

"I must have thought that he'd just follow me and get back on his own. I knew it wouldn't be nice for him, but I thought he'd manage. But when I eventually turned round, there was this dog on the rocks, barking at him, snapping at him. Then it suddenly leapt up, and Ted fell . . ."

"I understand so much about you now, Jenni," Klara murmured. "I understand why you've seemed so . . . guarded, as though you somehow feared exposure." It was true. This was why I always felt safer in the shadows. Invisible. "And is this why you don't want children?"

I didn't answer for a moment. "I don't trust myself to have them. I was angry, so I abandoned my little brother. What if I were to do that again, with my own child? What if I didn't take enough care, through incompetence—or worse, was negligent, as I was then? Because if I'd simply done as my mother asked, which was only what I should have done, then Ted would probably still be alive. I could have driven that dog off, or at least stopped Ted from falling, because I would have been holding his hand. But I *didn't* hold his hand, and he died." I swallowed. "And after that my mother never held . . ." My voice had caught.

"Your mother never held your hand?" Klara suggested gently.

I nodded. "She said I was too old, but I knew that wasn't the reason. She was punishing me for not holding Ted's that day."

"She blamed you for what happened?"

"She's always blamed me—which is why we're not close."

"But you were a little girl. Didn't she help you? Console you? You must have been traumatized."

"I was, of course. But she thought only of her own grief. She asked me how I could have walked away from Ted, on a beach. She asked me again and again—what had I been thinking? Why had I done it? She kept *on* asking—I thought she'd never *stop*." I exhaled, blowing out my breath. "So, finally, I told her the truth. But I soon wished that I hadn't. She just stared at me, shocked. Then she said the fact that I'd done it on purpose made it so much worse—impossible to forgive."

Impossible to forgive . . .

The words had echoed in my head for twenty-five years.

"Where was *she* when it happened?"

"At the top of the beach, with her boyfriend."

"So she was distracted."

"I think she was so glad to be with a man again after all her unhappiness that she focused on him instead of her children. She was very young—twenty-eight; six years younger than I am now."

"Young or not, she was the mother. Didn't she blame *herself* for what happened to Ted?"

"No. Or at least she didn't seem to."

"But parents are responsible for their children, and you were only nine."

I shrugged. "Old enough to have done the right thing."

"But you said that the tide was coming in; shouldn't she at least have been aware of that?"

"Maybe. I don't know."

"And she knew that your little brother was scared of dogs. Why should you take all the responsibility for what happened?"

"Why shouldn't I, when I abandoned him?" I drew the tissue under my eyes. "Ted would be thirty now. I think of him every day and wonder what he'd look like, and what job he'd be doing and how often we'd see each other. Then I think of him standing on the rocks, in his red trunks. And it's as though he's still there, waiting for me to go back and help him." I clutched the tissue. "And how I wish, wish, *wish* that I had!"

"It must have been very hard, afterward," Klara said quietly, "living with your mother. It must have felt as though a wall had gone up between you."

I looked at her in surprise. "That's *just* what it felt like."

"You couldn't comfort each other."

"No. But I longed for her to comfort me—but she couldn't, because she blamed me." At that Klara nodded knowingly. "Being so much in the wrong, I became withdrawn. I didn't want to get to know people in case they found out what I'd done. When I started at my new school, I called myself Jenni, as though the name Genevieve had nothing to do with me. I didn't make any friends. Because if I did, they might come to the house, and they'd see the photos of Ted, and I'd have to tell them what happened, and they would judge me for it."

"Do you really think they would have judged you?"

I shrugged. "My own mother had, so I felt sure that they would. She even said that the reason we'd moved was because she didn't want people in the village to find out that Ted's death was my fault."

Klara blinked. "She didn't spare you, did she?"

"No. So I didn't spare myself."

"Didn't she feel *any* responsibility for what had happened?"

I shrugged. "Not that she would ever admit to. When I was seventeen, we had this awful row. It was Ted's birthday; she'd had a couple of drinks and began crying. Then the blaming started. I couldn't bear it. I said that *she* should have been looking after us but that she'd been messing about with her boy-friend—a man she'd only just met—and who she never saw again. She retorted that I'd behaved in a wicked way. She said I'd deprived her of Ted, that I'd ruined her life. She said worse things than that—far worse." I couldn't bring myself to tell Klara what they were. "So as soon as I'd finished my A levels, I left home."

"That must have been a relief in many ways."

"It was liberating. After nine years of my mother's reproach-ful gaze, I could try to move forward and be *myself*. Since then I've seen her no more than once a year. We phone occasionally and send birthday cards, but we both know that we're just pay-ing lip service to our relationship."

"Poor woman," Klara murmured. "I feel sad for her. But did you ever talk to anyone about what had happened?"

I shook my head. "I didn't want any of my friends to know."

"I mean a professional person."

"A therapist?"

"Yes—or a counselor of some kind."

"No." I heaved a sigh. "People didn't do that back then. Maybe it would have helped, because with no one to confide in, I had to absorb all my unhappiness and guilt. You could tell me ten thousand times that I was only a child, but that would never take away my certain belief that I was entirely at fault for what I did—or rather, failed to do—that day. I've tried reading self-help books," I confessed. "But they only make me feel worse, so I get no further than a few pages."

"I think you were meant to come back to Polvarth," Klara said after a moment.

"Perhaps I was." I shrugged, then picked up my pen, hinting

that I was ready to shift the focus back to Klara. I wasn't sorry that I'd confided in her—in fact I was glad—but now it was time to move on.

"You talked about emotional honesty in writing a memoir," Klara persisted. "What if, fifty years from now, you were writing your own? Would you write about Ted?"

"Well, yes. It would be too huge a thing to leave out."

"But would you have the courage to tell the truth? To say what really happened, rather than just the surface story, that there was an accident?"

"I'm not sure that I'd be brave enough." I stared at her. "Why do you ask?"

"I . . . wondered."

"Klara, I'm here to write about *your* life, not mine. A week ago you asked me whether you'd get to know me, and you have, surely more than you would have liked." Before Klara could protest, I started the tape, with a sigh of relief.

Fifteen

Klara

It was still dark when we were woken for morning *tenko*. My mother, Peter, and I set out from the house in the pink light of dawn and walked out onto the street where hundreds of women and children were walking in silence. I caught a glimpse of Irene, Susan, and Flora, who was clutching her doll, before they were swallowed up in the vast crowd. The soldiers counted us, then the hubbub of conversation around us resumed as they moved farther on down the rows. It was two hours before we were dismissed, then Mrs. Cornelisse came and told us to send two women to fetch breakfast. This time my mother volunteered. Carrying the empty bathtub, she and Louisa set off along Laan Trivelli toward the *dapur*. An hour later they returned with the full tub, which they'd had to keep putting down because the metal handles cut into their palms.

As I helped them haul it onto the verandah, my mother gave me an ecstatic smile.

"I *found* them!" she whispered. "They were at the kitchen. We couldn't talk for long, but Irene told me where their house is and we'll go and see them this afternoon!"

I felt tears of happiness prickle my eyes. "I can't wait, Mummy. I just can't *wait* to see Flora!" Louisa ladled out the food as a hundred hungry faces crowded round for their cup of tasteless porridge and five-centimeter piece of hard gray bread. Everyone watched, gimlet-eyed, anxious that no one should get more than their share. The youngest children were allowed to scrape up the residue. I watched the twins do this, licking their fingers. They were nearly three but had the bodies of one-year-olds.

After breakfast Mrs. Cornelisse told us which work parties we'd have to join. There was a team to work in the *dapur* and another to help in the hospital, washing the linen and bandages. There was also a "hygiene" party to deal with the septic tank. The sewage first had to be stirred with a stick, then scooped out with little buckets and poured into the drainage ditch that ran along the *gedék*. Each house had a crew of young women to do this utterly disgusting job, and Kirsten now learned that she was to be one of them.

She stared at Mrs. Cornelisse in disbelief. "Are you saying that I have to stir *poo*?"

Mrs. Cornelisse nodded.

Kirsten clasped her hands in prayer, then looked up to the

sky. "Come on, God! It was one thing to make me eat snails, but *poo stirring*?!"

There was also a *kawat* team to fix the camp boundary, which was just rolls of barbed wire with wooden posts that often needed repair; to her relief, my mother was put in this group. I was assigned to the team that swept the streets and carried rubbish to the gate. We were told that from two P.M. until four, the hottest part of the day, was rest time.

"It's important to sleep," Mrs. Cornelisse told us, "to conserve energy."

I failed to imagine how anyone *could* sleep amid the noise and stress of these hideously overcrowded houses. In any case, my mother, Peter, and I were not even going to try. We were going to find the Jochens.

My mother had the directions to their house, and we set off. I was so excited, I wanted to run, but my mother made me walk. As we went down Ampasiet Weg, we saw a soldier coming toward us. We bowed deeply, then, once he'd passed us, we straightened up and hurried on. The houses here were smaller and less well built, though their gardens, strung with lines of ragged washing, had more shade. The street was deserted, but now we saw three figures under a tree. Unable to contain myself, I ran toward them, then stopped, shocked.

Irene's blue linen dress hung about her in deep, loose folds. Flora's sweet sturdiness had gone, and her hands and feet seemed too large for her rake-thin limbs. Susan's face was gaunt, her cheekbones sharp, her eyes huge. Her long hair had been ruthlessly cropped. I ran forward and gently hugged Flora, then Susan. My mother put her arms round Irene, and they stayed like that for a few moments, not speaking, just patting each other's shoulders.

Irene wiped away a tear, then laughed. "*Look* at us! We're like scarecrows—scruffy scarecrows at that!"

We shook our heads in bewilderment at what had happened to us; then, keeping an eye out for soldiers, we sat in the shade and talked.

Irene said that they knew that Wil had been in Tjimahi—they'd had two postcards from him, although nothing for a year now. "But we assume he's still there, as we haven't heard otherwise."

"Perhaps he and my daddy are together?" Peter suggested happily.

Irene stroked his cheek. "They probably are. I just hope my Wil's not bossing your dad about too much!" she added with a laugh.

"So, what happened after you left the plantation?" Mum wanted to know.

"We headed for Batavia," Irene answered. "Wil had booked passages to Singapore on the *Star of Asia*, but we missed it because our car broke down. The next day we were queuing to get on another boat when we heard that the *Star of Asia* had been sunk by a Japanese submarine that had been lying in wait off Bangka island." She shuddered. "I told Wil that we'd had a blessed escape and were *not* going to tempt fate any further. I told him that it was too dangerous to try and get to Singapore. We'd just have to take our chances on Java and pray that the Dutch army would hold out."

She went on to explain that they'd rented a house in Batavia so that they could be ready to leave if any safe passage could be found to South Africa or Australia. But then the battle for Java had begun.

"We saw it," Peter said, his eyes wide. "The sky was all red."

"We were right *in* it," said Flora. "We watched the Japanese planes fly overhead—they had suns painted on them. We saw a bomb being dropped—it looked like a bell. Then we heard this horrible explosion and there were these clouds of black smoke everywhere. We ran into an air-raid shelter, where we were given bits of rubber to bite on so that our teeth didn't shatter during the bombardment. It was so *loud,* even though we'd stuffed our ears with cotton wool."

On Peter's face was a mixture of awe and envy. "Amazing . . . ," he murmured.

"No, Peter, dear." Irene shook her head. "It was terrifying. We thought we were going to die. Then, within the week, Java fell. After that things moved very quickly. There were thousands of Japanese infantry marching through the streets, and surrendered Dutch soldiers sitting on trucks."

"Did you see Corrie's father?" I asked. "She's here as well— I meant to tell you. We came together—on this horrible train."

"Corrie's mum's dead," Peter blurted out. "The Japs killed her because she bought some eggs. One of the women found out that they'd hanged her."

Irene's hands sprang to her face. "Dear God . . ."

"Corrie has to look after her little sisters," I explained.

"She's their mum now," Peter added. He glanced at our mother, then at me, and I knew what he was thinking.

"We help Corrie as much as we can," my mother told them. "Another friend, Ina, does a lot for her, but it's very hard for the little girl."

Tears shone in Irene's eyes. "The poor darling," she murmured.

"Greta's here too," I told Flora. "With her *oma*."

"And how long have you three been here?" my mother asked.

"From the start of internment," Irene answered. "Two and a half years. But now tell us, what happened to you?"

My mother explained that we'd been able to stay on the plantation until May 1943. "But it's been unbearable, having no word of Hans. We're so worried about him."

"It's better to hear nothing," Irene said. "The way most people here learn that a loved one has died is if they have a postcard to that person returned with the word *Dead* stamped on it. Or they're sent a little parcel that contains the man's name, with a lock of his hair, his nail clippings, and his watch—it's brutal. So believe me, Annie, no news is *good* news."

"How was Arif?" Susan asked us. "Did you see him? Is he all right?"

"He was working for us until we left; he was fine," my mother replied. "But I don't know what's happened to him since—or to anyone else on the plantation."

"Susan still loves Arif," Flora declared. "Don't you, Sue?" Susan glared at her.

Peter was leaning against Mum's shoulder. He looked up at her. "Will we be going back home when the war's over?"

She kissed his head. "Of course we will," she answered, though I heard the uncertainty in her voice.

"We *have* to go back," Peter said. "I promised Jaya. And *don't* forget the chess set we're going to get him."

"I won't forget," she assured him. Now we asked them about Tjideng.

"At first, life here wasn't too bad," Irene explained. "We were allowed to cook, and to leave the camp during the day as long as we were back for evening *tenko*. We could hold church services and even concerts—the pianist Lili Kraus played to us a few times; she'd been on tour and got caught by the invasion. But then, on April first, like some hideous April fool, Kenichi Sonei arrived. One of the first things he did was to have all the pianos chopped up."

Peter blinked in astonishment. "What for?"

"The fuel for the *dapur* was running low. So all the furniture was burned—even the doors. He halved our rations and doubled the number of *tenkos*. He did utterly evil things too. He had all the sick people dragged out of their hospital beds."

"Why?" I asked.

"Because he didn't want them dying in the camp, as that would look bad for him in Tokyo. So he just dumped them outside the gates—elderly men and women—and left them there to die. It was dreadful. And *then* . . . "

Irene closed her eyes, as if preparing herself for some ordeal. "Many people had brought their dogs into the camp," she explained quietly. "One night Sonei had all the dogs put into sacks; then he gave the teenage boys cudgels and ordered them to club the poor creatures to death, or be clubbed themselves." She shuddered. "The boys were crying—we all were. Many of them refused to do it, and were badly beaten, but eventually, it was done."

Peter clenched his fists. "I'd like to put Sonei in a sack and club *him*!"

"Morale is very low," Susan said. "We count every grain of rice, and each drop of soup. We constantly accuse one another of stealing—clothes mostly, but also soap and food." She explained that if anything went missing, the Tjihapiters were usually prime suspects because they had fewer possessions.

My mother nodded. "That explains the hostile reception that we had at the gate."

Irene laughed bleakly. "But we're *all* paupers now. Think of what we once had! Now we measure our wealth in terms of spoons, cups, plates, or garments—even an old rag has value. Have you seen what a lot of the women here are wearing as tops—tea towels! They wear frocks made out of sheets, and most of us have no shoes, because they've fallen apart."

"Look how callused our feet are," Susan said, gesturing to hers.

I asked her what had happened to her hair. I was worried that she might have been shaved, but she nodded at her mother, then made a scissoring motion.

"I cut it," Irene explained. "I didn't want the soldiers to notice Susan. I'm going to cut Flora's as well soon, Anneke, and I suggest you cut Klara's."

Peter, clearly puzzled, asked why.

"Because the soldiers sometimes try and find girlfriends among the young women here," Irene answered carefully. "If they refuse, the soldiers force them. For that reason it's best for girls to look as plain as possible, and so Susan's lovely tresses had to go."

"Don't worry, Sue," said Flora. "It'll only take five years to grow back."

Susan scowled at her. "No need to rub it in!"

"I wasn't!" Flora wailed.

Susan tugged at Flora's hair. "Yours is going to be chopped off too, missy."

Irene pushed herself to her feet. "Don't fight, girls," she said wearily. "Life's quite hard enough. Come and see our luxurious accommodation," she said to my mother.

We followed them inside.

"It *is* luxurious, having a bedroom," Peter said.

"Yes, though it has no door," Irene responded. "But at least we have a little privacy."

On the way to their room we'd had to step around several sleeping women, and I noticed that two had the swollen legs of hunger edema. We went into the Jochens' room and sat on their mattresses. Flora showed me her dolls; the china doll, Lottie, had lost a hand, and one side of Lucie's smiley mouth had come unstitched.

Flora picked up Lucie, then put her finger to her lips.

"All our precious things are sewn inside her," she whispered. "Mummy's jewelry, and our passports. I take her with me when we go to *tenko* to keep it safe. I keep my other treasure *here*." She picked up her pillow, and out of it pulled a piece of wadded cloth. Inside was the brass lizard, gleaming softly. Impulsively, I ran my fingers over its sinuous beauty and, once again, wished that it was mine.

Irene asked us where on Laan Trivelli our house was. When my mother told her, a shadow crossed Irene's face. I thought this must be because she knew that it was so near to the gate, but that wasn't the reason. "You're living in the boys' house," she told us. "That's where the boys were held in the days before they were sent to the men's camps. The youngest were ten.

Some were holding their teddy bears as they climbed onto the truck."

"How heartbreaking," my mother murmured, "and how wicked to classify little boys as men."

"Annie," Irene said, "I don't want to alarm you, but there's something you should know . . ."

"Yes?" my mother said anxiously. "What?"

Irene drew in her breath. "Sonei's planning another transport of ten-year-old boys."

It was a huge comfort to have found Flora again. With so many women and children now pouring into Tjideng, I recognized other people as well. Two more classmates of ours arrived— Edda Smits and Lena Bosch. Lena and her mother were sent to Flora's house, and I worried that Lena and Flora would now become best friends.

Edda had been in a camp called Kampung Makassar. She told us that Miss Broek and Miss Vries had been there too. "But Miss Vries is *so* thin now," she confided. "She cries all the time because her fiancé was killed in an air raid."

One day my mother, Peter, and I saw another familiar figure. We returned to our house to see Marleen Dekker unrolling her mattress in a corner of the living room. We hadn't even known that she was in Tjideng.

My mother was taken aback but went up to her straightaway and greeted her. Mrs. Dekker ignored her—she clearly hadn't forgotten my mother's scolding her for being snobbish about Jaya and Peter's friendship on that April day.

"So she bears grudges," my mother whispered as we walked away. Before long we would discover that Mrs. Dekker was the type not just to bear a grudge but to take revenge.

We learned that she had been in Tjideng for a year, on Moesi Weg, but had made herself so unpopular with the other women in her house—they called her "Queen Marleen"—that her group leader had suggested she be moved. And so, a few days after we'd arrived, Mrs. Dekker appeared in our house. Her son wasn't with her, and someone told us that he'd been put on the latest boys' transport a month before.

"I feel sorry for her, Klara," my mother said. "She must be very worried about Herman; but I do wish that she'd gone anywhere else. I won't let it affect me though. I'm just happy that Irene and the girls are here."

Whenever we could, Peter and I would spend time with Susan and Flora. We'd all close our eyes and pretend that we were back at the plantation, gazing at the mountains. In Tjideng our eyes just hit the *gedék*.

Flora and I were both on sweeping duty, and sometimes we'd go for a walk while pretending to work. We'd go to the western side of the camp and peer through the rolls of barbed wire at the outside world. Often people would notice us and stare. I'd usually see shock on their faces, because we were so thin, and dirty, and looked like boys because by then Irene had cropped our hair. But sometimes I'd see satisfied smiles at our degradation; they were glad to see the privileged Dutch colonials brought low. But something else amazed me.

"Why aren't they thin like us?" I asked Flora.

She shrugged. "I guess they get more food than we do."

"So . . . are the Japs starving us?" I asked. "On purpose?"

Flora pursed her lips. "Some people say that they are. But I don't know."

In Tjideng, time seemed to stand still. I felt as if we were always waiting—waiting to be counted, waiting to go to work, waiting to be fed our meager rations or to go to bed. In our spare time my mother and Irene took turns to teach us, just as they'd taken turns to look after us when we were at school. We used to write on a tile with a piece of lead, or draw marks in the dust with a stick. Sometimes Corrie joined us for "lessons" while Ina and Kirsten watched the twins. We also played games. For the boys it was jacks, played with bits of bone; for the girls it was hopscotch, using white stones to mark out the squares, or we played ticktacktoe in the dirt, with our fingers.

Tenko was sometimes up to three or four times a day, because Sonei would call us out, without warning, at any time. At full moon he'd call us out in the middle of the night. Mothers would bring a blanket for their children to lie on, and if they saw Sonei coming, they'd quickly rouse them and make them stand. But *tenko* wasn't the worst thing about Tjideng; the worst thing about Tjideng was the gate. We called it *de Poort,* and were terrified of it, because that's where all the bad things happened. The gate was where the punishments took place—usually head shavings and beatings. Sometimes women were made to kneel with a length of split bamboo behind their knees, which cut off the blood supply to their legs; or they were suspended by their wrists, which were tied behind their backs, their feet barely scraping the ground. For serious "crimes" women were tied to a chair, in the sun, with no food or water, sometimes for days. Most women didn't survive, rapidly succumbing to dehydration and sunstroke. So to us the gate was a place of hell. We had come into Tjideng through it and knew that we would leave through it, most probably dead, we came to believe as the weeks went by.

By February 1945 people were dying in large numbers, not just from malnutrition but from dysentery, pellagra, whooping cough, and beriberi. Death became so common that we no longer even remarked on it. I might play with a child only to be told, two days later, that the child was "no longer alive." In the "real" world, such an event would be shocking. But I wasn't shocked because in Tjideng, death was a normal occurrence. There was even a work party that made bamboo coffins; Sonei seemed perversely proud of this.

Peter wanted to play with the other children, but our mother now made him stay in the house because she was increasingly worried that he'd blurt out his age.

"If anyone asks you, you must take a year off it," she whispered to him. "Do you understand?" He nodded.

"And, Klara, you must never, *ever* tell anyone how old your brother is. Do you promise me?"

"I do." I laid my hand on my chest. "I solemnly promise that I will never, ever tell anyone Peter's age."

For weeks nothing was said about any further transports, and I began to believe that it would never happen. Then, in March 1945, the axe fell. We learned that all the boys of ten and over, being a "danger to women," were to be transferred out of the camp.

Mrs. Cornelisse came to see my mother, holding a clipboard. "Our records show that your son, Peter, will be ten on the eighth of April," she began. "Is that correct, Mrs. Bennink?"

I saw a muscle clench at the corner of my mother's mouth. "No," she answered calmly. "He'll be nine." She added that when they'd gone to Garut to register, the official had mistakenly recorded Peter's year of birth as 1935 instead of 1936. "I wrote to the authorities about it," she went on coolly. "But they clearly didn't correct it. He'll be nine on that day," she repeated firmly.

Mrs. Cornelisse said that she would look into it and went away.

Peter, for his part, was confused. "I'd *like* to go to the men's camp," he whispered to me, "because then I'll see Daddy again."

"We don't even know where Dad *is*," I reminded him, "let alone whether you'd be sent to the same place. In any case, Mummy doesn't *want* you to go."

"But I—"

"Peter," I interrupted, "we both *promised* Daddy that we'd do whatever Mum said, with *no* argument. You'd better not break that promise because he'll be very upset with you."

So Peter agreed to do what our mother asked.

On 8 April, Mum made a point of celebrating Peter's birthday—as far as it was possible to celebrate anything in Tjideng. She gave him a bread roll that she'd saved, and we picked some red hibiscus flowers and arranged them in a jar. We sang "Happy Birthday" and did nine birthday claps. Later that day, Mrs. Cornelisse returned. She told Mum that as she'd been unable to clarify Peter's date of birth, she was going to remove his name from the list.

My mother received this news calmly, as though it was only what she had expected. Inside, though, she was elated. But her euphoria was to be short-lived. Two days later she got a letter saying that Peter Hans Bennink would be transported to a men's camp on 15 April. She ran to Mrs. Cornelisse, who told her that she'd have to discuss it with the camp leader, Mrs. Nicholson. So my mother went to the camp office, taking Peter and me with her.

Mrs. Nicholson was sitting behind a small desk, going through a list of names; just visible in the adjacent office was Lieutenant Kochi, who was almost as hated as Sonei. Engrossed in some paperwork, he took no notice of us.

My mother's face was very pale. "My son is nine," she told Mrs. Nicholson. She stood behind Peter, her hands on his shoulders. "Look how small he is."

"Most of the boys are small," Mrs. Nicholson remarked.

"True, but don't you think I'd remember when I gave birth to my own child? In any case, why has the decision been reversed?"

Mrs. Nicholson hesitated. "I'd rather not say."

"I want to know," my mother demanded. "I have the *right* to know."

Mrs. Nicholson stared at her before answering. "All right . . . It's because, since the original decision was made, we've received reliable information that Peter is ten."

My mother blinked. "From who?"

Mrs. Nicholson bit her lower lip. "A few days ago, Marleen Dekker came to see me. She'd overheard your conversations with Mrs. Cornelisse. She told me that her family had visited you on Peter's sixth birthday, and that this was four years ago."

My mother's face flushed. "Mrs. Dekker is mistaken. She and her family did visit us, but it was Peter's fifth birthday that day."

"Why would she be wrong?" Mrs. Nicholson asked.

"Because she's erratic and confused. I'm sure it's only due to the pressures of camp life, and it's very sad, but it means that her word can't be trusted."

I was suddenly aware that Lieutenant Kochi was looking at us.

"Peter," said Mrs. Nicholson. "How old are you?"

Peter reddened, then glanced up at my mother. Her fingers tightened on his shoulders. "I'm . . . nine."

Lieutenant Kochi came into the room, and we all bowed. In Malay, he said that he was tired of listening to us squabbling. *He* would establish the truth—"with help from the girl," he added, gesturing to me.

My mother looked stricken. "I don't want my daughter to be questioned," she said to Mrs. Nicholson. "Please, tell Lieutenant Kochi not to talk to her."

"I don't have the authority," Mrs. Nicholson responded. "I'm sorry, Mrs. Bennink."

My mother bowed to Kochi again. Then, averting her eyes from his face, she implored him, in Malay, to let me go. "She's just a child," she pleaded, her voice breaking. "She's very young—only twelve. Please, Lieutenant Kochi, I respectfully, and in the name of His Imperial Majesty the emperor, beg you *not* to . . ." But by then I was being led out of the office by Lieutenant Kochi. He marched me across the courtyard into the guardhouse.

I was taken past the rack of rifles into a bare room at the back of the building. It had only a table with two chairs, no windows. What light there was filtered in through the gaps in the bamboo, casting slatted shadows onto the dusty floor. Seeing discarded cigarette ends, I felt sick to think of the use to which they might have been put. Some women, I knew, had had bamboo pins pushed under their nails, or had had their toenails pulled off with pliers.

Kochi sat behind the table. I stood in front of him. My breath grew shallow. My knees trembled.

"How old is your brother?"

"My brother," I answered falteringly, ". . . is nine."

"How old is your brother?"

"My brother is nine."

"On what date was your brother born?"

"On 8 April 1936." Maybe Kochi wouldn't understand "1936," I fretted, because I knew that the Japanese calendar was different from ours.

"How old is your brother?"

"My brother is nine."

Kochi must have asked me two hundred times, sometimes pausing for a minute, or even two minutes, between each time. I stood there, terrified to show any emotion, staring at a corner of the table. Then another soldier came into the room—a man with round glasses, named Sergeant Asako. The two men conferred in Japanese; then Asako questioned me too, in Malay, but I said the same thing over and over.

"You are not telling us the truth," Sergeant Asako insisted. He took a pack of cigarettes out of his pocket and lit one. "So now we will try something else."

I don't know how much longer I spent in the guardhouse. I was aware that the room was getting darker and colder as the sun began to set. Then, finally, after the line of questioning had taken a much darker turn, my ordeal was over. They jerked me to my feet, gave me a message for my mother, and pushed me out of the room.

I was fighting back tears as I walked out. I dreaded seeing my mother, but there she was, watching for me from the front of our house. She ran to me, her face twisted with anguish.

"What did they *do* to you?" she whimpered as she helped me away. "What did they do to you, my darling? Tell me," she wept, as she looked at my arms and legs for signs of injury. "Please, Klara. I'm your mother; tell me what they did so that I can comfort you."

But my mother was the one person in the world that I *couldn't* tell. We got back to the house, and now, in a voice I barely recognized as my own, I gave her the message.

"Tomorrow morning?" she repeated faintly. "Peter has to be at the gate tomorrow morning?" I nodded. "So they've brought the transport forward?"

"Yes."

Her face filled with terror and despair. Then a different expression came into her eyes, one of disappointment. "So you told them his age."

"No."

"You *must* have done."

I tried to swallow but my mouth had gone dry. "I promised you that I wouldn't tell anyone, and I didn't. You have to believe me, Mummy." She didn't answer. But now, accepting that there was nothing to be done, she opened Peter's case. Into it she put some malaria pills, a blanket, the few clothes that he still possessed, and his bear, inside which she left the cherished photo of my father. She packed a small saucepan, a plate, cup, and spoon. Then she took down our *kelambu,* ripped it in half, and out of it made a new net for Peter, stitching it with thread that she'd pulled out of a dress. When it was finished she showed him how to hang it up and tie it, then she packed it. She sewed up the remainder, and the three of us lay beneath it, curled together, for one last night.

I couldn't sleep. Peter was awake too; I could see his eyes, shining in the darkness. Our mother, exhausted by despair, had drifted off.

"I'm sorry, Pietje," I whispered.

"What for?" he whispered back.

"For every mean thing I've ever said to you, or done to you."

"It doesn't matter," he murmured. "Anyway, I can't even remember."

"I bossed you around, and quarreled with you, and called you names."

"Well . . . you didn't mean it. Anyway, the war's going to be over soon, and Daddy and I will come back, then we'll all go home to Sisi Gunung."

Then we talked about the plantation. We remembered the day the bees came and how bravely Suliman had dealt with them. We talked about Sweetie and Ferdi. Then we shared other memories—our father squirting us with the hose on hot days; our mother's pink and white orchids in their pots; our games with Flora and Jaya; the panther padding past; the bats swooping out of the Indian fig tree at dusk.

The following morning we rose at first light. Peter got dressed and rolled up his mattress. Then he opened his case, took out his jacket, and put it on. It was the first time he'd worn it since the war started, but it still fit him because he'd hardly grown.

My mother smiled at him. "You look so smart."

"I need to," he replied, "because I'll be seeing Daddy. I shall run to him."

My mother nodded, unable to speak. She did up the gold buttons, then we picked up his things and went outside. As we came out of the house we saw small, solemn groups walking down Laan Trivelli. Each group was clustered around a little boy. Some women and girls were already in tears. I glanced at my mother; her face was pale but her eyes were dry.

Irene, Susan, and Flora fell in step with us as we walked to the gate. There a large truck was waiting, its engine running; the smell of petrol hung in the air. Boys were being herded into a lineup. Some were wearing their school backpacks; others carried worn-looking soft toys. Mrs. Nicholson shouted out names and numbers from her list, and as the boys answered, the guards hurried them onto the truck.

"Lekas! Lekas!"

All too soon, it was Peter's turn. His arms went round my mother, and he leaned into her as she held him tightly.

"This is just another part of the adventure," she promised him, "but we'll all be together again very soon." She kissed him, then laid her cheek against his. "I love you, Pietje," she whispered. "Goodbye, my darling. Goodbye for now."

I put my arms round my brother. "Bye, Peter. I love you too."

Irene, Susan, and Flora all hugged him, then my mother kissed Peter once more and handed him his suitcase; then he stepped forward into the line. As he climbed onto the vehicle Irene put her arm round my mother—they were both crying—then the tailgate slammed shut. Some boys were weeping, but Peter, in his smart jacket, was smiling and waving as the truck moved off, through the gate, out of sight.

Sixteen

The rest of Honor's visit passed quietly, my revelation seeming to have subdued her. On Friday we visited the small castle at nearby Caerhays, then later, while I was with Klara, Honor stayed in the cottage and read. On Saturday morning we went to Truro Cathedral, and then I took her to the station to get her train home.

"I'm so glad I came," she said as we waited on the platform. "And I'm glad you told me what you did," she went on. "But Jen, whatever happens with Rick, you should tell him as well."

If only it were so easy, I thought as Honor's train pulled in. Surely Rick would want to break up with me, because if I'd concealed something so huge for so long, then how could he ever really know me or trust me?

I waved to Honor as the train pulled away, then left and drove back to Polvarth. I worked all afternoon and early eve-

ning, transcribing Klara's interviews. As I reread it, tears sprang
to my eyes at the thought of Peter leaving his mother and sister,
not knowing whether he'd ever see them again.

But they had been able to say goodbye, and express their
love, I reflected enviously. And at least Klara wasn't to blame
for what happened to her brother, whereas *I* . . . I closed the
document and tried to pull myself together. After a few moments I looked at my emails. The first was from Nina.

Jenni, a card will be on its way soon, but Jon and I just
wanted to thank you and Rick for the beautiful silver
frame—we've already put our favorite wedding photo
in it. Speaking of which, a few snaps from the day are
attached. We had a great honeymoon, with lots of sunshine and wonderful food, very little of which I felt like
eating—as Hons will by now have explained. It's still
early days, but I can't help thinking that you and she
would make lovely godmothers . . . Speaking of godparents, I hear you're in Cornwall with my godfather's
mum—Klara's a remarkable person. Enjoy being there
and see you soon! N x

Godmother . . . I impulsively clicked to a number of baby-
wear sites and looked at pink and blue blankets, and onesies and
tiny hats and shoes. Like Honor, I had to fight the urge to buy
something straightaway.

I looked at the photos Nina had sent. There was the one that
the photographer had taken of Rick and me outside the church;
it was good, though our smiles didn't quite reach our eyes.
There was the group photo, Honor laughing into the camera as

she stood a few feet from Al, who at that stage she hadn't met. There was a candid shot of us all at our table; Amy and Sean were chatting to Rick; I was talking to Carolyn, while Vincent was looking at me with a thoughtful expression. That had been only two weeks ago.

There was also a message from Vincent's daughter, Gill.

I grew up knowing that Granny Klara had suffered dreadful privation as a child, and I was aware that the biggest issue in her life was food. Whenever we went to Polvarth we'd have to brace ourselves for her huge breakfasts, lavish lunches and sumptuous teas, the table groaning under the weight of her homemade sandwiches, flans, chocolate mousse, and meringues. I'd be in trouble if I took something then didn't eat it—Granny couldn't stand waste. I remember her once being furious because I'd told her that I was "starving." "You're no such thing!" she snapped.

She made me promise, when I was older, never to diet. "Just give thanks to God that you have enough," she'd say. Granny's always been tirelessly hardworking, a good neighbor, a caring friend, and a devoted mother and grandmother. She's taught me so much about growing things, and I think of Granny as being a "planter" too. When I was little I adored going into the walled garden— her "piece of paradise," as she always called it—and I still love being in there with her, to this day.

I was about to close the in-box when another message arrived. It was from Honor to say that she'd just got back to London.

"Thank you for a lovely stay," she wrote. "I also wanted to

say that I was on my iPad on the train back and found a website that you might want to look at, if you haven't already. It's called 'Tjideng Revisited' and has survivors' stories. Just thought it might be useful. In haste, and much love to you, H x."

I wrote down the name of the website—I would look at it later. But now, heeding Honor's advice, I picked up the phone, took a deep breath, and called Rick.

Afterward, I went down to the beach—the moon was enormous and so bright that I could see my shadow as I walked down the lane. I sat on the bench by the tea hut, looking at the lights of Trennick shimmering on the dark water. Rick and I had spoken for over an hour. I'd let him tell me his news—that half term had started but that he wasn't going to go away because he needed to write job applications. He said that he'd seen a head teacher's job advertised in *The Times,* for a school in Norwich. I'd said how nice that might be, with the Broads, and the Norfolk coast, and he'd said that he'd give it a shot. He wanted to know how the writing was progressing. It was going well, I replied, then I told him about Honor's visit and he asked what we'd done. I answered that we'd walked and talked, about all sorts of things. Then, somehow, I found the words to tell Rick what had happened at Polvarth twenty-five years before.

When I'd finished there was a silence so deep, I thought that he'd hung up. Then I heard him say that he now understood why I'd hesitated to go to Polvarth, and why I hadn't wanted my mother to know where I was. I told him that Klara had been there that day, and that I'd met her. Rick asked me how I could remember, given that it was so long ago, and I explained that I

aglow with lights, then unlocked the cottage door. I went upstairs, undressed, and got into bed, leaving the curtains open.

I slept fitfully, and dreamed of Peter, in the truck, waving goodbye.

Sometime before dawn, I awoke. I sat up, my pulse racing. There was someone with me in the room. I could sense it in the darkness. As I peered into the gloom my heart beat wildly, thumping against my ribs. Then it gradually slowed as I realized that there was no one there but me.

I pushed back the duvet, went to the window, and sat looking at the moonlit garden and the glimmering sea. I stayed there for a time, then went back to bed. As I got in, I looked at the painting on the wall. There was the churning sea beneath the marbled sky, the waves rearing and breaking, smashing the water into foam. But now I saw something that hadn't been there before. Standing on the rocks, clutching a net, was a small, fairhaired boy in red trunks.

I lay awake, seized by fear. Then I heard Honor's voice. For a moment I thought that she was still in the cottage; then I realized that I'd fallen asleep and that it was just the radio coming on. I pushed myself up, then stared at the painting. The figure in the red trunks had gone. Or, rather, it had never been there, I told myself sternly. My tortured mind had conjured it. I was going mad.

"Remember, the clocks go back today," Honor said. "So if you were about to drag yourself out of bed—don't! Stay snuggled under the covers for the second half of the show, in which we'll be talking about Halloween. What do you think of trick or treat?" she asked. "Do you enjoy it, enthusiastically carving pumpkins, spraying fake cobwebs on the windows, and dragging your kids round the block dressed as vampires and zombies? Or do you thoroughly disapprove of the whole thing and pine for the good old days of 'penny for the guy'? We'll be hearing your views on that a little later, but first here's Jason with the news . . ."

I went into the bathroom and showered. When I came back, Honor was chatting to the weather presenter; then, still focused on Halloween, she began talking about ghosts.

"Do ghosts exist?" she asked.

"Yes," I murmured.

"That's what we'll be discussing this morning, as a new survey shows that a whopping forty percent of us believe that they do. Joining us now is Barnaby Crewe, a professional 'ghost hunter.' Barnaby, welcome to the show—you're obviously a believer."

"Oh, I am," Barnaby responded. "I absolutely believe in ghosts, because I've seen them for myself on numerous occasions."

"What have you seen?" Honor asked as I pulled on my jeans.

"I've seen the ghost of a little Victorian boy; I've seen the ghosts of two monks, each holding a lighted candle; I've seen the ghost of an elderly woman sitting in a chair, knitting. I've seen the ghost of a young girl running down a corridor—I even heard her footsteps. I've seen things that simply defy any rational explanation."

Barnaby continued to list his ghostly encounters, then Honor said that she was going to take calls from listeners.

"You can tell us about your own experiences of ghosts, or

put questions to Barnaby," she explained. "And we have Cathy calling us from Sevenoaks. Good morning, Cathy. Have you ever seen a ghost?"

"I have," a woman answered firmly. "It happened thirty years ago, when I was ten. I saw my grandfather standing at the top of the stairs, smiling at me. I was surprised because I hadn't realized that he was in the house. What I didn't know was that he'd collapsed and died two hours before; my parents broke the news to me later that night. When I told them that I'd seen him, they said that I couldn't have done, but I *did*. I believe that my grandfather had come to see me to say goodbye."

"Ooh, you've made me go all goose bumpy!" Honor exclaimed. "Thanks for that, Cathy, and do stay on the line for a moment while we talk to Patrick, from Bath, on line two. What's your view, Patrick?"

"I'm skeptical. I think that once people are dead, that's it—we don't see them again."

"So you're saying that Cathy couldn't have seen her grandfather?"

"I . . . guess I am saying that, yes."

"Look, if I say I saw my own grandfather, then I did," Cathy retorted. "It's like if someone says that they've had a religious experience—a vision, say, or a visit from an angel. No one has the right to say to that person, no, you *didn't*. That would be total arrogance."

"Nonbelievers *can* seem arrogant," Barnaby agreed. "I'm with Cathy on this. If a person believes she's seen a ghost, or experienced an angelic presence, then that is that person's subjective truth."

"Yes," said Patrick, "*subjective* being the operative word. So, as I was saying, I don't believe in ghosts—but I *do* believe in hauntings."

"What's the difference?" Honor asked.

"I believe that under acute psychological pressure we can feel ourselves to be haunted, but that there's nothing really *there*."

"Which is to reduce it all to hallucination," Honor said.

"Or . . . neurosis."

"I don't buy that," Barnaby insisted. "Nonbelievers say that to see a figure float through a wall could never happen, because it defies the laws of physics—the person's 'seeing things.' But who's to say that a ghost isn't a manifestation from some *other* universe that has different physical laws from our own?"

"That's certainly food for thought," Honor said. "Pattie on line three—what do you think?"

"I think that the dead can leave behind an imprint of themselves," Pattie answered. "Like an echo that we can sometimes detect. I believe this is more likely if the person has died in a violent or traumatic way . . ."

I switched off the radio, not wanting to hear any more of the discussion. Remembering that Honor had recommended the Tjideng Revisited website, I turned on my laptop and found it. There was a history of the camp, with photos of the derelict houses, their gardens strewn with basins and potties and buckets and broken chairs, their verandahs strung with lines of ragged washing. There were haunting images of children with stick legs and huge eyes, and of lines of women, bowing, their arms clamped to their sides.

I clicked on the survivors' stories. A woman named Renata wrote of picking through the rubbish for anything still edible and of trying to catch grasshoppers to eat. A man named Max wrote of the thrill when, occasionally, they'd get an egg; he and his sister would share it, then their mother would grind up the shell, dissolve it in water, and make them drink it for the calcium. Katrin described how she once watched her six-year-old brother trying to make a toy out of two rusty nails—a memory, she wrote, that could still make her cry.

Now I read a posting by someone called Edda.

I was interned in Kampung Makassar and then Tjideng. What stands out most in my mind were all the punishments, for nothing at all—bowing a second too late, or looking a soldier in the face. I remember one girl being hung up by her wrists, because the guards had found a Dutch coin in her room. One woman in our house missed *tenko*—she refused to go because she was ill; so they tied her to a chair, in the sun, for two days, and she nearly died. There were interrogations in which torture was used; but in a bizarre act of courtesy, the soldiers would allow the victim to choose. Imagine being asked whether you'd prefer to be burnt with cigarettes or to have your fingernails torn off! These interrogations were carried out in the guardhouse. One day I saw a classmate of mine, Klara, coming out. I didn't know what they had done to her, but I have never forgotten her shattered expression. She looked as though the world had just come to an end.

Seventeen

Klara

It was now a month since Peter had left, and we'd heard nothing. We could only hope that he was amongst people who treated him decently, or at least didn't mistreat him. I consoled myself with the thought that wherever Peter was surely couldn't be worse than Tjideng; but perhaps that was just a lack of imagination on my part.

One morning, Flora and I were on sweeping duty when we saw the bread truck drive in. As it took its usual route up Laan Trivelli, we could smell the bread, and soon the children were rushing out of the houses and racing toward it with as much energy as they could muster. We waited for the truck to stop, but it didn't stop. Instead, it did a U-turn, went back down the street, and drove out of the gate.

"Why's it done *that*?" Flora wailed.

I shook my head. "I don't know."

A minute later the truck came back in, drove up Laan Trivelli again, followed by the children, only to turn round and go out once more. By the time it had done this three times, everyone stayed inside. We now understood just how determined Sonei was to make us suffer.

Later, Mrs. Cornelisse told us why Sonei had told the driver to do this. The day before, she explained, Sonei had seen the vegetable truck come in. But not one of the prisoners on the street had bowed to the driver—an employee of the emperor!

"Lieutenant Sonei feels that this was a grave insult to His Imperial Majesty. And so . . ." Mrs. Cornelisse paused, and I knew that bad news was coming. "I'm afraid he's going to withhold food from the entire camp for the next three days."

There were wails of despair.

"He can't *do* that to us!"

"We'll die!"

"He's *insane*!"

"Speak to him, Mrs. Cornelisse!"

"Yes—in the name of God, beg him not to *do* this to us!"

"I'm sorry," Mrs. Cornelisse said. "All the group leaders tried to dissuade him, but Sonei's mind is made up. We'll just have to cope as best we can."

The cries of anguish continued, but worse was to come. The kitchen workers were ordered to dig trenches and to throw into them all the porridge and bread that they had been about to distribute. Sonei himself was seen shoveling dirt onto it to make sure it was inedible. And so the food that would have fed ten thousand starving women and children was now destroyed!

That night it was impossible to sleep. The constant weeping rang in my ears. The twins kept crying, and Corrie screamed at them to be quiet, just be quiet, be quiet . . .

We heard the monkeys shriek.

"*They're* being fed," Kirsten said bitterly.

A deep despair descended on the camp. Some of the women, crazed with hunger, said they were going to break in to buildings and find food. There must be *something* to eat, they screamed, somewhere in this hellish, *godvergeten* place. They even said that they would sneak into Sonei's villa—there was always a smell of delicious food coming from *there*!

"My cousin has to cook for him," said a woman called Mies. "Sonei tells her to bring her children with her so that they can watch him eat—that seems to make it taste *extra* delicious, God damn that devil!"

We all slept as much as possible to avoid wasting energy. As I lay there I thought of all the things I regretted not having eaten in my life. I regretted not eating rice pudding at school; I regretted not having eaten cassava cake when I was at Flora's house once. I regretted turning up my nose at bread crusts, and buffalo milk, and the insides of tomatoes. I even wished that I had eaten more snails.

The medical staff handed out tiny quantities of bread and lentils, from their emergency supplies. But there was nothing to cook them on because Sonei had confiscated all the Anglos. So we ground them up with a rock, mixed them with water, and ate them with our tiny piece of gray bread.

My mother looked at her lentils. "We are now Stone Age people," she observed quietly. "This is what they have done to us."

The three days felt like three weeks. But at last Sonei gave the order for the *dapur* to reopen. While that happened we waited on our beds, too weak to do anything else. I had found a piece of cardboard and was fanning myself with it, but my mother told me to stop, as even this small exertion would waste precious calories.

"When can I see Flora?" I asked her. We'd been unable to see each other during the "hunger days," and I missed her.

"After we've eaten," my mother answered wearily.

When Mrs. Cornelisse's megaphoned voice once again summoned the food carriers to the kitchen, my mother and Kirsten hurried off with the tub. When they returned, my mother seemed upset, but she wouldn't say why; I knew that she was worrying about Peter, as we still hadn't heard from him. She gave me my cup of porridge, then, as soon as we'd finished, she told me that she'd seen Susan.

"Did you tell her that I'm going to go over there?"

"Yes. I did tell her . . . but . . ."

"But what? What's the matter, Mum?"

She put her hand on mine. "Klara," she said gently. "Flora's ill."

A warmth rose in my chest. "Why didn't you tell me before?"

"Because I was worried that you wouldn't eat."

I stood up. "I must go and see her."

"I don't think you should," I heard my mother say, but I was already halfway across the front yard. As I got to the gate I saw Irene and Susan, with two other women, hurrying up the road, carrying Flora on a stretcher. Flora had got too hungry, I told myself. She just needed some extra food; I would give her some of mine. But as she was carried past us toward the hospital, I saw that her skin was gray, and that her body was twisted in pain beneath the thin sheet. It wasn't hunger that had done this to her. In distress, I ran back to my mother and asked her what had.

She explained that the previous night, Flora and Lena had found some cakes of *bungkil* in an outhouse and had eaten some. *Bungkil* was animal feed, made of flaked soya beans.

"Why would that have hurt Flora?" I demanded. "Soya beans are good."

My mother explained that *bungkil,* though fine for animals, can be poisonous to humans. Lena had eaten only a little and would recover, but Flora was very ill. I asked my mother if I could go into the hospital to be with her, but she said that Flora was too unwell. I must just wait, and pray that she would get better.

I prayed morning, noon, and night, stopping only when Susan came by to give us news. By the end of the first day Flora was barely conscious; by the end of the second day she had slipped into a coma. On the afternoon of the third day, my mother and I were inside our net, dozing. I heard a *tokeh* and began to count its croaks, hoping against hope to hear seven, but it stopped at six. I'd have to start all over again. *One . . . two . . . three . . .* I opened my eyes and saw Susan standing on the other side of our *kelambu.* In my half-asleep state I thought she was an angel.

I sat up, my heart pounding. "How is she? How's Flora?"

Susan didn't answer. She knelt down beside me. "The doctors did everything they could," she whispered through the net. "They did their very best for her—they tried so hard to make her better . . . I'm sorry, Klara."

As if in a dream, my mother and I went with Susan to Ampasiet Weg, where we found Irene, cradling Flora's china doll, Lottie. The doll's face was wet with her tears.

"I didn't know," Irene sobbed. "I didn't know that the *bungkil* was there or that she would ever have *eaten* it!" She clasped the doll to her, rocking back and forth.

The next morning we all stood beside Flora's small bamboo coffin as it was loaded onto a truck with five others; then the gate was opened and the vehicle drove out, toward the cemetery.

My mother and Susan were crying, heads bowed. Irene was standing a little way in front of us, staring at the gate. I went and stood beside her. I wanted to say something, but didn't know what.

"She was my best friend," I whispered after a moment. "I'll never like anyone as much as I liked Flora."

A tear slid down Irene's cheek. "You'll have other friends, Klara." She swallowed. "But please, don't forget my Flora."

"I won't," I vowed. "I'll never, ever forget her."

For the next few weeks we hardly saw Irene and Susan. Then one day Irene came to our house. She told me that she wanted to give me something of Flora's as a keepsake.

"It's just a small thing," she said as she handed it to me. It felt heavy in my palm.

"Thank you," I managed to whisper as, in the saddest possible way, the lizard became mine.

By the end of May, thanks to a very brave woman named Henny, who had smuggled in a radio, we knew that Hitler was dead and that Holland had been liberated. We knew that victory had been declared in Europe, and that the Allies had retaken the Philippines and Borneo and many of the Pacific islands. A new mood took hold in the camp. Everyone whispered of freedom, not *if*, but *when*.

In early June my mother and I were overjoyed to receive a card from Peter. It was from Tjimahi and had been written six weeks before. He'd ticked the usual prescribed phrases stating that he was "enjoying excellent health," had "good fresh food," and was being "treated well" by the Forces of Nippon. In his twenty-five "free" words he'd managed to convey that he was "fine," but that he "still missed Daddy and Wil." At the end he'd added, "Herman's been kind."

Anxiety clouded my mother's face. "So Daddy isn't in Tjimahi. Poor Peter—he was so sure that he was going to see him. Wil isn't there either. I must go and tell Irene."

"Mum, Herman *is* there. Shouldn't we tell Mrs. Dekker?"

My mother stared at me. "I am *not* prepared to," she said. "If it weren't for that hateful woman, Peter wouldn't *be* there." I felt a pang of guilt. My mother chewed her lip. "But I suppose we should, in all conscience, pass that on. But you can tell her, Klara."

"I will."

After Peter had been taken away, my mother had been unable even to look at Mrs. Dekker. Summoning all her self-control, she'd ignored her, fearing that if she didn't, she might strike her. But Marleen hadn't liked being ignored.

"*My* son had to go, Anneke!" she'd shouted after my mother. "Why should you have got away with those lies about yours?"

Now, while Mum hurried to see Irene, I went to look for

Mrs. Dekker. Unlike my mother, I didn't blame her for Peter being transported; I knew that he'd been transported because of me. And after the war, when everything was all right again, I would tell my mother what had happened in the guardhouse that day, and she would not only understand, she would forgive me, and it would all be forgotten. That was my plan.

I found Mrs. Dekker in her usual space in a corner of the living room. She was lying down, and through the *kelambu* I could see that her feet and ankles were swollen with the beginnings of hunger edema. "Mrs. Dekker."

She pushed herself upright. "Yes?" she said warily.

"Mrs. Dekker, we've just had a card from my brother. He's in Tjimahi, and he says that your Herman's there too. I expect you know that already, but just in case you didn't, I thought I ought to tell you."

She opened the net, staring at me, clearly surprised at my friendly tone. "I did know," she said faintly. "But . . . thank you."

"Peter said that Herman's being kind to him."

Mrs. Dekker smiled. "Good. I'm glad to hear that—he *is* a kind boy. If Herman sends me news of Peter, I'll tell you, Klara."

"Thank you, Mrs. Dekker." I walked away but, on an impulse, turned back. "Mrs. Dekker, I just want to say that it's not your fault that Peter was transported."

She didn't answer for a moment, fiddling with the collar of her shabby dress. "I shouldn't have done what I did," she said softly. "I feel bad about it, but I was . . . angry."

"It's all right. I just want you to know that I don't blame you."

She looked puzzled. "Well . . . I'm glad. Thank you, Klara."

In a while my mother returned from seeing Irene. She sat on her mattress, took out a grubby card that she had been saving, and began to write. "It's so good to know where Peter *is*, Klara." She gave me a radiant smile. "And to be able to send him a card is just wonderful after all our worry."

"Are you going to tell him about Flora?"

"No. It'll make him too sad. We'll tell him when he's safely back with us, which, let's pray, won't be long now."

"I *do* pray for that." My mother could have had no idea how fervently. One afternoon toward the end of June, Louisa ran into the house.

"Sonei's gone!" she screamed. "He's gone. Sonei has GONE!!!" As we gathered round, Louisa explained that it was to do with the coming end of the war. "Isn't it wonderful?"

Ina sniffed. "I don't believe it. Our hopes have been dashed often enough before."

As for the war supposedly ending, we had no idea whether or not this was true, because our radio had been discovered. Henny, who had smuggled it in, had been tied to the chair. We'd managed to get a little water to her when the guards weren't looking. Even so, she'd died on the evening of the fourth day.

"It wasn't a punishment," Kirsten had said angrily. "It was an execution."

A few days after this, Greta's grandmother, Mrs. Moonen, hurried into the house. "I've just seen a new officer by the gate," she said breathlessly. "He's called Sakai, and he's Sonei's replacement. Someone told me that Sonei's been made a captain and has been transferred. That's why we haven't seen him— because he really *has* gone!"

A cry of unadulterated joy went up.

That night there were celebrations throughout Tjideng. Some women wept with happiness; others were so euphoric that they decided to go *gedekking*. They went to the northwest corner, right away from the gate. We heard afterward that they'd been in such a happy frame of mind that they didn't trade in the usual terrified silence but in an abandoned way, with conversation and laughter. Then the laughter had abruptly stopped.

We learned that while the women were still at the *gedék*, Sonei, who had been in town celebrating his promotion, returned and caught them by surprise. At gunpoint he marched five of them back to the guardhouse, where he beat them, then locked them in the interrogation room.

The next day the group leaders went through the camp with their megaphones and ordered all last night's *gedekkers* to report to the gate. No one came out of the houses. During evening *tenko*, one of the guards, a Korean called Oohara, advised Louisa to get volunteers to come out in order to appease Sonei, who was becoming *"gila"*—crazy.

We went out into the front yard to see what was happening. At first we saw a dozen women standing at the gate, but we were then told that Sonei had said it wasn't enough. Within an hour there were seventy, but he was still not satisfied. By midnight five hundred women stood there in the moonlight, motionless and silent. They were prepared to suffer for something they had not done, in order to save those who had.

Sonei, in his metal-tipped boots, strode up and down the rows. He stopped in front of one woman, pulled her out of the line, then began to slap and punch her. He picked out five others. With his guards, he marched these six women to the house opposite ours, which served as the air-raid building. He made them line up on the verandah, where, in the light from the one electric bulb that hung from the ceiling, I could see their terrified faces. The monkeys were screaming, as if they knew that something dreadful was happening.

"What's he going to do?" my mother murmured.

"I don't know," Louisa answered. "But it's going to be bad."

Sonei started haranguing the women in broken Malay. He called them "ungrateful sluts" who had dared to disobey the "divine will" of His Imperial Majesty, the emperor. He pushed the nearest woman onto her knees. She crouched down and covered her head with her hands, but he began to beat her with the butt of his rifle.

"Our Father," I heard Ina murmur, *"which art in Heaven . . ."*

As other women joined in the prayer, Sonei rained down his blows. We could hear them thudding against her body. Twice the woman staggered to her feet, but this only seemed to enrage him all the more. He threw her onto a chair and took a knife out of his belt. He grabbed her by the hair and pulled back her head. The blade glinted as he held it to her throat.

"My God," Kirsten breathed.

". . . and deliver us from evil."

Sonei sawed at the woman's scalp. As blood streamed down her cheeks there were screams and gasps. I covered my face with my hands.

My mother was sobbing. "If there's nothing we can do, surely we shouldn't watch."

"Yes, we *should*," Louisa shot back. "Because soon the war's going to end and then we'll tell the whole world what this devil did! We *must* watch—and remember!"

"How could we ever forget?" Kirsten wept as the woman fell to the floor for the final time.

Sonei beat and shaved the other women too. Then he ran down the front steps of the building. As he headed off toward the *dapur,* we all rushed forward to take the injured women to hospital. While we were doing this, Sonei was pushing over the drums containing the following morning's breakfast. Once the food was oozing over the ground, he went back to his villa, his work done.

This infamous night was Sonei's swan song. He left Tjideng before the sun came up. We never saw him again.

The next day the new officer, Lieutenant Sakai, took over. Almost immediately the atmosphere in the camp improved. We now had *tenko* only once a day, and over the next few weeks the rations increased, though not enough to prevent people from dying.

In mid-August Mrs. Dekker came to find me, walking with difficulty. She was holding a card. "I've heard from Herman. He says that Peter's fine."

I could have kissed her. "*Thank you,* Mrs. Dekker. I'll tell my mother."

"It's taken two months to get here," she explained. "He wrote it on June sixteenth. But I'm worried because in his free words he used the words 'I am going.'" When she showed the card to me, my euphoria died. *Aku pergi.* "I think he was trying to warn me that they might be transported again," Mrs. Dekker said. "Let's hope not," she added anxiously.

"Yes." I imagined Peter struggling to breathe in an overcrowded train.

Mrs. Dekker sighed. "This war is horrible, isn't it?"

"Horrible," I echoed.

"But the end *is* coming—very soon, they say."

"I pray for it, Mrs. Dekker."

What we couldn't have known was that the end had already come, a week before. In a final act of cruelty, we hadn't been told.

One morning in late August we assembled on Laan Trivelli in the usual way. To my surprise, we weren't made to line up, and Mrs. Cornelisse told us that we didn't have to bow. Then Lieutenant Sakai, standing on a stage, started to talk. Sounding subdued, he told us, through the translator, that this would be our last-ever *tenko*. A bewildered murmur rippled through the crowd. Sakai told us that the emperor had ordered the cessation of hostilities.

"A new type of bomb was dropped on my country," he went on. "It has resulted in hundreds of thousands of victims. His Imperial Majesty has therefore decided to end the war. You are now free."

We stood there, a crowd of emaciated women and children, and stared at Sakai. A new kind of bomb had been dropped on Japan and had killed hundreds of thousands of people? We could not begin to understand this. We understood only *tenko* and beatings and filthy latrines; we understood bedbugs and bamboo coffins, and fifty centimeters. We remained silent, too stunned to speak. Then a murmur started among us. A growing elation took hold. Someone started to sing the Wilhelmus, hesitantly at first, then with more strength; and now, with a gathering passion, others joined in. Someone brought out a Dutch flag; how she'd concealed it, I had no idea, but there it was, being openly waved—proof that the war really *was* over. A few Britishwomen were singing "God Save the King." Ina was crying; Corrie was kissing the twins and twirling them. They were laughing, heads thrown back.

My mother gripped my arm. She was smiling but her eyes glittered with tears. "Klara, we're going to go and find Peter. We'll go to Tjimahi, right now—this very minute. And after we've found him, we're going to find Daddy. They'll be *so* glad to see us! Come, my darling—we must go!" She hurried off toward the gate. As I followed her, I fretted that we should at least go back to the house and get our things; then I remembered that we didn't *have* any things. And how would we travel, given that we had no money? Nor were we strong enough to undertake a journey—my mother weighed forty kilos and could barely walk, plus we had no idea where my father was. And if Peter *had* been transported again, then God knew where he might be.

I was about to try to reason with my mother when Sakai spoke again; we all turned to look at him.

"Ladies," he said, "for the time being you must stay inside the camp. It is too dangerous for you out there. If you leave, you could be killed."

Here was more startling and bewildering news. The war with Japan was over, so if the Japanese no longer wanted to kill us, then who *did*?

Irene and Susan came through the crowd toward us. My mother told them of her plans to leave.

"Annie, please stay," Irene insisted quietly. "For the moment at least." She put her hand on my mother's arm.

"But I want my son and my husband." My mother was crying. "The war's over and now I want them back—I *want* them!"

"Of course you do." Irene touched my mother's face. "But Annie, it's not safe to look for them now . . ."

I soon understood why. We had been so cut off from the world that we had no idea that nationalism, encouraged by the Japanese, had taken hold and that an Independent Republic of Indonesia had been declared. Gangs of young men, called *pemuda*, were patrolling the streets with bamboo spears and saber-like swords shouting, "*Merdéka! Freedom!*" as they hunted for Dutchmen to kill. I tried to comprehend the idea that the people of Java, among whom we'd lived for so long, would now happily hack us to pieces. So although the war had ended, we were still confined to our filthy and overcrowded camp.

At the very end of August we had a second postcard from Peter. Like Herman's, it had been written on 16 June. In his free words Peter said that he had "enough to eat" and was keeping his "head up," but he made no mention of being moved. Perhaps he hadn't been transported after all.

My mother pored over the card as though studying runes. "He's fine." She looked up at me. "He has his malaria pills and his net and enough food, and now that the war's over, he'll soon be back with us."

One day I looked up and saw Australian bombers flying over—the first Allied planes that we'd seen since the start of the war. As we waved, the sky was suddenly filled with red, white, and blue parachutes that drifted down, like petals, square containers swinging from their cords. Within a short time these boxes had been picked up and brought into the camp; tins of food were opened, though we were repeatedly warned by the hospital staff not to overeat in our emaciated state.

Our Anglo stoves were returned; having no firewood, we gleefully ripped down panels of the *gedék* and began to burn those until Sakai arrived and made everyone stop. He warned that because of the rebels we needed the camp walls. So now we had to shelter behind these once hated screens as the gangs of *pemuda* rampaged around us. At night I'd hear gunfire and screams.

Some women decided to take the risk and left Tjideng, but most of us believed that we were better off where we were. In the camp we were not only protected and fed, but we could more easily find out the fate of our loved ones. Now the joy at the ending of the war turned to fear and grief as the death lists from the men's camps began to arrive.

The Red Cross lists were put up every day, at noon, and we'd all rush to the gate to check them. During this ordeal my mother and I would hold hands. First, we'd scan the *Alive* list, then, with thudding hearts, the list headed *Dead*. All around us we saw wives and children crumpling into sobs. Some just covered their faces and remained where they stood. Others turned and walked slowly away. In early September my mother and I were in the house when Susan came to see us. She was holding a letter, and for the first time since Flora's death, she was smiling. "My papa's alive!" Fighting back tears, Susan explained that her mother had received a card from the Red Cross. Wil had been sent to work on the Burma-Thailand Railway and was now recuperating in Singapore.

"Mummy started a letter to him, but she simply couldn't find

the words to tell him about . . ." Susan's voice trembled. "So . . .
I wrote it, and I'm just taking it to the office to be sent to him—
but I just wanted to tell you the news."

"It's wonderful news," my mother said. "But how strange,
to think that Wil was so far from Java."

Susan nodded. "All the time we thought he was in Tjimahi,
he was a thousand miles to the north. We're just so relieved that
he's survived; but he has to stay in Singapore for another six
weeks, as he's only a hundred ten pounds." I tried to imagine
the hefty Wil reduced to a husk, and failed. We all strolled out
together to the front yard. Susan said goodbye, then turned out
of the gate and stepped onto Laan Trivelli. She walked a couple
of paces, then stopped. Then she lifted her hand to her head, as
if to smooth down the thick blond hair that was no longer there.
As we followed her gaze we saw a tall figure walking toward
her.

"Arif," my mother murmured. "It's *Arif*, Klara." She smiled.
"He's come to find her."

"Of course he has," I said.

Arif's face lit up as he drew closer to Susan. Now they were
standing a few inches apart. She was staring at him with a look
of exhilarated bewilderment.

"There you are," we heard him say. "I've been looking for
you." He handed her the tiffin box he was carrying. "But you
must eat, Susan. You're so thin. You must eat."

Then he put his arms around her and she burst into tears.

Eighteen

On Monday Klara had to take Jane to hospital to see her specialist, so I took a little time off, walking along the coastal path to
Carne and back. As I looked at the sea I saw Adam, in his boat,
taking in his catch. It struck me that Klara's family knew almost
nothing of what she had been through. She'd coped with her
memories in silence, and despite her sadness had made a good
life for herself. I needed to do the same.

The following morning I returned to the farm. As I walked
down the track I saw Klara closing the shop door. She smiled
at me.

"Jenni, could you do something for me?"

"Sure—how can I help?"

"I need to cut the rest of the pumpkins and bring them up
here; would you give me a hand?"

"Of course." I put my bag down, then followed Klara across

the yard into the walled garden. I enjoyed just being outside with her, away from the intense atmosphere of the interviews. It was so still that I could hear only the drone of a bumblebee as it drifted by.

"It's always quiet in here," Klara remarked, as though she'd read my mind. "You can barely even hear the sea." She took her secateurs out of her apron pocket and cut the pumpkins off their vines. I lifted them into the wheelbarrow and pushed and pulled it back up to the yard.

"Thank you," Klara said as we unloaded them and put them on a table by the shop door. She wiped the earth off the skins with a corner of her apron. "There are lots of children here for half term."

"I saw some arriving when I took Honor to the station."

"They go trick-or-treating, so all these will sell. Now, which would you say is the biggest?"

The ginger cat was in the yard again, and this time it followed me up the stairs to Klara's flat, then curled up beside me, purring.

Klara made coffee. "I'm sorry I couldn't see you yesterday, but Jane has regular appointments in Truro and I always take her to them, as her son works in London."

I stroked the cat. "You're a very good friend to her."

"She's been a wonderful friend to me."

"And did you ever talk to her about Java? Given how close you've been?"

Klara shook her head. "Very little. I always felt I couldn't talk about it to anyone who hadn't been through it themselves." She got down the Delft crockery, opened a tin, and shook some biscuits onto a plate.

"I've had a lovely email about you from Gill," I said as Klara switched on the kettle. "And I'd like to get some reminiscences of you from Jane and was wondering when we might do that."

"She's coming to Adam's art show tomorrow evening, so you could do it there." She spooned coffee into the brown jug. "You are coming, I hope?"

"I will come, thanks—but that'll be my last night. I'm leaving the morning after."

Her face fell. "Well . . . I shall miss talking to you, Jenni."

"I'll miss you too, Klara. I feel as though I've known you for years—which in a way, after all these interviews, I have." I collected the tray of coffee things and put it on the table while Klara brought the jug.

"But there's something I want to show you," I said. "You don't use a computer, do you?"

"I never have done, and I feel too old to start now." She handed me my coffee. "Why do you ask?"

"Because there are a number of websites about the camps. There's one in particular that's about Tjideng."

"Gill did tell me about these websites, some time ago, but I told her that I didn't want to look at them," Klara sighed. "I find it hard enough dealing with my own memories, without having my mind full of other people's."

"I can understand that. But there's a memory of you on it, Klara. I think it's by a schoolfriend of yours, Edda. Can I show it to you?"

Klara's hand shook as she poured the coffee. "Yes."

I took the laptop out of its bag, opened it, then looked at the screenshot I'd saved of the page. I handed it to Klara. She balanced the computer on her lap, then reached for the pair of glasses on the table. She put them on and peered at the screen.

"Yes," she said after a few moments. "That's the Edda I knew; she gives her maiden name, Smits. She's living in Hilversum, it says here . . ."

"Yes."

"And that she has children and grandchildren." Klara removed her glasses. She was quiet for a few moments. "Thank you for showing me this, Jenni. It's good to know that she survived."

"But . . . do you remember the incident that Edda describes?"

Klara didn't speak for a moment. "Of course I remember it. I could never forget it."

A silence fell. "Klara, what was the terrible dilemma that you faced?"

She closed her eyes for a moment. "I was put in a position where I had to make a choice—one that has tormented me ever since." She looked at me. "But I'm not ready to talk about it, Jenni, even to you."

The wooden box was open. Inside it I could see the recipe book, the folded handkerchief, and some airmail letters. There was also a large brown envelope and something wrapped in white cloth. Following my gaze, Klara took this out and unwrapped it, and suddenly the lizard gleamed in my hand. I ran my finger along it from nose to tail, and imagined Irene giving it to Klara after poor Flora had died.

"It *is* beautiful," I said.

Klara nodded. "I felt guilty for ever having wanted it. Sometimes I just hold it and think about Flora, and what her friendship meant to me. But how I wish that it had never become mine!"

I handed the lizard back and Klara wrapped it carefully and returned it to the box. She took out the brown envelope and passed it to me. I lifted the flap, the glue of which was shiny and brittle, then gently pulled out a small painting. It was a portrait of a little boy with sun-bleached hair and laughing green eyes in a too-thin face.

"Peter," I murmured.

Klara nodded. "A few days before he was transported."

"Did Susan paint it?"

"Yes; she'd somehow managed to conceal her box of watercolors from the soldiers. But she caught Peter's expression exactly."

I studied it for a few moments, then handed it back. "Klara . . . why did Peter die?" In the silence that followed I could hear the tick of the clock. "*Was* it malaria?"

"It wasn't," she answered, "though that was what our mother had feared most." She touched the box. "Jenni, you told me, when we started this memoir, that I could choose how honest I wanted to be." I nodded. "But I still don't know. And now we've got to this point, I'm trying to decide whether to tell you the simple, 'on the surface' story about what happened to Peter, which would be easy, or the deeper, truer story, which will be agonizingly hard."

"Klara, it's *your* memoir. What you say—or don't say—is your decision." She slid the portrait back into its envelope, and I saw her struggling with herself. I didn't want her to feel pressured into telling me anything that she didn't want to. I glanced at my notes. "Perhaps we could talk about Arif. I was thinking how hard it must have been for him to recognize Susan."

"No. If you love someone, it's easy," Klara answered. "He

recognized her at once, but yes, he was shocked at her appearance."

"How had he known where to find her?"

Klara shook her head. "He'd had no idea where she was, or
if she was even alive. But the day the war ended, he began to
search for her."

"Wouldn't he have assumed that she was in Singapore?"

"No, because after the Jochens missed that ill-fated boat,
Susan had written to him, telling him that they would be staying
on Java. Then word spread that all the European women and
children had been rounded up and put in camps. Arif thought it
likely that Susan was in a camp in West Java. So he hitched a lift
to Bandung and went to Tjihapit, which was almost deserted.
He searched in Camp Karees, but she wasn't there. He got a
train to Batavia and went to camps Kramat and Grogol before
someone told him that Susan was probably in Tjideng."

"How long had it taken him to find her?"

"At least two weeks, I seem to remember, because without
any money, he'd had to walk everywhere. Often he'd had to
wait because the streets weren't safe—there were snipers on
every corner. He started carrying the red-and-white nationalist
flag, because by then the *pemuda* were killing not just Europeans
but any Indonesians they believed were pro-Dutch. But finally
Arif got to Tjideng. And as he went through the gate, the first
person he saw was Susan, walking toward him, a wraith."

Nineteen

Klara

It had been three and a half years since Susan last saw Arif. She'd had no idea if she'd ever meet him again. She told him about Flora; then, with my mother and me, she took him to see Irene.

We asked him about everyone at Sisi Gunung. Arif said that the Japanese had cut down most of the trees for fuel and then planted castor seeds, which the plantation workers had been forced to cultivate as *romusha*—forced labor. They'd survived by living off the land. Arif told us that our houses had been occupied by the Japanese, but that once they'd gone, both villas had been ransacked by a mob. I hated to think of our beloved home being looted and despoiled.

I asked Arif about our pets. He told me that Suliman and

Jasmine had looked after them for as long as they could, but that Ferdi had disappeared some months before.

"Peter will be sad," my mother murmured. "But we'll get him another rabbit. Or perhaps he'd like a dog. Yes, I think a little dog would be fun for him, don't you, Klara?"

"Yes," I agreed uncertainly. "What about my pony?" I asked Arif. He said that the Japanese had harnessed Sweetie for dragging logs, but that he hadn't seen him since the surrender. I felt tears sting my eyes.

My mother reached for my hand. "We'll search for him, Klara. Perhaps we'll find him."

"So are we going to go home?" I asked her. "To the plantation?"

"Maybe," Mum answered. "Though Daddy will have a *lot* to do there by the sounds of it; but we'll all help him, won't we?"

"Jaya will be glad to see Peter," Arif said. "He's really missed him. But where *is* Peter?"

"We have no idea," I answered.

My mother gave me a sharp look. "Of course we do, Klara." She turned to Arif. "Peter's in Tjimahi—a men and boys' camp, west of Bandung. We had a card from him not long ago, and he was fine."

I didn't like to remind my mother that Peter had written that card ten weeks before. I hadn't told her that he might be transported again. Now I just prayed that he'd soon return; it was awful having no news.

Nor was there any information about Dad. Every morning my mother and I steeled ourselves to look at the lists, and were amazed now to understand the scale of the transport—not just of soldiers but of civilian men. They had been in labor camps in

Burma, Sumatra, Borneo, and Manchuria. Many, we learned, had died aboard ships en route to Japan.

By mid-September we still hadn't heard. One morning we were standing by the gate when, to our surprise, we saw a Dutch pilot walk into the camp. He was the first Dutch serviceman we'd seen since the war started. He stared at the skeletal women and children who flocked to him, some of them bowing, as we still did, automatically, to anyone in uniform. The pilot told us that his name was Captain Arens and that his wife and young son were in Tjideng. He'd come to collect them in his seaplane, which was moored in the harbor. Someone rushed to find them, and when the man's wife and son ran to him and flung themselves into his arms, it was for most of us a bittersweet sight. But this man was so moved by our plight that he offered to take letters for us all, immediately, to post to Holland. We all rushed around looking for something to write on. My mother found a scrap of paper and a pencil stub and wrote a note to her parents saying that she and I were fine but that we were still waiting to hear about Hans and Peter.

By the time my grandmother received that note, we'd had news.

One day, in late September, my mother and I had gone to check the lists as usual, but as usual there was nothing.

"No news is good news," I intoned as we turned away. "No news is . . ." All at once the camp official came out of the office again, holding another list. As she pinned it up, my mother and I walked toward it. My mother reached for my hand and squeezed it, hard. Then I felt her fingers go loose.

Dead.

It was as though there was no other name.

Bennink.

My instant reaction was that it must be my father. But as we drew closer, we saw *P.H.* in front of it and, after it, *8 April 1935–10 Aug. 1945. Tjitjalengka.*

My mother's knees buckled. I held her—she felt so light—then we walked slowly away. With nowhere else to go, we went back to the house, closed the net around us, and let in the darkness of a life without Peter.

"I should have fought harder to keep him with us," she whispered.

"You did everything you could, Mum. You never gave up."

"I knew that I was fighting for his life. But I lost," she added bleakly. "I lost. But . . . why was he in Tjitjalengka?"

"He must have been transported there."

"Yes . . ." She blinked. "That would explain it. But I wonder what happened to him, Klara. We don't know what *happened* to him, do we? We don't know what happened to him or *why* he . . ."

Her thin body was convulsed by sobs that now turned into a keening cry that made my heart cave in. Then, as her weeping subsided, she began, as I knew she would, to blame Mrs. Dekker. She said that she *hated* her for what she had done. She would hate her until her dying day.

"If only I hadn't *upset* her that time," she wailed. "If I'd known where it would lead, I'd have kept my mouth *shut*."

"What Mrs. Dekker did was horrible, but—"

"It was *more* than horrible," she wept. "It was wicked; it was evil—she condemned my son to *die!*"

"No, Mummy. She didn't."

My mother stared at me through her tears. "Of course she

did, Klara. Without her interference he'd have stayed here, with us, and he would have survived." The logic of it, to my mother, was clear and unarguable.

"But it wasn't Mrs. Dekker's fault that Peter was transported."

"Of course it was her fault," my mother retorted angrily. "I don't know why you're arguing about it, Klara."

"Because . . ." I was on a precipice. I looked into the abyss, then jumped. "It was my fault," I whispered.

"What do you mean?" she demanded. "How? How *could* it be your fault?" She stared at me, her eyes red with weeping, then her expression cleared. "So you *did* tell them his age, that day."

"No. I didn't. That's not what I mean."

"What are you talking about, Klara?"

At last I told my mother what had happened in the guardhouse. The words came out in a torrent. "They questioned me for hours. Then they said that they were going to hurt me, and that I could choose. I thought they meant that I could choose whether I wanted to be burnt by cigarettes, or to have needles pushed under my nails, or to be hung by my wrists, any of which I would have preferred to—"

"To . . . what?" My mother looked confused.

I swallowed. "They said that they wouldn't transport Peter. I was so relieved and elated. I thanked them, again and again; I was almost crying with happiness. Then they said that instead, they'd punish *you*. They told me that they'd tie you to a chair for five days, maybe more. If I didn't want this to happen to you, they would transport Peter. My choice, they said."

My mother gasped. "So you chose for him to go?" I nodded.

"But you should have chosen me. You should have chosen *me*," she repeated.

"How could I, knowing that you'd die?"

"No. I'd have borne it."

"You wouldn't. Mrs. Tromp died after two days in the chair; Henny died after four. And you were already so *frail*, Mum. How could I have let them do that to you?"

My mother's mouth twisted with distress. "How could *you* have let them send Peter *away?*"

Tears pricked my eyes. "Because I believed that it was the lesser of those two evils."

I cast my mind back to that day. As I'd waited in the guard-house, I'd thought of Peter trying to fend for himself among hundreds of men and teenage boys. I thought of him being mistreated or abused, or not having enough to eat, or being cold at night, or getting malaria again, with no one to care for him. But then my mind would swing back to the image of my mother, tied to a chair in the blazing sun.

"Mummy, I didn't know what to do. Then Kochi said that if I *didn't* choose one, they would do *both*. Then he left me for two hours to make up my mind."

In that time I'd convinced myself that Peter would be all right. The war would surely soon end—within weeks, people were saying. I told myself that there might be some kind men in the camp who would take pity on these young boys and help them. I even persuaded myself that my father was there. Then the soldiers returned, and I gave them my answer. I prayed that I'd never have to tell my mother what it was.

———

When Herman Dekker returned to Tjideng in mid-October, he came to see Mum and me. We sat in a quiet corner of the house as he gave her Peter's suitcase. She opened it and took out my brother's shabby old teddy bear, then his jacket. She laid the jacket on her lap and ran her hands over the cloth. She did up the buttons. Then, clutching the bear, she asked Herman to tell her what had happened to her son.

Herman put his hands on his thin knees, as if bracing himself. He was only twelve himself and was visibly upset. He explained that in Tjimahi, Peter had been treated reasonably well. He'd been there for twelve weeks, and things were bearable— not least because their camp leader had done his best to make sure that the boys had enough food.

"If we'd been able to stay there, Peter might have been all right," Herman continued quietly. "But in July we were transported again."

My mother looked bewildered. "Why? The war was almost over."

He shrugged. "It seems mad, but the Japs had started to build a new railway line between Tjitjalengka and Madjalaya. In July they transported hundreds of us Tjimahi boys to work on it. We were in the middle of the jungle, living in a camp that was just bamboo sheds with no running water and almost nothing to eat. We had to work all day in the sun, just in our shorts, with no shirts or hats. Most of us didn't even have shoes, let alone the boots and trousers we should have had to do that kind of work."

"What kind of work?" my mother asked.

"We had to move stones away from where the tracks were to be laid. That's what we did, all day," Herman went on, "just lifting stones from one place to another. I was working next to

Peter, and he was managing all right—he was cheerful, even. He kept saying that it was an 'adventure.' Then one day he lifted up this big stone, and . . ." Herman closed his eyes. "There was a cobra." My hand flew to my mouth.

"But . . . Peter would have known what to *do*," Mum protested quietly. "We'd always taught our children to keep absolutely still."

"He did, Mrs. Bennink. I'd seen the snake too, and I froze. We were just waiting for it to move away. But then this other boy, Markus, picked up a stone, and before we could stop him, he'd hurled it at the snake. Then I heard Peter scream. It had bitten him on his hand, which immediately started to swell. There was a doctor in the camp, so I ran to get him, and he put a tourniquet on Peter's wrist to try and stop the venom from spreading, and we carried him back to the shed. But after a while the doctor took me to one side and he said . . ." Herman's eyes glimmered with tears. "We kept talking to Peter as though everything was fine, but I think he knew that it wasn't; he was becoming ill, and there was nothing we could do except . . ." Herman lowered his head. A tear fell onto his lap, darkening the pale green of his shorts.

"Did you stay with him?" my mother asked softly.

Herman nodded. "I didn't leave him, Mrs. Bennink. Not for one second."

"Thank you," she whispered.

"The doctor said prayers for him, and we sang a hymn . . . and then we . . ." He put his hand in his pocket, pulled out a piece of paper with some pencil markings on it, and gave it to my mother.

"His grave?" she whispered.

"Yes," Herman answered. "I made a map, so that you'll be able to find it one day. It's marked with a big stone, with his name scratched onto it." My mother stared at the map, her face blank with grief. "A few days later we were told that the Japs had surrendered and we were trucked back to Tjimahi. We had to stay there for another month, because of the rebels, then a group of us were brought here to Tjideng. I'm so sorry, Mrs. Bennink."

My mother gave him a half smile. "I always knew that he wouldn't come back. Deep down, I knew. But thank you for being such a kind friend to him, Herman."

As Herman left I wondered why he'd been so good to Peter. Had he found out what his mother had done and felt bad about it? Or was he just a decent boy, trying to do the right thing?

"You *should* have chosen me," Mum said again one morning as we were sitting on the steps at the front of the house.

I looked ahead, afraid to meet her gaze. "I didn't, because I knew that you'd die."

"*No.* My love for my children would have kept me alive!" She gestured at the emaciated women coming and going on Laan Trivelli. "Many of *these* women should have died; but they refused to die, because they *had* to stay alive, for their children, and I would have stayed alive for mine!" Her face was tight with pain. "So that's why you wouldn't tell me what had happened in the guardhouse that day."

"Yes. Because I knew that you'd have asked to be punished instead."

My mother put her hands on her knees. I could see every bone in them. "If I had known that Peter would live, I would have gone through the punishment—sacrificed myself for him, if necessary. But you didn't give me that choice. And I think that you chose for Peter to go because you needed me, Klara!"

"No," I whispered, appalled. "That's not true."

"I looked after you, and so you were more afraid of me dying than Peter."

"No! I didn't want *either* of you to die!"

My mother shook her head. "Poor Hans—he'll never get over it. *I'll* never get over it. *Never.*"

"Nor will I," I said fiercely. "Especially if you're going to *blame* me! You're making me feel as though I *killed* Peter!"

My mother stared at me; the color had drained from her face. I had shocked her, and shocked myself.

After that we didn't talk about Peter anymore. But as the days went by, I searched my conscience and wondered whether what she'd said might have been true.

I *had* been terrified of losing my mother. It was what all we children in the camps dreaded most. Had that been part of my thinking, subconsciously, when I chose Peter? I didn't know. I just wished, with all my heart, that I'd never had to *make* such a choice.

Twenty

"I've never told anyone what really happened," Klara told me. "Not even Harold. My family knows only that Peter died of snakebite. They've never known what led up to it, or my role in it."

"You were put in an impossible, agonizing situation, Klara—having to choose between your mother and your brother."

"Yes. This was how they tortured me—it was mental torture, and the pain is still with me to this day. In her grief and anger, my mother blamed me. And that is what you and I have in common, Jenni."

"It's not the same! You did what you believed was for the best. *I* did what I knew to be wrong."

"You hadn't meant any harm, Jenni. You were just a confused, angry little girl. But it happened a long time ago, and it does seem sad that there's still such a gulf between you and your mother."

"There always will be," I said stubbornly.

"Not necessarily. You could change that, if you wanted to."

I shrugged. "Did things change for you and your mother?"

"Not for a very long time. She could hardly bear to speak to me, or be with me. She said that I'd promised to help her keep Peter with us, and had then had him transported, behind her back. She told me that it was the most dreadful betrayal—that it was unforgivable."

Unforgivable . . .

"Klara, is that why you said sorry to Peter, the night before he left?"

"Yes—in case I never saw him again. But I believed that the chance of him returning was far higher than the chance of my mother surviving the punishment. But she didn't see it that way. Which made it impossible for her to accept what I had done."

"It must have been hard, just being with her after that."

"It was very hard. Sometimes I'd catch her looking at me with pain and bewilderment and I'd feel accused all over again."

"I know *exactly* how that must have felt, Klara. But these must have been such dark days for you, because you'd already lost Flora, which was bad enough, and then Peter. You must have felt that you'd lost your mother too."

"In a way I had, which is why I felt for you, Jenni, for what you'd been through."

"But how did you cope, day to day?"

"By distancing myself from her. I helped Corrie with the twins, and I played with Lena and Greta. I talked to Ina and Kirsten and spent time with Susan and Irene."

"Did Irene help you?"

"She tried. She spoke to my mother and told her that I couldn't have known what lay ahead. She said that she herself would have made the same choice. Then she warned my mother that she had lost one child, but if she wasn't careful, she'd lose both her children."

I felt tears sting my eyes. "That's what happened to *my* mother."

Klara nodded sympathetically. "But, Jenni, you could break down the wall that's between you."

"No. It's too late."

"As long as you're both alive, it *isn't* too late. And surely your mother must wish for that too."

"She probably does, but we don't know *how* to be with each other, so we keep each other at a distance. In any case, it's still there, the knowledge that I was at fault."

"If you could only forgive yourself, Jenni. After all these years, isn't it time?"

I shook my head. "I'll carry it with me all through my life." I swallowed. "But did your relationship with your mother ever recover?"

"In some respects, over time, though it was never the same. I knew that if she had my father back, this would help her. But we still didn't know where he was, or if he was even alive. Then, in mid-October, my mother received a card from the Red Cross. It informed her that in December 1943 Hans Roland Bennink, born Rotterdam, 1912, had arrived in Japan."

"You must have been . . . stunned, to think that that was where he'd been."

"We were astounded. We were so relieved that he'd at least

survived the journey there, because by then we knew that so many men hadn't. Now we could only pray that two years later, he was still alive. And a few days after that, I went to the camp office, as I did each morning, to check whether there was any mail for us—and I was given this."

Klara reached again into the wooden box and brought out a thick airmail letter.

I looked at the neat, looping hand. "This was what you were waiting for."

"Yes. With a cry of joy I ran with it to my mother, and she opened it with trembling hands."

"May I look at it?"

Klara passed it to me. "Of course."

The sky-blue paper was brittle with age and was stamped *Manila*. At the top of the first page Klara's father had drawn a four-leaf clover. There were six pages, closely written on both sides. It was in Dutch.

"Let me translate it for you," Klara said, so I handed the letter back to her and she put on her glasses then began to read.

My darling Anneke,

I have been in Manila since the 5th September but it's only now, six weeks later, that I'm strong enough to be able to hold a pen and write to you.

How are you, my darling—and our sweet children? Every minute of the day I pray that I will soon get a letter from you telling me that you are all in good health.

I am in a tented camp here; the food is good and there is lots of it, and I gain a little more strength every day. We do exercises to rebuild our muscles and to pass the time while we wait to be airlifted out. The most frail POWs go first, and so I, being "healthy," must wait, which is frustrating, as I long to be reunited with you and with our darling Klara and Peter. I've been out of my mind with worry about the turmoil on Java, and every minute I pray that you are all safe and well. It's impossible to believe that it is nearly three years since I saw the three of you, spoke to you, held you in my arms, all of which I long to do again soon! But let me now tell you what happened to me—the bizarre journey that I went on—after I left Sisi Gunung.

The truck took us to Bandung, to Tjimahi, where we stayed for five weeks. We then went to another camp called Adek, where we stayed for two months; then in mid-May we were told, to our amazement, that we would be going to Japan. At the end of August we went to Batavia, where we were held in a large school. In late September we sailed for Singapore on the Makassar Maru. *There were two thousand men in the hold of that boat—Ralph Dekker was one of them, and we were glad to have each other's company. On Singapore we had to build an airstrip, in the blistering heat. It was hard doing such physical work on such small rations, and some of our group died.*

In November we boarded the Maru Shichi, *which was to take us to Japan. It was part of an eight-ship convoy, and once again, we were packed in like sardines. There was no way for us to wash, and the toilets were a pair of crates that hung over the side; you had to hold on for dear life or get swept away!*

After three weeks we reached Formosa, where we were allowed to wash ourselves on deck with buckets of seawater.

But as we set sail again, the convoy was attacked by Chinese planes. Our boat escaped damage, but two of the other ships were sunk, and we took on survivors. Then, just before we reached Japan, we hit a typhoon. It was terrible sliding around in the hold as the ship pitched and tossed in mountainous seas. We survived that ordeal only to find that we were now freezing because in Japan it was winter and most of us were just in a vest and thin trousers. We sailed along the coast, then finally, on 3 December, we docked at Moji on the island of Kyushu in southern Japan. It was then that a sergeant told us that we were going to work in a mine. We were astounded; we had no experience of mining. At least it would be warm, one of the prisoners pointed out grimly as we stood there, freezing. Some poor lads were too weak even to stand. They just lay down in the snow.

The Japs made us walk to the train station, dragging our bags. We tried to help the sick as much as we could, by letting them hang on our shoulders, and so we marched to the railway station in this pitiful state. If you stopped even for a moment, a Jap would run up to you and hit you with the butt of his rifle. Some boys were in such a bad way that they lay down and screamed that they wanted to die, but we lifted them up and told them to think of their families. And so we somehow dragged ourselves to the station and were put on a train.

For once we were glad to be packed together like cattle, because that at least created heat. We traveled until we reached a small mining town called Miata. From the station we had to walk for half an hour before we reached a camp. Our beds were just thin mats on the floor. There was no *heating, and we were all so cold, despite our blankets, that we slept in our clothes. That first day many men died, and every day after that a few more died, from exhaustion, dysentery, and pneumonia. By now there were 400 men left out of our original 500.*

We had been told that we would be working in a mine near the camp. We each had our photo taken, holding a number, and were also fingerprinted, like criminals. We were treated like criminals and were severely punished for breaking any of the many rules. A single misdeed by anyone and the whole camp suffered terribly, including "hunger days," when men simply died. But I was determined to live so that I could see you and our darling children again.

I keep wondering how much Peter and Klara have grown. Has Peter still got the Spitfire that I made him? If not, tell him I'll make him another one when we are back at our home, which I pray has survived this terrible war.

In December we started work in the Nioroski mine, which was midway between Hiroshima and Nagasaki. We had to walk there every day, in the snow. They gave us an overall to wear with a miner's hat that had a little lamp on it. Then you stepped into a mine car and moved down a long deep shaft that was pitch black. Once we'd gone about 400 meters underground, we had to walk in single file for two kilometers. I kept thinking of a book I read when I was a boy, Journey to the Center of the Earth, *because it was just like that, with some tunnels going up, and some going deeper down. Finally we came to a tunnel that was a dead end, and this was where we were to work, pickaxing the coal. The tunnels didn't have enough props, and several times*

*the ceilings collapsed. One time there was a very bad cave-in
and two guards and five prisoners were killed, one of them,
I'm very sorry to say, Ralph Dekker, and this will be very
hard for Marleen and Herman. But this hellhole is where
I toiled for seven months. The rations were so poor that we
were getting thinner and thinner. They were just going to
work us until our bodies gave out. Then one day we were told
to work in another mine, the Ibigizachi, which was nearer to
our quarters. I remember on 6 August we felt huge vibrations
in the mine, and a lot of shaking and disturbance. We
assumed that it had been an earthquake. It wasn't. It was the
first atomic bomb being dropped on Hiroshima.*

*The end came a few days afterward when we were called
to tenko and a Japanese officer told us that Japan had
surrendered. He said that we were free but had to stay in the
camp until the U.S. military took over. During the weeks
afterward we were fed from the air, as American planes
came over and dropped crates of food. Then one day we were
taken by truck to Nagasaki. My darling, the sight of that
place will haunt me for the rest of my life. It was just a flat,
smoking landscape of vast emptiness, with only a few steel
columns still standing. We could not imagine the kind of
bombs that had been able to do this, and even when we were
told that these had been "atomic" bombs, we had no idea
what that meant.*

*And then it was the beginning of the end. Or, as I hope,
the beginning of a new beginning. At the harbor we were
taken through various buildings that had been erected by the
American army. We had to get rid of our clothes and shoes,
which were to be burned, and were given military clothing.*

We were then taken aboard the U.S. warship the Renville, *where we got our first civilized meal. It was only ordinary bread, but to us it was like delicious cake!*

We were flown here to Manila, where we are being given the treatment necessary to restore us to health. Many of us were half blind because of malnutrition. But we have yeast and eggs every day, and my sight is now improving, enough to be able to write to you at last.

Forgive me, darling, this letter has become a confessional, the words spilling out of me; but I'm so worried because I've no idea what has happened to you and the children while I've been away. I just hope and pray that you were able to stay at home, in safety. So please write to me, reassuring me that you are all fine, just as soon as you can. Two weeks ago the Red Cross gave us preprinted cards with which we could request information about our families. I lodged a card for you, Peter, and Klara, and these will be sent to Batavia, where any information that they have will be printed on it, and it will then be returned to me. So I hope to get good news of you all before long.

Annie, give both the children a big hug from their daddy and tell them that I love them so much. And you, my dearest wife; I want to hold you in my arms and never let you go. And if I have somehow survived, it was only because I wanted to stay alive in order to make you and our darling children happy.

With tender embraces, your loving husband,
Hans

Twenty-one

Klara

I wept to think of what my father had been through. I regarded it as a miracle that he had survived. My mother wrote back and broke the news about Peter to him. I had asked her not to tell him about my role in what happened, as I wanted to explain this to him face-to-face. She agreed. She gave him a brief account of our life in the camps. She recounted what had happened to the Jochens and to Flora. Finally she told my father that we would wait for him in Tjideng, where our lives were improving daily.

The Americans, who were in a caretaking role until the Dutch could return, supplied us with food and drinking water. They had also brought in a huge open-air cinema screen. One warm evening five hundred children sat cross-legged on Laan Trivelli—Corrie and I each had a twin on our lap—and as night fell, we all watched *Snow White*. For many of us it was the first film we'd ever seen, and I was enchanted by those magical images, glowing against the starlit sky. We saw other films too—*The Wizard of Oz* was one that I'll never forget. This entertainment was a welcome distraction from the increasing stress of the Bersiap uprising, which was now raging on Java. In a bewildering reversal, the Allies had ordered the Japanese to stay where they were and protect the people in the camps from the nationalist rebels.

"So here we are," Kirsten grumbled one morning, "liberated but not free; in peacetime but still at war, being protected by the very people who, until recently, starved and beat us." She put an imaginary gun to her temple at the absurdity of our situation.

"Do you think we'll *ever* get out of this dump?" Ina asked. "And if so, what will happen to us? Will we be able to go back to *tempo doeloe*?"

"To the good old days?" Kirsten translated. "I don't see how we can—those days are *gone*."

"I think we will," Mrs. Moonen countered, "once the Dutch come back and reestablish the old order."

"Well, they'd better hurry up and do it before the *pemuda* kill us all," Kirsten groused.

No European now dared venture onto the streets, especially after dark. One night a huge mob armed with bamboo spears and *kléwangs*—saber-like swords—made their way up Laan Trivelli screaming, *"Merdéka! Merdéka!"* As we all cowered inside our houses, it sounded like *Murder! Murder!* Suddenly I heard a splintering sound.

"The *gedék*!" Corrie screamed. She hugged the twins tighter to her. "They're tearing down the *gedék*!"

As the *pemuda* got closer we huddled together, the women shielding the children with their bodies, crying and whimpering. Many were praying. Then I heard shots and Lieutenant Sakai shouting. He and his soldiers were firing rounds into the air, which finally made the gang disperse. We slowly emerged, shaking with shock.

"To think what we've survived these last three years," Ina said grimly. "And now this!" She shook her fist at the sky. "Haven't we suffered *enough*, Lord? I'm losing patience with you here!"

It was little comfort to be told that Batavia was calm compared with the bloodbath that was taking place in East and Central Java. In one atrocity the *pemuda* slaughtered a hundred Dutch women and children as they tried to leave their camp in Surabaya. The conflict had become an orgy of killing in which all Europeans, *Belanda Indos,* Chinese, Japanese, and pro-Dutch Indonesians were targeted.

By now the talk was no longer of *tempo doeloe* but of repatriation.

"But Holland is in ruins," Ina said as we sat under a tamarind tree. "How can we go back there?"

"Because for most of us there's nowhere else," Kirsten remarked.

My mother, who was a little calmer since my father's letter, agreed with Kirsten. "When we've been reunited with Hans we'll go back to Rotterdam. Ruined or not, it will have to be our home. In any case, we could never be happy on Java again."

Irene nodded feelingly. "We'll go to England. From there we might go to Australia."

Susan scrambled to her feet, to collect drinking water.

Once she was out of earshot, my mother turned to Irene.

"If you go to England, what will happen to Arif and Susan?"

Irene gave a shrug. "They're both so young," she said. "He's gone back to the plantation now, as you know. He wants to go to technical college, but that will mean a lot of studying and Susan's missed four years of school. She'll need to catch up. So they're going to write to each other and see what happens. But as she'll be in England and Arif will be on Java, the circumstances are against them staying together."

"Do you think Wil would object if they did?" my mother asked.

"He wouldn't mind," Irene responded. "Not now." Then she showed us Wil's most recent letter, and pointed to a paragraph toward the end.

Irene my darling, having lost our beloved Flora, and having myself almost died amid scenes of utter cruelty that I will never forget, I no longer care about artificial barriers of race or class. I care only about the real, everyday things of life—having enough to eat, having shelter, and above all, having the love of family and friends. *Nothing* else matters.

In early November, Irene and Susan left. The RAF, who were evacuating British subjects, were to fly them to Singapore, where they would be reunited with Wil; from there they would sail to England. They said goodbye to all the women that they'd been with—Kirsten, Ina, and Corrie and the twins. Then they came to say their goodbyes to us. It was a dreadful wrench; my mother and I knew them so well, and we'd been through so

much together. But our sadness was lessened by the knowledge
that we would soon see my father again.

Finally that day came, in November 1945. Because of the turmoil on Java, families were to be reunited at Balikpapan. That
morning I put on the silk dress that I'd saved and my mother put
on the one good dress that she had been keeping, then we
boarded the tarpaulin-covered truck that would take us to the
airfield. We were told to lie on the floor because of snipers. As
we raced along, I prayed that the truck wouldn't be attacked;
but we arrived safely and saw the B-25 bomber waiting for us on
the runway.

Most of us had never flown before, and everyone was smiling
at the excitement of it, and at the fact that we would soon see our
loved ones again. The noise and vibration of the plane were tre-
mendous, and I tried not to scream as we rose into the air. As we
flew toward Borneo, I looked out the windows at the glittering
blue of the Java Sea.

As we stepped off the plane I saw dozens of men waiting. I
scanned the crowd for my father and felt a pang of disappointment that he wasn't there. Then, with a jolt, I realized that I was
looking straight at him. When I'd last seen my father, he had
been a young man. Now he looked old. His hair, which had been
fair, was the color of ash and very short. Where once he'd been
big and well built, he was now pitifully thin, his muscles wasted.
But as my mother and I ran toward him, his eyes were full of
love for us. We held each other tightly, and cried for our years
of separation and for what we had suffered. Most of all we cried
because Peter wasn't there.

At the camp there were hundreds of green tents, pitched neatly in long rows. I shared one with my mother because husbands and wives weren't allowed to cohabit. Her relief at being reunited with my father softened her mood. We had our first shower and were given soap and toothpaste, which we hadn't seen for so long, and clean towels. Just to have clean running water seemed like a miracle.

For meals we filed into a massive tent where the long tables groaned with food. We would stare at it, overwhelmed. Children were allowed to have whatever they wanted, with as many helpings as they could manage. I sat next to a little boy. He took a hard-boiled egg and ate it; then he anxiously gave the shell to his mother to crush up. She touched his cheek and told him that they didn't have to do that anymore.

As my father sat, smiling at us but saying little, I tried to imagine him pickaxing coal in the darkness and heat, then freezing above ground. I imagined him lying in the hold of a ship, with two thousand other men, in tumultuous seas. I imagined him feeling the shock of the bombs.

"What *are* atomic bombs?" I asked him now.

He shook his head. "I still don't really know. But I'm glad I was in the mine when it happened, as many of the prisoners were above ground and heard the terrible explosion and saw the lightning flashes and strange clouds."

One evening I told my father the truth about Peter. As his eyes filled with tears, I panicked that he'd also say that I'd done the wrong thing, made the wrong choice, betrayed Peter. But he took my hands in his, enclosing them.

"Poor Klara," he murmured. "What agony for you."

"I wish they'd pushed pins under my nails instead," I told

him. "Or hung me up by my wrists. I could have coped with that, but I can't cope with this! Mummy feels that I took Peter away from her. She said that I made the decision selfishly, because I didn't want anything to happen to *her*."

"She won't feel like this forever," my father assured me. "She needs time, Klara. We'll *all* need time. It won't be easy. Be patient with her." A few days later my father was discharged, fit, so we traveled down to the port of Balikpapan. During the battle for Borneo, two of the quays had been reduced to rubble; there was a slick of oil on the sea, and an acrid smell hung in the air. On the beach, among the shredded palm trees that littered the sand, were the burnt-out carcasses of Japanese tanks.

We boarded the SS *Noordam*, which would take us to Holland. It stopped first at Batavia, now renamed Jakarta, and we took on hundreds more evacuees. Because of the conflict we weren't allowed to disembark, so we said our farewell to Java from the ship. As I looked at the bustling dock, I suddenly remembered the joy on my father's face that day when Mum, Peter, and I arrived. I remembered the drive up to the plantation, when I'd first seen the curved terraces of rice fields, rippling like waves across the mountains, and the jungle-clad volcanoes with their deck of cloud.

As I heard the long blast of the ship's horn we leaned on the rails and watched the island recede. As it grew smaller, I cried, not for the loss of our home, or for what we had suffered.

I'd never leave Daddy on Java . . .

I cried because we were leaving Peter there.

We stopped in Colombo, Ceylon, then sailed on to Ataka in the Red Sea, where we were taken to a Red Cross clothing depot that had been set up to equip East Indies evacuees for a European winter. We traveled by train through the desert to a huge warehouse surrounded by sand that had been whipped up into dunes. Inside the building, a band was playing, made up of German and Italian prisoners of war, in shabby uniforms, with numbers stenciled on their backs. There were long tables laden with soft drinks and piles of sandwiches. I still couldn't get used to the idea that food could be there for the taking. After years of deprivation, abundance felt wrong.

The racks of clothes seemed to stretch for miles and gave off a strong whiff of camphor. It felt so strange, trying on these thick garments in the desert heat, but we each selected a winter coat, and my father chose a tweed suit, some shirts, a hat, and leather brogues, as well as long johns, vests, and ties. My mother and I selected worsted jackets, long-sleeved dresses, cardigans, hats, some underwear, and a handbag each. These garments had all been donated, and the idea that they could just be ours, without having to trade for them, let alone risk being shaved or beaten, seemed miraculous.

We returned to the ship with our new wardrobe, and our journey continued. We reached Port Said, where the boat was refueled for the final lap of the voyage, then went through the Suez Canal and into the Mediterranean, past Portugal and the west coast of France. Going through the English Channel, I gazed at the white cliffs and thought of the Jochens, who would be in Kent by now; then we entered the North Sea, where the ship pitched and tossed in the swell. Finally, on the evening of 19 February, we saw the glimmering lights of the Dutch coast. The *Noordam* was piloted into Amsterdam Harbor, and in the morning we all gathered on the decks to disembark.

A welcoming party had gathered; a band was playing the national anthem as the evacuees walked down the gangplanks and stepped onto Dutch soil. For the many *Belanda Indos,* it was the first time they had ever been to the "mother" country, which they had been brought up to think of as "home."

My parents and I took a bus to Rotterdam, three hours away. As I traveled over cratered, rubble-strewn roads, past buildings with no fronts and churches without spires, I realized these were the scars of a war that I hadn't known. This had been *their* war. Our war had been the war of *tenko* and dysentery, of *gedekking* and barbed wire, of bayonets and beriberi and head shavings.

We stayed with my grandmother, Oma, for a few nights. My mother was sad that she would never see her father again—he'd died, with thousands of others, during "the Hunger Winter," when northern Holland was blockaded. My grandmother had barely survived. They had burned their kitchen cupboards to keep warm, and their tables and chairs. She had very little left. But she had kept the photo albums that she'd compiled from the many pictures that my mother had sent home before the war. When my mother opened one I saw her eyes fill with tears, and I thought she must be looking at a photo of Peter. But then I went closer. I saw that it was the photo of me, dressed as Cinderella, barefoot and in rags. My grandmother gently shut the album, then put them all away. It would be a long time before they were opened again.

We discovered that we were to be accommodated in a "repatriates camp." The one we were sent to was a former army barracks in Nijmegen, close to the German border. We were allocated a living space and a bedroom, our beds were straw-filled jute sacks, which had to be turned before we could sleep on them. The whole camp was enclosed by a fence of wire mesh, and the man who owned it lived in a house by the gate. So it echoed what we had endured on Java, except that we were being fed, not starved, and were not baking in the sun but shivering in the bitter cold.

Our relief at having somewhere to live soon gave way to dismay. Crowds of local Dutch used to gather at the fence, shouting abuse. They called us *uitzuigers*—leeches—and Indos. Holland had suffered so much during the Nazi occupation and was now so impoverished that its people didn't want all these colonials, who had come back with nothing and were now expecting to be fed and housed. To make matters worse, we had double the food rations, because we'd been starved, and this caused deep resentment because the Dutch had been starving too. I used to go with my mother to a local grocery; one day, as she opened her handbag and got out her food stamps, there was furious tut-tutting from the woman behind us.

"Look at *you*," she shrieked, "coming here and asking us to help! While you were sunning yourselves in the tropics, *we* had the Germans. You people should look after yourselves!" I became very upset, but my mother told me to ignore her and we quickly left. This kind of incident happened several times, increasing our sense that we were once again isolated and unwanted. But it was worse for the *Belanda Indos*, who, in addition, suffered racial abuse.

I was enrolled in a local high school, where like the other repatriates, we were given a "bridging" education to try to fill in the huge gaps in our learning. Sometimes another evacuee, Carola, would try to explain to our classmates what we had experienced under the Japanese, but they didn't want to know.

"At least you were warm," they would say. "You weren't

freezing like we were. Or eating tulip bulbs or raw beets, or hiding in a ditch or being sent to die in Auschwitz like all our Jewish friends were."

To which there could be no answer. They'd suffered in their way, and we in ours, but where the Dutch children talked openly and volubly about the war, we now knew to keep quiet. As I cycled to school each morning, past scorched and shattered trees, steering my wheels around holes left by shells and grenades, I vowed to look only to the future.

We were in Nijmegen for a year. Then we moved into a village closer to Rotterdam, where we stayed in the basement of a large villa. These were "contract pensions" in which the Dutch government paid the owners of large houses to open up part of their homes to evacuees. Usually there was just one room per family. We were lucky. We had two rooms, and our own small bathroom; there was also a large garden, fragrant with roses. I used to watch my mother walking about in it, and I knew that she was thinking about her garden at Sisi Gunung.

During the day I didn't think about the plantation, but it would return to me in my dreams and I'd travel back there on a wave of memory. I'd be sitting on the verandah with my mother and Peter, watching the *tjik-tjaks* come out, or I'd be playing with Flora or riding Sweetie, or walking through the rubber forest with my father, trying to match his long strides. He had seemed a giant to me then, but now he seemed shrunken and old, a shadow of the man he'd once been.

My father wanted to work, but most of the jobs to be had were laboring jobs, to rebuild the shattered city, and he was quite unfit for this. The coal dust inside the mine, and the freezing conditions outside it, not to mention the lingering effects of being starved almost to death, had left him with fragile health.

We often heard from the Jochens, who were by now in Fremantle in Western Australia, where Wil had cousins. Wil helped my father get the pension due to him from the Dutch agricultural company that had owned the plantation; to my father's surprise it was enough for us to live on, albeit modestly. Wil also mentioned the growing demands for war reparations from Japan, but we knew that this, if it ever happened, would be years, if not decades, away.

I remember my parents avidly following the coverage of the Dutch War Crimes Court, and when, in September 1946, Kenichi Sonei was sentenced to death, we felt that the suffering of thousands of innocent women and children had been avenged. As I thought of him facing the firing squad, I could not summon one shred of pity for the man.

Even as late as 1948, the war for independence still raged. But in 1949 the flag of the Indonesian Republic was raised over the archipelago and the last Dutch officials left.

In that year my grandmother died. She had left her apartment to my mother, and this now became our home. I attended the Erasmiaans School, and now, at sixteen, I tried to put the war years behind me. My mother's relationship with me had improved, inasmuch as she was still a concerned mother, doing her best. But deep down her resentment toward me remained, and at times I saw it in her expression, just a glance, and I felt accused all over again. I had nightmares about the camps. In these dark dreams I saw again the train journey to Tjideng, and Flora's gray face, and emaciated women lined up under a full moon, their children curled at their feet. But I drew comfort from my father, who I knew still loved me unequivocally. He told me to look only ahead.

What should I do with my life? I wondered. Should I become a teacher, or a nurse? Perhaps I could train to be an interpreter— thanks to Irene, my English was good. With my planter's background I became drawn to the idea of working in the flower trade, as the Dutch bulb industry was rapidly reviving.

In September 1949 I went with a school friend, Mina, to a dance in a new music hall on Delft Street, where we jived to the Andrews Sisters and Buddy Clark. There were some boys there from our school, and while Mina was talking to one of them, an attractive man, two or three years older than I was, approached me. He asked me if I spoke English, and I said that I did. He then told me that his name was Harold and that he'd love to dance with some of these girls but didn't know how to ask them in Dutch. Could I help him?

"Of course," I answered. "It's *'Wilt u met me dansen?'* Or you could, if you like, say *'Ik zou graag met u willen dansen?'* Either would be fine."

"Your English is very good," he told me. "Or *are* you English?"

"No, but I grew up hearing it. Anyway, now you know what to say, and . . . good luck."

"So what I have to say *is* . . . " Harold frowned as he tried to remember. "Will you mit me . . . dancern?" He smiled at me. "And what should she say in reply?"

"Well, that all depends on how she feels. If it were me, I'd say *'Ik zou graag'*—'I'd be delighted.' "

Harold grinned, then offered me his arm. "I was hoping you'd say that!"

I laughed as we took to the floor.

Harold told me that he was a sublieutenant in the Royal Navy, and was in Rotterdam with the HMS *Vanguard,* on which he would serve for another two years.

"What will you do after that?" I asked as we sat out the next dance.

"I'll go and help run the family farm. It's in Cornwall."

"Is it a flower farm?" I asked. "Do you grow daffodils?"

"It's dairy, but we do have one small field of daffodils that we sell to local shops."

We danced and talked some more, and then Harold walked me home. As we stood outside the building, he asked me if he could take me out for supper one night. I said that I'd have to check with my parents. They gave me permission to go, but only if Harold came up to the apartment to meet them beforehand. So he did, and was charming, and I could see that my parents liked him. He told them that he'd been too young to serve in the war but had joined up as soon as he was sixteen.

"Why did you choose the navy?" I asked him later, as we had supper.

"Because our farm's by the sea, so I know about boats." Then he asked me about the plantation. "So you're a farmer too, Klara."

"I suppose I am."

The night before Harry's ship was due to leave, we went out one more time. Now he asked me more about what had happened to us on Java. His eyes were full of compassion as I described our lives in the camps. He sat very still as I told him about Peter, and then Flora. I told him about what we ate, and our struggle to grow food, and about my dream of having a walled garden one day.

Harry smiled. "You *will* have one, Klara. I know you will."

"How?"

"Because I'm going to build it for you," he said.

Harry returned to his ship, and we wrote to each other every week while he was in the Atlantic and I was at school. In this way we got to know each other very well.

My parents weren't worried that I was marrying so young. They wanted me to seize my chance at happiness; they knew too well how easily everything that we love or value can be snatched away. So in May 1952, Harry and I were married in Rotterdam's Town Hall, one of the few historic buildings to have survived the Luftwaffe. We had a wedding breakfast in a nearby hotel and honeymooned in Devon en route to Cornwall.

I will never forget my first glimpse of Polvarth. I looked at the headlands and coves, the patchwork fields, the light sparkling on the sea, and I drank in lungfuls of the wonderful air. Harry had told me the truth—it *was* a beautiful place—and I settled happily into my new life.

My parents visited me every spring. In June 1953 they helped me inaugurate the walled garden. It was Coronation Day, and Harry and Seb had just finished building it. We decked it with bunting and toasted it with champagne. Then my parents helped us to mark out the beds, my father rolled up his sleeves, and he and I planted the peach tree, which has thrived for sixty years.

I'd go to Holland every two years. If I ever tried to talk to my mother about Java, she would simply say that she "couldn't remember." But I'd get out the albums and sometimes she'd come and sit with me and I'd turn the pages, and we'd talk about Sisi Gunung. Gradually she and my father were able to look at the photographs and smile, and in 1955 they went back.

My mother had been in touch with the Netherlands War Graves Foundation, and in late 1954 she was informed that Peter had been reburied in the Ereveld Pandu cemetery in Bandung. The letter gave the number and location of the plot. So my parents bought second-class tickets on a cruise ship and went there the following spring. I couldn't go with them, as I was pregnant, but I didn't need to return to Java to have Peter in my heart. I was trying to put the past behind me, to concentrate on my new life with Harry, and on the new life that was growing inside me. But my mother wrote to me at the very end of the trip, and her letter is among my most treasured possessions.

We traveled there via Suez and Colombo, then went on to Jakarta, where we got the train to Bandung. Bandung is so much busier now, Klara, with far more people and cars and commerce. All the old Dutch street names are now in Indonesian, which confused us until we found our bearings. We saw your school and I thought of you and Flora, arm in arm on the steps. Then, since we were near Tjihapit, I took your father to Houtmanstraat, now called Jalaan Supratman, and showed him the house where we lived for that year. As I stood outside it, I remembered all the women and children and fancied that I could hear the noise and tumult all over again. I thought of what a good girl you had been, and of how brave you were, coping in such difficult, and often frightening, circumstances. I felt sad to think of the childhood that you should have had but which was taken from you.

The following day your father and I got up early and went to Ereveld Pandu. The cemetery is vast, and enclosed within it is the "Dutch Field of Honor"—not so much a field as a vast plain, filled with thousands of identical white crosses that stretch, in perfectly straight rows, as far as the eye can see. Many of the graves are those of civilians who died in the conflict, and as we walked along the neat paths we'd stop, as we noticed on this cross or that the name of someone we'd once known. We saw the name of your teacher, Miss Vries, and of Mr. Uys from Grindlays Bank, and of Roelph Smits, Edda's father. Just as sad was to see "Unknown," which we saw on so many graves.

Finally, we came to "our" plot. However much we had prepared for this moment, seeing Peter's name was a shock. We wept at the inescapable reality of it. Then we laid some pink and white orchids on the grave of our darling boy, who would have been twenty on that day, but who will always be ten. We stood there for a long time, neither of us able to leave; then we each kissed the cross and walked away. As we did so, we felt no less sad, but comforted to have at least come back to Peter, and seen the place where he rests. Being surrounded by so many graves helped me to view what happened to him in a different way—that Peter was simply a victim of circumstance, caught up in the tide of a terrible war. I'm only sorry that in my grief and rage I blamed you,

Klara. You will soon be a mother yourself, and I hope that this may help you to understand—and to forgive.

I had one last thing still to do. Your father had been reluctant to go back to the plantation, but he agreed to come with me, and so yesterday we drove through the gates of Sisi Gunung. There was Suliman, waiting to greet us! He looked much the same, though I can't say as much for the plantation, which is still recovering from the occupation. Most of the forest had been replanted, and it was odd seeing so many young trees. It was strange being there, Klara; I half expected to catch a glimpse of you and Peter running down to the stream. Suliman introduced us to the new administrator, Mr. Aceh, who kindly invited us to go up to the house. The garden was overgrown, which grieved me, but my beloved cherimoya was still there. Mr. Aceh asked us if we'd like to go inside, but we said that we didn't want to disturb his family. The truth was that we wanted to remember it as it had been. Then Suliman invited us to his home, and so we all walked down to the kampong, going slowly because of your father. As we were almost there we saw Jasmine, who ran toward us, hand in hand with Sushila, who is now seven and a lovely little girl—their late blessing. I cried to see Jasmine again. We went into their house and exchanged news in Malay, over tea and spekkoek. *But as we talked, all I could think of was two small heads, one fair, one dark, bent together on the verandah. Then we heard steps outside and suddenly there was Jaya— a handsome young man of nineteen. He's studying maths at a college in Garut and hopes to become a civil engineer.*

Jaya told us how sad he'd been about Peter, and that he often thought of him. I opened the basket I'd been carrying, took out the carefully wrapped parcel, and handed it to him. Puzzled, Jaya undid the string and pulled off the layers of brown paper. As he saw what was inside, he smiled.

Twenty-two

"Onyx and marble," I murmured. I looked away so that Klara wouldn't see that I was crying.

She nodded, then lowered the letter. "Onyx and marble. My mother had bought it in Colombo. She told Jaya that she'd looked at dozens of chess sets, and that this was the most beautiful one that she could find. She explained what had happened to his wooden set, and how upset Peter had been to have to leave it behind. She told Jaya about the promise that she'd made Peter, and said how happy she felt to have kept it at last."

"Jaya must have been . . . very touched."

"He was; he promised that he would always treasure it. Then my parents said their goodbyes and drove to Jakarta, to board the ship that would take them home."

"What about Arif?" I asked as Klara put the letter back into the wooden box. "Didn't they see him at the village too?"

Klara shook her head. "He'd long since left."

"What happened to him? Did you ever know?"

"Yes. He'd gone to a technical college in Tasikmalaya, living with relatives while he studied. He'd then been apprenticed to a printing firm, from which he'd gone on to become a typesetter at the *Jakarta Post*, an English-language newspaper."

"And Susan? What about her?"

"She went to school in Fremantle, then to art college in Perth, and became a graphic designer. At twenty-five she married a man she worked with, but he didn't treat her well and it ended. So there she was, divorced, at twenty-eight, and terribly upset. Her parents told her not to worry—she was still young; she'd be happy again."

"I hope she was," I murmured.

"She *was*."

Klara opened one of the photo albums, turned the pages, then showed me a photo of a tall, dark-haired man standing on a lawn with an attractive blond woman, in her late thirties, and two girls of about ten and eight.

"So . . . that's Susan," I said.

"It is."

"And that's . . ." I looked at Klara, puzzled. "Arif?"

"Yes," said Klara, laughing. "That was taken in their garden in Rockingham, just outside Perth."

"So . . . how did they . . . ?"

"Although she and Arif had written to each other for a while, their new lives, inevitably, took over, especially once Susan had married. But she'd never forgotten Arif. She kept thinking about the day he came to Tjideng; the way he'd walked for two weeks to find her, risking bullets and knives. So after her marriage ended, she wrote to him, hoping that his old address would still find him. She had a phone call from him within the week! Arif, who by then spoke English well, left his job and came to Perth, where he worked on *The West Australian*. He and Sue were married in 1958."

"I'm . . . *glad*. And did you ever see them again, Klara?"

"I did. They came to London in '65, and I went there with my boys, and we had a very happy reunion with them in Regent's Park. Arif died in 2004, Susan four years later; but I still exchange Christmas cards with their two girls, Florence and Bea."

"And what happened to Wil and Irene?"

"Wil was stronger than my father, and recovered well enough to work again. He was the general manager of a vineyard near Fremantle."

"Another plantation, then."

"Yes. He and Irene kept in touch with my parents—or with my mother, I should say, because my father died in 1957. After that, my mother came here more often, to be with Henry and Vincent, and with me. This was a time when she and I became close again, and we often spoke about Java. She died in 1981."

Klara talked about her life on the farm—driving the cattle in from the fields and milking them in the shed where the boat now was; the bed and breakfast that they'd done to make ends meet, the daily fishing, the cow that went for a swim. She talked about the pleasures of parenting, the friends she'd made through her children and at the church. She spoke of her gratitude for her long and happy marriage, and remembered the golden wedding party that she and Harold had had. She talked of her closeness to her sons and their families and of her hope that she would still be working when she got to ninety. Then I asked her for some final thoughts on her extraordinary childhood.

"My childhood wasn't extraordinary," she corrected me. "My childhood was stolen. We lost that time—time when we should have been at school, learning and reading and playing with our friends; it was taken from us, and we were forced to see and do things that no child should."

"How do you think your time in the camps has affected you?"

Klara sighed. "That kind of privation teaches you that everything has a value, however small or seemingly insignificant—a piece of string, a nail, a length of thread from an old dress. I still find it hard to throw anything away. I learned to value food, and in a way my whole adult life has been about food—growing it, distributing it, and making sure that none of it is wasted."

"Have you ever forgotten the hunger that you felt then?"

Klara's eyes were shining. "You *never* forget it! Even now the fear of not having enough to eat is never far from my mind. But the time in the camps gave me strength in adversity," she went on. "Whenever something bad has happened to me since, I've thought to myself, *I survived Tjideng—I can survive* this. Above all, I witnessed what mothers will do to save their children. I saw women who prostituted themselves to get food for them, or waded through sewage to fetch medicine for them, or held them, in their arms at *tenko,* for hours on end. I saw women who risked dreadful beatings and even death in order to trade through the *gedék* for the egg or the banana that might keep their child alive for one more day. And this has stayed with me all my life."

Finally Klara looked through the photograph albums again

so that she could select those she wanted to be printed in the book. She chose fifteen, removed them from their corners, and slid them into a stiff-backed envelope for me to take to London. I put it carefully into my bag.

"So what happens next?" Klara asked me.

"I'll go back to London and spend two weeks rewriting and editing the manuscript, and checking any facts; then I'll send it to you, for you to go through."

"You said that you'd take out anything that I'm unhappy about," Klara reminded me anxiously.

"I will. You've been very open, Klara, but I want you to feel comfortable with every word that's in it."

"Thank you, Jenni. So"—she took my hands in both hers, then looked into my eyes—"I shall *miss* our conversations, my dear. I feel . . . it's hard to describe *how* I feel."

"Unraveled?" I teased.

"I feel . . . as though I've been on a journey into myself. It *has* been cathartic—more than I could ever have imagined. And you, Jenni? What do *you* feel?"

"That I've been on a journey too—one that wouldn't have happened if it hadn't been for you. You wanted to tell your story, Klara, and it brought out mine."

"So . . . are you glad you came back?"

"I am."

At Lanhay that night I packed my suitcase and then got ready to go to the gallery. I was just changing when I heard someone knock. I went downstairs and through the glazed panels saw a small silhouette. There was another, more urgent knock, and I opened the door to find a diminutive Dracula with red-rimmed eyes and plastic fangs.

"Trick or treat?" The boy's mother, hovering behind him, flashed me an apologetic smile. "Trick or treat?!" the boy demanded again.

"Ask nicely," his mother said.

"Trick or treat *please*."

"I'm a bit unprepared," I said. "Just a moment . . ." I went into the kitchen and came back with a KitKat. "Will this do?"

The boy dropped it into his bag. "Thanks." Then he sped away, his long black cloak flaring behind him.

A minute or two later there was more knocking, and I opened the door again to find two small skeletons.

"Trick or treat?!"

I gave them my remaining KitKats, then waved them off.

I put on a little makeup, then glanced at the clock. If I drove to Trennick, I wouldn't be able to drink; in any case I was used to the walk, so I put on my coat and locked up.

In the lane, glowing pumpkins grinned at me from every house. I heard shrieks and laughter and saw witches and ghosts darting across the lane or standing expectantly at front doors. As I passed the hotel I saw flames at the bottom of the garden. In the field below the swings a bonfire blazed and crackled, sparks shooting out of it like fireflies. There was a crowd of small zombies, devils, and ghouls with their parents. Spider-Man was facedown in a bowl, apple bobbing. There was a smell of smoke, hot dogs, and mulled wine.

The moon was full but blanketed by the rain clouds that had filled the sky all day. I walked down to the beach, where the tide was halfway up, then went along the path into the village, where more pumpkins flickered.

As I walked up to the village square I heard giggles and running footsteps from the narrow streets on either side; the sound of door knockers rapping and bells pressed. I went past the general store, then to the gallery. ADAM TREGEAR: NEW WORKS had been stenciled across the windows.

I opened the door, and a slim, straight-backed woman introduced herself as Celia, the gallery's owner, and invited me to help myself to a drink. I hung my jacket on a coat stand, got myself a glass of wine, then looked at Adam's paintings. There were dramatic seascapes with boiling clouds lowering over wild seas; there were calm coastal scenes, the sun shimmering on placid waves. There were still lifes of lobsters and speckled plaice and wildflowers; and there was a large canvas of a rock pool, the clear surface whipped into ripples by a breeze that you could almost feel.

I approached Adam. "Congratulations. These are wonderful." I sipped my wine. "There are so many! How do you find the time?"

"I paint in the mornings, after I've staked the nets." He glanced around the gallery. "This is two years' worth of work. Don't suppose I'll ever make a living at it, but I enjoy it."

The door opened and a pretty woman with short brown hair came in, waved at Adam, then came over to us. Strapped to her in a sling was a baby boy. The whorl of dark hair on his head looked like a tiny hurricane.

"This is my better half, Molly," Adam told me. Molly smiled. "And this is little Leo."

I held my hand up and Leo gripped my forefinger. "You're beautiful," I murmured.

"Moll, this is Jenni," Adam explained. "She's been helping Gran with her memoirs."

"Oh yes, of course." Molly lifted Leo out of the sling, then Adam unzipped the baby's padded coat and pulled it off. "So how's it gone with Klara?" Molly asked me as she took off the baby sling.

"It's been wonderful; in fact I've just finished the interviews. So . . . are you a painter too?" Molly told me that she was an illustrator—she and Adam had met at art school in Falmouth five years before. "It must be hard to get things done with a young baby."

"Almost impossible unless you have child care, which we can't afford, so I try and do a bit of work when he's asleep. Not that I'm complaining." Molly kissed Leo, who closed his eyes and chuckled; so she did it again. She laughed. "He loves that, don't you, my darling? But, Adam, I'd love to have a drink and a chat—will you take him for me?"

"Sure." Adam took Leo from Molly and put him against his left shoulder. From this vantage point Leo looked about him benignly, sucking on his left hand.

As Molly went to the drinks table I glanced out the window and saw Klara getting out of her car. She went round to the passenger door and helped Jane out, then gave her her arm. The two old friends walked up the hill.

Celia opened the door for them. "Hello, ladies," I heard her say. "You're looking lovely, both. Good evening, Jane."

"That's right," Jane said. "Lovely. Lovely. Now . . ." She glanced around, frowning. "Have I been here before?"

"You have, Jane," Celia answered. "But it's always nice to see you. Adam's done some wonderful pictures. Can I take your coats?"

Henry and Beth arrived and came over to me.

"I'm sorry we've hardly seen you while you've been here," Henry said. "We've had a late calf arrive, and it's needed bottle feeding, so it's been a busy time; but I hear you've got on very well with my mum."

"I have—not that it was difficult; Klara's a wonderful person."

Henry glanced at Klara, who was looking at a large seascape in turquoise, cobalt, and white. "And was she forthcoming with you?"

"She was—more than I thought she'd be."

He smiled. "You probably know all sorts of things about her that we don't."

"Well . . . that's possible. But then, that's the nature of what I do."

"I hear you're leaving tomorrow," Beth said. I nodded. "Then do have supper with us tonight. Just knock on the door."

"Thank you. I . . . might."

"Now," said Henry, "let's look at the paintings." Henry and Beth drifted away, and Klara and Jane came up to me.

Jane fixed me with her bright blue eyes. "I *know* we've met . . . somewhere . . ."

"It was at St. Mawes," I reminded her. "Last week." Jane gave a defeated shrug.

"At the café," Klara prompted her. "We had tea together, Jane. Honor was there."

Jane's face lit up. "Oh yes. Honor! Now I remember *her*." She looked at me. "But what's *your* name again?"

"Jenni," I answered. "Or Genevieve. That's my real name."

"*Genevieve,*" she echoed. "Of *course.*"

The gallery was filling up, the noise levels rising as people chatted by the pictures.

"I like that lobster!"

"Porthcurnick Beach, isn't it?"

"Prefer the mackerel myself."

"You can almost feel the spray."

By now Leo was becoming fractious, emitting ear-piercing squawks, so Adam handed him to Beth, who cuddled him for a while, then she handed him to Klara, who bounced him in her arms.

Meanwhile, I persevered with Jane. "Jane, I was wondering if you'd like to say something to me about your friendship with Klara. This is for the book that I'm helping her to write."

"Book?" said Jane, looking astounded.

"Yes. Klara's been doing her memoirs."

"*Oh,*" she said, as though it was the first she'd heard of it.

"It's going to be published for her birthday in January."

"January the thirtieth," Jane said. "Her birthday's on January the thirtieth."

"That's right—and I'm collecting a few thoughts about her from her family and friends. So I just wondered if you could tell me what Klara means to you."

"Well . . . Klara is wonderful," Jane said. "She's a wonderful friend, yes, yes, of *course* she is," she added irritably, as though we'd been arguing about it. "I've known her so long—*so* long, but she's a marvelous friend, and it's ten out of ten for Klara every time, *every* time."

"That's a lovely tribute." I made a mental note of it. "Thank you, Jane."

I heard her sigh. "But it was *sad*." She shook her head. "He *died*, you know, in the war. Just once she talked to me about him, just the once. Fell and hurt his head, poor little boy."

Klara came over to us, still holding Leo, and I was glad for the interruption. "My arms are getting tired, Jenni. Would you mind holding the baby?"

"Sure, if Adam and Molly don't mind."

"Oh, they're fine. You've written a book about babies, so I'm sure you know what to do with one. Here." Before I could say anything, she'd placed him in my arms.

To my relief, Leo didn't cry. I enjoyed the feel of his solid little body as I walked round with him, pointing at the paintings. I was just wondering whether he was still comfortable or wanted to change position when I realized that he'd fallen asleep, his right cheek on my shoulder. I stroked his head, which was as soft as swansdown, and inhaled the sweet scent of his hair.

Jane was sitting on a small sofa in a corner of the gallery. The seat beside her was empty, so I carefully lowered myself beside her. As I sat there I could feel Leo's breath on my neck like a tiny zephyr, and his small rib cage rising and falling. His heartbeat was rapid, and I felt anxious until I remembered that babies have a fast pulse. Suddenly Jane's head slumped onto her chest. Alarmed, I waved at Klara.

She peered at her friend. "She's fine," she told me quietly. "It's her new medication—it makes her drop off. She'll wake up in a bit, fresh as a daisy. Did you get anything out of her for the book?"

"I did," I whispered. "She said some lovely things about you. She was quite lucid, and could remember the date of your birthday, but then she . . . got in a muddle again." I didn't explain how.

"That's the nature of it," Klara remarked. "Some days we can almost have a conversation; other days she makes no sense at all. But are you okay holding Leo? He's having a lovely snooze there, but I'll take him if you're tired."

"No, I'm fine, Klara. You enjoy yourself."

I sat there cradling the sleeping baby and listening to the party hubbub.

"Yes, carved pumpkins *do* look lovely," Klara was saying to someone. "But it's an awful waste because you can't eat them afterward, as they're all black and smoky from the candle!"

Now some trick-or-treaters were coming in to find their parents. There was a masked ghost and a girl dressed all in black with a silver cobweb painted on her face.

Suddenly Jane woke up, as alert as if she'd never been asleep. As she started talking to me, Leo began to stir. He pushed his hands against my chest and lifted his head, his cheeks patched with pink from where he'd rested against me. A thread of dribble hung from his lip, and I took out a tissue and wiped it. Jane peered at Leo, then at me. "He's got your eyes."

Now people were saying goodbye. Klara brought Jane her jacket and helped her on with it; then Molly came up to me and smiled at Leo. "You look happy there, my sweetie, but it's nighty-night time." She put his coat on him while I held him.

Adam came up to us. "Thanks for holding the baby, Jenni."

"It's been a pleasure. He's a little love."

"So let's get you home, Leo," Molly said. She lifted him off my lap, which felt warm from where he had lain against me, and suddenly hollow. "It's been great to meet you, Jenni. Perhaps you'll come here again."

"Perhaps," I answered. "I'm not sure. But it's been good to meet you too. And it's been a privilege to spend so much time with your grandmother, Adam."

He smiled. "Goodbye then, Jenni."

"Bye, and thank you for this evening." I stroked the baby's hand. "Bye, sweetie."

As they left, Klara came up to me. She touched my arm. "So . . ." She looked sad. "You're leaving tomorrow morning."

"Yes—at around ten. But I'll drop in to see you before I go. Bye, Jane," I added. But she was already heading for the door.

I walked down the hill past still-flickering pumpkins, then left the village behind. The clouds had almost cleared, though a few dark shreds marbled the moon. As I reached the tea hut I saw a sky lantern drifting out to sea, like an incandescent jelly-fish.

I went down the steps, to the water.

Evie . . .

I watched the waves roll forward, then draw back, then push forward again with a *shhhhhh*.

Evie . . .

I walked toward the rocks, jagged against the silvery sea, and climbed up.

Evie . . . wait . . . wait for me . . .

"Don't cry," I whispered. "I'm here now, Ted. I'm here. I'll help you. I'll help you. Come . . ."

Please . . .

I felt a small hand slip itself into mine.

That night I dreamed of Ted, with the usual longing, but without the piercing pain that had always accompanied my dreams about him. Then Ted faded and I opened my eyes. The room was light. I glanced at the clock. It was nine. To my surprise, I had slept the night through.

After I'd put my bags in the car, I went to take one last look at the beach. As I walked down the lane I realized that it was the first of November—the feast of All Hallows. Tomorrow would be All Souls, the day of the dead.

I took in the headland and the fields. From the top of the slipway I watched a cormorant dive into the sea like a small black missile, then I walked down to the sand. I picked up a smooth gray-blue stone and put it into my pocket, then I went back to the cottage and drove to the farm.

As I parked in the yard, a seagull was perched on the farmhouse roof, like a weather vane. The cat sat by the shop door, cleaning its fur.

I went inside, knowing that I'd find Klara there. She was standing beside the counter, in her white apron.

She smiled. "Morning, Jenni."

"Good morning, Klara."

"So . . . are you all packed?"

"Yes, and ready to leave. Here." I put the key to Lanhay on the counter.

Klara handed me a waxed-paper shopping bag. "I hope you can carry this." Inside were a pot of Polvarth marmalade, some apples, and a chocolate cake wrapped in cellophane and tied with a red ribbon.

"Thank you, Klara. That's very kind. And thank you for putting me up. It's been a lovely place to stay." My words sounded oddly formal and stilted.

"You're welcome to have the cottage anytime, Jenni. You only have to let me know."

"That's sweet of you. But . . . I'm not sure I'll ever come here again."

Klara gave a helpless shrug. "I do understand that, of course. But I shall miss you," she went on. "And I hope so much to see you again, if not here, then perhaps somewhere else, or . . . could we phone each other from time to time?"

"Of course we could," I replied, "and we will. I do want to stay in touch with you, Klara. How could I not, after all that we've . . ." I held out my hand, and she took it in both of hers. "Thank you for being such a great client, Klara—far more than a client actually. You've been a real friend."

Klara drew me into a hug, and we stood like that for a few moments. She patted my shoulders. "Thank *you*, Jenni," she whispered. As we drew apart she smiled. "I shall be thinking about you. You have some important choices to make."

"Yes," I murmured, my heart sinking.

Now we walked outside. I got into the car and Klara waved to me as I drove away. When I looked back in my mirror, she was still standing there, still waving.

On the train I gazed out the window as Cornwall receded, Klara's parting words echoing in my head. I turned my thoughts toward home.

One, I change my mind; two, you change your mind; or three . . .

Rick and I were still at three. I wondered whether we'd break up gradually, or find the courage to do it quickly but painfully, like ripping off a plaster. I didn't feel that our phone conversation had resolved anything. Perhaps Rick felt that he understood me a bit better? I wasn't sure that that was enough.

As I got the underground train to the Angel, I felt my pulse race. I walked down City Road, then turned onto Noel Terrace. As I put the key into the lock, the door drew back, and there was Rick in jeans, a polo shirt, and bare feet, smiling the blue-eyed smile that always made me feel weak.

"Hi," he said. "I heard you coming."

"Hi."

He kissed me on the cheek—the kiss of a friend, not a lover.

"You've had a haircut."

He ran his hand over his head. "Needed it. You look well," he added, as if to someone he was simply fond of.

The flat looked strange and unfamiliar, no longer *gezellig*. I glanced at the orderly shelves, clear floor, and plumped-up sofa. "It's tidy."

"In your honor. And I've made dinner."

"That's nice. Thank you. Klara gave me a cake." I opened the bag and put it on the kitchen counter. "We could have some for pudding."

Rick opened the fridge and took out a bottle. "Glass of wine? You probably need it after being on the train all day." He took the corkscrew out of the drawer.

"It was five hours actually, but yes, that would be great. I'll unpack first though."

I put my laptop in my study and placed the pebble on my

desk; then I went up to the bathroom, undressed, and ran a shower. I stepped into the stream and closed my eyes. When I opened them, Rick was sitting in the wicker chair. After a moment he stood up and pulled off his shirt, then unzipped his jeans, took them off with his boxers, then pulled back the glass screen and stepped in with me. He soaped me and washed my hair, twisting it in his fingers; then, as the water poured down, he kissed me. I stroked his chest and his back, then ran my hands over the swell of his buttocks, feeling his erection against me, springy and firm. We got out and dried each other, then, weak with desire, I followed him into the bedroom.

We were passionate and intense, in the way people often are when their relationship is ending. Afterward we lay entwined, not daring to articulate the sadness that we felt.

By now it was almost dark. Rick got up and drew the curtains, then put on his dressing gown. "Let's have that drink now, and then talk over dinner."

"Sure," I responded casually, though the word *talk* had filled me with dread. Not that there would be much to talk about, I reflected as I pulled on a clean T-shirt and some jeans. It would be a simple matter of discussing how we'd manage our breakup and who would stay in the flat and who would leave.

We went downstairs. Rick poured the wine and lit a candle; I set the table and made a salad. He took the lasagne out of the oven, gave me some, then served himself. Drips from my still-wet hair trickled down my shoulders into the small of my back.

Neither of us seemed to want to start the conversation. Finally I broke the silence. "So, did you apply for that job you mentioned? The one in Norwich?"

"Yes—I sent the form off yesterday. There are a few others I've seen—two in Sussex, one in North Wales, and there's a junior school I like the sound of in Bath."

"Bath would be great." I took some salad. "I can imagine you there."

Rick lowered his glass. "You can imagine *me* there? Is that what you meant to say, Jen?" he added gently. "Or did you mean that you can imagine *us* there?"

I stared at him, taken aback. "I meant you, Rick, because how can I possibly talk about us when we still have this huge problem—a problem that isn't going to go away? We want different things," I went on, "and they're completely incompatible, because you'd like to have children—"

"Yes, I would like to have children," Rick interjected.

I put down my fork. "I understand that."

"I'd love to have children."

"I know," I said, feeling impotent. "But I *don't*."

"So . . ." He exhaled. "It's going to be hard."

"It will be." I felt a sob rise in my throat. "It'll be *very* hard."

Rick gave another pained sigh, and I waited to hear the words that would finally bring our relationship to an end. I closed my eyes.

"But what I want, even more than children, is you." I looked at Rick, startled. "I've hated being without you, Jenni. Before you went to Cornwall I thought that we *could* break up—that we'd *have* to. But I don't feel like that now."

"Then . . . why didn't you say this straightaway? When I arrived?"

"Because it's such an important decision. And I was waiting to see how I felt when I saw you again, spoke to you again, held you in my arms again. Now that I have, I know that I don't want to lose you. I need you, Jen . . . for my happiness. I have to be with you."

"But . . . nothing's really changed between us, Rick. Except that now you know . . . now you know about . . ." The candle was bending and blurring. I lowered my head and let the tears come.

Rick reached across the table and wiped my cheeks with his fingers. "When you told me about Ted, I felt full of tenderness for you, Jenni."

I swallowed. "I thought it would make you think that you could never really know me. I thought that it would make it easier for you to leave."

"No. It's made me want to stay. And if I'm to build a new life, then I'd rather build it with you."

"Even though that would mean . . . not having what you want?"

"But I *would*, Jen, because I'd have you."

Over the next two weeks Rick applied for a number of head teacher jobs, all over the country. I had several ghostwriting inquiries, including an invitation to ghostwrite a science-fiction novel. In the end I accepted a commission to write the memoirs of an elderly man who'd been a Spitfire test pilot. I was keen to learn more about the Second World War.

In the meantime I caught up with Nina, whose bump was showing, and with Honor, who was aglow from her new relationship with Al. I was sleeping much better, and there was a new closeness between me and Rick.

I was still rewriting and polishing Klara's story and working out where the photos should go.

I spread them in front of me. There were photos of the SS *Indrapoera*, an aerial shot of Sisi Gunung, a snap of Peter and Jaya fishing, and one of Klara and Flora on the steps of their school. There were photos of Klara shading Peter with a parasol, and of their parents arm in arm on the lawn. There was the Bloemencamp handkerchief, Anneke's recipe book, the camp at Nijmegen, and the farm at Polvarth. The last photo was one that I had taken of Klara in her beloved walled garden. I had made a copy of it, and it now stood in a frame in my office.

In mid-November I sent her a copy of the manuscript. I wondered how she would feel, reading her own experiences, her fears, her happiness, her grief, and her regrets, reshaped and polished by me. A week later she phoned, and I knew.

"Well . . . I've read it," she began. "And . . ."

"Tell me," I said anxiously.

"I'm happy, Jenni."

I felt a wave of relief. "But . . . is there anything that you want me to take out?"

"Nothing," she answered. "Not one word."

"So . . . that means that you're happy about the guardhouse at Tjideng, and about Peter going to Tjimahi, and about what happened at Tjitjalengka?"

"Yes. I am happy. Or rather, I'm content for those things to be in the book. They're an essential part of my story, and I couldn't live with myself if I had glossed over them."

"I'm glad, Klara. It's brave of you."

"I feel more at ease, telling the truth." Then Klara told me that she wanted to dedicate the book to her parents, in Dutch and in English.

I noted both. "What about the title? Have you decided on that?"

"I have." She told me what it was and I wrote it down.

Shadows Over Paradise.

I looked at it, taken with its blend of beauty and menace. "It's very evocative, Klara. So . . ." I gave a shrug. "That's *it*. We're done. Next time you see the book, it'll be a bound hard-back with your name on the cover. I'll have them couriered to you the week before your birthday."

"I will then give everyone their copy when we go to the hotel for my party. I wish *you* could be there, Jenni."

"Thank you, Klara. I'll be thinking of you, and I shall raise a glass to your next decade."

"So how's everything with you, my dear?"

"Well . . . it's fine."

"And Rick? I hope you don't mind my asking."

"I don't mind at all. I feel I could tell you anything, Klara. But yes, Rick's well, too."

"That's good. I've been thinking about you both. You're still together, then?"

"We are. And we've decided that we want to stay that way."

"I'm delighted. So . . . did you change your mind?"

"No. He changed his."

"Well, that must mean a lot to you, Jenni. That he loves you enough to do that."

"It means the world," I said.

Epilogue

Nailsford, Gloucestershire

It's an Indian summer's afternoon, and in my arms is a baby with bendy arms and legs, dancing blue eyes, a cowlick of fair hair, and a single tooth in her shiny pink gums.

"Smile," says the photographer.

"I *am* smiling," I say with a laugh.

"More, please. It's a christening, not a funeral."

"I don't think I *can* smile more than this. Can I, Rick?" Rick, standing next to the photographer, looks at me, then shakes his head. "She's at maximum happiness, I'm afraid."

"Me too," says Honor beside me. "My cheeks are aching."

"Okay, then, ladies, hold still." The photographer takes a couple more shots, then turns and takes a bigger lens off a nearby tombstone and slots it onto the camera.

"Just a few more . . . lovely."

"Now it's my turn to hold her," Honor says. "Come on, Jen. Hand her over." I smooth the baby's lace gown and pass her to Honor, then we compose ourselves for the next photo.

When this has been taken, Nina steps forward. "That's the godmothers done. Can we have the godfathers in the next shot?"

Al goes and stands with Honor, and Jon's brother James stands beside me. There's a volley of clicks, then Nina and Jon go into the center. Honor hands the baby to Nina, and more pictures are taken.

The photographer peers at the back of his camera.

"Very nice. So what now?"

"We'll go in for the service," Nina says.

And so, a year to the day after their wedding, Nina and Jon lead us back into Saint Jude's for the christening of their baby, Clementine. The congregation is about fifty strong, and Jon's younger brother, Tim, who is reprising his role as usher, hands us all an Order of Service. The organist is playing another Bach partita, and Rick and I sit in the same pew where we'd sat before. But instead of the tension and sadness that we felt then, we are relaxed and happy. Rick gives me a smile and takes my hand. I lean in toward him.

We look at the stained-glass window, of Jesus with the children. The sunlight pours through its colored panes, spangling the walls with little rainbows.

Hearing steps behind, I turn. Vincent Tregear is arriving. He's holding a silvery gift bag. Seeing me, he lifts his hand and I lift mine. In a strange way, what's happened has been thanks to him.

Now the vicar welcomes us back to Saint Jude's, then we stand and sing "All Things Bright and Beautiful."

"The birth of a child is a time for celebration and thanksgiving," the vicar says. "Many parents want to give thanks to God for their child." He calls Nina and Jon to the altar, and they hand Clemmie to him. She bats her arms, then blows a raspberry, and we all laugh. Still smiling, the vicar turns to Nina and Jon. "Do you receive Clementine Alexandra as a gift from God?"

"We do," they respond.

"We now ask for God's blessing on Clementine," the vicar goes on. "We all give thanks for her, and we pray for her parents as they commit to the responsibility of raising her."

We bow our heads for the prayer, then the godparents are called and Honor and I and the two godfathers proudly take our places by the font.

"Wasn't that lovely?" Honor says to me afterward as we go out into the churchyard again. "I adored having to reject Satan," she adds with a giggle.

"And all his works," I remind her.

"Yes—most of them, at any rate."

"*And* all his empty promises."

"Okay—that goes for you too."

We pose for a few group snaps, then we stroll across the field to the house. Jon holds Clemmie, and the lace of her christening robe lifts in the breeze.

The walls of the Old Forge are once again clad in pyracantha and Virginia creeper, the borders aglow with scarlet dahlias. The christening tea is served outside, and we sit on chairs on the lawn, thankful for the late-summer sun that makes this possible.

Clementine is passed round, and Honor and I do our best not to fight over her.

"She was so good in church," Honor says. "Weren't you, darling?" As Honor puts Clemmie on her lap, the diamond on her left hand sparkles in the sunlight. "To think that a year ago she barely existed." She turns to Al. "And to think that a year ago I hadn't met *you*. We'd better not break up," she adds with a laugh. "As we're *both* godparents, it could be a bit awkward."

"I think we'll be fine," Al says with a smile.

"So when's the wedding?" Nina's mother, Betty, asks them as she cuts the christening cake.

"In June," Honor answers. "We're just planning it now. So is that the first layer of the wedding cake?"

"It is. Carefully kept for this occasion." Betty hands a piece to Rick. "I hear you've got a new job."

"I have," he answers. "I just started this term."

"Rick's a head teacher now," Nina tells her.

"How wonderful," Betty responds. "Is that in London again?"

"No, it's in the New Forest," he answers. "Not far from Romsey. We're still getting to know the area."

"It's beautiful," Betty says. "You're only a few miles from the sea—and Southampton's close. What a good move."

"I could have got a job in Norwich," Rick explains, "but we decided on Romsey so that we'd be nearer to Jenni's mother."

"That's nice for her."

"And for us," Rick says. "We see her fairly often." I think of my mother's face when Rick and I first visited her last November. She was happy to see me, and to meet Rick, who has gone out of his way to be friendly to her, bridging the gap between us.

As my mother and I sat on the sofa, Rick had looked at the photos on the sideboard. "Jenni's told me about Ted," he'd said quietly.

My mother nodded. "It was very sad. It was just one of those terribly sad things, wasn't it, Genevieve?" She put her hand on mine, and, as I took it, I felt that I had started to forgive myself . . .

Now Betty passes me a cup of tea. "So, have you and Rick found somewhere to live?"

"Not yet," I answer. "We're renting for now, but hope to buy before long."

"Seen anything you like?" Nina's father, Derek, asks.

"There's one house that we love," Rick responds, and he's about to say more when Vincent approaches, then sits on the empty chair next to me. He opens the silvery bag and hands Nina his gift. "A small present for my sweet grand-goddaughter." He smiles at Clemmie, sitting happily on Honor's lap.

"Thank you, Uncle Vincent," Nina says. "Can I open it now?"

"Of course."

Nina does so, helped by Clemmie, who grasps the paper. Inside is a cut-glass trinket box with a silver lid. "It's beautiful," Nina exclaims. She smiles at Vincent. "*Thank* you."

"I thought that you could put her first tooth in it," he suggests.

"Well, when it comes out, that's where it'll go. You lucky little girl," she says to Clemmie, and kisses her.

Then Vincent starts talking to me. "It's nice to see you again, Jenni."

"It's good to see you, Vincent. Funny to think that it was exactly a year ago that we met."

He nods. "I'm so glad that we did. I know you've been in touch with my mother, but I just wanted to say that you did a wonderful job with her memoirs. You brought her story out so well."

"Thank you. It was a story that she wanted to tell. But we had a very good rapport, and I think that helped."

"It must have done." Vincent smiles. "She told us that you were a lovely 'ghost.'" He puts his hand in the bag again. "But I was at the farm last week and told my mother that I'd be seeing you today . . ." He takes out a small parcel and hands it to me. "Before I left, she asked me to give you this."

I look at it, puzzled, as he hands it to me. "What is it?" It feels heavy.

Vincent shrugs. "I've no idea. She'd already wrapped it and wouldn't say. She just said that it was something she wants you to have."

I untie the string, and as the paper falls away, my heart skips a beat.

"She wants me to have this?" I murmur.

"She does." Vincent looks at it. "Is this the lizard that she talks about in the book?"

"It is." It gleams softly in my hand.

"Then I know how much it's meant to her."

I try to speak, but the words won't come. "Please thank her," I manage to say. "I'll write to her, but please, please thank her, and tell her that I shall treasure it."

"I will. She'll be happy to know that I saw you; you're looking very well."

"You are," Nina says. "You're positively glowing, Jenni." I smile, still gazing at the lizard, unable to believe that Klara had wanted to give me something so precious. I force myself to tune back in to the rest of the conversation. Nina is asking Rick about the house that we're interested in. "You were going to tell us about it," she says.

"Oh yes," he answers. "Well . . . the house itself is nothing special—it's just modern—but the garden is fantastic, with a big, wide lawn. It'll be great for entertaining," he adds, but I know that Rick is really thinking, longingly, of children, playing and laughing. And I can see them too. But now, instead of fading like ghosts, they're running toward us. Running across the grass.

I open my arms.

Acknowledgments

In the U.K., I would like to thank Thalia Suzuma, for her brilliant editorial guidance and for her unfailing support of me as a writer. I'm also grateful to Kate Elton, Martha Ashby, Claire Palmer, Katie Moss, Jaime Frost, and everyone at HarperCollins. Huge thanks, as always, to my agent, Clare Conville, and to the team at Conville & Walsh. In the United States, I'm indebted once again to my wonderful editor at Random House, Kate Miciak, for her invaluable editorial input and for her inspiring enthusiasm and warmth. At Random House I would also like to thank Evan Camfield, Julia Maguire, and Margaret Wimberger. Maria Adriana Boerstra and Louise Staël von Holstein generously shared with me their memories of internment on Java in camps Solo, Muntilan, Ambarawa, Tjihapit, Kampung Makassar, and Tjideng. In Cornwall I'm grateful to Charlotte and Simon Taffinder of Curgurrell Farm for illuminating me about life on a coastal farm, and to Robert Pepper of the National Coastwatch at Pednvadan Point for telling me about tides. I'm indebted to my friends and neighbors at Rosevine, especially Jo and Alan Mullet, Jane and Julian Noad, and Tim and Hazel Brocklebank at the Rosevine Hotel. Roland Bosch corrected the Dutch translations, and Louise Clairmonte and Eliana Howarth kindly read the manuscript along the way. Finally, huge thanks and love to my very patient and indulgent family—Greg, Alice and Edmund, and Freddie and George.

The following books provided helpful background during the course of my research:

Archer, Bernice. *The Internment of Western Civilians Under the Japanese 1941–1945: A Patchwork of Internment.* Hong Kong University Press.

Berg, Jan. *My P.O.W. Story.* Published by Jan (John) Berg.

Bonga, Dieuwke Wendelaar. *Eight Prison Camps: A Dutch Family in Japanese Java.* Ohio University Press.

Crofts, Andrew. *Ghostwriting.* A & C Black.

Hillen, Ernest. *The Way of a Boy: A Memoir of Java.* Penguin Books.

Hollander, Inez. *Silenced Voices: Uncovering a Family's Colonial History in Indonesia.* Ohio University Press.

Huie, Shirley Fenton. *The Forgotten Ones: Women and Children Under Nippon.* Angus and Robertson/HarperCollins.

Kogel, Paula. *The House at Ampasiet.* Matador.

Krancher, Jan A., editor. *The Defining Years of the Dutch East Indies 1943–1949*. McFarland & Company.

Leffelaar, Hendrik L. *Through a Harsh Dawn*. Frederick Muller.

Ockerse, Ralph, and Evelijn Blaney. *Our Childhood in the Former Colonial Dutch East Indies*. Ralph Ockerse and Evelijn Blaney Publishing.

Oort, Boudewijn van. *Tjideng Reunion: A Memoir of World War II on Java*. Trafford Publishing.

Pilgrim, Phyllis. *The Hidden Passport*. Pilgrim Publishing.

Priesman-Bogaardt, Louise. *Dark Skies Over Paradise*. Trafford.

Tyrer, Nicola. *Stolen Childhoods: The Untold Story of the Children Interned by the Japanese in the Second World War*. Weidenfeld and Nicolson.

Wilbrink, Jannie. *Java Lost: A Child Imprisoned. Parts 1 and 2*. Friesen Press.

Shadows Over
Paradise

ISABEL WOLFF

A Reader's Guide

A Conversation with Isabel Wolff

Random House Reader's Circle: What drew you to write about what happened in Java during World War II?

Isabel Wolff: When planning my novels, I always start with what the heroine does for a living, because from this, everything else will flow. Once I knew that Jenni would be a ghostwriter, I had to work out what the story that she "ghosts" was going to be. I decided that it would be a wartime memoir, not of the conflict in Europe, which has been written about so much, but of the war in the East instead. I've always been very interested in the Pacific war. I remember, as a child, learning that my parents' friend Dennis had been a POW on the Burma-Thailand Railway. My mother told me, in hushed tones, that Dennis had suffered terribly and seen "dreadful things," although she didn't want to say what those things might have been. As a teenager I used to avidly watch the TV drama *Tenko,* about a group of British and Australian women interned in a jungle camp on Sumatra. I was moved by their struggle against disease, malnutrition, and the capricious cruelty of their captors. I was also fascinated by their desire to help one another but also, at times, to betray one another. And I'd read *A Town Like Alice,* set in occupied Malaya, a novel that has stayed with me all my life. So I decided that my ghostwritten story would be a memoir of internment in the Far East. There were many locations in which it could have been set: civilian men, women, and children were interned right across the region, in Singapore, the Philippines, China, Malaya, and Hong Kong. I decided to set the novel in the Dutch East Indies, on Java, where the camps were most numerous. They were also, by and large, the worst.

RHRC: Parts of Klara's and Jenni's stories are very painful to read. Were they painful to write too?

IW: They were, largely because I write in the first person and so I have to "become" my characters in order to convey what they've been through in a believable way. Klara's story required a great deal of research. First I interviewed two women who had been interned on Java as children and whose memories of the camps were still vivid, seventy years on. I also read the memoirs of Dutch survivors, whose accounts of the appalling conditions, cruel treatment, and the atrocious train transports were distressing. So I immersed myself in their remembered world of a paradise that had become a living hell, and into this I placed the fictional characters of Klara and Peter and their parents, the Jochens, and the vengeful Mrs. Dekker. Jenni's story was also painful to write, but in a different way: She is a captive too, though her prison is an internal one of profound remorse at the fatal mistake she made on the beach that day.

RHRC: Was it difficult writing from two very different women's points of view? Who did you feel closest to, Klara or Jenni?

IW: I didn't find it difficult because I was so interested in them both. I knew that I'd simply have to inhabit their characters completely in order to summon their memories and feelings as though they were my own. In Klara's case this meant doing the detailed historical research about her life in Holland and on Java, which would enable me to relate to what had happened to her in an authentic way. I felt close both to Klara and Jenni, because, like them, I have lost a brother, and know all too well their sense of irreparable loss, the feeling that a part of one's very self has been wrenched away.

RHRC: Klara and Jenni are thrown together by a twist of fate, or by random chance. On the surface they seem to have little in common, but memories play an important part in both their lives. Was memory—its function, its legacy—something that you particularly wanted to explore in the novel? How powerful do you think it can be in forming personalities, forming lives?

IW: It's true that these two women, one old, one young, seem to have little in common. However, as the interviews progress, they realize that they do. The twist of fate that reunites them is Jenni's meeting Klara's son Vincent at the wedding. Despite the mental terrors that Polvarth holds for her, Jenni decides to return, in order to confront the past, and to try and lay to rest the ghost that has haunted her for twenty-five years. So yes, memory is a key theme, particularly how we cope—or don't cope—with very difficult memories. Jenni has chosen a job that lets her take refuge in the memories of others, because her own memories are a source of such pain. The novel is also about the power of memory, in that we are our memories—the sum total of all our experiences, held in our minds, to be retrieved and reflected upon, making us behave in this way or that. If dementia takes away our memories, it robs us of our personality too.

RHRC: Klara is quite literally a prisoner. Jenni is a bit of a prisoner too, in a prison of her own making. Do you think many people are trapped by the burden of guilt? How does one break free?

IW: Klara has been imprisoned by an occupying force, but Jenni has been imprisoned by her own conscience. She feels completely culpable for what happened to Ted. That tragedy and its legacy have shaped her personality, making her gravitate toward the shadows, concealing herself, happy that few people even know her name. It has also led her to shun family life, because she believes that she doesn't deserve to have a child. I felt very sorry for Jenni. In real life, perhaps therapy would have helped her come to terms with what happened. But she exists in a novel, and I decided that Klara would help her start to break free of her past, enabling her to view the tragedy in a different way.

RHRC: You describe Cornwall and Java in great detail. Are these places you know well? Are some locations in the novel fictional?

IW: The rubber plantation, Sisi Gunung, is made up, but all the other places on Java are real and are described from my research, and from a trip I made to Java. Polvarth is fictional but is based on the coastal hamlet of Rosevine, where I spend many holidays. Trennick is modeled on the fishing village of Portscatho, nearby. The Cotswold village of Nailsford and the Church of Saint Jude are invented, and I created one or two of the characters that feature in Tjideng. Lieutenant Sonei, Mrs. Cornelisse, Mrs. Nicholson, and the Korean guard Oohara all existed, but I have invented Sergeant Asako and Lieutenant Kochi. I have also transposed the worst punishments from camps Kampung Makassar, Banyu Biru, and Ambarawa to Camp Tjideng.

RHRC: How long did the novel take you to write, and were you consumed with thoughts of the Second World War in the Far East all the time you wrote it?

IW: The novel took eighteen months to write, largely because of all the historical research that I had to do. I *was* fairly obsessed by thoughts of the war in the Far East. I'd close my eyes and try to imagine what it must have been like to be in a house with eighty or even a hundred other people, with no possibility to be alone, in peace and quiet. I tried to imagine the hunger that prompted these desperately thin women to write out recipes for delicious dishes that they knew they would never get to eat. I tried to imagine what it would be like to have my head shaved, or to stand at *tenko* for hours at a time with a child in my arms. What these many thousands of women endured is not widely known; I wanted to write a novel that would have their ordeal, and their courage, at its heart.

RHRC: In some ways *Shadows Over Paradise* is a departure from your previous novels. For one thing, the main thrust of the novel isn't a love story. Was this intentional?

IW: *Shadows Over Paradise* is first and foremost a story of survival, and so to have focused on romance would have felt wrong. Having said this, there is some romance—the growing love between Arif and Susan, for example, and the faltering relationship between Jenni and Rick. But the main thrust of the novel is about how women coped in such atrocious conditions, how they kept sane, not knowing where their husbands and sons were, or if they were even alive. It's also about how they tried to maintain decent standards of behavior when they were living with so much fear, and when every basic comfort had been taken away. As for *Shadows Over Paradise* being a departure from my previous novels, this is true. The earlier romantic comedies such as *The Making of Minty Malone, Out of the Blue,* and *Rescuing Rose* have given way to stories in which I blend present and past. This is something that began with *A Vintage Affair* and continued with *The Very Picture of You. Shadows Over Paradise* maintains that process of change. I very much hope that the readers of my earlier books will enjoy these later, semi-historical novels too.

RHRC: For those who would like to get to know more about Java in the time of the Second World War, what resources would you recommend?

IW: I've listed many books on the subject of the Japanese occupation of Java. Of these, I particularly recommend Jannie

Wilbrink's *Java Lost,* Boudewijn van Oort's excellent and
scholarly *Tjideng Reunion,* and Ernest Hillen's moving memoir, *Way of a Boy.* There are also some very informative websites, notably Elizabeth van Kampen's Dutch East Indies site,
www.dutch-east-indies.com; the East Indies Camp Archives,
www.indischekamparchieven.nl; and the Tjideng Camp website, members.iinet.net.au/~vanderkp/tjideng.html.

Questions for Discussion

1. Jenni and Klara each suffer the loss of a sibling early in life. Compare and contrast the circumstances surrounding these tragic losses.

2. Jenni carries a heavy burden of guilt and responsibility over Ted's death; do you think her feelings of guilt are justified? Does the fact that she acted out of anger on the day Ted died influence your feelings?

3. What choice would you have made if faced with Klara's decision in the camp? What do you make of Klara's mother's assessment that her choice was motivated by a self-interested desire to preserve the protection and support of her mother?

4. How would you react if you learned a life-changing and long-concealed secret about a close friend or lover? Would you, like Rick, feel a renewed sense of tenderness and closeness toward that person? Or would you, as Jenni feared, question whether you could ever really know the person at all?

5. Jenni and Klara both feel haunted by the memories of their brothers. What do you make of this? Do you believe in ghosts?

6. Who, if anyone, was responsible for Peter's fate?

7. In a relationship, how much would you be prepared to compromise in order to be with the person you love? What do you think of Rick's choice to give up his dream of being a father in order to be with Jenni?

8. Compare and contrast Jenni and Klara's responses to the traumatic events of their childhoods. In what ways did their experiences shape the course of their adult lives?

9. Why do you think Jenni chose to return to Polvarth? Would you have taken the job, if you were in her position?

10. Jenni's ability to form attachments and maintain close relationships was heavily influenced by the early loss of her brother. What, if anything, could she or those around her have done differently to mitigate the impact of her brother's death?

11. In reading about life in the Japanese-run internment camps during World War II, what feelings came up for you? What was your or your ancestors' experience during this tumultuous period in the world's history?

12. What did you think of the Dutch people's reaction to the colonials when they returned after the war?

13. Discuss the significance of Flora's lizard to Klara and to Jenni.

14. What do you think of Mrs. Dekker's actions? The women in the camp are described as often fighting with one another and turning on one another. Did you find this surprising?

15. This story focuses a good deal on memory; how important do you think memory is in forming a person?

16. Klara defines *paradise* as a walled garden. What do you think of this? How do you think Jenni would define *paradise*? What does *paradise* mean to you?